## About th

My dear, dear father, Paul Holbrook, the author of this book, lives in North Yorkshire with his wife, Kathryn and his two amazingly talented and beautiful daughters. We also have two gluttonous and stupid cats, and a dog who is alright, I guess. Surely after a couple of books, you'd think he would have realised what a huge mistake it was giving me, his wisest, most impressive and obviously funniest daughter, the power of writing this section. Alas, here I am again to torment you.

Paul has lived a long life of fighting crime and keeping the streets (all of them) safe, this hobby started when he broke out of Luton. What does he do to the villains he defeats? Well, I'll tell you right now, their life force is absorbed, and he keeps these stolen souls in his calves, very unassuming, very smart. His life goal is to become Immortal Overlord of the universe and Dad, if you're reading this, it's not going to happen mate, NOT IF I GET THERE FIRST. Why else do you think I'm spilling your secrets, I'm catching up.

As a cover, Paul works for Ryedale Special Families alongside his writing, which you shall be reading in a couple of pages. His passion truly is in writing, his love for horror being directed into the thrilling books *Memento Mori* and *Domini Mortum*, both of which I have not read and might read in the future, but I don't know what the future holds, I'm not a scientist. A book of his that I *have* read and loved was *The Love of Death*, check that baby out ASAP. I have been very eagerly awaiting this book though, whimsical, fantastical, funny, oooOOOOOooooh. You want to read this book so bad, I can tell. I'll let you get on with it then.

Ta-ra love,
Eve x

Also by the author

Memento Mori
Domini Mortum
The Love of Death

# DOLORIAN BOOKS

ISBN: 9798852964137

© Paul Holbrook 2025

Published by Dolorian Books 2025

Printed in Great Britain
Outside of the United States of America, this book is sold subject to the condition that it will not, by way of trade or otherwise, be lent, re-sold, hired out or circulated without the publisher's prior consent in any form of binding or cover other than that in which it is published and without a similar condition including this condition being imposed on the subsequent publisher.

# The Love of Time

## Paul Holbrook

Liz
Hope you enjoy!

**DOLORIAN**
BOOKS

*For Kathryn,
Because you know that I would follow you through time*

*Special thanks also to Louise Moore and Ian J Williams for their test reading services, wise advice and constant support*

# Amelia
# The Battle of Sunningdale

## Finlay – present day

Nothing like it had ever been witnessed at Sunningdale in the ten years since the retirement village had opened in the small Scottish town of Finlay. It was normally such a quiet and happy place, never before seeing anything of the violence and fury which Mrs Amelia Hawke had displayed. Sunningdale prided itself on being the perfect place for older ladies and gentlemen to move into in their later years, a place where they were still able to live independently in their own homes, but also feel safe in the knowledge that there were staff nearby able to come and help at a moment's notice. It was not a place where you would regularly see an older lady launch into such a sudden and blistering physical attack on one of her neighbours.

The staff didn't have to hold on too tightly to her arms. Amelia's rage had more or less subsided once they had got her down the corridor and into one of the side rooms of the reception area, leaving other residents open mouthed, and the neighbour in question Maureen shaking in fear. Amelia still shook with anger, but her torrent of foul-mouthed expletives had simmered down to a mutter, the words of which no one could clearly hear. David, George, and Sophie sat down with her, the men glancing nervously at each other, obviously uncomfortable in the situation, Sophie stroking Amelia's arm saying soothing words in an attempt to bring her around.

Quite what had brought about Amelia's sudden and violent attack on Maureen, who had been sat in the chair next to her in the cafe, they did not know. One moment they had been happily sat together sharing a pot of interminably weak tea, the next they were a blur of blue rinse and knitwear, Amelia bringing Maureen's intellect and promiscuity into question combined with a flurry of arthritic fists and slippered feet. Of course, they were aware of how Maureen could sometimes rankle people and stir them into anger, Amelia and Maureen however had always been close; they could often be seen sat in the cafe chatting and sharing a pot of tea. If anything, Amelia was one of the few people who allowed Maureen to get up their nose without annoyance or outburst. In fact, Amelia herself was known as one of the jolliest and kindest ladies that you could hope to meet at Sunningdale; something which made today's incident all the more unusual.

Sophie knew why Amelia was a little testy. Today was the anniversary of Amelia's husband Alan's death, five years previously, and the beginning of events that led Amelia to selling the cottage she had shared with Alan for forty years and moving to the retirement village. Today was the one day of the year that Amelia did not wear a happy face; in fact, Amelia had told Sophie before how she had even been happy and content at Alan's funeral, she showed little or no sign of grief or sadness whatsoever, even wearing a smile at the remembrance service, 'I knew it was only temporary,' Amelia had said. 'I knew we would be together again soon.' Sophie found this statement a little gloomy to say the least, but had put it down to Amelia's notoriously dark humour. She was well known for making odd and sometimes shocking statements about her own and sometimes other's mortality, which would then be followed by a mischievous grin. Sophie watched her now; Amelia appeared a shell of her normal self.

David, manager of Sunningdale for seven happy and, until today uneventful years, straightened his trousers and tucked in his shirt, which had been pulled free of his belt during the melee, exposing what his wife referred to as his biscuit belly. This situation was all very uncomfortable and hardly something that he wished to be involved in. Of course, he knew that sometimes the residents of the retirement village would need some emotional support, all people did no matter what their age, but a full-blown assault by one little old lady on another was not something that they had a policy to deal with at Sunningdale. He stepped towards the door and gestured to George to follow his lead. George did not need much encouragement; he was just the village handyman. Semi-retired himself he had not signed up for this type of thing, and had only happened to be present for the violence because a lightbulb needed changing in the café area. Usually, the most dramatic event he had to attend to was if the tea urn stopped working, or someone's telly had gone on the blink during Countdown.

'How about I go and make us all a nice cup of tea, eh?' David said. 'I'm sure I've got some biscuits hidden away somewhere, Amelia. Why don't you just sit for a while with Sophie and get yourself calm again.' As he opened the door to leave George hurried after him, mumbling something about helping to find the biscuits and a broken toilet in flat 39. The door closed behind them, and Amelia spoke clearly for the first time.

'We are beings of light; these are just the bags we live in,' she said, gently pinching the skin on Sophie's arm. 'That's how I think of him. How I see Alan, not as a person but as a ball of bright energy.'

'Yes,' Sophie replied. 'He certainly was a lively sort of fella your Alan.' Sophie had obviously never met him but, since beginning to volunteer as a companion at the village nearly three months ago, she had spent many hours listening to Amelia talk about her husband.

Amelia simply looked at the young girl and rolled her eyes. She didn't understand, and she would not, not unless Amelia explained it, not unless the whole story was told from the beginning. She sat for a couple of minutes, trying to recollect all the events, the order they came in, and how each moment of the story held a special place within her heart.

Sophie watched her, Amelia looked so far away, and Sophie was reminded of the looks on the faces of some of the people that she visited at Sunningdale; lost and trapped within their own minds, sometime visitors to the world's reality. She reached out and clasped Amelia's hand within her own and, for a brief moment, she felt suddenly very dizzy, as if stood at the top of a skyscraper leaning over the edge. She pulled her hand back quickly, as if she had touched a flame. Amelia smiled.

'You have it within you, young lady,' she said, her eyes suddenly bright and piercing. 'I can see a light in you, feel the energy within. You could have it all you know. If you were brave enough to take the leap.'

Sophie broke her gaze from Amelia, there was something about the way that the old woman looked at her that suddenly felt intrusive, as if the whole of Sophie's innermost thoughts and feelings were there to be inspected and analysed.

The moment was broken as the door opened, and David came back in carrying a tray with cups and a teapot. 'I found them,' he said, placing the tray on the table and cheerily holding up a packet of Fruit Shortcake biscuits before attempting to open them.

Sophie poured the tea and passed a cup and saucer to Amelia, who took it smiling.

'Our souls first met when I was a 12 year old boy and he was the oldest woman in the village,' said Amelia suddenly.

David dropped the biscuits.

# Amelia
# Her First but Definitely not Last Life

## Finlay's Hollow - 632CE

In the first of Amelia Hawke's lives she was a boy called Brid. He was a painfully thin child, with a shock of spiked dark blonde hair, an explosion of freckles on his bright face, and a knack for unintentionally disappointing his mother at every turn.

Finlay wasn't so much of a town at all back then, just a little village really; a collection of small wooden houses, a bakery, a blacksmith, and overlooking it all was the hall of the Laird, his uncle. It was a quiet and peaceful place, kept secluded from the outside world by the shelter of the surrounding hills, and content to go its own way at its own pace. Of course, the people of Finlay did have some contact with other villages and towns. A carriage was sent to Glenleven twenty miles to the south once per month for supplies of salt and grain and it was also where animals were bought and sold. Glenleven had a river running next to it, which brought goods from further afield than anyone in the little village of Finlay could ever dream of visiting.

Back then the village wasn't even called Finlay either; it was Finlay's Hollow, named after the giant, Finlay McBray, who had come down from the mountains in the north many years before, in search of a wife and a place to call his own. Nowadays there is a statue of Finlay McBray standing in the centre of the marketplace, it is fifteen feet tall and made of bronze. The real Finlay was a great deal taller, and his skin was tougher. Taller than twenty men and broader than ten carthorses, Finlay was a huge being, even for a giant. A great wiry nest of thick red hair sat atop his wide and bumpy head, and he had a mouth so large he could eat a fully grown pig in a mouthful. His arms could almost reach the stars if he stretched, and they ended in wide fists capable of brushing aside the trees as if they were nothing more than feathers. McBray came across a Loch on his travels and looked at the surrounding hills deciding that here would be a good place to settle. At the head of the Loch, where Bein Aghlos Dur now stands overlooking Finlay, there was only a small hill not a mountain.

But he dug away at its side with hands as strong as iron, piling the earth onto the top to create a clearing for his house, and a strong mountain to look down and protect it.

Each night he would sit by the Loch and sing out for a partner, as this was the way all giants found a wife. His father had warned him about leaving the safety of the mountains to find a partner, but he had also told him the legends of how once the giants had lived in the low country many miles away. They had all lived together in great cities, the sons and daughters of the Watchers. That was before the monsters came down from the sky, before the great flood when the giants had scattered, running to the far corners of the world and the safety of the mountains. He would sing the song that his Father had taught him, the song that had been sent down through generations of giants back to the first ones. It was the song that had brought his parents together, and though his voice was a little cracked and coarse, it was deep enough to send ripples across the Loch, and a shudder through the trees in the hills surrounding the water. Each night he would sit by the Loch and sing his song, the sound echoing around the hills, and he hoped that his love would come to him.

During the day he would continue to dig at the hill creating a hollow, and slowly as the days passed all of the hills and mountains surrounding the Loch were created; Bein Aghlos Dur to the north at the head of the Loch, and Fuamhairean a Leum the ridge that overlooks the town, now known as Giant's Leap.

Days turned into weeks, weeks into months, every night he sat, and he sang his song, his voice echoing for miles around, but still no wife came to claim the giant. It was said, by the older people of the village, when they sat at night around the fire, that eventually Finlay McBray died in sadness. He never did build his house and instead, in the space he had dug under the gaze of Bein Aghlos, forlorn and broken by his efforts, Finlay McBray curled up into a ball and died of an unloved heart. Finlay's Hollow was created.

Brid's Uncle Earchan had once said, as he sat on his large sheepskin covered chair in the hall of the Laird, that the first men had come to the Loch many years later and found the remains of the giant. They had decided to stay, as the hills which Finlay had created made good pasture for their sheep and cattle, and the Loch which he had sung over was rich with fish. The giant had also left other gifts in his passing. Finlay's bones had been used to form the foundations of the great hall where they now sat on a night and from where the Lairds over the years would rule and govern the people; Finlay's hair had been used to make the thatch that covered the houses and kept the rain out, his hands were the small boats used by the first men to venture out onto the Lòch each day to catch fish, and his heart had been buried deep within the earth under the village, as everyone knew that there was magic in the heart of a giant, magic that would bring luck and long life to all those who lived nearby. When time allowed and her old legs would carry her, Amelia still visited the spot where the old village stood, not ten metres from where his statue stands today, and if she was very still and closed her eyes, she could feel the strength and magic of Finlay McBray's heart in the earth below her.

Brid was not a strong boy, thin and pale like a weak sapling tree, he did not have the strength or the energy like the other boys of the village who all seemed to be a good head taller than him no matter what their age. Brid's father blamed the sickness for this. When Brid had been very young, he had been struck down with a fever which had affected the whole village. Not a family in Finlay's Hollow had been left unaffected by the sickness, many had died, many bigger and heartier than the skinny boy. For weeks he had been unwell, drifting in and out of consciousness as his mother and father bathed him in cold water from the Loch to prevent him from overheating. They fed him a broth prepared by Analla, the ancient healer of the village, who also visited daily. Analla had sat by Brid's bedside in those few weeks, encouraging him to drink and placing a specially prepared poultice on his forehead, which she claimed would draw out the sickness.

It was a strange time, Brid slipped in and out of a dreamlike state, unsure what was real and what was imagination. Throughout it all though, even hundreds of years and many lifetimes later he remembered Analla, by his side, tending to him. Her lank iron-grey hair hung low on each side of the grizzled and textured skin of her face, her thin lips whispering ancient words into his ear, and drawing him back to the world when the child faded into dreams. Sometimes Brid spoke to her, his voice cracked and weak. He would ask her to tell him stories, and she would, in a fashion as often her tales would be of far-off lands and places which she could not have visited. Brid knew very well that she had lived in the village for all of her life; Brid's mother had told him that she had tended to her as a child. Brid decided that Analla's stories were whimsical fancies, that of an old woman making up tales to entertain and distract a sick boy.

Eventually Brid recovered but never fully regained his former fitness, being prone to tiredness and lethargy, and unable to engage in any strenuous physical activity without collapsing with a wheezing, hacking cough. This was a disappointment to his father, who was a proud strong man, as Brid was his only son. Brid knew that his father loved him, but he could see the look of sadness in his eyes whenever the boy tried to help him with carrying the logs that he had split, or attempting to run with the other boys in the village. His father had hoped that one day Brid would take over as Laird of the village from his Uncle Earchan, who was getting old and had no surviving sons of his own, but knew that the village would never accept a weak and sickly leader, no matter who his family were.

Brid's father, Cormag Brothaig was killed when the boy was ten years old. He had been one of fifteen men sent by the Laird when the King had called on each of the villages to send men to help him repel the foreign invaders who had ravaged and plundered the lands to the south. Of the fifteen men who left to join the battle only two returned. They told Brid and his sisters that their father had died well, that he had been strong and brave in the battle against the Danes and had been pulled down by their axes whilst protecting the king himself. They had won the battle though, killing many invaders and sending the rest back to their boats, bloodied and sore. It had been a great victory but at a terrible cost for many in Finlay's Hollow. Brid was given his father's sword and an arm band of silver taken from one of the invaders, which he had always worn, and which Amelia still kept. When the news came back to the village his Uncle Earchan asked Brid's mother and family to move up into the hall to live with him, which they eventually did and, despite the loss of his father whom he loved and missed dearly, Brid enjoyed living with the Laird in the largest building in the village.

As he grew older Brid spent many of his days in the company of Analla the Healer. Ever since his sickness, he had felt a close bond to her and enjoyed her company. He was keen to learn about the herbs and other plants that she used in her medicines, and he would follow her when she took trips into the forest to collect them. For her part she abided the boy, and nothing more. At first she found him to be an annoyance, constantly questioning what she was doing; why was a particular shrub useful for stomach cramps, and how the bark from a tree could stop headaches. Eventually however she found him convenient to have around; he could reach up to the tree branches for the freshest leaves, and dig for useful roots, or even into ant's nests for their eggs, which would later be pulped and added to wounds as a pain reliever. Despite the boy's young age he was taller than her already, although this was mainly due to her crooked back which was bent almost double most of the time. Brid did not know how old she was, no one did. His mother said that Analla had been old when she was a little girl, and that she had even treated Brid's grandfather when he was a young man.

Each evening they would return to her cabin and the boy would help her by sweeping the floor, or cleaning her never ending collection of dirty pots. Her small house was always warm and dark, no matter what time of day, as she kept out any natural light – 'It fades the power of the plants,' she would tell Brid, gesturing to the many branches, leaves and dried flowers which hung from her ceiling. The smell of her rooms was cloying and earthy, but it was not unpleasant. Even now if Amelia closed her eyes she could smell it, and it was comforting to her still.

'Could I be a healer like you when I am older' Brid asked Analla one evening, while she stirred at a pot over her fire. The boy didn't know what she was making but it smelled awful, it was caustic and sharp and burnt Brid's nostrils. Thankfully it was not for eating but rather a poultice for putting on wounds.

'No,' she said. 'There will be no healer in the village after me. There will be no one left to heal.' She carried on stirring slowly, and staring into the flames, as if her words had not been said at all.

'What do you mean, no one to heal?' Brid said, 'will everyone stay healthy? Are we all to die?'

She did not answer and, knocking her wooden spoon against the side of the pot and removing it from the heat, she sat herself down in her chair in the corner with a large sigh. 'No more questions, no more. I am tired now, Brid,' she said. 'Run home to your mother and tell her that I will need you again tomorrow before sunrise, the flowers I need to make ointment for your uncle's back must be picked while they are still closed up.'

The boy leant the broom he held against the wall and left her, her eyes were closed, and she was snoring before he had time to pull shut the old wooden door behind him.

The following morning, in darkness, Analla and Brid left the village and headed into the forest. The dew glistened in what little moonlight there was, giving the forest a silver, ghostly sheen.

Analla seemed happy that morning, excitable almost, her voice had lost its normal low gruffness and when she spoke it was in a musical tone which reminded Brid of how she whispered to him during his fever. There was a light spring to her step that belied her age, as she tripped and skipped over the tree roots which adorned the forest floor. The boy struggled to keep up with her in fact, and had to call her twice to stop so that he could take a moment to regain his breath.

After an hour of walking as the sun began to rise, she suddenly halted beneath a huge Sycamore tree and grinned broadly. The tree was huge its branches seemed to rise to the very top of the forest's canopy. 'Here,' she announced. 'Here are the flowers we need.'

The lad looked around but could not see any hint of a flower anywhere on the forest floor, just patches of grasses, moss, and pine needles.

'Are the flowers invisible?' He asked mischievously, causing Analla to laugh.

'Invisible to you it seems,' she said. 'But you will see them shortly, once you climb to the top of this tree for me.'

He looked upwards. The tree must have been one of the tallest in the forest, its leaf laden branches reaching up to the sky and covering most of the early morning sun, which was struggling to pierce its blanket.

'I can't climb this tree.' Brid laughed. 'You know that I can't, it is too tall, I would be breathless before I reached halfway up.'

Analla looked upwards and examined the trunk. 'Then you must try to get halfway up it, regain your breath, and then climb the rest of the way. It is simple.'

'But I have never climbed a tree this high before, what if I fell? I could die.' A cold sweat had begun to form on the boy's forehead, and his stomach twitched and turned.

'You are not going to die today. No tree will cause your demise. Now go and get up that tree, the sun is rising and I need you to collect the flower buds before they open. Go on, up you go. You have the energy within you, you have it within you to do a great many things that you thought impossible. I have known this for a long time, since I brought you back from the brink when you were young, do you remember?'

'I remember being sick,' Brid said. 'I remember you sitting at my side and talking nonsense. I remember sleeping a lot and dreaming that I was a tiny fly caught in a spider's web, and that you came to save me from the spider when he came to eat me.'

'The fever was a strong one,' she said, 'and must have confused you, for that was no dream. The web was real, as was the spider, and a tasty fly you would have been for him too, you'll know it all soon enough. Now go, up the tree before you totally waste my morning.'

He looked at her quizzically, there was no humour in her voice. She just stood there and waited for him to start climbing. The boy knew it was an impossible task; his arms would not be strong enough to pull himself up, and he would fall to his death. Analla's face was immovable though, she expected him to do it.

With a swear word that he had heard his uncle say, he began to climb. When he had told her that he had never climbed a tree that high, he was not lying. This was because, to be quite truthful, he had never tried to climb any tree before. The other boys in the village laughed at him because he would not, but he knew that he was weak and that he would never be able to hold on. He would ignore their laughter, better to be laughed at than dead.

He was surprised however to find climbing easier than he thought. He concentrated on finding handholds and places to put his feet and found that after a short while he was about ten foot up the tree. His breathing was ragged, and his hands hurt from clinging on to the rough bark, but he had made a start.

'Stop and rest for a moment,' Analla called. 'You are doing well but you have a long way to go.'

He did as he was told and regained his breath before continuing to push himself upwards. His stomach still rang with nerves, but he found that he was actually beginning to enjoy the feeling and decided that he would perhaps climb more trees from then on.

Handhold after handhold, step after step Brid continued to rise. 'Stop again!' Analla shouted from below and he did, but this time he made the mistake of looking down towards her. Suddenly a dizziness came over him, his fingers felt weaker, and he found himself throwing his arms around the tree and holding it tightly.

'I'm too high!' The boy shouted. 'I'm going to fall!'

'You are not going to fall,' she said. 'I've already said that you will not die from falling from a tree. Take a moment, compose yourself and start climbing again, you are over halfway now.'

Brid took a glance upwards and saw that he was nearing the forest's canopy. The tightness in his chest increased, a pounding sound rang in his ears, and he realised that it was his heartbeat. He would not be beaten he told himself, and he thought of how he would surprise his mother and uncle when they found out what he had achieved today, and of how proud they would be. He also thought of the pride his father would have shown if he could see him.

He pushed upwards with tired legs and found more handholds, inch by inch, foot by foot, he climbed until... daylight. He had reached the top of the canopy and saw a bunch of flower buds growing from a vine on the uppermost branch. He settled himself into a wedge at the top of the trunk and plucked the buds, dropping them down to the forest floor, where he knew Analla would be waiting for them.

With the last bud picked Brid took a moment to look around. He was indeed at the top of the tallest tree in the forest, the canopy spread around him like a green carpet, miles wide. In the distance he could see the top of the mountains and from here it seemed as if he was as high as them. Brid had never felt so alive.

He did not know how long he stayed up there, it might have been five minutes, it might have been an hour, but eventually Analla disturbed him from his dream and told the boy to come down, which he did. She had told him that he could do it and he had, she had told him he would not fall and die, and he hadn't, and it was with a greater confidence that Brid Brothaig descended from his new home in the clouds. When his feet touched the floor he was both relieved but a little disappointed, he wanted to go back up. He had never felt so happy and strong.

'I'm going to be the greatest warrior to ever come from Finlay's Hollow,' he suddenly declared.

'You're nothing more than a weak minded fool with delusions of grandeur, boy.' Analla laughed.

Brid had absolutely no idea what she had just said, he knew however that he had been put back in his place.

Analla ruffled through her basket and brought out some fruit cakes, and the boy suddenly realised that he was ravenous.

'How did you know I wouldn't die, Analla?' he asked hungrily devouring the cake. 'Were you just saying it to make me do it?'

Analla shook her head and stood up, placing herself in front of the trunk of the tree.

'Look at this spider web,' she said, pointing to a large web attached to branches on the tree, glistening with morning dew. 'And here, look at this one.' She motioned to her left, where another web of similar size hung from the tree. 'Now watch,' she said and reached out both of her arms. The tips of her fingers touched the centre of each web, a hold so gentle that neither broke. Slowly she drew them together, so that the centre of each web touched and, with a quick twist of her fingers, joined with the other. When Amelia remembered it now, it was one of the most beautiful things that she had ever seen in all of her many lives, but back then, as a twelve year old boy, all she could think of was how the owners of these webs would ever work things out between them. Analla spoke again.

'This is the best way I know, of how to explain life and death to you, Brid. One day you will see the concurrence for yourself, we all do, and you will understand. This web on your left represents death. Our deaths occur at each tiny crossroads in the web, our souls depart our bodies and we enter the web, most of us travelling on a path to the centre, a huge orb of light and energy. On your right is the web of birth, our souls journey from the centre up the paths to a crossroads where they exit the void and become life as we know it. We are born into this world, and will stay here until the fates decide that it is our time to enter the web once more and travel back to the light at the centre of the void.'

Brid stared at the two webs joined in the middle and marvelled at the wonder of it all. If Analla spoke the truth, she was giving him a glimpse of the afterlife, a view of what awaited them all when they died and passed over, the centre of the web being what those with faith imagine Heaven to be. Back then Christianity had not come to Finlay's Hollow and the people of the village still believed in the Gods of the first men, the spirit kings and queens who governed and represented nature and the seasons. They believed that upon death they returned to the earth from which they were born, their souls joining with the hills and lochs, and they would become part of the land. At that moment Brid knew what was happening, Analla was telling a tall tale to a young boy, she was quite obviously a mad old bird.

He stood up and walked around the webs, a smile on his face. 'How would you know this? Only someone who has died would know what the afterlife is like. Mother tells me you're old, but you're certainly not dead yet.' He reached up and touched one of the webs, just gently enough to make it shake a little and cause some of the dew to drop onto the moss which carpeted the forest floor.

'You think I am lying to you?' She laughed. 'Do you think I would make all of this up? How do you know I have not been to the void a thousand times already?'

'Because you are here stood in front of me. You said yourself that when a person dies they travel to the centre again.' Brid motioned to the web drawing his finger along one of the lines which led inwards.

'I did say that, you're right. But I didn't say that this was the only path, it is simply the strongest, most comfortable one to follow once we pass from this life. Look closer to the web, there are other paths. Imagine this place here,' she drew her finger to a point in the web where the strands crossed. 'If what I am telling you is true, then this is a point of death for a person. When their soul leaves their body they appear here on the web, and most of us travel inwards towards the centre. But there are other paths, are there not?'

Of course she was right, Brid had seen a web before, and he knew that other strands led from crossroad to crossroad, sometimes straight and concentric and sometimes diagonal.

'What if when a person died and their soul entered the web, they decided not to take the easy path,' she continued. 'What if they chose not to head towards the light, but to go a different way? And if they stayed in the void long enough, they would be able to see all of the web, every death and birth that has been and is yet to come. That is how I knew you would not die from falling from the tree.'

Brid thought for a moment. 'You called it something different when you started to describe it, what's a conncunney?'

'The concurrence,' Analla laughed. 'Its's the true name of the web, a French version of a Latin word. I wouldn't expect you to have heard it before, I'm not sure the word has even been properly invented yet. I would try to explain it to you, and why the web is named so but it would be far too much for your little mind right now. Ask me again in a hundred years. I've told you more than enough for today.'

Brid was entranced by the image in front of him, He could almost imagine this giant web that Analla spoke of, and he imagined himself travelling along the different lines of the web. He shook himself from the daydream. No, surely she was telling him a tale. 'You are making no sense,' he said, 'If this was real then everyone would be doing it, wouldn't they?'

'Not true,' she replied. 'Only the brightest lights, those with the most energy have the power to move about the web. I have it, and you have it too, although I am seriously starting to doubt how bright you actually are.'

'But what good would it do to move around the web?' He said. 'You'd be dead and taking another path would only lead to another place of death, there would be no reason to do that, there is nowhere to go.'

Analla smiled. 'No,' she said. 'Perhaps you are right, Brid, there would be no reason for it whatsoever. Everything I have told you is just in my imagination, and if that is what you wish to believe then I will leave it there, and you can find out for yourself when your time arrives. Come, we must be heading back to the village, your mother will have jobs for you.' With a nimble twist of her fingers the two webs sprung apart once more, taking their places on opposite sides of the tree. He saw tiny movements at each of their edges as their owners crept out from the branches to survey their handiwork. Analla swept up her basket and began to walk away.

'But I don't understand.' The boy scrambled after her, struggling to keep up with her quick steps through the forest. For an old lady she could cover a lot of ground very swiftly. 'Now you're saying you made it up, and I don't know if that's a lie too. Tell me more, I don't mind if it's all lies.' But Analla would speak no more about it, and did not reply to any more of his questions that day, giving just a smile or a small snigger, as Brid's questions became more desperate.

When they reached the village, his mother did indeed have chores to be done, but Analla's words stayed with him the whole day, he could not shift them from his thoughts. He was distracted by them, and indeed that night he dreamt of a spider's web reaching for as far as the eye could see. Small fires burst into life at each crossroads and people appeared to float off towards a bright light at the centre of the web. He was floating in that web but did not travel along the paths, he remained motionless, hovering, and watching the deaths of many, and their journey towards the light. It would be fair to say that he was disappointed when he awoke. He had become comfortable in the void, it seemed like a natural place to be, even if it was all part of Analla's vivid imagination.

Brid visited the old healer later that day and found her, pottering around in her small cabin which stood on the outskirts of the village. She was placing items in a chest, which she then locked.

'What are you doing?' He said, making her jump as she had not heard him enter. As she turned to face him he could see that she looked concerned, worried even.

'I er... I'm having a tidy, my house is a mess.' She flustered. 'You never know when visitors will come – especially those who do not announce their arrival.'

'What have you put in the chest?' The boy asked, sitting down in her chair by the fireplace.

'I have locked up the last little idiot that asked me personal questions,' she snapped. 'Get out of my chair, Brid, I need to sit down. These old bones of mine are nearing the end of their days. I shall be glad to get some new ones.'

He looked at her confused, but jumped up to allow her a seat, which she slumped into with a long groan.

'If you must know I have put my precious things in the chest, things that might seem ordinary and useless to anyone else but mean something to me. Do you not have things like that?'

Brid sat himself down at her table and began to fiddle with a collection of small bones, which had been arranged neatly in a pile. 'I don't know really,' he replied, 'I suppose my most precious things are my father's sword, and his silver arm ring which he had taken from someone in battle. I have a wolf that I carved once from a piece of Oakwood, I would be upset if I ever lost that.' His thoughts were far away, trying to work out where the bone he held was from, perhaps a jawbone of some kind, maybe a shoulder.

'Badger leg!' Analla suddenly shouted, stunning Brid from his daydream and causing him to jump in shock and almost fall off of the bench.

Analla giggled, 'I am collecting my precious things so that I can put them somewhere safe, and retrieve them later on. I will need your help later to dig a hole. Do you think you'll be able to do that without falling on your arse?'

'You're burying it?'

'Of course, find somewhere remote, bury your things, and they'll be there later for you to collect when you want them – no matter how many hundreds of years that is.' She grinned at Brid then, a wide beaming smile that showed him just how many teeth she was missing. She was quite obviously crazy, and he laughed with her.

Analla's chest of precious things was not large, or even that heavy, and he was able to carry it without too much difficulty, although she made sure that he was able to have rest stops along the way. They made their way out of the hollow into the hills which surrounded the Loch. From there it was possible to see for miles all around and they stood at the edge of the huge drop known as Giant's Leap. They paused for a moment for Brid to regain his breath looking out over Finlay's Hollow and the great loch beneath them.

'I've been right back to the beginning, you know,' she said absent mindedly, gazing out over the valley far below them. 'Back to when the giants roamed these lands. I was here after the last of the giants died, and the world was given over to men. I have even been so far forwards that I witnessed the end, when it all comes to a sudden stop, and the time of men was over.'

Brid did not know what to say to her. He was used to her ramblings, of course, he could put up with them a lot better than most. In the last two days however, she had really gone beyond.

'You are ancient then, and only just a little older than I thought.' He said, picking up her chest once more.

'I am!'. Analla laughed. 'There's still a bit of life in me yet though. You'll see soon enough. Keep going, my tree isn't too much further.' There was a small copse ahead and she sped up as she saw it, talking to herself and causing the boy to have to run a little to keep up with her. The collection of trees was not large, but it was dense and overgrown, and he tripped over roots as he tried to keep up with the muttering old woman ahead of him.

'Here!' She shouted suddenly and he ran into the back of her. 'This is my tree!'. She circled it, almost in a dance, wearing a wide smile on her face, and patting the trunk.

The tree was old, but no more so than any other in the small woods. It was only as Analla knelt by it and began to dig at the soil with her hands, that he noticed a symbol carved into its base; this was her tree indeed. She scrabbled down into the dirt until she felt something solid beneath her fingers. 'A-ha!' She said and pulled back a flat rock underneath which was a hollow large enough for her chest to fit into. She took the casket from him, placing it on the floor and opening it up. The chest was full of trinkets and jewellery, and she rummaged around pulling out a piece of parchment which she looked at quickly, mumbling under her breath, before slamming the chest lid shut again. Reciting, a collection of words and numbers which meant nothing to Brid, she placed the chest within the hollow, lowered the flat stone over it and with the boy's help began heaping dirt on top. By the time they had finished it was impossible to tell that there had ever been any disturbance made to the ground by the tree. 'That's it.' She cried. 'Come on, back to the Hollow, there are other things I need to do before tomorrow.'

Brid was confused. 'Analla, what were those words you were saying, it was in a language I didn't understand. Was it a witch's spell?'

Analla laughed, loud and hard. 'No, it was not the spell of a witch. Although if you understood the words and what they meant, you would realise the magic that they can do in the right hands.'

'What were they then?' Brid asked wondering what riddles the old woman would come up with next. Analla looked about suspiciously before bringing the boy in closer to whisper in his ear.

'Did you see the piece of parchment in the casket, the one I read quickly?'

'Yes.'

'Well, that piece of paper is a map, it is a puzzle that I must follow. A riddle I must solve. I just wanted to make sure I knew where to head next.'

'I'm sorry if this sounds rude, Analla, but sometimes it would be less confusing to me if you just didn't answer my questions at all.'

Analla screamed with laughter, a dry cackle which echoed in the trees around them. 'You are a funny boy,' She exclaimed. 'I look forward to seeing you with new eyes, to see if you are the same when you are a grown woman.' She continued to laugh as she set off back towards Finlay's Hollow.

Brid followed her, shaking his head, and deciding that perhaps it was not wise to aspire to be a healer like Analla, as it was obviously a recipe for madness and odd behaviour. They trudged back to the village, and he found that, for once, he had less to ask the old woman than normal. He left her at her cabin, but she stopped as she opened the door to enter. She looked at the boy and then at the rest of the small village of Finlay's Hollow, her eyes rheumy and wet, it looked as if she was trying not to cry.

'What is it, Analla?' He asked. 'Why do you look so sad?'

'The transition from one life for another is usually always a time of sadness. It is hard to lose the ones you love and who have been part of a lifetime.'

'Are you leaving, Analla?' He said, his voice strained. 'You said that the map was telling you where to go next. Do you mean to die?'

Suddenly she broke the moment with a mischievous grin. 'Die? Me, die? I can assure you, Brid that I intend to go on living for a very long time indeed, I've got too much to do. Good night!' She disappeared into her cabin and shut the door behind her.

That night Brid could not sleep. There was something nagging at his mind, tugging at him, and preventing him from drifting off to dream. All he could think about was Analla's web, her bizarre behaviour, and their trip to the copse. He decided that he would tell his uncle about it in the morning. The laird had known Analla for years, perhaps he knew if her words could be trusted or not. Still sleep would not come though, and finally Brid got out of his cot to dress and, collecting his most precious things, padded out into the night to start his own burial stash.

Brid was woken at dawn by the distant sound of screaming and crying. He turned over in his cot, pulling the sheepskin over his head, perhaps being awake for most of the night had not been a good idea after all. The sound didn't go away though and, as he began to stir himself, he realised that the sound was not far away at all. It was coming from the outside of the hall. He could hear his younger sisters, and he looked over to see them sat in their cots on the other side of the hall whimpering. His mother was nowhere to be seen. The doors to the hall were shut, but he could see smoke seeping in under the wood and, as he ran towards them, he could hear the screams and cries ever clearer.

He opened the doors to a scene of horror; the village of Finlay's Hollow was ablaze, and men in mail shirts and iron helmets were running through the houses killing everyone in their path.

'Stay in your beds!' Brid screamed to his sisters. 'Do not leave until Mother or I come back for you!' he went outside and pushed closed the doors.

The men of the village were trying to defend their homes, but they were farmers with no armour and without proper weapons to threaten the invaders with any real purpose. Most of them carried hoes and scythes which, no matter who wielded them, were no match for the axes and swords that they were faced with. Brid wished that he had his father's sword to hand, although he knew it was too large for him, and that he would not have been strong enough to use it against those that were destroying the village.

Smoke and flames engulfed the houses, stinging his eyes, as the raiders ran from house to house, slaughtering any man that they saw and dragging women and children screaming from their homes. He ran down the steps of the hall, unthinking of his own safety, as he desperately searched the scene for any sign of his mother. He screamed for her as he dodged between horses and villagers, trying to make his voice heard over the cacophony, but it was useless, she was nowhere to be seen.

Suddenly he fell, his feet catching on something on the floor and he landed heavily, his hands breaking his fall, and sending him skidding through the dirt. He rolled and looked behind him at what he had tripped over and saw that it was his uncle. He was laid on his back; his chest was a mass of open wounds, his arms outstretched, his hand still clutching his sword. Sobbing Brid crawled back to him and shook him in a futile attempt to revive him, but he was gone.

He heard a scream in the distance, the voice of his mother, and he scrambled to his feet running in the direction of the sound. He shouted to her, telling her that he was coming, telling her that he would find her, until through the smoke and fire, he saw her.

Three men towered over her. They threw her roughly to the floor and the largest of the men began to loosen his trews, grinning at the thought of what was to come.

'No!' Brid screamed and they all turned to him. 'Leave my mother alone!' He clenched his fists and prepared to fight them to save her.

If Amelia closed her eyes, even now, she could see the largest of the men, as if he were stood in front of her. He was so huge he would have dwarfed even the Laird, he seemed to be built of solid muscle. His head was partly shaved and covered in blue ink, and an angry red scar ran down the left side of his face. He looked at Brid for a moment, his eyes piercing, cold and blue. He laughed loudly and turned back to the boy's mother, dropping to his knees, and grabbing her legs with his huge bloody hands. Brid's mother screamed and he struck her across the face. 'Kill the boy.' He said without turning back to Brid, and his companions advanced on him drawing their weapons.

Brid frantically scanned the floor, before picking up a pitchfork, his shaking hands pointing it at his killers. He knew that his death was coming, and suddenly he thought of the void described by Analla, the web into which he would shortly be thrown.

One of the men used his axe to strike away the pitchfork, which flew from the boy's weak hands. Brid stepped backwards and fell over his own feet, and they stood over him, their axes raised above their heads ready to strike.

And then they stopped.

Their eyes shifted and they stared past the boy, their mouths agape.

Brid turned to see what they were watching, and he saw Analla walking slowly from her cabin. He was not sure, even to this day, hundreds of years, and many lifetimes later, if his eyes were true at that time, but he was quite sure that light emanated from her body. It was as if she glowed with a bright yellow luminescence. Could the men see what he was seeing? Was the old woman really magic after all?

Analla walked towards where the boy lay, kneeling and reaching out her arms as she neared, enveloped him within them. Her mouth touched his ear and she whispered, in a bright almost melodic tone.

'Time to leave. We're going on an adventure together.' She looked up at the men wielding the axes, as if to witness the things that would end her life.

The axes fell, Brid felt a sharp and powerful blow to the back of his head, and then darkness.

'So you died, and you were reborn as you are now. That's amazing.' Sophie said, still holding on to the old lady's hand.

'Oh no,' laughed Amelia, 'A lot more happened in between my life as Brid and where we are now, all kinds of fantastic things. Some terrible ones too, but for the most part all my lives had been wonderful, in their own way.'

'That's really interesting, Amelia.' David said, draining his cup of tea. 'You really know how to put a story together, don't you?' He stood, as if to leave, but Amelia waved her hand towards his chair, and he felt compelled to sit again.

'If you'll pour me another tea, dear.' she said smiling, 'I'll let you into the secret of what happens when we all die.'

David picked up the teapot and poured, perhaps another few minutes would not hurt.

# Helel
# The Tall Man
## Gökhem, Sweden 3127BCE

In another place in the world, far away from the Sunningdale Retirement Village, and at a much earlier time in history, a tall warrior rode his horse into a village on the edge of extinction.

He was angry, but that seemed to be a permanent element of his personality. You see the problem with being intent on revenge and destroying the world for thousands of years is that your hatred had to be deep rooted, an obsession, a single unwavering goal, you had to really want it. For the tribesman though, holding a grudge was something that he did very well, he had many years to practice, and the time had only intensified the need to fulfil his plan.

He had been released twenty years ago from his cell in Gehinom and sent out to cause havoc in the world. Gehinom, or what is generally known to most other inhabitants of this foul plane as Hell, had been his prison for thousands of years, and in all of that time he had sat patiently biding his time, planning his revenge on the world, and those who governed it.

As the tall man now entered the village, which was really no more than a small collection of huts, it was clear to him that he had arrived at the perfect time. Perfect for him that is, for the residents of Gökhem it was the worst time imaginable.

Helel Bene Elim had been travelling for two years, originally setting off from the Mugodzhar Hills and the vast steppes that surrounded them, and riding and walking for nearly two thousand miles.

He had left the nomadic tribe where he had long been the chieftain, in the middle of the night, silently killing two of the sentries at the edge of the camp before they could wake the rest of the tribe. He regretted killing the men, they had been good brothers to him, and their mother would be distraught to wake the next morning to find that two of her sons were dead and the other had fled the plains never to be seen again. It was important that he left without any fuss however. He had tried to leave twice in the past, but had always been persuaded to stay for just one more year, one more movement of the herds to better pastures. He enjoyed the life with his tribe, but he knew that he had other more important matters to attend to.

He had taken two of the ponies and enough food and supplies to last him for a couple of weeks slowly making his way north, always keeping his mind on his final goal. Tribal life had suited him well, it reminded him of the time before his first death, before Gehinom. Back in his very first life, in the desert into which he and the other Watchers had been placed, he had been the oldest and greatest. The Watchers were his brothers and cousins, his powerful children, a family which had been powerful; feared and respected by those around them. Unfortunately for those around them Helel and his family had also been very fond of killing or enslaving those that they saw as lower than them, which was basically anyone who wasn't a Watcher or their children.

Helel loved this time in Earth's history, violence as a tool to meet ends was still totally acceptable, and it was almost frowned upon to increase your power and prestige without using unnecessary force and cruelty upon others. It was, in his mind an almost peak point for enjoyment in a world which subsequently walked a long path towards achieving your goals through diplomacy and politics. Better, Helel, thought, to be a hammer crushing your enemies than a sugared tongue lying your way to greatness. But such was the way of things, and the so called evolution of the filth known as humanity.

For all its violent benefits however, if there was one thing about the Neolithic era that really annoyed Helel it was the dirtiness of it all and he sniffed disdainfully as he walked past the bodies which lay scattered in the mud.

He thought about the last time he had been in Sweden and longed for a return to his life as a software algorithm engineer, where he had set about destroying the world through his part in the invention and promotion of social media. He knew that eventually giving people the idea that staring at their phone for hours on end, and envying the fake lives of others would eventually do a fantastic job at dismantling the world, through the pretence of 'bringing the world together'. It was just a small explosion however, from the many little bombs he was intent of placing throughout history.

Eventually, he knew, that these little fires set around the world at various points would cause a blaze that would see the world burn, but it was a long heavy task, a more brutal version of which had caused him to return to Sweden at this time. When he was last here he had all the amenities available to a successful person in the early twenty-first century. He missed his spotlessly clean eighth floor apartment in the centre of Gothenburg, his beautiful views over the city, his UHD TV, and his internet; Oh, how he missed the internet! He promised himself that his next stop would be a return to the twenty-first century, and the first thing he would do was order himself a pizza and eat it in the bath whilst drinking a bottle of dry white wine. He closed his eyes for a moment dreaming of the feeling of a hot bath followed by soft towels and a comfortable bed. For now he was stuck in the dirty, cold, smelly late Neolithic era where he itched from lice, ached from his travels, and would quite literally kill for a double expresso almond mocha.

He wondered if his brothers and sisters, also freed from Hell, were staying true to the path, and had not just settled for a clean, luxurious life far in the future. He knew that Azazel was as much of a zealot as he, when it came to the cause, her twin sister Sariel too, but the others? Armaros had always been soft on the humans, quick to profess his undying love, Samjaza, the youngest of the siblings was greedy, and would be strayed from the task easily once he realised just how much of the world and its benefits were at his disposal, and finally Penemue, the oldest brother, he was the sharpest and most knowledgeable, but he also had a terrible and distracting need to learn more. How would Penemue have coped with the modern world of Assiyah with all of its books and understanding. What would have happened when Penemue had discovered the wonders and terrors that the internet brought, with its vast volumes of information, both true and wildly inaccurate. All of his siblings had made an oath to support him in his revenge, every one of them had promised to fight with him and bring back what they had lost. He hoped that they would stay true to this and be there to stand beside him at the end. They knew the punishment if they failed him.

The end however was far in the distance, much needed to be done before then and for now Helel was here in the muddy, and plague ridden filth of Neolithic man. The village of Gökhem was in its last days, the residents had stopped trying to rid themselves of the dead now; for those that had not been afflicted their only thought was to survive. Many had fled to other villages, only worsening the problem, which was already devastating the known world, some simply shut themselves away and prayed to their primitive gods for forgiveness and mercy. Helel Bene Elim knew the true gods of this world though, he had met them on the battlefield, and he knew that mercy was not something that they were terribly fond of.

He approached one of the bodies, one that looked as though it had recently passed. He took the sample he needed and placed it in his knapsack. He would take the sample as far as he could before he started to sicken himself. There he would make sure it was safe before he died again. It was to be a slow process, and this was just the start of it. Bringing an end to the world would be worth all the time it took to achieve, and time was not an issue.

# Zophiel
# The Last Yetziran

## Finlay's Hollow – 632CE

When Zophiel landed in the centre of the village and folded her wings, Finlay's Hollow was in a state of frozen chaos. All around her perfectly still Viking raiders with angry faces waved their axes and plundered the small village. Messengers such as her lived in a time different to that of the Newmans whose life force they collected. Time on Assiyah ran around them at about the speed of wet paint drying, or a bank answering a telephone call. It needed to run this slowly to allow the messengers to get around the world collecting the souls of the imminently dead without having to rush too much. It also meant that they could go about their work unseen to the Newman eye.

Zophiel Melaku had a very singular claim to fame amongst the Yetziran people. It wasn't the kind of claim to fame that you could live off, nothing that made her really that special, but perhaps the kind that would get mentioned in passing and her friends might remember for a bit. A couple of hundred thousand years ago she was the last born Yetziran. She forgot the exact number of years, to be fair when you have lived that long, birthdays aren't really something special anymore. Newmans seemed to lose interest in the annual celebration fairly quickly into their brief lives and resorted to only commemorating the round numbers, until they got to a hundred when it became some kind of watchable marathon for others to see when they would finally peg it.

Zophiel was born at a time when the people of Yetzirah were at their evolutionary peak, they had conquered death, had embraced immortality, and had been so caught up in their own brilliance that they almost didn't realise that no more of them were created after Zophiel Melaku. That's the problem with evolutionary peaks, there's only one way to go once you've hit the heights. For a short while, when they finally did realise that she was the last winged baby, she was a bit of a scientific wonder. Her name was well known to those that were interested and as a small child she became the poster girl for the demise of Yetzirah; not something you would particularly want to put your name to, but, there was a famous Yetziran saying which roughly translates as – 'Fate bears no thought for who it decides to give a bloody good kicking.'

The brief interest in Zophiel ebbed away at a fairly quick pace however until she was nothing more than an old news story, forgotten by all but the saddest of news geeks. Zophiel didn't mind though, she was able to move on with her life, and when Assiyah was created as a new source of life force for the Yetzirans to farm, and the opportunity arose to be part of a new and exciting project, she jumped at the chance to become a messenger.

Zophiel loved her job. There was something satisfying about knowing that you were playing a vital role in the universe, moving life forces on to a new adventure whilst also keeping her people alive at the same time. She treated today's mission, as she treated each time she was able to visit the Newman world, with great excitement, and it showed in her bright ice blue eyes. She was tall, even for a Yetziran, her hair was tied into a long, plaited tail which ran down her back, a black woven line which divided the large golden feathered wings which sprouted from her shoulders. Yetzirans rarely used their wings to actually fly to get around, there was no need and most Yetzirans were inherently lazy. Wings were seen mainly as a status symbol, something to use for flying as a hobby. They came in a variety of colours dependant on the current fashion or preference of their owner, but it was generally accepted that the larger and more naturally golden a pair of wings were, the better you were as a Yetziran. Millions of years of evolution had still not completely weeded out the desperate need to be superior to your peers.

Zophiel hummed a song to herself as she dodged her way through the frozen in time Vikings who, axes raised, were fully engaged in pillage mode. She stepped over the bodies of the villagers who had already fallen foul of the axes, and who had small brown cloth bags sat beside them which had been left by the collector, a being known to the Newmans as the Grim Reaper amongst other things. These bags contained the extracted life force which the messengers would then pick up and take back to Yetzirah with them. There the life force would be processed and pruned. The 'trimmings' would be sent on to maintain the lives of the Yetziran people, and the basic life force essence would be sent to create new life on the planet by being given to the newborn on Assiyah, there it would grow, and develop until it was time for collecting and harvesting once more. Zophiel likened it to a beautiful flowering plant which she maintained as a gardener of sorts.

Each time she visited Assiyah on a collection trip she was given a specific 'mark' to find. Today she had been given a small boy and it was not hard to find him in spite of the frozen flames, sharpened axes, and angry Vikings that seemed to litter the immediate area. The boy was knelt on the floor head bowed, an axe blade within a hairs breadth of striking the back of his head. Knelt by his side was an old woman, her arms around him and her lank grey hair covering his face like a curtain. Stood over them was another messenger, looking very confused indeed.

'Hey, Totfiel,' Zophiel chirped as she ducked under an axe and knelt by the boy to collect his bag. 'We are on a time limit here, you know. Don't be hanging around, we only have 60 heartbeats to collect our bag and leave or there'll be trouble.'

Totfiel Okiro, a white winged messenger, who Zophiel always thought looked like he could do with a good meal, simply smiled back at her.

'Yeah, good luck with that.' He said, folding his arms as she searched the floor around the boy and old woman. The two messengers had been good friends for longer than either of them cared to remember, they had both joined the messenger service at a young age, they were both just over three hundred thousand years old and had bonded immediately during the training programme.  She liked his slightly rebellious dark attitude, whereas he enjoyed her absolute desperate need to do things by the rules.

'What's going on?' Zophiel asked. 'These bags are empty, have you picked up the full ones, Toti?'

'No,' said Totfiel sitting down in the mud without a care for his pristine white robes. 'I'm waiting for one of the bosses. There's a problem here.'

Zophiel continued to scrabble around on the floor around the about to die couple, the full bags must be there, the bags were always there. 'This is weird, Toti. Do you think there's been some kind of mistake? Are we in trouble?'

'The answer to that is far above my pay grade, I'm too smart to have to worry about it,' Totfiel said, grinning. 'We can't be blamed for not collecting something which isn't there in the first place though, surely.'

'You mean you actually get paid?' Zophiel laughed as she lifted the cloak of the old woman just to check that the bag containing the life force was not hidden. 'Paid work was banned thousands of years before we were born, don't tell me they've reintroduced it just to get you out of bed in the morning.'

'It's a figure of speech, idiot,' smiled Totfiel. 'Any moment now…'

Suddenly a shaft of light hit the ground not far from where they stood, it was so bright that it blinded them for a moment and when the light faded, a tall red haired Yetziran being with the most golden wings Zophiel had ever seen floated in front of them. He had a long angular face that looked never far from a sneer, and sharp cheekbones that looked as though they would break through his pale skin at any moment. With a strange popping noise, like a cork being pulled from a wine bottle, he dropped to the ground. It was Araqiel Mardero, the deputy Arch in charge of life force collection this week, and his face was angry.

'You do realise I was in the middle of an important call with one of the Arches. She is not in the habit of being curtailed so that I can come down to sort out incompetent messengers. I am expecting to hear the greatest story ever as to why neither of you have collected your bags and returned to Yetzirah. Impress me.'

'There are no bags, sir,' Zophiel said. Trying not to sound too smug.

Araqiel let out a snort. 'No bags? Of course there are bags, I can see them. Look, there! Now pick them up and get yourselves back to Yetzirah. Quickly.'

'These bags are empty,' Totfiel replied. 'We've looked for full ones. Thoroughly. They are not here. Here are the Newmans, obviously about to die, but there are no bags containing their sucked-out life forces. Do feel free to have a look for yourself.' Totfiel's manner showed that he was not as good as Zophiel at hiding his smugness. Araqiel shot him a hard stare.

'If I may, sir,' asked Zophiel. 'Perhaps the collector missed his appointment. There's a lot of dead people here, maybe he forgot these two.

Or perhaps he didn't tie them up well enough and the life forces got out of the bags somehow'.

'The collector does not forget, nor does he make mistakes. The collector never misses an appointment,' Araqiel touched his hand to his head in complete bemusement. 'Wait here. Do not move from this spot.' He looked up at the sky and the beam of bright light shot down from the sky again. When the light faded the deputy Arch was gone once more.

'Well, this is awkward. You need to be careful,' said Zophiel. 'You don't want to give yourself a bad reputation with the bosses. Especially an idiot like Mardero, he has a terrible temper, proper Old Testament. You'll get yourself sent to the other place.'

Even Totfiel shivered at the thought of this. The other place 'Gehinom' was a world created for the unwanted waste of the life force business. It was where the sullied and irreparable souls went, the 'wrong Newmans' that had used their time on Assiyah for cruelty and terrible actions, soiling their life forces and making them almost worthless. It was staffed by Yetzirans of similar quality, those that had besmirched the goodness of the people of Yetzirah through bad behaviour. They processed and tortured the bad souls from Assiyah, draining every last bit of life force from them in order to survive themselves. For a messenger to be sent there was the worst punishment imaginable, worse even than being made a Newman and forced to live on Assiyah.

Araqiel Mardero reappeared in the same manner as before, a flash of light from the heavens and an unedifying pop as he landed on the ground. A nervous smile was on his face, and he no longer looked as though he wanted to disintegrate them in a torrent of holy fire.

'Ok, nothing more to do here, you two,' he said. 'Get yourselves back to Yetzirah.'

Zophiel was confused, where had his anger gone? 'But, sir, what about the missing life forces? Are we in trouble?'

'No, you're not in trouble, yet. The missing life forces are not your concern. Time to go.' And in a flash of light the Deputy Arch was gone again, leaving the messengers in shock.

'Weird,' said Totfiel. 'But there you go, obviously something we shouldn't be concerned about.'

'Does it not worry you, Toti? Doesn't it freak you out. It's not right, surely it's not right.'

'Why should it worry me? Nothing to do with us. It's only a little life force. There's plenty more to go around.'

'Yeah, but where's it gone?' she said dramatically throwing her arms out, an action which automatically spread her golden wings wide.

'No idea, and to be honest I don't really care either. Come on let's get home.' Totfiel placed his hands together in front of his chest and shot upwards in a streak of light leaving Zophiel stood on her own.

She paused for a moment, whistling a tune as she took one last look around the now ruined village of Finlay's Hollow, before placing her hands in front of her and leaving Assiyah by shooting into the sky.

# Amelia
# Her First but not Last Afterlife

## The Concurrence

The being first known as Brid, and in a later life as Amelia, was no longer human, not in the sense of anything recognisable. They had no arms or legs, no head, there was no body in fact. All that there was of them was light and thought. They looked around and saw other flashes of light floating in the blackness, it was as if they had been transported into the night sky and had become a star. There was a pattern to the stars around them though, each piece of light travelled in a line, and they saw that in the far distance sat a bright white orb, the destination of the stars. The path felt warm and comfortable, the white centre seemed to exude this heat along its strands, inviting all of the smaller lights towards it. It was a web! The web which Analla had described, she had been right all along. Brid had been killed upon the earth and had entered the next phase - this was the afterlife.

The being first known as Brid turned briefly to see where they had appeared from and saw a hole in the blackness behind them. From a distance it would have seemed like just another light, although larger than the lights which came out of them, but up close as they were, they could still see Finlay's Hollow through the hole. They were high above the village and could see that it was on fire, and murder was still being done as short bursts of light were appearing from it, just like Brid had.

The being first known as Brid felt the pull of the centre of the web and began their journey towards it. The warmth of the orb invited them, and they went without question, floating slowly towards their goal. They could not tell you how long they floated in the void, time was of no matter there, they simply floated, painless and alone. At times, if they did not keep totally true to the path they felt the cold of the black void alongside, gnawing and threatening them, a place of danger which they were not meant to venture into. Along the path other holes in the web appeared and as they passed, the being that would eventually be a little old lady called Amelia glanced into them seeing other villages like their own, but also great cities of stone and metal, forests and jungles, endless deserts, and lakes so wide that they could have been oceans. Lights appeared from them, the souls of others killed elsewhere in the world, and together they created a strand of a seemingly infinite web.

Suddenly their name echoed through the blackness. They could have said that they heard it, but that is too blunt a term for the sense that they experienced. It was as if the word appeared within them, a voice inside the ball of light that now made up their being.

'Brid.' It called, or was it Amelia, or perhaps Mohammed, or Kyung-Sook, or Francois? They owned so many names although did not know it then. Their name was called again, and they fought to recognise the voice calling it. There was no tone to the voice, no accent or volume, but they knew that it belonged to Analla – or was it Alan, or Lydia, or Jyoti? The being once known as Brid tried to respond but did not know how. Panic stirred and they spun around as if to see Analla floating beside them. She was not there.

'Brid,' it called again. 'Move to the edge of the path, fight against the cold no matter how much it burns you. I am waiting for you in the void. Come to me.'

For the first time Brid looked beyond the path, into the inky blackness between strands of the web, and it was there that they saw a ball of light alone in the dark. They turned to looked longingly at the centre of the web, the orb still glowed beckoning them in. It was where they felt they were meant to go, they were not meant to move from the path, they should stay on course. There was something though, a nagging feeling within and they found themself edging towards Analla, and away from the path. The coldness bit, like a master would chide a dog that misbehaved, and they flinched somewhat. It did not stop them though they continued into it, and the coldness grew and surrounded them.

'I can't do it,' they thought, and wondered whether Analla would be able to hear them. 'It hurts too much I cannot join you.' They looked into the void where the light of Analla awaited. 'I have to go back, it is impossible.'

'It is not impossible, just difficult,' responded Analla. 'It is a barrier to hold you within, but it can be broken. I am not cold. Come to me.'

The being first known as Brid pushed forwards again, throwing themself into the coldness, fighting against the knives of frost which sliced at their light, and threatened to leave them an icy ball forever floating in the darkness.

'It's too much, too hard,' they called, and that is when Analla moved forwards, coming close as if to pull them towards her.

'You're nearly there, Brid. Just one more push'

Brid pushed again, although it felt as though they were trying to run through a boulder. The pain was immense, but then it was... gone.

A sudden warmth enveloped them, and they threw themself towards Analla's light. They were free.

'What do we do now? Where is there to go?'

The soft warm glow of Analla was now around them now as they were drawn inside.

'I told you before you were killed, Brid, we are going on a journey. We are going back to the world.'

'But I am dead.'

'You were. That body, that life is gone now. It's time to start a new one. Let's go.' And they floated across the void heading towards another hole in the web. 'Those that are brave, those that can break free of the comfortable path, can find another life should they wish. I have done it for centuries, there are a handful of us that know the way back; some are good beings enjoying their multiple lives and helping those around them, however there are some who follow darker paths, mischievous and deadly, touring through their many lives causing chaos and terror, I pray you never meet them. This gift, this knowledge that there are choices, and that death is not the end, I am sharing it with you. If you follow the other idiots, blindly heading towards their destruction you can end it all here if that is what you wish. Do you want to return to the world? Do you want to live on the earth again?'

'Yes, I do. I'm not ready for it to end yet. How do I get a new life? Will I be born again?'

'In a way, yes. You do not control who you go back as. You may return as a baby, but not through birth.' There are dangers though, Brid. There are those that try to prevent us from borrowing lives, we call them

Reapers for once they have caught you, then you are truly dead to the world. I have known friends in the long past be taken forcefully and led straight into the centre of the web, to prevent their return. That is the choice you must make, another chance at life, or an eternity of the unknown. If you want to change your mind, I will not blame you. Think carefully.'

'What is at the centre of the web? Perhaps it is not so bad.'

'Perhaps not, but think of how I demonstrated to you in the forest what the web looked like.'

'Yes, you drew two webs together.'

'And tell me, Brid. What normally lives in the centre of a web?'

'A…a spider?'

'Yes, a spider but more likely it is a creator of sorts. The being that devised and built the web in the first place. Now some would happily fly down the strands of the web in order to meet their creator, but I, and others like me are not ready for that yet, some might never be. Some take the spider analogy a step further and ask the question; what does the creator of the web do with those caught within it? Now tell me, do you wish to trust your fate to the chance that it is a benevolent and neutral creator, or is there a niggle inside of you that fears a different fate for those floating mindlessly towards the spider?'

The being first known as Brid did not give it a moment's thought. 'I wish to go back. I'm not ready to give up just yet. Take me back.'

Their journey slowed and they came to a small hole in the blackness. 'Here is an opening; a light will be appearing from here very soon. Analla said. 'This one will do for you. It is all just a matter of timing.'

'But aren't you coming too?'

'I must take another path, Brid. But I will find you.'

They felt themself being pushed towards the hole in the void. They came free of Analla and found themself hovering above the entrance to their new life. They looked down into it and saw a darkened room with a large wooden bed in the middle. People stood around the bed, watching a small figure laid on top of the blankets. The people seemed sad, a tall man dressed in black robes stood at the head of the bed, he held his arms in front of him and seemed to be talking although they could not hear his voice.

Suddenly a bright light appeared at the edge of the hole. It was glowing white and seemed to crackle with life.

'Now! Go!' Analla called, and pushed the ball of light first known as Brid into the hole. Falling towards the bed at great speed, they hit the small form on the bed and took control of the body. They opened their eyes, and spoke the first words of their new life.

'Oh shit, I'm a girl!'

# Helel
# The Weird Son
## Kaffa, Crimea 1345CE

The on and off siege of Kaffa by the Golden Horde had so far lasted for two years. Kipchak Khan Janibeg's warriors had besieged the trading port and had been on the verge of breaching the walls back in 1343, when the Italian relief force had arrived and strengthened the Genoese army, causing the great Khan to retreat home and lick his wounds. Undaunted he had returned two years later, grinding down the defenders, continuing to send his men forwards day and night, uncaring as to the numbers of men that he lost in the endeavour. The Khan now sat in his tent surrounded by his most trusted warriors and secretly hoped that for once they would be honest with him.

The Khan studied the faces of the generals stood around the tent. Each of them looked towards the floor. None of them were stupid enough to lie to him anymore, and not one of them wished to raise their head above the parapet and admit that the Horde were failing, and that retreat was the only strategically sound response. They had seen how he treated failure when he had been forced to retreat before. Of his generals in that last failed campaign only the ones that were his close family had kept their heads, and they considered themselves lucky. He had enough bravado and history to have survived that last defeat with his crown. To fall back to Sarai a second time? He may as well declare his eldest son the Khan and put the blade into his own chest. He could not run away again,

'Will we win if we remain here?' He asked. Can we take the port?'

Only Berdi Beg his oldest son was willing to speak up and say the words. Perhaps it was because he had the most to gain from the Horde's defeat.

'Father, if we do not breach the walls of the port within the week our men will be crushed, and the army forced to head back east to recover. The plague is killing more of our men than our enemy, if we do not take the port soon our numbers will no longer be enough.'

'A week you say. Is the disease really that bad?'

'We are losing over a hundred good men a day. Our cause is unsustainable if we do not win soon, Father. I say we return to Sarai and build the Horde once more. We can return in two years, perhaps three.'

Janibeg looked around at the others, still they did not raise their faces and look at him, there was silence in the room apart from the sound of loud chewing.

'And what of you Qulpa?' Janibeg said to his youngest son who was the only one in the tent other than the Khan not stood. The tallest and strongest of the Khan's legitimate offspring, he lounged out on furs at the back of the tent eating olives and fruit and seeming to be very disinterested in the whole situation. Of all of his sons, even the many illegitimate ones, it was Qulpa that Janibeg feared the most. He knew it would only be a matter of time before he murdered his way to the position of ultimate power and took what Janibeg had himself killed his own father and brothers to get. Janibeg had considered killing Qulpa first, he had learned from his forebears that a pre-emptive assassination of one of your progenies by a Khan could delay any attempt at rebellion for at least a couple of years.

'What do you have to say, my son? You are not normally this quiet, you seem to have spent the majority of this campaign telling others behind my back how I have been doing things wrong. What brilliant idea do you have for saving my skin now, or do you wish to see me defeated and humiliated so that you can begin the ascendence that I know you covet?'

Qulpa finished his mouthful before speaking, an act which he knew would aggravate his father beyond words.

'Dear Father,' he said finally, his voice smooth and musical. 'You know that I respect and admire you above all others. How could I even think of taking your place; no one could. You are the great Khan, you rule over the Golden Horde with strength and love, and your name will be remembered for eternity, even those that have died in your name will serve you. I do have an idea but I'm sure that it is nothing that you haven't already thought of and dismissed.' He reached out and grabbed another handful of olives, enjoying the fact that all eyes in the room were now on him.

'Go on,' the Great Khan said.

'As I said, your men will serve you, even in the afterlife. I suggest stopping the burning of plague bodies immediately. Let the dead horde serve you once more.'

'Are you talking of magic?' Berdi laughed. 'Really, Qulpa I thought you a sharper mind than to rely on superstition and necromancy. What do you propose, raising the dead and having an unkillable army marching into Kaffa?'

'Not at all, dear brother. There is no magic necessary. I simply say that we share the terror that has been bestowed upon us. Load up our plague dead heroes onto the slings, throw them high into the air, into the centre of the port. The disease will do all of the fighting for us. All we have to do is sit and wait. The city will fall.'

The Great Khan thought for a moment. To treat the dead in this way would surely be seen as disrespectful, it could lead to rebellion if word of the deed reached Sarai. The situation was dire however, failure to take Kaffa would be an even more dangerous threat to his reign, and besides the horde were pledged to serve him in this life and the next.

'Let it be done, the sacrifice of the heroic dead will not be forgotten, they will bring us victory, although their bodies are plague ridden and the task will most likely be lethal for all those involved.' He stood from his chair and his generals immediately sank to their knees; their heads bowed. All except Qulpa, who continued to eat. 'Qulpa, my new favourite son. It is a good plan and one that will surely give us victory. In recognition of your innovation, I put you personally in charge of the collection and... distribution of the plague dead. Start immediately.'

If Janibeg had expected to see fear and horror on his youngest sons face he was to be disappointed. In fact, the sly grin on Qulpa's face widened and he popped one last olive into his mouth before standing and bowing to his father.

'It would be a pleasure, my Khan,' he said striding out of the tent to begin his grim work.

For a brief moment in the tent every face shared a look of outright bemusement, even the Khan himself looked incredulous. Qulpa had taken on this death sentence of a task with no more worry for his own safety than if the Khan had asked him to tether a horse. The moment ended in a flash though as everyone remembered their place in the grand order of things and the Khan's generals stood bowed and backed slowly out of his tent, leaving the great Khan, leader of the Golden Horde to wonder if he had succumbed to the plague himself and was currently in a feverish dream.

For Qulpa it was simply the next stage of the grand plan. By sending the plague ridden dead flying through the air and into the centre of the city he would of course spread the disease through the defenders causing them to collapse within days. Those that fled Kaffa however would do a much greater job, they would board their ships and escape the horror, but they would be taking the plague with them. They would take it to Constantinople where the death caused would bring the city to the brink of annihilation, and they would take it to Italy, where it would decimate the great Italian cities and spread north throughout Europe killing millions. Biological warfare at its most simple and devastating.

It was a very basic task, two days of catapulting plague-ridden bodies into a port under siege, but the effects would resonate throughout the known world. And if Qulpa died in process of carrying out his task, it did not matter, He was Helel Bene Elim, why should he fear death? He would simply move on to the next life and the next part of the grand plan.

# Zophiel
# An Evolved World

## Yetzirah

An ancient race of seven-foot tall, winged idiots Yetzirans had somehow survived for millions of years and had actually managed to evolve. This evolution, a painfully slow process held up by the fact they had the very human quality of trying their best to destroy themselves and their planet at every opportunity, continued up to the point where they actually became immortal, not just very, very old like an American Billionaire, they actually cured death, and carried on living without end. This may sound great, to those that had never experienced it, and the people of Yetzirah were initially overjoyed and annoyingly smug with their brilliant evolutionary development, but there were a few big drawbacks.

Firstly, they quickly became bored and discontented. Living for thousands of years on end, surrounded by the same people day after day made for very unhappy Yetzirans. The average Newman living on earth for their brief lives were well known to become frustrated, angry, and short tempered when being in close company with another of their kind for more than a couple of days, for some it was hours, and, for the unlucky, just a few minutes with others left them internally raging and ready to commit a ghastly murder.

The terms 'I will always love you' and 'We will always be together' have all the right connotations, and they, and other equally drippy pledges of love, have certainly cemented otherwise strained and doomed relationships throughout history, but can you actually imagine being stuck with even your nearest and dearest for a lifetime without end? It was a nightmare of infinite proportions and length, and the Yetzirans only had themselves to blame.

Secondly, despite their incalculable knowledge and extensive scientific abilities they became infertile, for want of a better phrase, 'the well ran dry', there were no more Yetzirans on the horizon. At first this was not a problem, less Yetzirans meant less mouths to feed, and more resources for the greedy Yetziran race to wallow in. They would live forever, it was fine, why was there the need to create more of them?

This was until they began to die again.

It was not a sudden thing, the first few that popped off the mortal coil drew a bit of alarm but, as has already been noted, the Yetzirans were, like the Newmans on Earth, a greedy race; self-serving, arrogant, and cursed with a love of short-term gains over long term happiness. The deaths continued, over the course of a thousand years until, this once populous and busy race were left with just a couple of hundred thousand who suddenly began to wonder if they were next.

They did what any normal beings would do in this situation and panicked. A lot. They cried, they raged, and at the height of their agonies started writing really terrible nihilistic poetry, they were in an awful mess. Finally, they set their great knowledge in motion, employing their greatest scientists (those left alive) to try to find a cure for their impending demise.

It was a pair of young Yetziran scientists, Sustina Homvettiner and her husband Malik, who made the greatest and most important discovery in the millions of years that Yetzirah had existed, since the first baby Yetziran had flapped their little wings and demanded feeding. They discovered the secret of creation, the essence of life itself. They took this newfound knowledge and developed it until they realised that they could actually grow life. A small amount of this precious life force could be used to create a new race of beings 'The Newmans'. This new race could be given a world to live on, which they called Assiyah – the world of action, but the Newmans called Earth. On Assiyah the Newmans could be moulded, nurtured, and essentially farmed. As the Newmans grew, the life force within them would develop and strengthen, and then, like some kind of all-powerful farmer with a massive scythe, the Yetzirans would cull them, take back the fully grown life force, and feed on it to keep the Yetzirans alive.

It was a brilliant plan. Not only did it sustain Yetzirah and stop its people from dying, but it also gave them something to do, it gave them a purpose, something that they had been lacking for a very long time.

The alarm awoke Zophiel Melaku from a sleep which was in no way as good as it could have been. Her mind had been racing when she had gone to bed wondering about the missing life forces. A contraband wooden clock hung on her wall, its loud tick filling the room and soothing Zophiel into the day. Her face was hidden by long black ringleted hair, which covered her like a curtain shutting out the interminable white light which seemed to shine from everywhere on Yetzirah and in which, for the most part, the Yetziran people lived quite contentedly. She had queried this inherent obliviousness to a migraine inducing environment many times with her friends and others; why the obsession with white, white walls, white floors, white gowns worn by everyone, Zophiel found it a constant strain on her eyes and wondered why others did not see it the same.

'The world of Yetzirah is as colourless as we can make it, to demonstrate our purity of purpose.' She was told by one of her teachers at the messenger academy, when she had questioned it. 'We are one people, and our uniformity is a blessing.'

'But it is actually very dull.' She replied. 'What is wrong with expressing yourself? Wouldn't it be more fun if we just coloured things up a bit?'

'Miss Melaku, the Yetziran race is beyond all that, we have evolved from such needs. Besides our hair is different colours, as is our skin, and our wings are various shades also, is that not enough difference for you?'

'Boring.' Zophiel said. Slumping down in her chair and folding her arms.

'When you are older you will appreciate how the Yetziran people have outgrown such basic fancies, Zophiel. For now you would do better to concern yourself with your studies and not your frustrations at a world you cannot change.'

Zophiel had never outgrown her frustrations though, it was a problem that had got her into trouble countless times over the years and something which she still would not back down on.

For a Newman the first thing that they might do, before even moving from their bed would be to check the time. Yetzirans however had long since dismantled and forgotten about the concept of time as a construct with which to run your life by. They had gentle alarms to wake them, these were not set to any particular time, but were aligned with their internal body clocks to ensure that they woke at exactly the time when their bodies had rested enough and were ready for a new day. This meant that there were no more people grumpy at being woken up too early which in turn led to less arguments, less tensions, and to a much more relaxed and comfortable lifestyle for all. Yes, perhaps some things did not get done exactly on time, but hey, they were immortal they had all the time in the world.

Time was just one of many things that the people of Yetzirah had evolved out of existence. Other notable concepts and ideas which had met their demise for the sake of a more peaceful and comforting existence were, paid work, public transport, regional government, competitive sport, religion, small yappy dogs, ear and nose hair, surprise parties, improvised comedy, and clowns. Their world was a safer and happier place all around, although they made sure that each of these things were added to Assiyah purely for their personal amusement of seeing another race suffer as they had done.

Zophiel loved her world, she loved the Yetziran people, despite what she saw were their obvious flaws, and she loved most aspects of her life, but she missed some of the things that millions of years of so called evolution had stopped her from experiencing. The thing she loved the most was her job, as this meant being able to visit Assiyah with all of its life and colour, despite the fact that it was seemingly static every time she was able to go there to collect life forces.

She climbed from her bed, making her way over to the kitchen cupboard to get out her breakfast. Her apartment was fitted with a replicator which could, Zophiel supposed be used to make food or drink, but no Yetziran ever used it for that purpose. Food was something that the Yetziran people had evolved away from requiring. Zophiel's breakfast was made up of a collection of four tablets, each of which had a special daily role in maintaining her bodies health, but eradicated the need for anything which the Newmans would call 'toilet business'.

Eating and drinking was not something that Zophiel ever missed, mainly because she only experienced it once and never wanted to relive the whole terrible process. She knew that the Newmans required it, she had attended Assiyah many times to attend deceased Newmans who had choked on their food, or literally drunk themselves to death, often in town centres on a Friday evening. She had also been there when Newmans had expired 'per latrina', something which made her retch slightly even at the thought, despite there never being the possibility of engaging in full scale vomiting. These factors however were enough to ensure that the consumption and expulsion was a part of Assiyan life that she had no desire to engage in.

Zophiel was not due for messenger duty during this waking cycle, it was to be a relatively quiet death day down on the Newman world, so she had taken the opportunity to take a day off. She knew that Totfiel was also not on duty and had arranged to meet him at the Flightosphere.

When she arrived, he was already in the air. The Flightosphere was, as the name suggests a huge domelike structure where Yetzirans were able to spread their wings out to flap, swoop, and dive without fear of crashing into things. For many years, as the Yetziran race developed, their wings became nothing more than status symbols, the bigger the wings the more important you were. That is until they realised that they could no longer use them to fly, as is often the case when a race of beings become too caught up in their own selves to realise that they are actually losing something of great importance.

It was one Yetziran, Mamlaketi Stormhorn, who one day was so bored with living his perfectly evolved life that he tried to flap his wings and take flight. He managed to extend them somewhat before tiring so much that he had to go for a lie down for a while.

He was not one to be beaten though, and the next day he tried again. His wings were tight, and they hurt when he stretched them out, a little further than the previous day, but he felt a small degree of progress. Mamlaketi then did something quite extraordinary, that the majority of beings either on Yetzirah or on the Newman world who have ever joined a gym or decided to get fit would have baulked at. For despite waking the next day feeling like his wings were about to fall off he went outside and tried again, and he continued day after day, a little at a time.

The other Yetzirans laughed at him, because even a race that has been evolving into perfection for a hundred million years cannot help but belittle someone for doing something different. But still he continued until he finally got to the stage where he could fully extend his wings and flap them, lifting himself off the floor by a full two inches. It was quite remarkable and the Yetzirans suddenly began to take him a bit more seriously. Mamlaketi Stormhorn kept going until eventually after many months of hard painful work he was able to fly like the Yetzirans of old, flapping swooping, diving, and gliding like a veritable seabird, squawking with joy as he did so. The whole Yetziran race now took him very seriously indeed, perhaps there was actually some benefit to having fully working wings, that they were not just a status symbol?

In true Yetziran fashion the powers that be set their greatest scientists the task of returning flight to the people of Yetzirah. Mamlaketi Stormhorn offered his help and advice, he had achieved the impossible after all, he had turned back the clock, although many Yetzirans had forgotten what a clock was. The scientists listened carefully to him, as he laid out a day by day exercise plan, with short term easy targets that any Yetziran with wings could accomplish. The plan would be beneficial to the whole race as they would relearn a skill that they had lost, whilst increasing their sense of self worth and achievement.

It was then that they decided that it sounded far too much like hard work, dismissed Mamlaketi as an idiot, and instead created a pill that flooded their wings with life and energy. The Yetziran people could fly once more, without the need for any effort. Success!

Mamlaketi could still be found at the Flightosphere, most days soaring amongst the pretend clouds whilst being laughed at by other high flying Yetzirans.

When Zophiel arrived in the sphere she peered up into the clouds to see if Totfiel had already made it and taken flight. She could just make out his skinny white winged form gliding in a circular fashion like a buzzard catching thermals before it dives towards its prey. Zophiel spread her golden wings wide, gave one flap and took off up into the air. The air in the Flightosphere was carefully processed to enhance any attempts at flight, but it still took a while for Zophiel to reach the giddy heights of her friend up in the fake clouds. She was tired by the time she came close to him and took advantage of the warm air being pumped into the upper sphere to spread her wings and relax.

'Hey!' she called angling her way towards him. 'Have you been here long?'

'Quite a while,' he said flipping over onto his back and putting his hands behind his head as he glided, 'I woke early, obviously wasn't in need of much sleep last night. You were by the looks of it. Looks like you could go straight back to bed.'

'Yes, I was awake thinking about the thing yesterday. I can't get it out of my head. I don't like it when things don't go to plan.' Zophiel stretched out her arms enjoying the feeling of weightlessness that flight gave her. How could her people have given this up this feeling before?

'You worry too much,' Totfiel laughed. 'It's honestly nothing for you to worry about, it happens quite a lot you know. I was speaking about it with Caphriel just now, you'd be amazed at how often. He said it's happened to him a few times.'

'Really?'

'Really, come on, it's Caphriel, he's never lied or even expanded the truth in all of his years. It would kill him to try.'

'Is he still here now?'

'Yes, down there, look.'

Zophiel looked down to where Totfiel pointed to see the broad silver wings of Caphriel as he danced and swooped in the air. Caphriel was large, even for a Yetziran, standing a good head height above most others, and was known to be one of the strongest in all of Yetzirah. Zophiel pulled in her wings and dived down to where he flew.

When he saw her coming towards him, he immediately stopped his mid-air antics.

'Hi, Zoph, long time no fly, where have you been hiding yourself?'

'Oh, I've been around, working a lot of extras. Mainly doing solo jobs, I don't get to see much of anyone lately.'

'I hear you had a no show yesterday. Annoying when that occurs. Never mind, it happens to all of us.' He suddenly stretched out his huge wings and with a flap shot high into the sky. Zophiel gave chase.

'It doesn't bother you?' she said as she came alongside him once more. 'Doesn't it niggle with you that there are dead Newmen down there with no life force to collect.'

'Oh, I feel for the Newmen, obviously, but the upper Arches know about it, and they're not bothered. So why should I be? I've spoken to quite a few messengers that it's happened to, it's not a thing, Zoph, really it's not. I know what you're like with these things, but I'd just get on with my job if I were you, no questions. I reported it at the time, and that's where my interest ended. If it was really that much of a problem there'd be a fuss of some kind. Don't be the one making that fuss.'

He closed his wings tightly behind his back and plummeted towards the floor, spreading them wide and missing the ground at the last moment. Zophiel thought for a moment about copying the manoeuvre but knew that she didn't have his strength. She waited until he came up towards her again.

'You said the Arches were aware of it, which ones?'

'Erm… Araqiel Mardero has been down to see me a couple of times, Gadreel Netzach once but I think it's because Araqiel was on holiday then. Forget about it, move on, we're not here to make problems for ourselves.' He dived once more, this time straight towards the exit of the Flightosphere where, just before crashing his huge frame into the doors, his feet touched the ground, and he walked out.

Zophiel shook her head and headed back up into the clouds towards Totfiel, who was flying past a grey haired Yetziran and calling him a loser.

# Amelia
# On Becoming a Girl

## Dolorburgh 720CE

The newcomer opened their eyes to a room full of people in strange clothing. There was a sudden cacophony of noise.

'Praise God, she's alive. It's a miracle!' shouted the Priest throwing his arms into the air in the kind of joy and delirium that only the religious or those that have taken class A drugs know.

'It's a blessing, a blessing from above!' cried their new mother, jumping forwards and pulling them into an embrace.

'The Lord has indeed saved her.'

'Oh shit! I'm a girl.' the small child shouted, and the room fell suddenly silent, all eyes upon them.

There was an uncomfortable emptiness, wide eyes on every face and so the child spoke again. 'I mean, I am well again, I have been... saved.'

The room returned to noise and commotion.

The being first known as Brid was born again as a six year old girl, something which took them some time to get used to.

She was hugged by her new parents, given small sips of water, and had her long red hair brushed by the maids. It was all very strange. She was also on the receiving end of a sharp look of disdain from a small scruffy looking boy, who peered over the end of the bed, just high enough so that she could see him stick his tongue out at her. She later discovered that he was her little brother, Leofric, and that before her death and rebirth they had hated each other, and constantly bickered. The girl stuck her tongue out in return. Little Weasel.

Her name was Elswyth, and she was the daughter of a landowner in what would now be called Northumberland, in northern England a little north of the site where Alnwick now stands. They had a small castle, which was built on a cliff top overlooking the sea on one side and the town of Dolorburgh below it.

There is no sign of the castle or the town now, not even a stone to say that the castle stood there. Amelia visited the site in the 1970s and stood on the exact spot where the kitchens were at the rear of the castle. This was the strangest thing about living many lives for her, seeing things age and decay until they are no longer there at all. That of course includes the people she had known, but more deeply she was shocked at changes in landscape, whole towns and villages disappearing and appearing, and the loss of the forests and woodland, when the seemingly immovable and permanent seem to disappear in the space of a couple of hundred years.

Her life, as the daughter of the castle was easy enough, easier of course than being a weakling boy in a poor Scottish village which was all she had known before this. She had servants who helped to dress her in the morning, she ate well, and had the freedom of the castle to roam around, something which she did on a daily basis soon getting to know everyone within the walls. It didn't matter if they were a soldier in her father's garrison of guards who protected the castle, the town and the surrounding countryside, or the cooks in the kitchen who prepared meals every day.

She was also lucky for the time, as her father engaged monks from Lindisfarne to come regularly to teach her how to read and write in Latin. Such activities were thought by many to be heresy, women had no reason to learn such things meant only for men of a higher stature, but her father was a man who was not to be led by others and gave generously to the Bishop of Lindisfarne for allowing her to learn - and of course to say nothing to anyone else on the subject. There had been no books or writing in Finlay's Hollow, there was no interest in it, but now she had been given this newly found power she loved to read whatever manuscripts or books which came within her reach. Reading was a blessing that Amelia had embraced throughout every life she had experienced, wherever it was possible.

Elswyth spent her time riding horses when the weather was fair, and doing tapestry and needlepoint on colder, wetter days, of which there were many. Riding a horse was something very new, there had, of course, been horses in Finlay's Hollow but they were large stocky things, bred to pull ploughs and carts, not the kind that could be ridden lightly. She proved herself to be an independent girl and, despite her parent's protestations loved to go for rides alone out in hills and on the beach near to the castle. At first Elswyth knew that they had her followed for her own safety, but as she grew older, they knew that she was proficient enough a rider to be able to avoid any trouble when out alone. Elswyth loved to ride, especially when she had the opportunity to gallop free and feel the wind on her face. She only did this out of view of the castle, if her parents had seen her on a horse at full pelt, they would have stopped the daily rides immediately. It is true to say that she enjoyed her new life following the rebirth into a healthy body.

The experience of being a twelve-year-old boy from a small village in Scotland to suddenly waking up in the body of a six year old girl, with long red hair, who lived in a castle, and had handmaids answering to her every whim, was not one that they would recommend, however. For a start you were expected to behave differently as a girl, and especially as a high-born girl, with all that the role entailed. Rules of etiquette and manners were not something that they had ever had to think about in Finlay's Hollow in fact they often wondered what their uncle would have said if they had told him that they had to dress for dinner, and not just use cutlery but also hold it in the correct manner. And then there were the physical changes. Their body had altered completely, a shock to the system indeed.

Apparently Elswyth had been struck down with a sudden sickness before her 'death', it had been rife throughout the castle and surrounding village, and all but the strongest had died as a consequence. Her recovery from the point of death was truly seen as a miracle and, for a few years afterwards, she was seen as a bit of a religious icon. Elswyth had passed to the other side and returned, perhaps she knew the secrets of heaven.

Priests from around the country would visit the castle to meet and pray with her, something which her father, an austere and frugal man, saw as an opportunity, charging fees to the churchmen for their time with her. Elswyth played the role well, telling them how she had passed on to the afterlife and seen Heaven and Christ himself with her own eyes. It was all lies of course, she was no more a Christian than she had been as a boy in Finlay's Hollow, but saw the benefits to herself and her new family of being an attraction. As Elswyth grew older, the visiting priests lessened as other miraculous individuals sprang up around the country with tales of seeing Jesus in their visions, it was a booming industry. After a couple of years, she began to return to a relatively normal life, which she was glad of as she had tired of the attention.

For every new person she met however she looked for a sign within them that they were Analla. She promised her she would find her, and although Elswyth believed this with all her heart, as the years passed, she began to wonder if Analla had forgotten and would ever return. As a second life however, Elswyth could not complain, she saw the people that lived in the village and surrounding countryside and knew that she had struck gold in terms of quality of life at that time. She also now knew the secret of new life after death. This would not be her last life.

When Elswyth turned fourteen she was told that she was to be married. A match had been made to a young Saxon lord from Eoferwic called Alwin. She was assured by Mother that he was very handsome, and that it was a good match. Mother said that the young girl would grow to love him eventually, as indeed her mother had with her father, and that once in Eoferwic, which Mother described as 'a beautiful city with high walls and lofty towers', she would soon forget 'our little castle by the sea'. Father had arranged for Elswyth's future spouse to visit, with his parents, who Father wished to take as much of a dowry from as he could.

Elswyth was not convinced though. She had not the slightest intention of marrying someone that she did not know, no matter how handsome he was, and she resolved to escape from this fate at the earliest opportunity. She had been giving a lot of thought to Finlay's Hollow and that tree where Analla buried her special things. Perhaps Analla would be there, waiting for her. Elswyth decided that she could not wait to be found any longer, she would go in search of Analla herself. Now that she felt old enough to make her way there on her own, she would slip away one night, taking a horse and riding north.

In the week prior to her future husband's visit she would steal down to the kitchens at night and collect together provisions for the journey. During the day she would take her bounty out into the woods beyond the river which flowed past the castle into the sea. There she would stash it high up in a tree in a handled hessian sack which she had stolen from the stables.

She was awoken on the day of her fiancé's arrival by her mother, who brought a tray carrying a jug of pressed apple juice and some honey cakes.

'It is going to be a great day for you, Elswyth,' she said, directing the maids to pull the heavy linen drapes from the windows and open the shutters. 'A great day for this family also. You will finally meet your Alwin and fall in love, just as I did when I first laid eyes on your father.'

Elswyth suppressed a snort and covered her face in blankets for a moment. Mother was a slim, clean, perfectly maintained, and always beautifully dressed lady. Father however was, and by all accounts had always been, a man who had two outstanding physical features. Firstly, there was his size; he was so round that he resembled a barrel, there was not an ounce of fat on him however, it was solid bulk. The other distinguishing feature that set him apart from the rest was his face. It was red, pock marked, and had tufts of bright ginger hair sprouting from random places about his cheeks and chin. If it truly was love at first sight for Mother, then Elswyth guessed that the first thing that she espied on him was the size of his purse, and the fact that he owned a castle.

'He's not *my* Alwin!' the girl shouted from beneath her bedclothes.

'Of course he is, Elswyth. You are promised to him, and he to you. It is a good match.'

'For who?' Elswyth groaned, her red hair slowly appearing from the bedclothes, as her eyes grew accustomed to the light which now invaded the bedroom.

'For everyone, dear.' Mother said, placing the tray upon the girl's lap and perching on the edge of the bed. 'You must understand your place as a daughter of this household and the importance of a joining of our families to your father. You are carrying out the service you were born for. It is not something you can refuse.'

'When will his party be arriving?' Elswyth grumbled, tucking into the honey cakes.

'Your father says that Alwin and his parents should be with us by the evening, they will have been travelling for a few days so will be in need of a feast when they arrive. You must spend the day preparing and making yourself look presentable. I'll have a bath drawn for you.'

The girl took a sip of juice. 'Perhaps I could go for a ride first this morning. You know how much I am going to miss our home. I feel that a ride on the seashore will give me a memory to take with me, when I go to live with this man in Eoferwic.'

'Of course, Elswyth. You know that we will miss you too, but you are not gone yet. I think that Alwin will be staying with us for a week or more before you leave with him and his parents. I'll ask one of the maids to lay out your riding clothes, and the stable boy to prepare a horse. Do not go far though, I want you back by the afternoon, you have much work to do.' She looked her daughter up and down, sat with her hair plaited into a messy nest on her head, and greedily stuffing cakes into her mouth. 'Much to do.'

Elswyth grunted and continued her breakfast.

An hour later she left her bedroom for the last time and crossed the courtyard to the stables. She had hoped that her favourite horse, Penda, had been saddled ready and was not disappointed as Jarod, the young lad who lived and worked with the horses led Penda out to meet her. Jarod was a year older and had been as close to being a friend to Elswyth as she had allowed anyone since arriving at the castle eight years earlier. He was a funny boy, he made her smile, and she felt comfortable in his company. Some evenings she would visit his house where his mother, a seamstress at the castle, would make them supper and teach her stitching and needlework while they sat by the fire and talked. Elswyth didn't enjoy the needlework, but it was worth it to spend time with Jarod and his mother, who always liked to tell them stories. It reminded Elswyth of being back in the Laird's Hall in Finlay's Hollow, where they would sit in the warmth of the hearth fire and listen to their uncle's tales of the first people.

A couple of years earlier, Jarod had been kicked in the head by one of the horses, he had spent the next two weeks drifting in and out of a murky consciousness, the swelling on his head not going down. Elswyth had visited him daily and sat by his side, until finally, just when it was thought that he would not return to them he opened his eyes.

'He's a bit skittish this morning.' Jarod said, handing her the reigns. 'I'd be careful not to push him too far, he's in a devilish mood. Where are you going?'

'Out.' She swung herself up into the saddle, shifting into a comfortable position and placing her feet in the stirrups.

'Out where?'

'Just out, you are nosey this morning, aren't you?'

He smiled in return and brushed the hair out of his eyes. 'Not nosey, just concerned. When Penda throws you from the saddle I want to know where to look for your body.'

Elswyth laughed. 'There'll not be a body for you to find today, Jarod. Look after yourself. Goodbye.' She tugged on the reigns, and Penda resisted a little. Jarod had been right; the horse was in a funny mood. Perhaps he knew something she didn't. She rode through the castle gates for the last time and headed north.

Two hours later she was laid unconscious at the base of a tree, blood covering her face.

When Elswyth finally opened her eyes, it was night and the light of a small fire shone orange onto the branches of the trees which surrounded her. Her horse Penda was tied to a nearby tree next to another horse which she recognised from her father's stable. A rabbit, skinned of its fur, and stuck on a small branch, hung over the flame.

'I told you he'd throw you,' the stable boy said from the other side of the flames.

Her forehead hurt and she reached up to find a strip of cloth wrapped around her head; a blanket covered her body.

'The bleeding has stopped now,' he continued. 'But I would keep that on for a while longer. The bump will go down, but you'll be left with a good scar.'

'You followed me.' Elswyth said with a groan, pushing herself upright.

'Of course I did,' he replied, turning the rabbit over the fire. 'I knew that you would end up in trouble and that you had no intention of returning. Any fool could have seen it.'

'What?'

'You were leaving today.' He laughed. 'You were running away from home because you didn't want to get married.'

'I had other reasons too,' she said, looking for her sack which she had retrieved from the tree soon after setting off. It was laid at her feet, and she pulled it towards me.

'Other reasons? What other reason could you have than not wanting to get married to someone you've never met?' He picked the rabbit off from the fire and took a tentative bite before offering it to her.

'No thanks,' she said, curling her lip, 'I've got some bread and cheese here. Do you want some too?'

'I'll stick to rabbit, thanks. You're going to need as much food as you can get if you're ever going to make it home.'

'I'm not going home though, am I? You guessed as much, and going by your own words that must make you a fool.'

'Fair point,' Jarod smirked. 'That's not the home I'm talking about though.' The stable boy looked at me straight in the eye.

'How do you….' Elswyth cried, before stopping herself and looking down at the floor. 'I don't know what you're talking about,' she continued, 'And anyway don't you need to be getting back to the castle? Your mum will be fretting about you, out this late.'

'She will. But like you, it is time to move on. Do you miss Finlay's Hollow that much, so you really want to go back? It may be a very long trip to be disappointed.'

She stared at him open mouthed.

'There's not much left of it now, you know.' He continued, 'Nothing that you would recognise, it's been over a hundred years since you last saw it, and no one has lived there since. It's amazing how the passage of time can change things.'

She stared hard at the stable boy sat on the other side of the fire, and saw the light glint in his eye.

'Analla?'

'No. Jarod. Just as you are now Elswyth and not Brid, the little nephew of the Laird, who wheezed every time he tried to break a sweat, and who asked too many questions. I told you I would find you.'

'But... but I've known you for years, ever since I arrived here. And all this time you've never said a word to me, never told me who you were. You are cruel, I could punch you.'

Jarod giggled and it was then in that giggle that Elswyth knew the truth, he had Analla's mischievous humour. Her face flushed in anger, and she threw her food at him, an action that only made him laugh harder.

'When I left you in the void, I did not follow you straight away, I had other business to attend to first. It was for the best, honestly it was. I have been playing this game for so long that I attract the Reapers, I am wanted by them, and you know that if we die by their hand then our journey is over. If I had joined you straight away they would have felt a vibration in the strands of the web and would have come after us. They came for me and so I led them a merry dance away from you, through a few other lives, and places, until I was clear of them, and it was safe to find you again. Jarod's kick to the head was fortuitous and happened just at the right time.'

'A few other lives?!' she exclaimed. 'How could you do that? It will have only been six years between my arrival and yours as Jarod.'

Jarod ate the last of the rabbit from his stick and stood, stepping over to where she sat, crouching next to her, stick in hand, he drew a web in the dirt at her feet.

'You obviously have less intelligence than I gave you credit for,' he said. 'Look at this web, each line to the centre is a passage of time; at the centre is the end of all things, and on the outer reaches of the web are the time that has passed before. The further you travel along the lines of the web to the centre, the further into the future you will go. But you have already seen that, with will and the strength, it is possible to break free from the web's strands and travel elsewhere. Tell me what this means?'

She looked at the web for a moment, and it came to her. 'That it is possible to travel backwards as well as forwards?'

'Indeed. Would you be so astounded to find out that, in the eight years you have been Elswyth, I have lived for over one hundred years in other people's borrowed lives?'

She thought on his words. Everything made sense to her now; the web, the centre, the creator, everything. 'So that is why you don't want to travel to the centre, because that is when time ends?'

'Exactly!' He leapt to his feet again. 'I have discovered a way in which our world, and all of the time in which it has existed and will exist for us beings, is at my disposal. Why would I want it to end? I'm having far too much fun, there is so much to see, and to learn. I do not intend to give up so easily. This world has so much in it that I haven't had the pleasure of experiencing, and there are other worlds out there too.' His face was animated now, his eyes bright and wide. 'What if I told you that further down the line of the web towards the centre there are opportunities to travel up there among the stars?' He pointed upwards to the thousands of tiny pin prick holes in the night sky.

'Then I would say that you are an idiot who is playing games with me, and takes me for more of a fool than I am.'

'I could show you if you like,' he grinned.

'Show me what?'

'Other worlds, fantastic planets, millions of miles away from our own. Just say the word and we could go.'

'But we would have to die first, fool.' she snorted.

'Yes, that's the easy bit. Look I have a knife, all I have to do is quickly slit your throat followed by my own, and…'

'Enough!' She snapped. 'I am not letting you anywhere near me with a knife! Do you think I'm mad?'

He laughed. 'No not mad, just a little rigid in your thinking, and untrusting of those that wish to help you. I would have thought that you would be a little more adventurous now you have an understanding of how it all works.'

Elswyth sat for a moment looking into the flames. The thought of suicide was not appealing in the least, but the idea of travelling to different places, and living other lives intrigued her. 'So, what do we do now?' She said. Do you have a plan?'

'Of course not, I have lived for over two thousand years through other people's bodies, I have never had a plan, where would be the fun in that? My only plan at this present time is to add another couple of sticks to the fire and get some sleep. In the morning we'll start another journey.'

'Back into the web, I'm not sure I'm ready to die again yet?'

He could see the sudden fear in her eyes. 'And I will not force you,' he said, taking her hands in his.

For a moment they sat in silence, their eyes locked together. A rush of warmth which did not come from the fire shot through Elswyth's body, a feeling that, although being new to her, was not uncomfortable.

It was Jarod who broke the moment. 'If you wake tomorrow and want another adventure in another life, then I'm afraid there is only one way to start it,' He drew a finger across his throat, 'but if you want to go back to Finlay's Hollow...'

'I do. If only for the fact that I don't fancy attempting to die again, not just yet.'

'Then it is decided,' he said standing from the fire and pulling a blanket from his saddlebag and tossing it to her. 'We leave at first light in the morning. There is nothing there, but it would be nice to retrieve my things from the base of the tree. Now go to sleep, we have a few long days of travel ahead of us and we will need to move swiftly, your father will have men out looking for you, you are an expensive asset to lose so easily.'

Elswyth thought of her own things, Brid's things, which he had buried between some rocks at the edge of the Loch on the night before their first death. She closed her eyes and fell asleep, dreaming of travelling to other worlds.

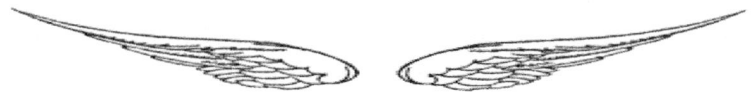

A soft scratching sound woke Elswyth, she opened her eyes to see Jarod hurriedly gathering up his blanket. He saw that she was awake and immediately raised a finger to his lips.

'What's going on?' she hissed. He did not respond, but pointed towards the horses. As slowly and as quietly as she was able, she got to her feet and, staying low, crawled over to Penda. Jarod was just behind her.

'Your father's men are near,' he whispered. 'We need to lead the horses to the other side of the copse, climb into the saddle and when I tell you set off at a gallop. It's our only chance of getting away from them.'

Elswyth could hear the men in the distance, even recognising one of their voices, a gruff soldier named Seward, who Elswyth had always been fearful of. She took Penda's bridle in one hand whilst resting her other hand on his neck and followed Jarod's lead. She could see the edge of the trees ahead of them and she started to climb into the saddle, seeing Jarod do the same. Seward's voice was getting louder, they were running out of time. Jarod nodded to her, and she kicked the horse's flanks setting off at speed.

Penda was a fast horse, and she was a good rider, but she struggled to keep up with Jarod who was ahead of her. They sped out towards the hills ahead of them. Elswyth could hear her father's men behind them, they had been spotted and were now being chased. She turned to see a group of five men on horseback break free from the trees.

She saw the arrow strike Jarod in the back and saw him fall from the saddle, his horse thundering on without him as he hit the ground. For a brief moment she thought of carrying on, of continuing to ride until she was free of the men, but she knew that she would not get far on her own, and she was suddenly very afraid of losing him again and being alone. She pulled hard on the reins and as Penda stopped, she jumped from the saddle.

'Jarod!' She screamed running to where he lay on the floor. He was motionless on the ground, an arrow sticking out from the centre of his back, and pulled on his shoulder, turning him over. Blood came from his mouth as he tried to speak, but she could not understand what he was saying. A thunder of hooves rang in her ears as her father's men reached them.

'Got you, Missy. Time to go home,' said Seward, as she was grabbed roughly by the shoulders and pulled from the dying stable boy.

'Get off me, you pig!' she cried, but was struck across the face. The last thing she remembered before her eyes closed was seeing one of the men approach the dying stable boy on the floor and drive his sword into him. Jarod had entered the web once more. As she was thrown over the saddle of a horse, she lost consciousness.

The ride back to Dolorburgh was short, the men obviously keen to return to the castle to show off how clever they were at capturing the runaway. Elswyth was tied to a horse with a cloth gagging her mouth which had been placed on her to block the torrent of abuse which she directed to her captors when she woke to find herself attached to the saddle. For the first hour they revelled in listening to the young girl curse them, but it soon became an annoyance, and the gag was put into place.

When they reached the crest of the ridge one mile to the west of Dolorburgh she was taken from her laid position over the saddle and sat up, her hands tied to the pommel, the gag remained however until they passed through the gates of the castle and into the courtyard of the keep.

Her parents came out to meet her, thanking Seward and his men for returning their daughter and preventing any further shame on their already damaged name. Elswyth was lifted from the saddle and her mother rushed forwards. 'Mother!' She cried, as she waited for arms to surround and comfort her. Her mother stopped before her however and the only greeting she got was a hard slap across the face.

The bruise on Elswyth's face was still evident two days later as she was led down the aisle by her father in the chapel at Dolorburgh. She had not spoken a word since being brought back to the castle and could not even look at her future husband as he waited for her with the priest. She pitied the poor boy for being placed in this terrible position and was glad that the whole messy affair would soon be over for him.

Later that night, when locked in her chambers awaiting her new husband and the terrible prospect of consummating the marriage, she threw herself from the window into the courtyard fifty feet below and found herself hurtling into the web once more.

# Cheerful Charlie

## The Palace of Whitehall, 1664CE

There's a common misconception, brought about usually by blockbuster movies or box set television series that the extinction of the human race, and the end of the world will come about through human idiocy or error. You know the type of thing, perhaps it's some crackpot scientist or lunatic inventor that creates or discovers something that they think will be of great benefit to the world. All is fine at first but then it subsequently ends up being not what they thought, and goes on to destroy the planet and everything on it. There's a standard list of potential extinction catalysts, nuclear weapons, artificially intelligent robots, a viral pandemic, or Facebook.

Perhaps it is not just one incident that brings an end to the world as we know it, but the human population as a whole, a group-clutz type thing, nothing really intentional but something that happens quietly over a long period of time through lack of human understanding or dumb short term thinking, such as global warming, stupid politicians, or line dancing.

Other ways in which the world ends are completely out of human hands altogether, perhaps an asteroid careers into somewhere on the Asian continent covering the sky in a thick cloud of dust, blocking out the sun and causing the planet to turn into a giant ball of deadness, like Neptune, or Ipswich.

Maybe it's not an asteroid at all, perhaps its alien invaders intent on eradicating all human life after watching them prove themselves over thousands of years of warfare, religion, and awful theatre to be totally wasteful of their chance in the universe.

Whatever the wild misconception thought up either as visual entertainment for the masses, or just a prayer to end it all by those who are actually able to see the bigger picture, nobody ever really gives much thought to the idea that the human race will be turned to dust through an act of pure love.

But it was love that drove the tall man as he walked into the Palace of Whitehall for a meeting with Charles II, King of Scotland, England, and

Ireland, it was love for his lost people that had driven him for thousands of years. It was misguided, twisted, and dangerous, it would end in the destruction of billions of lives, but it was love all the same.

The halls of the Palace of Whitehall were strewn with courtiers, sycophants, and hangers on, these were heady days for the royal entourage and those who lived within it. The days of austerity, piousness, and going without were behind them now. Those lucky enough to be caught up in the whirlwind of endless parties, sumptuous feasts, and rich living were determined to take as much from it as they could, for who knew when another Cromwell could pop up out of nowhere, and it would all be taken away from them once more.

It had taken a long time for Helel Bene Elim, who currently called himself Gustav Toussaint, to get a face to face meeting with the King; nobles had been courted, purses fattened, and indeed men had been killed to give the tall man the opportunity to finally meet the monarch.

The Banqueting Hall was full of courtiers as he walked through the double doors and was presented with the absolute sumptuousness of it all. Two long tables were laid at either side, running down the windowed walls besides which huge Grecian pillars stood. Each table was laden with food, the like of which Gustav had never seen with his own eyes, but Helel had himself only witnessed once when at a feast held by Caligula in his heyday.

Huge whole roasted boars, turkeys, geese, and pies as large as cartwheels littered the tables. Tall sugar sculptures, meticulously decorated cakes, and freshly baked bread loaves and plaits lay within the seated reach of all at the table, and Gustav was reminded by his stomach and salivary glands that it had been a while since he had eaten. It would have been easy to have just sat down and taken his fill, the mood in the room was of loud discourse, resounding music and laughter to the extent that his entrance had not been noticed, even by the pike bearers who lined the walls, and he wondered whether just anyone could have walked in and started to help themselves.

Gustav was well dressed though, he did not look out of place among the Dukes, Earls, Countesses, and Ladies, and he was grateful to the Earl of Thanet, John Tufton who he had visited earlier in the month at his residence, Lord's Place, and relieved the Earl of his clothing, a large amount of cash, and his life.

As he approached the throne, he kept his head lowered in due deference to the monarch, but a quick glance confirmed the suspicions that had brought him here. He took one knee as he reached the King, who had not even noticed his approach until looking down to see the kneeling noble before him. Charles whispered to a courtier stood at his side, they held a short but hushed conversation before the courtier spoke for the King.

'His Majesty wishes to know who you are. Today's feast is a birthday celebration and only friends, family, and loyal supporters were invited.'

Helel kept his head bowed but spoke clearly. 'My name is Gustav Toussaint, I am an architect and engineer, his Majesty will be aware of my work, I am sure.'

There were more whispers between the courtier and the King before the King spoke for himself.

'Master Toussaint, I have indeed heard of your work, especially the splendid designs currently being constructed for our brother in France. You are most welcome, but tell me, what brings you to my court, when you are obviously such a busy man?'

Helel raised his head and began to stand as he spoke.

'Your Majesty, your brother Louis sends his regards, all of your brothers wish to send you their regards. I am glad they find you well, Samjaza.'

The King's face dropped when he heard that name, to such an extent that his royal guard immediately reached for their weapons, but they were stopped by a wave of the King's hand, and his laughter. His sharp eyes met those of Gustav Toussaint, and if anyone had studied them closely enough, they would have seen a touch of fear.

'Welcome!' he cried in his loudest most jolly voice. 'You are indeed most welcome, Monsieur Toussaint, Are you well? Have you eaten? You must have a drink.' All eyes fell on him, and he stood from his throne, causing everyone else in the room to pause their feasting and stand also. The King descended the two steps and embraced his visitor with both arms. 'Let us go somewhere more private, my brother.' He whispered into his ear. 'We cannot speak freely here. I have a presence I need to maintain'.

The King put an arm around the shoulder of his visitor and led by a small but bemused entourage left the Banqueting Hall.

In the King's private rooms, Charles dismissed his followers and offered his visitor a seat. Once he was sure the doors were closed, he finally spoke.

'It is good to see you, my brother. It has been many years. I trust you are keeping well. How do you like my palace, I've done a lot to it myself since taking over. This is quite the life you know…' He stopped speaking immediately when Helel rose his hand.

'What are you doing, Samjaza?' Helel said, idly brushing his finger around the rim of the goblet handed to him by his brother.

'Pardon?'

'What are you actually doing?' Helel said. 'Did you forget our arrangement?'

'The arrangement? Oh, yes, the arrangement, of course I didn't forget I've been working hard on it.' He spread his arms. 'Look, I'm the bloody King of England! I'm very important, it makes it easier to get the work done.'

'Does it?' Helel's voice was calm, but Samjaza knew better, and a small bead of sweat ran down his powdered face, creating a dark streak.

'Well of course, how much more important can I get? There's nothing that I can't do, you know. You'd be amazed.'

'How long have you been a King here, Samjaza?'

'A couple of years.'

'Thirteen.'

'Pardon?' he said again.

'Thirteen years, Samjaza. You took over the body of Charles when he was killed at The Battle of Worcester. You took the body and fled the city, escaping through St Martin's Gate. What have you done other than hold parties and father bastards?'

'Is it that long? Well, you know, time flies and all that.'

'That's a very twentieth century idiom, Samjaza. You need to be a bit more careful how you speak. We're here to destroy history not just alter the language a bit.'

'Me? Oh, I'm terribly careful, although there are times when I would just love to have my iPhone, I still often reach for it in a pocket.'

'Trust me, brother, if we could take things with us, I would have just collected nukes and done the job in one go myself. But you were telling me what you've been doing, during your time here as King.'

'Oh yes, well it's not as straightforward as it sounds being king, but I've been doing the usual, having wars, expanding our territories and all that.'

'You need to do better, brother. I've brought you a little present, delivered it to St. Giles in the field, but you really must do better. And if you can't do better here, then move on and try somewhere else. You know the penalty if you fail us.'

The colour quickly drained from the normally jovial King's face. 'Of course, brother. I will not let you down.'

'I expect to hear great things from you when we meet up with the rest of our brothers, do I make myself clear?' Helel turned on his heel and walked out of the room, showing his back to the King, an action which if carried out by any other person would have seen them publicly flogged and sent to the Tower of London for a very long time. Not with this one though.

The King's wig had suddenly begun to feel very heavy and itchy. He poured himself another drink, and wished he'd found a better hiding place from his brother.

# The Concurrence
## Yetzirah

Zophiel whistled all the way to her friend Hariton Molechi's flat, the noise making heads turn in the pure white corridors of the apartment building. Throughout Yetzirah peace and tranquillity was of paramount importance. Imagine the traditional view of what heaven would be like, the only sounds perhaps the gentle harp playing in the background resonating through the clouds, angels and those that have passed wander smiling forever comforted in eternal happiness and sublime goodness. In reality there were no clouds, they had done away with that weather nonsense a long time ago. There were no recently passed people who had earned a place amongst the angels, they were being processed, farmed, and sent back down to Assiyah. The only sound was of quiet footsteps, gentle discussion, and absolutely nothing else. If a harpist had tried to resonate Yetzirah with their twanging chimes they would immediately be arrested for breaching the peace, their instrument would be sawn into tiny splinters and they would count themselves very lucky if they were not sent down to Gehinom, where the bad ones go.

Those that heard the happy whistling of the tall messenger, immediately turned in anger at the intrusion on their peace. It was only then that they realised who it was and tutted, shaking their heads, before resuming their activities. Zophiel was well known in Yetzirah as 'the odd one'. There had been many complaints about her irresponsible behaviour over the thousands of years that she had polluted the blank soundscape with her noises. Each complaint was met with a polite response stating that it was a medical condition and not an intentional attempt at annoyance, however she also happened to be the favourite niece of the Yetziran Leader Tertira Grammaton, and as such had a certain degree of protection.

Hariton's apartment was on one of the upper floors of the apartment building, which in itself was a huge structure comprising of housing for Yetzirans and their families as well as its own entertainment facilities, and something which on Assiyah would pass as shops, but in actual fact were places to collect free stuff.

Yetzirans had abolished the idea of currency thousands of years ago when they decided that money was indeed the root of all evil, causing more anxiety, sadness, and violent conflict than a primary school sports day.

It was not just money that they did away with, organised religion got the chop for similar reasons, it being a major cause of misery and bloodshed. Weirdly they decided not to step in when the early Newmans on Assiyah decided to worship invisible, make-believe characters, as they decided this would be a great way to help them stop wondering where they came from and their place in the universe. If only they knew that their actual place was to be the equivalent of plant pots, growing life force within them before being regularly pruned of the majority of their energy and re-potted as seedlings once more.

Zophiel travelled in the elevator up to Hariton's floor whistling and humming all the way, much to the great annoyance of those whose peace she disturbed along the way. Hariton lived in a very large suite, given to him as reward for his work with Sustina and Malik Homvettiner on the creation of Assiyah, which essentially saved the Yetziran race. Hariton was a scientist by nature but one that worked in the field of what Newmans would refer to as computers.

The Yetziran computer was a confusing, infuriating and rarely rewarding piece of equipment, very much like their counterparts on Assiyah. The secrets of how they actually worked, and how to make them do what you wanted without swearing, threats of violence, and regular tears were known only to a few blessed Yetzirans, who were treated with great respect by their people, some of whom thought they were true magicians. Hariton had told Zophiel many times that this really was not the case, there was no magic involved, just the ability to gain enjoyment from the dullest invention in the universe. He no longer worked as such anymore. He had been retired soon after the creation of Assiyah after rumours that he was a sympathiser to those that wanted a return to a more democratic approach to Yetziran governance.

Democracy was another thing that had been abolished as a thoroughly bad idea by the Yetziran leader, strangely enough shortly before her last term as democratic leader was about to expire. The Yetzirans had always had a rocky relationship with democracy however, when it had been discovered that if you give enough stupid people a say in how your society is run, combined with even greater fools in power who lie to people, that all you get is bad decision making, and misery.

Unlike the other supporters of democracy, Hariton had not been banished to Gehinom, but lived a comfortable life in a self-imposed imprisonment in his apartment. He could leave, he could go where he wanted on Yetzirah, he just didn't care to very much anymore and spent his time submerged in his computers.

The door to Hariton's apartment had a scanner which picked up her whistling from along the corridor and briefly studied her face once she stood in front of it. There was a moment's pause before it slid open with the words 'Welcome Zophiel Melaku' announcing her entrance. The reception room was bare, but for a single white chair and she hummed her way into Hariton's lounge where she found him sat upon a sofa, deeply ensconced in what she imagined to be a very geeky activity. He was hammering desperately away on a keyboard on his lap and swearing furiously under his breath, he did not look up but stopped cursing momentarily to greet his visitor.

'Morning, Zoph, have a seat I'll be with you in a moment,' his voice was quavered, whatever he was doing was very stressful. He returned to his colourful mumbled profanities briefly before slamming his hand down on the keyboard and chucking it across to the other side of the sofa.

'Trouble?' Zophiel asked, a wide grin on her face.

'Ha! No, no trouble, well maybe a little bit. You would think that after all the millions of years of evolution, improved comprehension of our place in the universe, and higher learning that we would learn to understand the mental workings of our family members, but no, it's impossible to believe just how many idiots can be bred from the same gene pool.' He smiled at his visitor. 'You cannot choose them, something made worse with immortality because it's so much harder to shake yourself free of them. Thankfully we have friends who we can choose.

Come and sit down.' He smiled at his guest, and gestured to the chair opposite which Zophiel sank into.

'I've got a question, Hari, it's a weird one though.'

'Go on. You know I like weird things. It's why we're friends.' He laughed.

Zophiel ignored the dig and continued. 'Life force. What happens to it after it's put in the little brown bags?'

'Ah, it goes into the concurrence, a self-contained life force farm. A little invention of mine I think you'll find. It's the reason I am where I am today, actually. I worked on a number of things with the Assiyah project, but the concurrence was my crowning glory. I didn't do any of the world building stuff, I couldn't be doing with all that rubbish, mountains and volcanoes are for geologists, terribly dull people if you ask me.'

'I quite like mountains,' said Zophiel.

'Of course you do, of course you do, but it's a very different thing admiring and enjoying the idea and sight of mountains and spending half your life designing and doting over them. That stuff's for other people. People with no personality.'

Zophiel was a little hurt, the thought of being able to create her very own mountain was very appealing. 'You're wrong, but I'll let it go for now. What is the concurrence? What does it do?'

'It's basically a portal. The collector on Assiyah travels around, doing his thing, hanging out with people about to die and all that, at the point of death he drains the life force out of the unfortunate Newman.'

'Ooh, I've always wanted to know. How does he actually do that?' Zophiel said leaning forwards.

'It's a closely guarded top level secret actually. Only the greatest Yetzirans are given this knowledge.'

'Really?'

'Ha! No, it's not really. We just say that to people to stop us having to tell anyone. The reality of the extraction process is actually quite disgusting and, trust me you really don't want to know. Just be content in knowing that if you ever arrived early on Assiyah and saw the act taking place it would haunt you for eternity. Once seen and never forgotten.'

'Well, now I'm really intrigued. Perhaps I will set off a bit early next time.'

'You won't thank me for the experience, Zoph.'

'Probably not, but I like to make my own mistakes thanks. Tell me about the concurrence, what do you mean when you say it's a portal.'

'Exactly that.' Hariton said expecting Zophiel to know exactly what he meant. 'Once the life force is extracted, the Collector puts it into the bag and leaves the bag by the deceased.'

'Where I find it. I know that much.'

'Yes, where you find it, Zophiel. Although as soon as you arrive and attach the bag to your belt the life force starts on its way. You see the moment the life force enters the bag it connects to the concurrence, once it comes into contact with you it travels directly back to Yetzirah for processing. When you set off back to Assiyah the bag is already empty.'

'Excuse me?' Zophiel liked to think that it took a lot to shock her. This however was something quite new. 'So you're telling me that I'm not actually transporting life forces back to Yetzirah. The core task which I'd been under the impression that I had been doing for thousands of years?'

'Ha ha!' With the drop of Zophiel's jaw, Hariton slapped his sofa in glee. 'I'm afraid you are over inflating your importance in the whole process of keeping Yetzirah alive. You're just there to inadvertently flick an invisible switch, and obviously to collect the bags.'

'What?'

'I'm sorry, Zophiel you're a collector of empty bags not a whole lot more. Do you realise how many Newmans pass on every day? Hundreds of thousands. We can't be having all those bags left behind littering Assiyah. The Newmans would be waist deep in them before they knew what was happening.'

'But I can feel the life force in there, it's how I know that I'm not just picking up a random bag.'

'Well of course you can feel it. The essence of life itself has been placed in that bag. You'll still feel the weight of it, probably see it if you looked in there, but trust me the life force's journey to processing has already begun.'

'I'm actually distraught.' Zophiel's face was the picture of horror and confusion.

Hariton laughed. 'I'm so sorry, Zophiel. Your life isn't totally without worth, consider yourself a highly intelligent litter picker.'

'I hate you, Hari.' Zophiel was smiling, but it was not a happy smile.

'Of course you do, and if you find some sort of meaning to your life by an eternal hatred for me then, I am happy to be of service. Otherwise the only other meaning for your existence is as a bag collector.'

'I thought you were my friend. We've known each other for over two hundred thousand years. Why didn't you tell me before?'

'It's because we've been friends for so long that I didn't tell you. Trust me, you need friends like me that will happily not tell you things to protect your precious ego.'

'Thanks, I think, you git.' Zophiel said, wilfully demonstrating that Newmans didn't hold a monopoly on insulting finger gestures, and used an old Yetziran one which would have been quite impossible for stubby Newman fingers. She suddenly threw her arms up in the air, causing Hariton to jump. 'But hey!' she shouted. 'Empty bags! Empty bags! That's exactly why I'm here.'

'What do you mean?' Now it was Hari's turn to be confused.

'Well it's empty bags that I came to talk to you about. What would you say if I told you that there have been occasions when highly intelligent litter pickers such as myself have arrived to pick up bags that they thought contained a life force, but they actually felt empty.'

'That's impossible.' Hariton laughed.

'No it's not because it's happened to me, and I know of other occasions when it has happened.'

Hariton leant forward. 'Tell me more.' he said.

'There's no more to tell. On a number of occasions, glorified rubbish collectors such as myself have gone down to Assiyah, found a recently passed Newman, picked up the bag and have found that they are empty.'

'Are you sure?'

'Of course, I'm sure, I'm not a total fool. You said yourself you can feel the weight of the life force in the bag.'

Hariton didn't reply but gave her a look that Zophiel thought was just a bit longer than it needed to be, as if he was trying to work out if this was all a clever joke to get him back for saying that her life was worthless.

'But that would be impossible, the system is fool proof. The life forces enter the bag, and they can't go anywhere other than to processing, there's no escaping the bag, or the concurrence. Have these empty bags been reported.'

'Of course they are, every time. Do you think any of the messengers would be brave enough to keep that kind of information to themselves. It's reported every time to the powers that be, who are obviously not bothered.'

'Well speaking as someone who is a member of the powers that be myself, I've never been contacted about it. You would think that if there was a problem with the concurrence, the first person they would come to would be the one that actually invented the bloody thing.' Hariton's face was one of both confusion and annoyance.

'And this is why I'm convinced that something weird is going on, there must be more to it.' Zophiel said. 'You said it would be impossible, what do you mean?'

'Well, there's no escaping the bag, but they could get free to wander inside the concurrence. I don't know what the point of that would be though. Give me a couple of days, let me look into it, and I'll let you know if I find anything.'

Zophiel stood. 'Thanks, Hari. You are actually a real friend, even if I do hate you for ruining the very point of my existence.'

'Trust me, Zoph it's truly been the highlight of my day,' he replied.

Zophiel left the apartment to the sound of Hariton's laughter.

# Attack of the Cat People

## Pelusiam, Egypt 525BC

Helel Bene Elim awoke in a sea of bodies with his left arm hanging from his shoulder by a thread and an Egyptian khopesh jutting from his chest. For any normal being this would be like something from a terrible fevered nightmare, but Helel felt like he had come home. The huge sword sticking out of him was not a worry. He had taken over enough dead and dying bodies to know that he had a grace period of around two hours, during which he was invulnerable to any injury or death, and injuries caused to the previous occupant of the body would recover themselves at an alarming rate. He did not fully understand why this was the case, but thought that it may be because the Grim Reaper had already done his job and would not return in a hurry to a body that he thought he had only just dispatched. It was a theory, probably not a correct one, but at the end of the day it worked for him.

The only reason when this was not the case was in decapitation, as he had found out during a visit to Paris in 1799 when he had been rash enough to take over the body of someone who had met their end through an appointment with Madame Guillotine. Heads would not re-attach, and the resulting chaos that ensued as he ran around the wooden platform in desperation trying to find the lost noggin was something that, although hilarious, was not an experience that he would like to take part in again. After finally finding the head and trying to balance it on his neck, whilst the screams of terror and cries to God for mercy rang in the ears that were attached to the decapitated bonce, the body expired once more and Helel was able to return to the great web to try and find a better receptacle to inhabit.

He was upset that the battle was now over though. Throughout his many lives, back to his very first, Helel had always enjoyed the chaos and horror of conflict. He had sought it out wherever he could and had always loved finding an enemy worthy of him. He always engaged them with a broad smile across his face in a fight for life and death. Unlike his foes however Helel did not fear death, why should he? To lose in battle, to be struck down by your enemy was more of an embarrassment than a disaster. When he was killed in battle he would simply move on to the next life and continue the fight elsewhere.

Obviously, this lust for war and conflict was secondary to his overarching goal, but it was a fun part that he enjoyed, a hobby if you like, the way that other people engage in self-destructive and meaningless pastimes like plane spotting, jigsaws, or jogging. Over his many years and lives Helel had made himself a master of warfare and fighting. Of course each vessel that he took over was a different bag of bones, with its own particular limitations and abilities.

It was this game of chance when borrowing and renewing the spent life of another which made the game more fun. Could he for example take a disabled child who would normally be abandoned in the forest for the wolves to feast on, and turn them into a successful warlord, leader of men, and ruthless invader of countries? Well, his time as Ivar the Boneless had shown him that this was possible. Could he take a mute child who bangs their head against the wall when they get sums wrong, and screams when their parents try to touch them, and turn them into the multi-billionaire public face of a Californian tech company. Again, easily done.

When a life force moved on and a new one took over the body, a little something always remained. Nothing major, no huge personality traits, memories, or disgusting habits, but there was always something. A good example was when Helel had inhabited the recently deceased body of Harold Turnpike, money lender and 'gentleman', who was both the scourge and the lifeblood of Hoxton in the late 1870s. Always to be found lurking around the bounds of Hoxton Square, Turnpike was a man that you did not want to fall into bad grace with. A broad man, he had started his days as a boxer, and not one who followed the Marquis of Queensbury's rules. Dirty Harold as he became known was just as likely to bite your ear than deliver an uppercut, and it was this reputation as a vicious and merciless bruiser that initially gained him both money and notoriety. As he began to age, and the fights became tougher Harold decided to invest the money that he hadn't spent on bad living and start his own business, lending money to the poor and unfortunate who scraped a living in the slums of Hoxton. It would have been impossible however for a man with the life and history of Harold Turnpike to not have made a lot of enemies along the way, either through his fighting days or from his swindling and exploitation of those desperate enough to have required his money lending services. Almost inevitably one of these many enemies finally caught up with him outside the Angel and Crown on Roman road.

To have your throat slit from ear to ear is normally the end for most people. Most people however do not have their just dead bodies inhabited by an entity who had spent thousands of years in Hell and now roamed freely on the earth appearing throughout history. So when the very clearly deceased body of Harold Turnpike stood up, and announced 'Tis but a scratch' before plunging his own dagger into the heart of his assailant, this feat only enhanced the fear and respect with which he was held.

So, what little element of the original owner remained when Helel Bene Elim took on his life? What essence of Harold remained? Well in his case it was the love of music hall songs, the bawdier the better, and a sudden and violent nausea when smelling fish. Weird traits, and probably not what Harold Turnpike really thought would be all he passed on when he died, but there you go. There was no sense or justice in how the whole life borrowing deal went as far as Helel could ascertain. In each life he took over, in each different bag of bones that he took control of, there was always something and Helel always enjoyed finding out the particular quirk of the recently passed. It wasn't much but it was a hobby of sorts.

The thing that Vidarna Walagash, Spada and foot soldier to Cambyses II left for the new inhabitant of his mortal frame however did not take long to discover as Helel awoke in his body on the battlefield.

He had a terrible fear of cats.

Now you would not think that the battlefield would be a place that you would normally find our feline overlords. Yes, cats do generally go where they want, do what they want, and laugh hysterically at human attempts to befriend and have mastery over them, but a battlefield where the screams of the dying and the cries of the wounded ring through the air? Surely not. But on this day in Pelusiam it was not just one, but hundreds of cats littering the aftermath of a terrible massacre. Wherever Helel looked they were there, daintily scampering in between the bodies, standing unceremoniously on the faces of the dead, and deep inside Helel felt true fear. At first, he thought that his mind was playing tricks on him, he had never feared cats before, he had even owned a few throughout the various lives he had lived.

Of course, it is common knowledge that no person ever truly owns a cat. If a cat lives in your home, sleeps around your house, and eats the food that you provide for it, do not think for one minute that you own this beast. They own you; you are their lapdog; you are the incredibly grateful pet in this scenario, and you should feel lucky to be so.

As he fought back the urge to scream at the top of his lungs, whilst a black and white four-legged representation of evil rubbed itself against his arm, which was slowly re-attaching itself to his shoulder, Helel thought of the very first cat that had allowed him into its life.

Mr Tubby was, as his name suggests, a rotund and generously built feline unit. His fur was long, black, and always had something attached to it, be it a leaf, a twig, or the feathers of his latest kill. His legs were thick and straight, and he always gave the impression that he was walking on his knuckles. If Helel Bene Elim was once a Victorian moneylender, then you can be sure that Mr Tubbs was once a silverback gorilla. He loved Mr Tubbs but at this moment in time, in this life, in this mortally wounded bag of bones, he grew goosebumps the size of garden peas all over his body at the slightest thought of his old, solid fat cat stomping his way towards him, licking the air as if on the scent of blood, as he fantasised about eating his tenth favourite human (Do not ever think that you are the favourite of a cat. There will always be at least nine others in front of you in the queue).

Helel cursed his new body, quietly so as not to draw attention from the wandering cats obviously and, after removing the sword from his chest, slowly crawled his way to the edge of the battlefield over the bodies of his dead comrades and adversaries and, when he felt he was a safe distance away from the feline evil, he stood and made his way into the victorious Persian camp.

Polyaenus, the second century Greek author and military strategist later claimed that reason for the cats' appearance on the battlefield was a strategic masterstroke and early success of psychological warfare by the

Persian King Cambyses II. He had marched on Pelusiam against the Egyptian soldiers with a cunning plan in mind. He knew that the Egyptians had learnt very early on that the cat is a very powerful, and sacred animal. He knew that Egyptians would never wish to harm a cat for fear of pain and suffering in the afterlife, and so Cambyses had ordered his men to march towards the Egyptian line holding cats out in front of them. Helel could only wonder at the levels of fear and outright panic that Vidarna Walagash must had felt as he was forced, probably under pain of death, to actually hold a furry spawn of the devil himself, and he was quite sure that the battle hardened Persian warrior would have welcomed his quick demise on the battlefield as a way of escaping his cat based misery and putting an end to a terrible day at work.

As he reached the camp he found it to be mostly empty. The victors of the day had entered Pelusiam and were, he assumed, running riot in the city, dispatching the last of the defenders, looting to their hearts content, and taunting Egyptians with cats who at this point just wanted to go and curl up next to a fire somewhere and sleep off their exhaustion at having to do any work. He found the captain's tent and, seeing that it was empty let himself inside. On a table in the centre of the tent he found what he was after. He studied the map momentarily and saw that he was about 4 miles from the coast and the main port, it was here that he had arranged to meet his contact. He was around two years too late but the art of jumping through time was one which often owed as much to chance as anything else, and his contacts will have waited patiently for him, family did that kind of thing. Six siblings, six points in the web, hundreds of explosions in time and space that would see an end to this whole petty affair. It was a complicated undertaking, one which had required hundreds of years of planning, but soon it would all be over.

'What are you doing in here, Spada!' a voice from behind interrupted Helel as he scanned the map. He turned to see a Persian officer stood in the doorway of the tent. 'Explain yourself. This area is off limits to a foot soldier like you, who do you think you are, one of the Immortals?'

Helel strode towards him. The officer did not see the dagger until it had entered his stomach and was pushed upwards. He died gasping for breath.

'An Immortal? Yes, I think that I just may be.' Helel laughed as he let the officer's body drop to the ground. He wiped the blade on his tunic and left the tent, heading north to find his sisters who he had not seen for nearly two hundred thousand years.

# A Mad Old Bird?

## Sunningdale Present Day

Amelia studied the faces of Sophie and David as she finished telling the story. She had not told anyone her secret for a very long time and wondered just how believable the whole thing was. Not very, she thought, by the look of David. Sophie was however a little more receptive.

'So now you both know, and you have to make a judgement; am I a time traveller, whizzing backwards and forwards in a giant spider's web, borrowing the lives of those that have died, breathing new life into a recently vacated body, and having a relationship with someone for over a thousand years?' She paused for a moment. 'Or perhaps I am just a mad old bird with a very vivid imagination who has constructed an elaborate theory about life, death and the history of the universe to help her cope with the demise of her husband?'

There was silence for a moment before Sophie spoke.

'I don't think you're a mad old bird. I think I believe you,' she said, reaching out and clasping Amelia's hands. 'I think it's a wonderful story, and if that is all it is, just a story, then that is fine, but I want to believe.'

Amelia smiled and turned to David, 'And you? What do you believe?'

David coughed and looked at his watch, avoiding any eye contact with the women on the other side of the table.

'I believe that it's been very interesting listening to you Amelia,' he said getting up from his chair. 'You tell a good story. But I'd better go and see if George needs a hand. I understand that one of the flats has a problem with its boiler.'

'Yes, of course,' said Amelia. 'I have taken up too much of your time. Thank you for the tea, I feel much better now thank you. I think I'll just return to my flat now.' She stood and walked towards the door. 'I'm glad you believe, Sophie. One day I hope that you get to see the truth. Perhaps if I see you again, I could tell you a little more.' She left without another word.

As the door closed David let out a long sigh. 'So sad when that happens isn't it? We've seen it so often in the past few years.'

'You don't believe her then?' said Sophie.

'Of course not, its utter claptrap. Time travelling and giant spider's webs. A love story that transcends time. It's a fantasy, can you not see it?'

'But it all seemed so real.'

'Oh, she tells a good tale I'll give the old girl that, but surely you're not taken in by her?'

'I think I'd like it to be true, I think I'd like to think that there was something else out there and that relationships can last forever.' Sophie's eyes were filling, not that David would have noticed.

'Really Sophie, you should know better. One day you're fully compos mentis, sharp as a pin, and fully in control of your faculties, and then Bam! Old age finally hits you, and you think you're a time traveller.' He chuckled at his observation but cut short when he finally read the look on Sophie's face. 'Look, I'm sorry. Perhaps I'm being too harsh on Amelia. Erm… a few of the staff are off out to The Forester's for a drink later if you'd like to join us?' he continued 'I thought it would be a good idea for team building and all that. I know you only volunteer here once a week, but you'd be more than welcome to join us.'

'No thanks.' Sophie replied. 'I've got something on, places to be, you know. Her eyes looked far away; her mind was not in the room.

David left her, sat at the table, deep in thought.

Sophie Pratman had never been lucky in love. There had been things in the past, just things though, nothing that she would ever have called real love. At twenty six she had begun to think that she would never find it, especially not in Finlay. Life in a small market town can turn pretty lonely when you know everyone around you, and you have already crossed off the list a long but not expendable list of potential partners. From her first boyfriend in school Alex to her most recent partner Maeve, there had always been something missing for Sophie. That spark of knowing, that tiny ember of love that seemed to have evaded her at every turn. In the last few months, since Maeve moved out of their flat and away from Finlay, Sophie had given her life and her future a lot of thought, perhaps an unhealthy amount of thought in fact, and she had come to a fork in the road. She wondered whether to follow Maeve's example and make a fresh start somewhere else, or to somehow become content with the knowledge that she was meant to be alone, apart from a lot of cats.

After hearing Amelia though, suddenly a new perspective had been put onto things. If only what Amelia had told her hadn't just been an elaborate fantasy as David had said, then perhaps the one for her really was out there, just not in this place and at this moment in time. Sophie's mum had told her that there was someone out there for everyone, sometimes there were more than one, as her own parents second marriages had proven. It was just a case of finding them, of not giving up, and of simply opening your eyes a little wider in the search.

Sophie collected the teapot and cups and saucers together on the tray and, after one final biscuit which she had earlier promised herself she wouldn't eat, she left the room and it's stories behind.

Half an hour later Sophie left for the day. She stepped outside the doors of the reception, her breath immediately visible in the cold air. The nights were beginning to draw in now and, despite it being only five o'clock, it was already starting to get dark. The orange streetlights which lined the roads of the Sunningdale retirement village were blinking on one by one. 'Lights,' thought Sophie, 'That was what Amelia had said we were. Lights floating in a web.'

She walked the short distance towards her home thinking of nothing else but Amelia's story. Just a story. It had to be. Nothing more. It made Sophie feel bad for Amelia, living alone without the love of her life, and dreaming of a time when she would see him again. As she reached the end of her road, the noise of the thoughts began to grow like a steam train inside Sophies head. The little medieval village where a little boy and his friend the old witch woman lived. The castle at Dolorburgh and the tower that Elswyth threw herself from. Amelia said that their story had been so much longer, and that they had shared many years and lives together.

There was something about Amelia's story, something that rung so true with Sophie, she almost felt that the old lady was telling her something she already knew but had somehow forgotten. It was a strange feeling, every time she tried to concentrate on the thought, every time she felt that she was recalling a memory, remembering something very important, the memory seemed to dance from her grasp, as if she was not meant to see it.

The feeling did not leave her all evening, it niggled and bit at her. It would not shift. After two hours of restlessly wandering from room to room trying to get on with other things, she grabbed her jacket and left the house. It was not too late in the evening, and she knew she would not rest until she knew more. She walked back to Sunningdale Retirement village and Amelia's flat.

Sophie reached the apartment building, pressing the buzzer for flat 23 where Amelia lived. After a few moments there was a crackle followed by the old lady's voice.

'Hello?'

'Mrs Hawke... Amelia. Hi, it's Sophie, I'm sorry to disturb you. Would it be ok if I came up to see you for a little while?'

There was no answer, but the door buzzed, and Sophie was able to open it and step inside. She found Amelia sat in a high-backed chair in her living room. By the side of her chair was a small side table upon, which was a short lamp which gave off a gentle yellow glow.

'You'll excuse me if I don't get up dear,' Amelia said. 'These bones are old now; I will be changing them soon.' She let out a small giggle and her eyes shone brightly and mischievously. The kettle has recently boiled if you fancy making yourself a cup of tea. What can I do for you?'

Sophie sat herself down in the chair opposite the old lady. 'No, I'm fine for tea,' she said. 'Any caffeine at this time of the evening and I'll still be awake until the early hours. I wanted to ask you something, if that's ok?'

Amelia smiled and closed her eyes. 'Of course you do, young lady. After what I told you this afternoon, I am guessing that you have many questions. The first being, is Amelia Hawke a mad old bird?'

Sophie laughed. 'I wouldn't be so rude, but yes. I want to know if what you said was true.'

'It was, and what I told you was not even the half of it. My Alan and I had many years and many lives together. You said that you believed me. Do you?'

'I do, I think,' Sophie said. 'But I want to know more. I need to know more. I want to hear it all. There's something about your story that is driving me crazy and I don't think I'll be happy until I know it all. I want to know what happened next after you threw yourself from the tower, how you found each other again. I want to know what happened afterwards; I want to know about your other lives together.'

Amelia took a sip of her tea and laughed. 'Trust me, young lady, if I were to tell you all of it we would be here for a very long time, probably longer than I have left in this life.' She settled back in her chair once more. 'After the tower, though? Well, I certainly can tell you that this evening. After the tower is where the Venetian soldier enters the story, and where I discovered my love for the first time.'

# The Sisters of Mercy
## Menton, France 1645

Every family has a dark secret. It could be something small like that time your iffy uncle did two years in Wormwood Scrubs for breaking and entering and now was the go-to person if a family member ever got locked out of their house. Or perhaps it's the great grandmother that was always rumoured to have got rid of her cheating first husband by lacing his food with sleeping tablets and staging an apparent suicide. It could even be the time your second cousin decided he was the messiah, bought a farm in the middle of nowhere and assembled his own heavily armed cult, who met their demise in a hail of police gunfire after threatening to blow up Buckingham Palace and the lizard overlords who lived there. You know the sort of thing.

Anyway, each family has one, a story told in hushed whispers at Christmas and funerals, a deep shame which is hammered into a family tree with a copper nail, slowly causing the leaves to fall and the roots to wither.

In many cases having a family member such as Helel Bene Elim would be enough to do it. He was no house breaking uncle, murderous granny, or crackpot death cult leader, but he was intent on the destruction of the world and killing of every human on it, as well as causing the slow painful death of the beings who looked over it. He was definitely the crazy relation that you warned your children away from at an early age, the one who would tighten the spines of everyone when they turned up uninvited to a family barbecue. He was however not the most brazenly dangerous member of the family. That badge of honour would go jointly to his sisters, Azazel and Sariel, the twins.

Azazel and Sariel had travelled together through the centuries, haphazardly causing pain and suffering on the world with a murderous abandon which would make even the most fervent dictator baulk in terror. They never stayed in one life for long, their wild reigns of horror meant that they were always brought to justice and killed for their terrible crimes fairly quickly. Through the years they had been burned at the stake, beheaded, crucified, and even once buried alive in a tomb so deep in the earth that it would be impossible for them to dig their way out. They didn't care, why should they? The sisters had their fun – although it would be a sick mind indeed that classed their exploits as in any way enjoyable – they were caught, or overthrown, and they would be killed for their violent and abhorrent deeds. It was not a problem however, as they would simply enter the concurrence once more and find another place in time, another spot in the world ripe for terror, entering the fray again, cackling wildly as they did so. There were no consequences for their actions, and this suited them just fine.

They had been at the convent for almost two years now, Azazel leaping from the concurrence into the body of the Mére Supérieure when the previous occupant, Brigitta Martín, had expired following a particularly bad bout of typhus. Her death had seemed like a long time coming, she had taken to her bed, where she spent over a week soaked in fever and drifting in and out of consciousness. The nuns of the convent had attended to her fastidiously, but they knew that it would only be a matter of time before she passed. In the second week of her illness things had taken a turn for the worse and she slipped into a comatose state. Somehow however her body held on, it was as if God was not ready yet to receive her into his large and benevolent bosom. Over the next week the young postulants bathed her body daily, and passed small amounts of water into her mouth through dry lips, her body wasting away by the day.

It was early on the Sunday morning of the third week of her sickness, as she was attended by a postulant named Marie Agnes de Fleur, that Brigitta, bathed in the Lord's early morning light which shone down on her through the window, finally left this world to join the almighty.

Moments later she opened her eyes, her body returning to the world but with an altogether inherently evil host.

At first the Holy Order of the sisters of St Cecilia, were overjoyed at the return of their Mére. Their little convent on the French Italian border had truly been blessed by the heavens. A sign from God himself that the good work of their order had great things ahead of them. Their leader, who had been close to death, had sprung from their bed full of life, sprightly and laughing hysterically in joy at their salvation.

It was indeed a rapturous time in the convent, full of happiness, laughter, and godly bliss. Yes, the Mére Supérieure was a little odd in her behaviour, often to be seen dancing excitedly in the gardens of the convent in the middle of the night, and perhaps a little prone to admonishing the nuns with a playful nature, almost as if she was enjoying reprimanding them. Overall, though, these small changes to her personality were nothing when tempered by the joy to have her back from the edge.

Things changed for the worse two months later however, with the arrival at the convent of a new postulant, Hildegard Meyer who appeared at the gates one day, saying that the Virgin Mary had appeared to her in a dream in her home in Prussia and told her to travel the 300 miles on foot to their little convent. She had been welcomed with open arms by the Mére, who had greeted her at the gates herself, and embraced her tightly as if she was a long lost family member. Surely, this was a second blessing from above in a short period. First their beloved Mére had been returned from borders of heaven, and now the Virgin herself had sent them another miracle. They were so very wrong.

Within days the Sacred Order of St Cecilia became a very dark place indeed. Gone was the peace of daily prayer meetings and time for silent contemplation, cast out was the feeling of sisterhood that had been developed over decades. Instead new rules of behaviour and expectations were introduced, which in turn brought cruel punishments such as enforced isolation of those daring to step out of line, and beatings in front of the gathered sisters, a warning and a lesson to others. There was whispered talk of Satanic rituals and other more ghastly terrors that went on behind the closed door of the Mére Supérieure's office, and eventually there was a death within the convent. At first it was thought to be a terrible accident, a punishment gone wrong, but the laughter heard coming from the Mére's room told another tale.

It was Agnes de Fleur, the same postulant that had borne witness to the rebirth of the Mére, that took it upon herself to flee the convent one night, scaling the walls to do so, and running barefoot to the nearest village to tell a torrid tale of cruelty and violence within the supposed holy place.

The great and powerful might of the Catholic church in Rome was brought the news of the evil deeds taking place in the convent within days of the nun's escape, and immediately leapt into action. After many very important meetings between the lower clergy and eventually the Holy See they sent their most experienced investigator to Menton - just over a year after receiving the news.

By the time Arturo Colombo-Bianchi finally approached the gates of the convent at Menton, the regime of evil which had started when Brigitta Martín awoke from her deathly sleep, had been running wild for eighteen torrid months. A soft faced man who was well respected and loved throughout the Papal court, Colombo-Bianchi had been the obvious clergyman for the job. His unyielding love of the church, knowledge of Christian history and the teachings of the bible, combined with his personable and kindly nature had meant that his work was never done. He had spent the last twenty years travelling around western Europe at the behest of the Pope attending incidents where the Catholic church's mission had been called into question. Sometimes it was claims of misdeeds of priests, other times clashes between local churches and landowners, Father Art as he was known within the confines of the recently completed St Peter's Basilica, was a man who was always able to calm tensions, resolve whatever crisis had arisen, and restore the authority and respect for the church through his jovial nature, wise words, and unbending faith.

The tales of witchcraft, Satanic worship and cruel violence occurring within the convent at Menton were not a task he had ever faced before, but it was felt that no other priest within the ranks of the Holy See would be better able to repel the works of the devil, bring the Sacred Order of St Cecilia back to their holy mission, and assuage the locals.

The gates to the convent were locked when he arrived, he rang the bell. Looking through the bars onto the walled garden inside he could see that it was unkempt and unloved, with high weeds, vegetables rotting on the ground, and a general feeling of abandonment. The door to the chapel at the end of the path was gingerly opened and a short woman stepped out and shuffled towards the gates. As she came closer, he could see that the woman looked a great deal older than her years, with bags of tiredness hanging below her eyes, dry cracked lips and a hunched uncomfortable gait, as though every step was painful to her. Arturo guessed that she was would actually be no older that thirty years of age and wondered just what horrors had befallen her and her sisters to cause such a terrible change in her overall countenance. She stopped at the gate and eyed him with a mixture of fear and suspicion.

'What do you want?' she asked. 'We do not take visitors, if you are delivering a message, speak it to me or pass it through the gates, we are a private order.'

'Sister,' the priest said, his kind eyes shining brightly, and a warm smile causing his voice to sound soft and comforting. 'I have come from the Holy Father in Rome himself to meet with you and your order. Please open the gates, that I might come in to speak.'

The sound of his voice, the softness of his face struck a light within her soul, and at first the priest thought that she was going to break down and weep in front of him, such was the effect. There was joy locked deep within her, but it was met with a weight of sadness.

'Our Mére would not allow anyone inside, whoever they are and even if they were sent from heaven itself,' she whispered. 'She would not be happy with me if I were to open the gates to you, not happy at all.' Her eyes twitched a little, her hands wrung together.

'Then I shall not ask you to dismay the Mére,' he said softly. 'Simply put the key in the lock on your side and I will let myself in. You will not be at fault for any transgression of mine that follows.'

She looked at him longingly for a moment, obviously trying to balance the potential risk to herself with the benefits which his entrance to the convent could bring, and for a short second the priest thought that she might run straight from him. She did not however, and instead quickly pulled out a large iron key dropping it at the foot of the gate, before fleeing back along the path and into the chapel once more.

Arturo leant down and reached through the gate to collect the key and within moments had let himself within the walls of the God forsaken convent. As he reached the door of the chapel, he was pleased to see that the nun had left it slightly ajar. He stepped inside.

In all of his days he had never seen anything like the view which met him as his eyes adjusted to the dimly lit darkness within. All was unholy chaos. The chapel was a terrible mess with its wooden seating overturned and smashed, stained glass windows broken, and at the head of the main aisle the cross itself had been pulled down onto the floor, hacked at, burnt in places and the effigy of the messiah which had once been part of it, pulled free and dismembered. The stone walls were daubed with unholy words and signs and a small fire burned at the altar. The priest's mouth fell open at the horror of it all, and he crossed himself, whispering a short prayer. The devil himself had visited this place.

Lost in both place and time, he did not hear the person approaching him from behind, and almost did not feel the blow which struck the back of his head. It was as he sank to his knees, blood trickling down the back of his neck that he then saw the bodies which lay before the altar. Mercifully Artur Colombo-Bianchi lost consciousness then and met his end.

Death had not come to this body. His eyes flickered open, and although blurred he could make out the figures of two nuns standing over him.

'What should we do with the priest, sister?' One of them said. 'If they have sent him then others will come. We do not have long left here.'

'Good. I was beginning to bore,' said the other. 'I was thinking that it was almost time to move on.'

Arturo's vision began to steady, and he saw that as well as the pair stood over him, the last remnants of the Sacred Order of St Cecilia were now gathered in the chapel.

'I would say that you have well and truly outstayed your welcome, Azazel.' The priest muttered, suddenly sitting up in front of them and causing many of the other assembled nuns to drop to their knees in prayer.

In that moment the two sisters Azazel and Sariel knew that they were in trouble. The priest sat up from where he had laid dead moments earlier. 'I came to find you in Egypt,' he continued. 'But you had already left those lives. I endured the cats of Pelusiam for you – do you know how horrible that was for me?' Helel noticeably shivered just to mention the name of his feline oppressors. 'I even found your bodies, they had been hung by their ankles on the streets of Alexandria for all to see, a warning to those that would do evil.'

'How did you find us here?' gasped Sariel the younger of the nuns.

'What? You think that you were so well hidden from me, sisters? You really think that I do not know my way around the concurrence enough to find you. You leave a huge mark wherever you go. Look at the trouble you caused in Constantinople. Taking the bodies of Emperor Justinian and John the Cappadocian were hardly subtle disguises, you should have moved on though after starting the plague. You hung around for another fifteen years!'

'We were hated, by those we ruled over, they wouldn't play the game,' smiled the Mére Supérieure.

'Thankless idiots they were, Sariel,' muttered to her sister. 'Didn't know when they had it good, we made that city rich beyond compare.'

'I agree,' said Helel. 'However, I think the mindless slaughter of innocent citizens, kind of outweighed the money side of things. And that is exactly my point! If you had controlled your urges, you could have created an empire. Once you had that power and control you could have killed as many as you liked. Of course, eventually it would have ended the same, with the pair of you strung up by your ankles, or nailed to a tree somewhere, but you could have taken your great work to a much greater level.'

The two nun's eyes met, as if blaming each other for their current situation. They knew that they were being chastised. They shrunk somewhat awaiting the next bout of verbal admonishment. It didn't come. Helel sighed and pulled himself up to his feet, his voice softening and his hands laid on their shoulders. The congregated nuns around them were now a quivering mass of fear and holy doubt.

'There is a pattern here, my sisters,' he said. 'Each place you visit you just take things too far.'

'But you told us that we had to spread death,' said Azazel. 'I think you'll find that we've done more of that than any of our brothers. I'm sure Armaros hasn't caused half as much damage to the human race than we have, he's too soft on them. Penemue would be the same, far too caught up in his books to be slaughtering the innocent and butchering his way across continents.'

'Of course,' said Helel. 'I do not deny that you've been doing a sterling job, your deeds are legendary, the chaos you create second to none, and I commend you for your efforts. But that is the problem, it is born in chaos. If you just relaxed for a bit and concentrated on your endeavours a tad, you could do even more.'

Azazel was silent for a moment, evil cogs whirring furiously inside the Mére's twisted mind. 'But it wouldn't be as much fun,' she muttered. 'It would become… dull.'

'And we can't have that,' Sariel said, her voice a little whiney, like a toddler who had dropped her ice cream. 'It has to be fun. You know we bore easily.'

Helel sighed. 'And that is why I gave each of you a plan to stick to. I literally mapped out where to go and where to bring death. If you just stick to the plan then all of this will be over before you know it, and we will be free once more to take charge of this rotten world. Then you can have all the fun you like - for eternity.'

'We kind of lost our plans though,' mumbled Azazel, the Mére's face now resembling a naughty child. 'We buried it somewhere like you told us too, but we've forgotten where. We were very drunk at the time.'

'Then I shall write you a new one and you can get back with the programme. Yes?' His hands moved from their shoulders and lifted their chins so that they were forced to look him in the eye.

'Yes,' they both muttered in unison, before Sariel added, 'Are we going now? Do we have to leave straight away?'

'Oh, not right away,' the priest smiled. 'We are on a schedule, but there is a little wiggle room for fun still.' He pointed to the weeping nuns praying for their souls and winked at his now laughing sisters.

# The Venetian Visitor
## Finlay's Hollow 1288CE

Galasso da Molin had travelled for two years, finally reaching the village late in the evening, his torchlight showing little of the place where he had been born over six hundred years earlier. Finlay's Hollow seemed to be a ghost town, and he did not see anyone in the village as he walked past the small houses and animal sheds on his way to where the Laird's Hall stood. It was as he entered the village square that he heard the noise and knew where all of the villagers were. Laughter and music rang out from the hall, and he stopped for a moment not far from the exact spot where he had first died in the arms of Analla. The village looked very different now, the houses made from stone, there were lanterns hung from poles throughout the village, and there was an overall feeling that Finlay's Hollow was a happy and contented place to live, even more so than when he was a young boy two lives ago.

He still counted himself as a young man, as far as he could tell he was either twenty-seven or twenty-eight. He had lived four different lives since leaving the body of Elswyth, each of them quite different, either in age or gender, and each of them interesting and educational in their own peculiar way. Taking over a new body is similar in feel to what people in the modern age would feel like getting into a new car for the first time. The general layout is the same, perhaps some bits look different or are even in different places, but it is only when you start the car and set off to drive that you really feel the difference, in handling, strength and ability.

The first life after Elswyth was a short one. They had found themselves in the body of a slave on a Roman galley. For three months they had toiled beneath deck, chained to an oar and mercilessly whipped and beaten. It was a valuable lesson, albeit a painful one on the importance of choosing a potential new life carefully, rather than just hurling yourself into a hole in the web willy-nilly. This life ended quickly enough, when the galley sank to the bottom of the Mediterranean. In all of her many years after this experience Amelia had always held any body of water with a knowing mistrust. After this she was a 19th century dairy maid named

Heidi in the Austrian alps, who had miraculously survived being trampled by cattle, only to be lose her life from consumption five years later. She returned to the farm for her next life, as a young sheep herder in early twentieth century Wales. This had been one of their favourite ever lives; simple but rewarding, for fifteen years they spent their days wandering the hills and valleys, Daffyd Thomas was well liked in the local village and enjoyed a life of many friends and an even closer family. Unfortunately for Daffyd things took a turn for the worse after deciding to sign up to the British army in 1915. Daffyd did not even make it to Belgium as he was accidentally shot during training. Never clean a loaded gun was another great lesson still kept dear by Amelia. Prior to becoming Galasso de Molin they had lived in early twenty-first century France, Paris to be exact as Clarissa DuPont a software engineer for a computer games company. Clarissa was another of Amelias favourite lives, mainly due to the great shock of just how different the world was, and how less filthy everything seemed to be. For fifty years they enjoyed this life, finally entering the web once more when Clarissa died happily in her sleep, surrounded by her family. In each life they waited for contact from their friend, in each life there was none. Perhaps it was time to seek them out, and so back in time they went determined to this time head to Finlay's Hollow to look for a sign.

Galasso had awoken in the middle of a battlefield just outside a castle on the Greek island of Syros. The shock of being in a man's body was not unexpected, the light being once known as Elswyth had looked down through the hole in the web and seen where she was heading. It was the accumulated little things that were more of a change for her. There was an arrow wound in his side, which although now a bit niggly and painful on damp mornings, at the time had been the cause of his death.

Galasso was a thinly built man, with dark, tough features that gave the impression of someone who had lived a troubled life. Thankfully the body's current owner had not been forced to go through this hardship.

The body of Galasso da Molin that had been 'reinhabited' had been the victim of a conflict between the rival Ghisi and the Sanudo noble families. The warring families had begun fighting with each other over the ownership of a donkey. It would appear, he later learnt, that pirates had stolen the donkey from the Ghisi family and sold it on to William Sanudo Lord of Syros. When the Ghisi family found out, they laid siege to William's castle and only ended their warlike ways when King Charles II of Naples intervened to negotiate a peace between the two great families. Over 30,000 men had lost their lives in the so called War of the Donkey, Galasso being one of the lucky ones who had survived but only through that fact that his body had been reinhabited by a young girl from Northumberland who had recently thrown herself from her bedroom window. It was never ascertained what happened to the donkey.

Galasso made his way up the rebuilt steps to what had been his uncle, the Laird's house all those years ago. The main frame and size of the building remained; however it was clear that whoever had taken over the role of Laird had made many changes to the hall.

The Hall was a sumptuous and wild place, very different from the scant decoration, hard dirt floor, and hay beds that had been there when Brid lived there such a long time ago. It would seem that the new Laird, whoever it may be, was much more of a lover of the extravagant. Thick red cloth hung on the walls and from the dark beams on the ceiling. Long tables lay down each side of the hall, all filled with copious amounts of food which just the sight of would have sent Brid's uncle apoplectic with rage, as he was not one for such gaudy displays of his wealth.

The door closed behind him the hall, which until that time had been awash with the loud noises of music and laughter. The cacophony stopped immediately as all eyes in the room fell on the newcomer. Galasso looked to the end of the hall to see a well-dressed man on a large chair looking down towards him. The man was a large and imposing figure, dominating proceedings around him, and enjoying his place as the centre of attention. He had never laid eyes on the man before, but there was something about him, something which was confirmed to him moments later when the man spoke.

'Ah, my friend you do not know how long I have been expecting you. You are welcome to my house, I am Robert. Come, eat and drink with us, we have much to talk about.' Sound returned to the room as suddenly as it had left, and Galasso was handed a large flagon of ale as he walked toward the man at the head of the hall. As he reached the Laird, a seat was brought for him which he took gladly, he had travelled many miles to get to this point, and return to a place he called home.

'Tell me, after I left you did you end up marrying the boy from York?' The Laird said, failing miserably to hide the amusement in his face.

'I did, although it was brief, our marriage lasted less than a day. I died on the evening of the wedding. Jumping from a high window will do that to you.' He took a large gulp of his drink and wondered if his characteristics and personality were as evident to the Laird as the Laird's were to him.

'A falling death? Wow, that's hardcore, I've only ever done that once - never again.' The Laird had a round red face; his pockmarked cheeks partially hidden by an impressively large beard. He spoke with an accent which was definitely not local, and it was clear to Galasso that his friend had also travelled back to Finlay's Hollow from elsewhere.

'Wow? Hardcore?' Galasso exclaimed. 'I don't fully understand what you're saying, but I get the intention of your words.'

'You don't know the words because they've not been invented or spoken by anyone yet except for me. It's one of the little benefits of the strange lives you and I lead, we cannot bring the physical with us, but we can bring other things, words, ideas, learning. You'd be amazed at how many things I have brought back and introduced to the world.'

'Amazing me seems to be your life's work,' Galasso said.

'I try, and always will,' the grinning Robert replied with a sharp twinkle in his eye, which brought a smile to the Venetian's face and a redness to his cheeks.

'You're an idiot, and always will be,' Galasso laughed. 'Did you not like the feeling of falling? I found it quite exhilarating.'

Robert took a large swig from his tankard and shook his head. 'No, I have always had a fear of heights, they make me feel quite shaky.'

'Hence why you prefer to send small boys up trees for you?'

'Exactly.'

They both smiled and took a moment to bring their flagons together. After two years of wandering a war torn Europe working as a mercenary for some of the richest, most respected, and ultimately most corrupt families, trying to return to true home, Galasso was immediately eased by being back in the company of the only person that he could call a trusted friend. The closeness brought a warmth back to him, something which he had missed terribly.

'So, you've obviously been here a while then?' Galasso said remembering how hungry he was, and taking some food from the table.

'Oh, many times. When I first got back here four hundred years ago it was deserted, just as I said it would be. I decided to stay for a while, but ended up spending the next thirty years here. I rebuilt the Laird's Hall, and I travelled to Glenleven nearby telling them that Finlay's Hollow was being rebuilt. Soon others came to rebuild and live in the empty houses. Finlay's Hollow became a working village once more. I even married a local woman. I was happy and content with my life for the first time in a very long time, although I knew, at the back of my mind, that one day it would be time to move on and begin again. It was as I was starting to feel old age in my bones that I decided that it was time for a change. You obviously were not returning anytime soon, and it didn't matter anyway, I could return to the village whenever I wanted and see if you had returned. I would have taken myself up to Giant's leap and thrown myself over the edge but, you know… heights and all that. A knife to the neck is a brutal way of leaving one life to start another but I prefer it every time to the screaming and flapping arms when you dive from a height. Twelve times I have returned here, in between other lives, at other times, and in different places. I can't remember exactly how long it has been since I last saw you, but I am guessing it to be well over two hundred years.'

'What? But to me it has been less than seventy.'

'You still don't get it do you? How time works for us. You remember what I called the web, don't you?'

'The con something…'

'The Concurrence. It is there and in place, all times running together, don't you understand? I can flip about as many times as I like and still return to you the next day in a different body after living a thousand lifetimes. I watched for you all over the world, throughout time, but I knew that you would always return here to find me, and here you are.'

'But how did you recognise me?'

'I could ask you the same question. How is it when you entered my hall that you knew that it was me sat here waiting for you?'

'I don't know I sensed it; I wasn't sure but there was something at the back of my mind.'

'It is a skill that you are only just learning from your time in the concurrence. Sooner or later you will not see people's skin at all when you look at them, you will only see their life energy. The light within them. Where other people will see Robert Turner, Laird of Finlay's Hollow, you see Jarod the stable boy.'

'You really do talk a lot of rubbish, you know.' Galasso smiled. 'If anyone else heard what you were saying you would be taken to the Loch and drowned. In fact, I'm quite tempted to do it myself.'

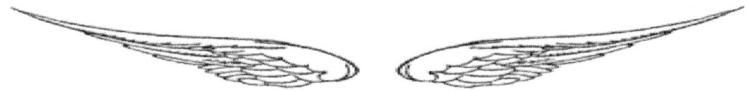

Galasso remained in Finlay's Hollow, moving into the Laird's Hall, and helping Robert to turn Finlay's Hollow from a small and unremarkable village to a bustling market town. Galasso enjoyed being back in the place that he had grown up in hundreds of years earlier, although so much had changed since his first life.

The friends became close for the first of many times throughout their countless lives. No one raised an eyebrow to this in Finlay's Hollow, why would they? To the townspeople the Laird was a good man who provided them with the means to make a happy and prosperous life for themselves, who cared who he took to his bed? And besides the Venetian that came visiting one night and decided to stay made the Laird smile a lot more than he used to.

The time to move on came on a winter's night fifteen years after the Venetian had first walked into the village. The snow had come heavy that year and the village had been grateful to have set aside stores during the autumn to help to feed them and their animals. For days at a time they were trapped in the village, as large drifts blocked the pass out of the valley. They made it a happy time though, in some ways Galasso preferred those days, all of the villagers huddled in the hall, telling stories singing songs and sharing food. It is a feeling that Amelia had struggled to find anywhere else, in the hundreds of years that she had travelled the world and its times.

One of the villagers, a stout man named Doran, went to check on the horses in the stables at the side of the hall. Suddenly a scream was heard from outside and Robert and some of the other men picked up their swords and ran outside to find the body of Doran laying on the snow covered floor. Standing over him were three tall, winged beings dressed in clothes of pure white, so bright they stung the eyes to look on them. They each wore helmets but shining through were bright eyes of blue fire that looked like they belonged to the devil himself. Each carried a white staff which ended with glowing blue head. As soon as they saw Robert they leapt into action springing forwards, weapons pointed at their quarry, they were unnaturally quick.

Unaware of the danger, Galasso stood inside, at the back of the hall.

'Reapers!' Robert shouted as he came running through the doors, and Galasso knew that it was time to go. He gave his adopted daughter Elise a hug, telling her that he loved her, and that he would see her again and ran to Robert who stood waiting for him in the centre of the room. They embraced. Galasso drew his knife and Robert drew his. The Reapers burst into the hall, screaming a high pitched squeal, which rang in their ears, and which Amelia still heard in her nightmares.

'As we planned, Galasso. Now!' Robert cried and he plunged the knife home in the nape of his lover's neck, as Galasso did for him.

# A Poisoner's Trick

## Hnevin Castle, Most 1598CE

It was a very strange scene that Zophiel found herself transported into, possibly in her top ten of weird death scenes that she had attended. Number one on that list had also been the one that gave her the most nightmares. In 1326 in London, Zophiel had arrived to find a body floating in excrement. The deceased in question 'Richard the Raker' had fallen through the rotten floorboards of his privy into a very full cesspit of his own making. Thankfully the collector had left the cloth bag at the side of the pit and Zophiel didn't have to go digging around for it, but she felt sorry for the collector himself who would have had to submerge himself to collect the life force from poor Richard.

Zophiel found herself in a cell block in the dungeon of a castle where the occupant had recently expired through poisoning. What would be weird about that I hear you ask? Prisoners in sixteenth century cells died daily, either through exotic and ingenious methods of torture such as the rack, the iron maiden, or the horrendously named Fork of the Heretic. In fact, in terms of dispatching your enemies the sixteenth century dungeon was often the best place to do your worst, whilst gaining weird enjoyment from watching people suffer at the same time. Of course, by the time Assiyah had reached the early twenty first century the use of such things as The Pear of Anguish was frowned upon, and if you wanted to see your enemies fall and revel in their suffering, all you had to do was make up something about them on social media and actively encourage a pile on. Apart from death it was a much more effective way of destroying a person and didn't include all the blood, guts, and messiness.

What was most strange about this particular scene which she suddenly found herself part of was that the recently deceased had taken the poison willingly in front of an audience which included what Zophiel thought may be his wife and children such was the horror on their frozen faces. Quite why a person would want to do this in front of their family was completely beyond Zophiel's comprehension, although she had long since decided that the Newman race were ultimately doomed to extinction by their own hand, such was their determination to destroy themselves and everything around them. She approached the body and looked for the cloth bag which she expected to find at his feet, but it was nowhere to be found. Surely it hadn't been collected already it had been a reasonably quiet waking cycle and she knew that she was one of only a few messengers on duty. She had seen the others descend to Assiyah and none had been heading here.

She was about to take a seat and wait for the visitation of a deputy Arch to scold her for her tardiness when she saw, in the gloom at the back of the dungeon, another body, that of a tall guard who was slumped against the wall. She made her way through the audience which were a collection of the opened mouthed in horror and the open mouthed in happiness and saw that this was obviously her job today. The guard had expired in excitement at the sight of the self-poisoners demise. She picked up the cloth bag only to find that it was empty. Her disappointment at a wasted journey was tinged with a little excitement, and a touch of happiness which was shown by the wide grin on her face. She had around twenty heartbeats left until an alarm went off in Yetzirah, and so decided that rather than wait graciously next to the body, she would take a seat in the audience and put her feet up to rest on a nearby 'Spanish Donkey'. Thankfully the iron donkey did not have anyone sat on it and screaming in pain. She had just got comfortable when the member of middle management arrived with a dull pop.

'You again?' Said Araqiel angrily when he saw the messenger lounging with her feet on an instrument of torture. 'What are you doing, and why in Her name have you not collected your bag and returned to Yetzirah?'

Zophiel remained in a relaxed repose feeling quite pleased with herself. 'It's happened again. I must be either very lucky or very unfortunate, but it's happened again. Empty bag.' She ran her fingers through her long black curls and waited for his response.

'An empty bag?'

'Yep.'

'Are you sure, it's empty? Have you checked? Stand up for Her sake!' Araqiel looked a little unnerved and Zophiel couldn't work out whether it was the lack of life force in her possession or her languid manner. Either way it was entertaining to her. She took her feet off of the Spanish Donkey and stood up, showing a touch more respect.

'Yes... sir. Of course I have checked it's my job. Tell me, does this happen a lot? Its twice for me now, and from what I hear it's a bit of a thing.'

Araqiel's face darkened, 'It's nothing. Nothing to be worried about at all. Now get yourself back to Yetzirah immediately.' He went to place his hands together at his chest to leave but stopped himself. 'What do you mean it's a bit of a thing?'

'Well, I've been doing some snooping around and it seems like this kind of thing happens a lot. Now are you sure that it's nothing to worry about, or should I be speaking to someone above your pay grade about it.'

For a moment Zophiel thought she could see a little fear on the eyes of the deputy Arch. It was momentary, but it was there.

'Snooping around? I can assure you Melaku that you do not want to get yourself the reputation of a troublemaker. This is not the kind of occurrence that you would be wanting to talk to anyone about, least of all one of the Arches. They are aware of this; it's a minor anomaly of no importance, and any talk of major problems and accusations of mis-dealings are not looked kindly upon. I would think that if you went marching into an Arches office with any talk of this you would be finding yourself on a very sudden trip to Gehinom. Do I make myself clear?'

Zophiel straightened herself, the smile immediately wiped from her face. 'Of course, sir, I fully understand. I shall of course return to Yetzirah straight away and shall talk no more of it.'

'Good,' said Araqiel. 'Off you go, and I hope not to have to come down and deal with you again.'

'Yes, sir,' Zophiel said. She placed her hands in front of her chest, but they did not immediately touch. 'Interesting though,' the smile returned to her face. 'I didn't say anything about major problems or mis-dealings, I just said it was a thing.' Her grin widened and, as her hands touched, she left Assiyah in a shot of dazzling bright light.'

Araqiel stood for a moment in the dungeon, his face impassive, his mind busy, before touching his hands together and leaving the Newman world.

As time resumed and the world of Newmans returned to its normal state, the dungeon was suddenly full of screams, shouts, and chaos. Both from the self-poisoner's wife and children, and from the castle guards who realised that one of their own had also died, seemingly also from ingesting poison.

As his body was picked up by rough hands and carried out of the dungeon, up the stairs and into the courtyard of the main castle, master alchemist, professional occultist, psychic medium, and ultimately confidence trickster Edward Kelley was pleased that his great act seemed to have gone to plan. He had been getting bored of his time on the continent and wished for a return to England. He had spent two years in the cells of Rudolf II, who had lost patience with Edward's constant excuses as to why he had not been able to create gold and untold riches for the Holy Roman Emperor. He had arrived in the castle with a great reputation, it was said that he could commune with angels and receive messages from God, something which initially intrigued the emperor. These communications with the almighty and the production of gold did not materialise however, and he was locked away.

When he was told by a guard of Rudolf's plan to have him executed to stop him from escaping and sharing the secrets of Alchemy with Elizabeth back in England, he was surprised when Rudolf had agreed, as a favour to an old friend, to allow him to choose the nature of his own death. He was even more surprised when Rudolf had allowed him to mix the poison with which he would commit suicide himself. The ingredients were difficult to find, and it was necessary to ensure that the guard who he had persuaded to help him switch the bottles did not survive. It was a shame as the guard had spent many hours in his company whilst in the dungeon, questioning him about his communication with angels, and how someone could contact the seraphim and cherubim. Poor fool, Edward didn't have the heart to tell him that it was all a ruse, part of his patter; angels did not exist.

His apparently lifeless body was dumped by the castle gates where, once his self-induced paralysis had worn off, he would creep out to the woods on the outskirts of Most, where he would meet once more with his family and escape back to Britain. His wife and children had put on a good show this evening, they were naturals, not as dramatic as his own particular show, but it all added to his successful escape. Edward Kelley never knew just how close the angels had come to him that day.

# Lair of the Bookworm

## Bodleian Library, Oxford 1603

Sir Thomas Bodley sat in the peaceful solitude of Duke Humfrey's library above the Divinity School, in the library which had been recently named after him. He looked up from the medieval manuscript which had had been taking all his attention, and gazed around the room wondering if life could ever get any better. In the last fifteen years he had achieved all he had ever wanted out of life. He was renowned, respected, revered, and now, in the past year, had cemented his place in history by having the greatest library in the modern world named after him. He allowed himself a rare smile, closing his eyes and enjoying the moment.

The moment was ruined by a voice which, although he had never heard it before, he recognised immediately.

'If you wished to hide brother you would have done better than to place yourself in the centre of a pile of books. You make my task too simple by far.'

Bodley sighed, he had not been called brother for over a thousand years. 'Was I that easy to find, brother?'

'Fairly,' Helel replied. 'I had a list of likely places I might find you; this place was fairly high on the list. I did think you would have chosen something more modern though. If it is knowledge you crave the 21$^{st}$ or 22$^{nd}$ centuries have much more available. All at your fingertips at the touch of a button.'

'You misunderstand my love of the written word, brother. Nothing could ever take the place of a book, or a manuscript held within your hands. I am happy at his time in history, the written word still has authority and meaning here, and it hasn't yet lost its sense of mystery.'

'Books though, Penemue?' the voice said. 'You really think that books are the answer to everything?'

'I think that the world, any world, is better for them, brother. How could it not. Do you not remember that even after millions of years of Yetziran culture we never gave up on books. There is nothing quite like the power and joy that can be consumed when a good book is physically within your hands. Can you not remember sitting somewhere quiet on Yetzirah and becoming engrossed in a good read?'

'I remember nothing of my life in Yetzirah. I have cast it from my memory. That cursed world is a dead place, and I will see it erased from the universe.'

'My, my, dear brother. You really do hate them, don't you? Why can't you just leave them be? There is plenty on this world to enjoy, you can go anywhere you like, at any time in history. You could be happy.'

'There is no happiness for me while I know that the killers of our children still live. There is no happiness for me while I know that they go unpunished. You made a vow to serve me, Penemue. You made a promise on that day, that you would follow me, and we would see our revenge. Do you not remember?'

'Oh, I remember, Helel. We all say and do things when we're a bit excited don't we? It was a very emotional moment wasn't it. I mean we were all a bit het up with what was going on. It was thousands of years ago now. A lot has happened since then. I've lived a lot of lives here on Assiyah, there is beauty here, brother, beauty, and happiness.'

'And books?'

'Yes, there are books.'

'And what if I burnt your books, and indeed this whole library to the ground?'

'You wouldn't dare!'

'Dare? I mean to turn this whole world to ash, and you're worried about a library. You really don't understand do you, brother. There is no place for us here building things. Whatever we build now, wherever in time we are, it does not matter. Everything will change once we act, and our plan comes to fruition.'

Penemue placed his palms on the desk and sighed. 'This library has been my life's work.'

'Our plan should be your life's work. Follow me, do what you promised back in Shulon, and I promise you that there will be a place for a library even greater in our new world.'

'You still want that then? That's still the plan?'

'But of course, everything will be as we wanted. Our children will return, and we will have our own world to live on in peace. Do you think I'd forsake that?'

'I'm never sure with you Helel. You always did have nihilistic streak.'

'Oh that. Well, that's just a show, a mask that I wear. You know me better than others, brother. How are we going to achieve our goal if the Yetzirans do not believe we would be mad enough to go through with it.'

Penemue looked at his brother, he made a good argument, but like Helel had said, Penemue knew him better than most, they were the two oldest of the six sibling generals, and he knew for a fact that the madness that Helel claimed to be just a mask, ran deep within him. Helel would see this world burn even if it meant taking everyone else with him.

'I am happy here. I have achieved so much. I can achieve so much more.'

'Your promise.'

'But I won't be able to take them with me, will I? I will have to leave all of this behind.' He waved his arm, gesturing to the countless shelves, heavy with thousands of the world's greatest written work. 'Look at it all, brother! Such beautiful words written over thousands of years and think of what is yet to come. In the next four hundred years alone there will be Dickens, Twain, Austen, Tolkien. All of it will be lost.'

'It can be re-written. Greater works will be created in our new world. Listen to me brother, take what I am offering you, because you should be assured that the alternative is not one that you would want. I will not only destroy your library, but I will also make sure that none of these so called great works are ever created. I will travel through the concurrence finding and killing authors for fun, before they can even learn to write their first word. I will do all this and then I shall consign you to that same concurrence where I will find you and eat your eternal soul. How do those terms sound to you?'

Penemue stared at his brother for a moment, looking for a hint of compassion within his eyes. There was none.

'It makes me feel awful, obviously, he said. 'Tell me brother, will you really see this through to the end even if you have to destroy everything even your family, even those that love you?'

'Don't doubt my resolve, Penemue,' Helel smiled. 'You know the time and the place. I expect to see you there after completing your task. Don't let me down, I will find you if you do. You know I will.'

Helel stood, idly picking up a book from the table as he did so. 'Is this precious?' he asked, flicking through the pages and enjoying the fear in his brother's eyes.

'You know very well that it's the Histories of Troye. It's one of the first to come off of Caxton's press. Currently it is indeed precious, but in years to come, if looked after properly, it will be priceless.' He recognised the nature of his brother's smile and spotted the quick glance to the fireplace. 'Don't do it Helel. I beg of you!'

'Brother, please. What do you take me for? I am not a complete animal, and I am not that easily fooled. I know that there are two copies here.' He lazily tossed the book into the flames and left the room laughing, as Sir Thomas Bodley thrust his hands into the fire and cursed the day he had ever made the promise to his brother.

# The Soul Eaters
## The Concurrence

The being that would one day be a little old lady, seeing out her days in a retirement village was a ball of light again, but this time there was no thought of following the path towards the centre of the web. The being that had just been Galasso da Molin immediately searched for his partner who was nowhere to be seen, and they began to wonder how many years it would take for them to find each other again.

Thankfully this time there would be no huge search, as a quick glance to the distance found the light that had been Robert floating towards them. Galasso thought for a moment that Robert's light was brighter and somewhat larger than it had been the last time they saw it.

'Where have you been,' asked the light as it came close.

'I literally haven't moved; I just came out of that hole in the concurrence. 'Where have you been?'

'Oh, I arrived here a while ago, I've been hanging around for ages waiting for you to arrive. You're very slow, you know.'

Galasso did not rise to the bait. 'Where next?' they asked.

'I was thinking perhaps of taking you a little further forward, perhaps we could visit some friends of mine in the Americas.' The light that had once been Robert replied, 'Someone who has been doing a bit of work for me hopefully. It was something I set up a long time ago, but should be coming to fruition about now.'

'I've never heard of the Americas, and I don't know what you're talking about. Can you not just talk normally to me? You always talk in riddles, and I don't think you realise how annoying it can be.'

'That's because it is far from Finlay's Hollow and anywhere that you have been before. It is too much for your tiny country bumpkin brain to conceptualise.'

'Again, using words I've never heard of, and acting like some kind of idiota compiaciuto.'

'Of course, I apologise, I don't mean it in a cruel way, I find your simpleness cute, and don't take the word simple as an insult either, it is not meant like that. And remember that I was once an Italian merchant. There are no insults that I don't know. We'll need to travel laterally for a while though in order to change our position. Are you ready to see the far side of the web? It's a long way away but I think you're ready for the journey.'

'I'm not so sure, is it dangerous?'

The light that once was Robert pulsed with laughter. 'Everywhere is dangerous, everywhere there is the danger of death. It should not worry you though, I thought you would have realised that by now.'

'Then let's go.'

The journey across the web took some time, all the while they felt small vibrations echoing around them.

'What is that?' The light that had been Galasso asked. 'I've not felt anything like that before in either time that I've been here.'

'It's just a vibration through the concurrence, they happen every now and then although this is stronger than normal.'

'Are we in trouble?'

'I thought you would have learned by now that we are always in trouble, my love. Perhaps we should pick up speed a little. Stay close.'

They floated onwards, not at a great speed, but fast enough for the light that was Galasso's liking. At times it was difficult to hold on to their partner's light, to stay together, and they began to feel that if they lost hold and drifted behind, that they would not be waited for. All through the journey the light of Galasso questioned their partner, questions that only seemed relevant in the web.

'I've been meaning to ask you for a very long time.' Galasso said. 'Do you remember your first life? When was it?'

Robert did not answer immediately, and for a moment Galasso thought that he wouldn't respond at all. Finally, he spoke.

'I was born for the very first time on our world a very long time ago indeed, thousands of years ago, in times of legend really. You would not believe what the world was like back then, it makes the world we have just left look very hi-tech and fancy. The only records of these times are inaccurate musings, nothing like what really happened.'

'Have you ever thought to write it yourself, to tell people how it really was?'

'I could I suppose but there would be no point, it would only bring me pain and misery no matter in what point in history I told it. I would be seen as blasphemous, you see. Some would believe me I'm sure they would, but for the most part the human race is very happy to live in their ignorance with their made-up gods and idiot religions. It's a terrible fault of man, their reliance of superstitious nonsense to justify their existence. If they knew the real truth of it all I think they would be able to move on a lot quicker. Unfortunately, I have been to the very ends of time, as close to the centre of the concurrence as I dare, and it is something that they never manage to free themselves from.'

'Oh, really? That makes me want to know more. Will you tell me?'

'Perhaps one day. It's not that special, all very dull really and not something for you to concern yourself with.'

Suddenly they stopped. A light, somehow larger and brighter than either one of them could be seen in the distance, it was fighting its way out of one of the strands of the web, and pulling itself out into the void between.

'Is that another wanderer like us.' Galasso asked. 'Do you know them?'

'Be quiet and move back!' Robert hissed, there was real fear in the voice. The bright light ahead had now freed itself from the herd and was powering through the void towards them, its speed was terrifying compared to theirs. They shifted back until they touched a strand of the web, Galasso felt the icy pull of the web at his back. When the light hit the strand it sent the life forces, which included those of Galasso and Robert, scattering like nine pins. Most of the lights sent out into the blackness of the void went straight back to the strand of the web, some of the lights however flickered with the impact, and to Galasso's horror disappeared completely.

'Out of my way, sheep!' cried the bright light angrily, as it forced its way through the gap in the lights and out of the other side, disappearing into the distance, their light somehow brighter than before.

'Who was that?' asked the light of Galasso when they had moved back into the void and continued on their journey.

'Do you remember many years ago when you were Brid and before you had entered the concurrence for the first time, that I talked about the dark ones?'

'Vaguely,' replied Galasso. 'You said there were others and that some used their gift for mischief and cruelty. Was that light one of them?'

'It was, and pray that you do not get any closer to them than we just did. They would put out your light in an instant. Stealing your life force to strengthen their own.' They paused for a moment. 'Did you see the lights go out?'

'I did, does that mean they are gone?'

'Yes, they are truly dead, their light is snuffed, their life force inhaled by the dark one. There is no coming back once you have been absorbed. The dark ones are the one thing in this universe that truly scare me. They are tyrants on the real world, and soul suckers in the concurrence. You saw how large he was? It's a sign of just how many poor lost souls have been taken by him.'

'But you are bigger than most lights, does that mean you are a soul stealer too?'

'I will not even answer that. I thought you knew me better, and I am disappointed that you should even think it. I am larger because of the lives I have inhabited; I have lived thousands of years slowly growing with each life.'

'Of course, I'm sorry.'

'We will forget the conversation. Enough of them anyway, we must away to our destination, and there is far to go. We will talk no more about it.' The being that had last been Robert, and before that Jarod and Analla, shot away with considerably more speed than before, leaving their companion chasing after them.

They continued onwards, the being that had been Galasso in their last life now nervously scanning the horizon for larger, brighter lights.

Time passes differently in the concurrence; a day could feel like a minute and the next one like a lifetime. A single hour could pass in no more than a blink of an eye, not that those within the concurrence needed eyes to see.

Finally, they began to slow on their journey, and the being that had once been Robert spoke.

'We are approaching our destination, we need to be very careful, can you feel that vibration getting stronger still?'

'Yes, what is it?'

'We are being searched for. To take the analogy further, it is like a spider tapping on the web to feel for flies. They did not like that we escaped them in Finlay's Hollow, they scent our blood. Travel gently.'

'Travel what? We are floating in a huge void how do you travel gently?'

'Just go steady, no sudden movements, float naturally. We will travel on their paths where we can, lose ourselves in the throng a little.'

'Oh right, float naturally. It's not something I've ever had to do before, but I'll see what I can do.'

They continued on their path crossing between strands when it felt safe to do so, travelling with the other lights who were on their way to the centre of the web at other times.

'Look up ahead, we are here. We will take this strand here and enter the world at a point slightly closer to the centre of the concurrence.'

'So, we are going forwards in time. How far ahead are we going?'

'A little over two hundred years, we need to be exact in order to find the time and place where my friend is.' They stopped suddenly. 'There, over there, do you see that hole, it is bigger than the rest and there are many lights coming from it. It should provide excellent cover for us; they will not find us there.'

Galasso could feel the vibration running through the web, thrumming all around. They could feel it and somehow, despite the apparent empty silence of the web hear it also. The vibration seemed to be becoming stronger, and Galasso could see that even the normally placid and compliant lights, who had entered the web without knowing any better and mindlessly followed the herd towards the centre of the web, were becoming restless and unnerved by the disturbance. By the time Galasso and Robert had reached the hole the vibration had reached an almost deafening crescendo.

'Go now!' called Robert. 'They are getting closer!' Galasso hurled themselves towards the opening in the web, fighting their way through the crowd of light coming the other way. Wherever they were going it was obviously going to be a scene of terrible death, and for the briefest of moments Galasso thought about turning around and finding a more peaceful entry point back into the world.

They were not wrong, looking down onto the world Galasso saw a scene of terrible desolation, body upon body, death upon death. Galasso turned to ask Robert if this was really a good idea, but Robert had gone. They were alone. They looked down and saw the light of a soul leaving a body, they had no choice. Diving downwards Galasso da Molin took the body of a woman who had just had a large spear thrust through their chest. They felt the pain of the wound, but they were alive, and in the world once more.

# Nearly Ice Cold in Alex

## Alexandria, Egypt 1348CE

The streets of the once great city of Alexandria were now nothing more than a plague infested wasteland. Zophiel whistled her happiest tune as she tiptoed through the lines of bodies laid out in the market square in preparation for burning. It was strange, she thought, that she was here to collect a recently drained life force, as it looked like the bodies here had been dead for days.

The level of death had been terrible here, Zophiel had lost count of the amount of times she had visited Assiyah recently. Herself and her fellow messengers had never known anything like this before in the history of Assiyah. Senior management had been understanding and had insisted that messengers took regular breaks from their work and had a least one full waking cycle off every couple of weeks, but it was fair to say that the life force collection department was at full stretch.

They had known pandemics in the past, disease was something that was always going to happen on a primitive world; they had even considered them temporary bonuses, a sudden influx of life forces to keep the coffers full, if you like, but this one was unprecedented. Millions had passed on already and millions more would follow them as the Black Death spread from Eurasia to the so called civilised world.

Zophiel did not have to wonder long where her bag for collection was, as at the edge of the rows of dead was one set slightly apart, a man on his stomach as if put with the bodies too early by mistake, but who could not ever fully escape their fate.

Inside Zophiel was counting her heartbeats, she quickly collected the bag and attached it to her belt and, knowing that she had a little time, took a moment to look around.

Alexandria, if it had not been littered with the dead would be a marvellous place to have the time to look around, and Zophiel wished that she could have the chance to fully enjoy the sights, sounds and smells of Assiyah. The Newmans, although primitive, destructive, and capable of doing terrible things to each other, were also able to build beautiful buildings, and great cities which were a wonder to behold. It made her sad to think that her only instances of experiencing the Newman world were to see it frozen in time, silent and without any movement or life.

She was distracted for no more than a couple of heartbeats and so did not notice the movement to her side, the tall figure rushing towards her. In a world without motion there can be a delay to senses when you are suddenly pushed to the ground, and it was the shock which caused Zophiel to freeze, even when the darkened figure stood over her and plunged a dagger into her chest. Her vision swam and she began to lose consciousness, her assailant leaned over her body, their face covered.

'Greetings from the Brotherhood,' they hissed through their mask, before escaping from the scene and running off down one of the small alleyways which circled the market square.

Zophiel lay dying amongst the plague ridden dead of Alexandria and called for help to people frozen in time who could not hear her. For a reason that she could not explain, she reached down and touched the cloth bag at her belt.

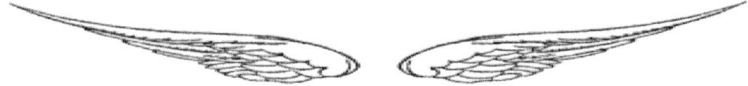

There was darkness, and then suddenly a flash of light causing Zophiel to close her eyes to protect them from the brightness. When she dared to open them, she was aware that she was floating, a ball of light in a vast inky blackness. There were other balls of light, milling around her and as they began to move, she found herself drawn along with them. She turned to see where she had come from and saw a hole in the blackness and through the hole the bright sunlight of the Market Square in Alexandria. The line of lights that she had joined felt comfortable, felt right, and she wanted to follow them.

She stopped however, suddenly as if grabbed from behind. Zophiel tried to move forwards, to follow the others but she couldn't. Something had hold of her and she was being pulled backwards, back towards the hole in the darkness, back down to Alexandria once more. She fought against it, but the pull was too strong, and she found herself falling into the hole. With one last look into the void, she caught her fullest glimpse of it yet. Thousands upon thousands of streams of light, all moving towards a common goal, all heading to the centre of the void, but there were others, just one or two that were larger and brighter than the others. And they floated alone in the blackness, they did not follow the path like the others. She left the void.

She hurtled downwards striking her physical body hard on the ground with such force that it forced her eyes open once more. She was laid bleeding, a hole in her chest where the dagger had been thrust. There was a dark shape above her, and for a moment she thought that her attacker had returned to finish the job.

'Breathe, Zophiel. I've got you. Breathe. Don't you die on me!' There was a rush of air around them as she was transported back to the safety of Yetzirah, and then there was nothing.

When Zophiel awoke she was laid on a bed and felt something she had never experienced before, pain; sharp, excruciating and incredibly nauseating pain. Nausea too was a new one on Zophiel and she wondered if this sicky feeling was what it felt like after drinking heavily as Newmans were very prone to do. Ever since discovering how to create alcohol the Newmans had added it to an ever growing arsenal of ways in which to ruin their lives and kill themselves slowly. Apparently, it created some pleasant effects but ultimately it shrivelled bodily organs, and when used consistently shortened their lives in such a way as to be alarming to anyone who did not partake, including Zophiel who was experiencing what Newmans referred to as the spinny room. She cried out, more for the spinning than the deep pain in her chest; this was horrible!

'Don't move! Try to stay calm, Zoph, you're safe now.' Totfiel was stood by the bed, his hands on her arms in an attempt to stop her from sitting up. 'She's awake!' he shouted and immediately another came to her bedside, an older Yetziran with a shock of white hair who Zophiel recognised as Hermatiel an Arch.

'Hold still,' he said. 'You've had a… shock.' Hermatiel produced what looked like a small, brushed metal gun from the fold of his gown, which he pressed against her arm. Immediately the pain and the nausea abated.

'What happened?' Zophiel said, her words a little slurred. 'I don't understand.'

'You were injured on Assiyah somehow,' The older Yetziran said. 'Thankfully your friend Toti found you and brought you back and straight to me. You must have tripped and fallen, landing badly on a weapon. You could have died.'

Zophiel looked over to Totfiel who had backed off when Hermatiel had entered. He gave her a small wave, 'Hermatiel was the only one I thought could help you,' he said. 'Turns out I was right.' He gave a weak grin which struggled to hide his obvious concern.

Hermatiel Metfornial was one of the oldest Yetzirans living, and in his day had been an expert in medicine, back when Yetzirans needed that kind of thing. He had been at the forefront of the research that had led to the discovery of the death gene in Yetzirans and had, as such in one smooth stroke both changed the evolution of Yetzirah as a world and made himself redundant in the process. He now lived in happy retirement, recounting old stories from hundreds of thousands of years ago about the old days when Yetzirans got sick and died. Anyone who spent any considerable time with him quickly found out that his stories were limited in their number and were repeated often. Thankfully he was also known as a kind, gentle and wise soul, so it was worth listening to the same story for the fifth time, each time increasing in drama and general exaggeration just to spend time in his company. He also happened to be Totfiel's uncle and so Toti had heard the stories more than most.

'I was attacked,' Zophiel said. 'Someone attacked me in Alexandria, I remember.'

Hermatiel shot Toti a glance. Before producing his small gun again. 'Lucky I still had this lying around the place.' He said waving it in his hand. 'It will take the pain away until you recover fully, thankfully I keep a store of old medicines. Don't worry they're not out of date. These things last forever you know.'

'Didn't you hear me. I said I was attacked. Who would do that to me?' Zophiel could feel the pain gnawing in her chest, along with another feeling she was unaware of. Was this fear? Anxiety? She felt like she was about to throw up.

Hermatiel seeing her growing distress gave her another shot in the arm from his gun, and immediately Zophiel began to calm again. 'My dear,' he said. 'It would be quite impossible for someone to stab you on Assiyah. All the Newmans are frozen, their time is slowed massively. It could not happen.'

'But it happened I can remember it clearly. It was a large being very tall, almost as tall as a Yetziran.'

'Well then it can't have happened.' Said Hermatiel. The only other Yetziran messenger within a mile of you was Totfiel here.

'That's right,' said Toti, 'and I know you can be really annoying, but I would never go so far as sticking a knife in your chest.' He gave a small smile and let out a nervous giggle.

'You are healing well, but the medicines I have given you will still take a little while to work,' said Hermatiel. 'There can be side effects from the medicines also, amnesia, hallucinations. Once you are fully better, I'm sure it will all be clearer to you. Now you must rest, the wound in your chest is almost closed and sleep will only aid a quicker recovery.'

Zophiel felt something press into her leg and before she could fight it, she was asleep once more. She dreamt of Alexandria, how beautiful the city was, and of how the being that meant to kill her still roamed there.

# The Girl who Lived
## Tenochtitlan, Americas 1520CE

The battle, if you could call it that, was very short lived. The soldiers led by Francisco de Balboa had known of the large settlement to the north of their camp for a while now, but had learned in the past that just marching into Aztec lands and not expecting a fight was foolish and likely to lose you men. Francisco de Balboa had no wish to lose any more soldiers than he had to, as there was potentially a long way to go on this expedition yet and he would need as many as he could keep. For this settlement his group had done things differently since setting out.

They had started by sending a small force upstream of the settlement to poison the water. By the time the people in the village had started getting sick, and begun to suspect that they were in trouble, they would already be weakened. The next part of the plan was to send their quickest men to the edges of the settlement and draw out the Aztec warriors into the trees where they could be ambushed and slaughtered. After that it was just a case of walking into the settlement, dispatching any warriors left behind and enslaving the women and children. It was a simple plan but one that had been very successful so far on this current expedition. It helped that Francisco was a man with an uncanny knowledge of the Aztec people, although this was his first expedition.

By the time he walked into the settlement the battle had almost finished, and he had to step over many bodies on his way to the temple where he hoped his target would be found. This was the fourth settlement they had conquered, and each time his plan had been the same, quell the township, find the temple, hunt down and kill the Priestess. His men wondered at the religious zeal he seemed to show in this seemingly personal crusade. In normal times he was seen as a respected commander, known for his friendly affable nature, and for his kindness towards the men under his command. In battle however, and when faced with the priests and priestesses of the Indian tribes, he was bloodthirsty beyond compare, violent and cruel to levels which shocked even the most enthusiastic Conquistadors.

As he approached the doors of the temple his personal guard, who remained by his side throughout every battle, knew what was to come. The temple would be taken in the most vicious of fashions, their commander running through the building as if in a desperate hunt for blood. For some of them it was sickening and shocking to see, but their victories were fast becoming famous amongst their peers and the rewards gained with each battle would ensure that they would all be very rich men when they finally returned home.

Today was different however, today, when they had entered the pyramid, they had found only one priestess who had been stood in front of the altar at the far end of the high ceilinged temple. She had not moved at all when the men entered, and only when Francisco de Balboa ordered the men to leave the temple immediately and they started to back away, did she turn to face them. She simply stood, serene and silent, in her hands a short golden sacrificial blade which she held to her own throat.

She was a stunningly beautiful woman, glowing in light which shone down from the gap in the ceiling created to allow the rays of the sun to fall on the altar. Tall for an Aztec, she had long black hair tied into plaits which ran back from her shoulders, her arms were adorned with golden rings, and on her head was a headdress of brightly coloured feathers. Around her neck and across her chest she wore a collar of gold, intricately carved and studded with jewels. Francisco de Balboa looked down to her bare stomach and, seeing the wide scar which ran from one side of her body to the other he knew that he had found who he had been looking for so long.

Atlacoya, although relatively young, was already a legend among the Aztec tribes. Her name spoken around the campfires of even the smallest village, spoken with reverence and wonder at the miracle she was the centre of. The stories told of a brave, young girl who had fought hard against the foreign soldiers who had raided her village ten years previously. When others around her had cowered in fear when the men in armour had razed her village to the ground, Atlacoya had taken up her father's macuahuitl and charged at the soldiers, finding gaps in their armour with the sword and killing four men before their blades finally brought her down. It was as she lay amongst the bodies of her family and those she had killed that her legend was born. Despite many cuts to her, including a spear in her chest, and the slice that had opened her stomach, slowly she started to rise again. Those who witnessed her rebirth, claim to have seen a ghostly golden light within her, as she stood once more and screamed at the invaders, who ran from the village in fear at the devil's magic that they had seen.

It was as Atlacoya stepped down from the altar and out of the sunlight, that Francisco saw that same golden light flowing from within her. For a moment he simply took in her beauty and felt grateful to have finally found her. He sheathed his bloodied sword before he eventually spoke.

'Well, I was beginning to think I'd never catch up with you again.'

Atlacoya smiled at him, seeing that he had a golden glow of his own which she recognised in an instant.

'Same here, 'Atlacoya said. 'Have you even been looking for me?'

'Of course I have. Do you really think that I would just abandon you to your own devices and let you fall victim to the Reapers?' Remember you really are not a lot more than a twelve year old village boy still.'

'Idiot! I've lived at least eighty years since I left the world as Brid. I think you'll find that I've grown up a lot since then. I've had to.'

'Of course, but every now and then, when I look into your eyes, I still see that weedy boy too scared to climb a tree.'

'You do know that's really weird, right. I'm a young woman now and it's a bit weird to know that when you look at me you see a boy. Especially considering our... history.'

'No weirdness intended. What I meant was that I can still see every life you have lived in your eyes, be that Brid, or Galasso, Elswyth or, as you are now, Atlacoya. Have you not got over the whole sex and gender thing yet? Really, I thought you would see beyond the skin bags by now and see the light.'

'I do, I mean I'm starting to. It just still sounded weird, that's all.'

The sound of Francisco's soldiers outside the temple door disturbed them.

'Well, we can't hang around her chewing the fat forever.' He said. 'I supposed it's time we moved on.' He pulled a short knife out of his belt.

'Good, I was getting very tired of this life. So, tell me, what's the plan?'

'Plan? I told you before, there is no plan.'

'Yes, but we need some sort of plan. We can't just go skipping around through history running away from Reapers forever.'

'Well, it's worked for me for a few thousand years. What's the matter are you scared?'

'Of course I'm scared, you oaf! I am literally living every moment expecting huge, winged aliens armed with pointy staffs to appear out of thin air. I am constantly on edge; every moment could be my last.'

'Isn't that true of any life though?'

'I suppose so, if you want to get all philosophical about it, yes that is how every living being on the planet feels deep at the back of their mind. But the problem is I've now seen more, I've realised that death doesn't have to be the end for us, that it is possible to live forever.'

'Unless you get caught by a Reaper.'

'Exactly! I blame you for all of this, you know. I was meant to die as a twelve year old boy in a small Scottish village, but now, because of you, I've suddenly got all these dreams and aspirations, places I want to go, people that you've told me about that I want to meet throughout history. I mean, bloody hell, have you actually been to the twenty-first century?'

'Of course, I've spent many a life there.'

'Well then, you know how hard it is to live in the relative comforts of that era and then have to give it all up in a heartbeat to go back to living in squalor, just because some aggressive winged nasty is chasing you and trying to send you to eternal oblivion. There must be somewhere we can hide that's better than this, where we can have some of the finer things in life, and don't have to be continually looking over our shoulders.'

'There are a couple of places we can try. Nowhere is completely safe but trust me, finding somewhere to hide is fairly close to the top of my list of things to do, and not just from Reapers.'

'What? Who else do we have to be afraid of? What are you not telling me?'

'Nothing to concern you,' Francisco said waving his hand. 'There are just some other wanderers like us that I'd rather steer clear of if I can help it.'

'Really?' Laughed Atlacoya. 'Do you mean to say that you've annoyed others and not just me? You really never fail to surprise me.'

'Yes, yes, you're very funny. Come on I'll see you in the web.' And he thrust the blade into his chest.

Atlacoya paused for a moment. Who else was after them? As much as Atlacoya cared for them, there was always a feeling at the back of her mind that she was never really being told the whole truth.

Francisco de Balboa's men entered the temple once more and saw their fallen commander dead at their feet, a blade in his chest. They would have had their revenge on the Aztec priestess if she hadn't quickly followed him into death.

As she entered the web once more Atlacoya cursed loudly. Once again, the being later to be known as Alan Hawke, husband of Amelia had disappeared.

# The End of a Grand Story
## Sunningdale – Present Day

'How did you find each other again?' Sophie asked.

Amelia smiled and picked up her teacup, draining the last of it, before carefully putting it back on its saucer.

'It took time, but that's the one thing that there is never any shortage of. Turns out he had entered the web and come face to face with a group of Reapers. He had run far away into the concurrence to lead them away from me when I entered. I headed off to somewhere a bit more comfortable to live for a while, Georgian England I think it was, and he came to find me, approached me at a ball and asked for a dance I seem to remember. He was a terrible dancer, but looked very dashing in his uniform, I was a more accomplished dancer, but struggled to successfully pilot a ball gown.

'We have lived countless lives together since then, and been on the run for a thousand years or more. Each time we escaped our fate, and each time we journeyed to a new life and found each other along the way. We have seen all of history together; borrowing lives, borrowing time. We have ruled countries, dined with emperors, we have fought in countless wars and helped make the peace again, we travelled to the furthest reaches of the world together. We have sailed across oceans and, if you dare to believe all that I have told you, even travelled far into the future beyond the realms of Earth to visit other worlds. For every life however, for every adventure, the result is always the same; eventually we die, either by our own hand, by others, or through illness and accident, and we return to the concurrence, the web, where we find each other once more and continue our journey together. Sometimes we would drift apart and lead separate lives but more often we always found each other and lived long happy lives together. Often we return here to Finlay's Hollow, where our story together first began, it's a special place and we have watched over it through the centuries.' she paused for a moment, her eyes glazed over a little and Sophie wondered where her mind had wandered to.

'Amelia? Are you ok? You look a little lost suddenly.'

The old lady looked up at Sophie, and forced a smile. 'I am sorry, dear, it is not a good day for me. You see, this part of our adventure is over. I do not know where he has gone, and may never meet up with him again. After a thousand years together, it is not something that I can ever really come to terms with.'

With effort, she leaned down and picked her handbag up from the floor, placing it on the table next to her now empty teacup. Her hand reached inside and reappeared holding an envelope. 'I was not upset when my Alan died, because I knew it would not be forever, but a couple of weeks ago I decided that it was time to go and find him. I went to visit the special spot under the trees where Alan and I had always kept our mementos from our lives, to pop a couple of things in, but when I opened my box, I found this letter. It was meant for me, but he never gave it to me himself. I imagine he couldn't bring himself to give it to me in person.' She carefully pulled open the envelope which looked as though it had been opened and sealed many times over, and pulled out a letter on thin notepaper passing it to Sophie, who unfolded the paper and began to read.

*My dear Amelia,*

*I have spent more than a lifetime in your company, and have been luckier that any person on this earth to have done so, but I have finally decided that there should be no more time. I was old when we first met in Finlay's Hollow, and you were just a skinny, wheezy boy. I am feeling even older now all these hundreds of years later.*

*I am tired, Amelia. I have seen more of this world than anyone who ever lived, and I have no further wish to remain here. There is nothing left for me to see, and I've decided that it's time for my next great adventure. I have resolved that I will follow the path into the light and face whatever meets me. Perhaps it will not be as bad as I have been telling you all these years, perhaps there is something better in the end. Maybe there is not a great and ravenous spider in the middle but heaven after all. Until I find out I will not be content, and so I must leave you for the final time. I could tell you that you were the love of my life, but this would not be true, you are the love of all of my lifetimes. You have given me so much joy and happiness, but you are still so young in your journey, and I so old. I must follow my heart although in leaving you I break it.*

*I have written and rewritten this letter a thousand times over, each time tearing it up and throwing it away. This one you will finally get to see.*

*Please forgive me, think fondly of our time together.*
*Yours for all time*
*Alan*

Sophie handed the note back to Amelia, who carefully folded it and returned it to the envelope.

'Oh, Amelia.' She said. 'Does this mean that he is finally gone for good. That there will be no more lives after this.'

'I really think so, dear. When Alan died, at first I thought it was just a joke, that he had got bored, and disappeared, sooner or later appearing again at my door as an emo teenager, or a bus driver, something random. Just another prank like I had come to expect from him. I could never bring myself to follow him into the void to chase him and catch him out before the joke was sprung on me, and I decided to carry on in this life for a while, enjoy old age a little, have a little time on my own.' She paused for a moment playing with the shiny silver catch on her handbag. 'But, after finding this I was in shock, I didn't know what to do. It was why I got so upset with poor Maureen. You remember, when I first started telling you my story. I really do think that he went on purpose. I really do think that he's gone for good. Perhaps I just have to end this life and find out for sure.'

Sophie shifted uncomfortably in her seat. Until now listening to Amelia's story had been fun, it had been a pleasant if slightly odd diversion from the tedium of her normal life. Suddenly however it had taken a dark turn. Suddenly all of this could end with an old lady actually taking her own life, and if everything that she had told Sophie was a convoluted lie then it really would be the end for Amelia.

'Don't do it,' Sophie said. 'Please, Amelia don't do it. You have years left yet, and there is still so much you could do in this life.'

Amelia laughed. 'Do you think? Really, Sophie, when you've lived for as long as I have the list of things still to do begins to run a little short. Perhaps you're right though. Forgive me, I'm just in a funny old mood today, just an old lady feeling down on life and prattling on about nonsense. Don't worry about me, sweetie.'

Sophie left her friend's flat, after making sure that she had everything she needed for the evening, and many more promises that she would not do anything stupid. All the same Sophie would make a call to David just to make sure that the staff working that evening popped in on Amelia to check that she was ok later. As she walked back to her house, her mind was spinning with thoughts of Amelia's travels. She thought of David's words, Poppycock he had called it, the outlandish mind wanderings of a lonely old lady missing her dead husband. Sophie was not a betting person but if she had been asked to place a large amount of money on the truth in Amelia's words she would be inclined to agree with David, but there was something about it all, something deep within Sophie's conscious which told her to believe the elderly storyteller.

Sophie was not expected to visit the retirement village tomorrow, but resolved to return to see Amelia, if only to make sure that she was ok. She didn't sleep well that night and instead spent the evening staring at her phone and scrolling through supposed true life stories of people that claimed to have met time travellers. There were copious amounts of tales, often with photographic proof of time travelling visitors, but as these stories were often accompanied by accounts of alien abduction, journey to other planets, and very painful sounding probes, she decided that perhaps the internet was not the greatest place in the world to find the truth.

# A Genomous Problem

## Yetzirah

The message pinned to the door of her apartment was intriguing, and an extremely old school way of getting her attention, but gain her attention it did, and Zophiel was immediately excited at the prospect of meeting up with Hariton again.

Hariton had become a bit of a recluse, he never answered the door to his apartment anymore, often the action of ringing the doorbell only caused a recording to sound stating that he was far too busy today to meet or talk to anyone, if it was an urgent matter leave a message, and if not try again in a week. Zophiel always left a message, and he never got back to her, it was both intensely annoying, whilst also making her realise how her parents felt when they tried to get in touch with her.

The message was handwritten, which was also very odd as far as Yetzirah was concerned. Pens and the like had slowly faded into obscurity many thousands of years ago with the invention of the screen and the touchpad. They were never used for any official business and only ever owned by collectors, pen nerds known as ink spotters, and that person who was the grown up version of the annoying kid in class who always had an array of them in their breast pocket. Even the physical act of writing was a long distant memory for most now, and if you asked any Yetziran to simply write their name the result would be a spidery scrawl not resembling any recognisable letters or symbols. Very much like when Newman children returned to school in September after along summer break and had to teach themselves how to hold a pen again and make it work.

The message was simple. *Fat Gehoriel's Bar and Grill when you're ready, text me when you've arrived.* Zophiel was not due to be on duty during this waking cycle, and even if she was, the thought of meeting up with Hariton to question him further about missing life forces would have nudged even her in the direction of pulling a sickie. Although quite how she would do this when illness, injury and being run down were something that the Yetzirans were very proud of also having almost eradicated from their lifestyle. It was these advances in Yetziran science and medicine that had finally seen the last of bugs and viruses, protected them from organ failures, and as demonstrated in the case of Zophiel, meant that life threatening injuries like a knife to the chest which severs a major artery can be fixed and recovered from in a very short length of time. All physical ailments and threats were a thing of the very distant past. Mentally however, the damage to Zophiel could not be given an easy cure. The attack and its immediate aftermath had left her with nagging fears and worries that she had never had before. The act itself had in the first instance made her scared for her own mortality. She had actually thought that she was going to die and, with her dreamlike visit to the concurrence which she still swore to have actually happened, she did for her few moments in the web, think that she was actually dead.

The idea of mortality was one that Newmans of Assiyah lived with every day. There is a birth and a beginning, a life of varying lengths in the middle, and then at some point potentially at any time, there is an end, a death. The beings of Yetzirah had lived for a very long time without this inherent knowledge about themselves. They had cut the end bit out of their existence, and, through some twist of fate, in doing so had inadvertently cut out the birth bit too. So now they just had the middle bit, which may seem ideal but actually it could be very dull indeed.

The beings of Yetzirah now laughed at the Newmans and their constant back of the mind 'fear of death'. They found it hilarious in fact, mainly because they didn't have to live with it anymore. Imagine being a Newman and being told that as of tomorrow you will live forever. That even if you are horrifically injured through some such act as jumping out of a building, wrestling a shark, or questioning a lollipop lady's authority, that you will have an almost 100% chance of a full recovery with no lasting damage to your body. Would you immediately try doing one of those things? Would you become a base jumper, or apply for a job as a crash test dummy? In most cases the guaranteed answer would be no. There would always be some clever idiots that would immediately sign up to be a polar bear jockey, or a crocodile dentist, but you can guarantee that even without the blessing of an immortal life that those idiots would still be first in the queue. It's about that tiny lump that lives in the brain that tells you that going up to a drunken squaddie and telling them that their mum is of loose moral character, and their dad is impotent and prefers the company of sheep, may not be the greatest idea. Some people just have better access to it, and the beings of Yetzirah thought they had eradicated it altogether. Zophiel had discovered that it was still in there, and it was very real indeed, she could actually die, and she was lucky to be still living.

The name of the place where Zophiel headed to meet with Hariton, Fat Gehoriel's Bar and Grill was obviously a joke. Yetzirans didn't eat or drink anymore and so would not need to sit somewhere listening to mid twentieth century Italian American music, whilst they were served by a waitress who had never been close to a New York lower east side restaurant in her immortal life. The joke however went deeper than this for Yetzirans in the know as it was opened by Gehoriel Barakon, a retired messenger in a direct reference to Fat Georgie's Bar and Grill on Hester Street in Little Italy, a venue famous with Yetziran messengers in the 1980s and early 1990s.

That particular restaurant had been opened as a small kitchen serving home cooked food from the old country by Georgie Esposito who had got off the boat at Ellis Island in 1910, young, fresh faced and enthusiastic to start his new life as an American citizen. Initially for Georgie, life in the new country was hard, he worked long hours in the markets, running errands and deliveries during the day and working in bars during the evening. Eventually he saved enough money to open his own kitchen which he did in 1924.

As the years rolled on and the kitchen expanded Georgie enjoyed great success in the 30s and 40s until his restaurant became the place to be seen if you were anyone in New York who enjoyed surrounding yourself in the warm Italian family run restaurant experience.

This success continued until 1977 when at the grand old age of 98 and still being the life and soul of the restaurant, the collector finally arrived during a vigorous rendition of '*Ho un sassolino nella scarpa*', took the life force from him and left it in a cloth bag at his feet. For a while Georgie's children kept the family business going until it fell into the sole hands of Giancarlo, the great grandson of Georgie and friend of some very unsavoury neighbourhood characters. It would be fair to say standards dropped in the restaurant, and iffy stuff went on in the back rooms, to the point where the Grim Reaper was such a regular visitor that he thought that perhaps his photograph should go up alongside the hundreds of photos of Tony Bennett, Tony Danza, John Gotti, and many others all posing with Georgie and framed on the walls of the restaurant.

At one point messengers from Yetzirah would argue over whose turn it was to visit the restaurant this week to collect the cloth bags of the unfortunate souls who had choked on a chicken bone, suffered a sudden heart attack, been shot in the face, or other ingenious and colourful ways of buying the farm.

The game was up for Giancarlo Esposito in 1995 when he allowed one too many dubious dealings to be held in the back room, which came to the attention of the FBI. Giancarlo disappeared shortly after this and it was never known whether he went on to live in a witness relocation programme, or had his feet put into a bucket of concrete and went to visit the bottom of the Hudson River.

Gehoriel Barakon upon his voluntary retirement from messenger duties had opened up the Yetziran version of Fat Georgie's many years ago as a tribute to the Legendary New York restaurant. Of course Yetzirans did not eat and drink so the whole idea of opening a restaurant and drinking house was completely preposterous, but it became a popular place to meet up with friends and enjoy a virtual plate of braciola, or a make-believe glass of Valpolicella, all delivered to your table in the form of a small piece of rice paper which, when placed in the mouth, gave the taste and fulfilment of the real thing.

Zophiel loved coming to spend time in Gehoriel's, mainly because unlike the rest of Yetzirah which was white, dull, and seemingly drained of life, Gehoriel's was full of life and happiness no matter what time of day you entered. It was beautifully decorated just like Fat Georgie's, with pictures on the walls of the owner Gehoriel posing in black and white pictures with photoshopped 1950s film stars and crooners.

When she arrived at the bar, she was greeted by the man himself.

'Miss Melaku, where have you been? I don't think you've been down to see me here for too long, too long.' His faked New York Italian accent never failed to amuse Zophiel. Accents as a whole were few and far between on Yetzirah disappearing slowly over a number of years prior to the invention of Assiyah when the number of Yetzirans dwindled and they found themselves all living together in one large group rather than the disparate cities which they had enjoyed on the past.

'Hello, Gehoriel.' Zophiel said. 'I'm supposed to be meeting Hariton here. Has he arrived yet?'

'Arrived? Arrived? He's been sat over there at my best table taking up space and hardly ordering a thing off the menu for over an hour now. Get over there and tell him to order or get out, will ya?'

Zophiel laughed and followed Gehoriel to a large round wooden table with a red chequered tablecloth. She took a seat opposite Hariton who still had not looked up to greet her.

'Look at this guy,' Gehoriel laughed, slapping Hariton on the back to his obvious annoyance. 'You'd think his whole life was dependent on what was in that tablet. We should go back to the old days before all this technology stopped us talking to one another.'

Hariton's eyes did not divert from the tablet in front of him. He swore under his breath.

'Charming.' Said Zophiel. I don't hear from you in a couple of weeks, and this is how you greet me.'

He looked up. 'Oh Hi, Zoph. Get a fake drink, if only to give this old ghoul something to do. I'm almost finished here.' He swiped and tapped furiously at the tablet, his fingers almost a blur.

'Can I have a whiskey sour please, Gehoriel.' Zophiel said smiling. 'Make it a large one, I can tell I'll need it with this one.'

Gehoriel laughed and left them, muttering something about fishes and sleeping which Zophiel did not understand at all.

Hariton swore again and slammed the tablet down on the table, shaking the glasses which no one would drink from.

'Problem?' asked Zophiel.

'Definitely.' Hariton muttered. 'I haven't been idle while you've been laid at home putting your feet up.'

'Recovering from a stab wound.' Zophiel said.

'Yeah, whatever, Miss Martyr.' He allowed himself a smile. 'Anyway, I've been trying to log in to the concurrence, to have a look at the stuff you were telling me about, the empty bags and all that stuff, but it wasn't as straight forward as it should have been. Far from it in fact.'

'What do you mean?'

'Well in the past I've just been able to monitor the concurrence through a screen at home. Simple really, I just clicked a button on my device, the concurrence would come up on my screen, and I could zoom in on particular areas of interest and see what was happening. You know, life forces in life forces out. However, after your 'occurrence' down on Assiyah....'

'The attempted murder.'

'Yeah that. Well, this time it wouldn't allow me in, I tried all the normal processes for getting onto the system, even some abnormal and very illegal processes, but nothing. I had to go down to the machine in person, I haven't had to do that in years. I...' He fell silent as a waitress came over with a small plate containing the essence of a whiskey sour with ice.

Zophiel waited until the waitress was out of earshot before speaking. 'But you designed the whole thing why would you be blocked from it?' she said.

'Well, I haven't logged into it for a very long time, I didn't need to. I told you it's a concurrent system. I designed and built it back in the formation of Assiyah. Set it off when the Newman world began, and have only really ever had to return to it once when the great reset happened. You know the flood thing.'

'What do you mean it's a concurrent system? That doesn't make sense.'

'To you maybe, but that's because you're not on my level of genius.'

'Thanks.'

'Not a problem. Do you really want me to explain it to you in less intelligent people terms?'

'Well, I might just hit you in a minute, but yes it would be nice. It could be important.'

Hariton sighed. 'Ok, listen very carefully I'll only be telling you this once and I'll try to do it in a way that you'll understand. I hate repeating myself. We, as a people, do not like taking risks with anything. Am I right?'

'Yes, I suppose so, we have reached a point in our evolution where risk and threat are all but extinct. That's why everything is so boring.'

'Exactly, just the way that most normal Yetzirans like it. You are very un-normal Zophiel. But that's not the point. When I designed the concurrence as a tool for farming life force, I decided to eradicate all risk and make it something that was utterly fool proof, and decided that the best way to do this was to make it a concurrent system. It took a bit of work originally, but I'm an immortal genius, so of course I managed it.'

Zophiel raised her hand slightly. 'Can I ask a stupid question?'

'I am expecting many,' Hariton laughed.

'How is it concurrent?'

'Not a stupid question really, and I was coming on to that. The best way to explain it is to say that the world of Assiyah was created, and its beginning and its end decided, by me and a group of other Yetziran scientists all sat around a workbench in one of our labs. What happened in the meantime was up to the Newmans themselves, their history was of their own making. However, in the concurrence, time as a rolling concept does not exist. There is no beginning or end, there are just life forces leaving the world of Assiyah, being taken and trimmed by us and then being put back in at random times in Assiyah's existence but with no memory of their previous lives. Everyone that has ever lived or died on Assiyah never leaves. The world of Assiyah was born and it ends with the destruction of the planet and the end of all life there, but actually it doesn't really matter because it all happens concurrently, it all happens at once in the concurrence.

'It was our way of making a self-sufficient life force creation machine that just runs forever no matter what is happening throughout Assiyah's history, whether it be in Ancient Greece or 25th century Brazil, medieval Britain, or 20th century Australia. Yes, on Assiyah the world runs through time, hundreds of thousands of years, but in the concurrence, it doesn't matter, it all happens at the same time. That way we have an everlasting source of life force to farm and there is no risk to us at all. Do you understand?'

'No, not really and my brain hurts. But what you're saying now is that there is actually a risk because something is happening in the concurrence that you didn't create or plan for?'

'Exactly! My word, she's got it!'

'So that's why you've been logged out of the system, because somebody is up to something.'

'Yes, someone is using the concurrence for their own ends, although I'm not sure what these ends are, and it seems that we've come to the attention of the wrong people. It must be serious stuff. You were nearly killed.'

'Ah, finally, you admit it.'

'I never denied it. I just didn't want to play into your whole victim thing.'

If Zophiel had had an actual glass in her hand, she would have slammed it down on the table. 'Excuse me how about you get stabbed next time?' She sneered.

'Ooh no, I'm far too important to kill. Anyway, you're changing the subject. The point is that I went down there and had a look in person. I managed to log back in and accessed the concurrence again.'

'So why are you swearing at your tablet.?'

'Because I was obviously being watched, and in the time between leaving there and getting here to you I've been locked out again.'

'Weird.'

'Very, but while I was there, I did notice a few anomalies on collections.'

'Empty bags.'

'Exactly, but also something else which is a whole lot weirder.' He paused for dramatic effect.

'Go on.' Zophiel was in no mood for any more mystery at this point.

'Genomes!' Hariton exclaimed.

'Excuse me?'

'Genomes. That's the answer to your empty bag mystery.'

'Oh, I'm really confused.' Zophiel clawed at her face. 'I came to tell you that there was something very wrong happening down on Assiyah as life forces were going missing, and you're telling me that the answer is little bearded garden statues?'

Hariton did not bite. 'Zophiel, do you know what a genome is?'

'Er... no.'

'It's a signature, a marker, a very individual code which every life force that enters or leaves the concurrence carries with them. We created them when we created Assiyah, as a way of labelling life forces and tracking them. Except we didn't end up tracking them. We started to at the beginning, but it was a dull job, and things seemed to be working well so we were glad when the orders came from above to stop tracking life forces.'

'So, you have no idea who's actually in there.'

'Well roughly we do, but I ran an algorithm when I logged back in and I noticed something very odd.' Another pause for dramatic effect. Hariton was really enjoying his moment here.

Zophiel growled.

'We have some lurkers.'

Zophiel hit her head on the table. 'I don't even know what that means!' she sobbed.

'Some of the life forces that went in at the beginning when Assiyah was created, have never come out for processing!'

'They've never died?'

'Oh yes, they've died, countless times but they were never farmed. They just disappeared off and started a new life somewhere. The only time they were ever properly in our hands and trimmed of their life force was after the big flood reset, but since then nothing, they've just never come out again.'

'Erm... Is that supposed to happen? Surely that can't be right. Where are they going?'

'They aren't going anywhere. Either they're lurking in the concurrence, or they've found a way to get back down to Assiyah. Either way this is very dangerous, it goes against everything that the concurrence was set up to do. They are growing in size with each life they inhabit and live. They're eating lives and getting stronger each time they do. If they keep going then very soon our source of energy will diminish, and the

Yetziran people will start to die again. Starved of the life force we need to stay immortal.'

Suddenly Zophiel's newfound fear of death was no longer just a niggle in her mind. Suddenly the fear of her immortal life ending was very much at the forefront of her thinking. Wow, she thought, this must be what Goths on Assiyah feel like all the time!

'That's terrible,' she cried forgetting now that they were in a very public place and could be overheard. 'We should tell someone. We need to stop this from happening, we should go to the Arches!'

'Will you keep your voice down!' Hariton hissed. We have no evidence without getting into the concurrence's system again.'

'But you logged back in, didn't you?'

'I did and now I've been logged out again. There's something very suspicious going on here. I think that there are some beings in quite high up positions that are aware of this and are positively encouraging it to happen. I have no idea why, but I think we've uncovered something very nasty indeed. Without getting back into the concurrence's system we can't prove anything though. What we need is someone to go down to Assiyah, and put a tracker drone on a life force, anyone will do, just as long as they're someone who's just died on Assiyah. Drop the tracker drone into your cloth bag before you attach it to your belt. The tracker drone will then enter the concurrence, through the backdoor. Once the drone is in the system, I can control it from here and find our lurkers. Now I can make the equipment for this, but I can't leave Yetzirah. I think I'm already being watched, so it'll have to be you. It won't take much, just get back to work. Take the tracker with you each time you make a visit to Assiyah for a collection, and when you see your chance. Take it.'

'Oh yeah,' Zophiel laughed. 'Me, who isn't suspicious at all, and who didn't just get stabbed for poking her nose into the wrong places. Me, who's already been warned off from prying. Me, who most of the deputy arches hate already. I know you're just the geek with the gadgets, but I'm sure you could actually be a little more proactive in this. It seems like I'm just the idiot blindly putting myself at risk here. Do you want me to actually die?'

'Not yet.' Hariton whispered. 'That will be Plan B.

# Sophie Pratman meets a Ghost
## Finlay – Present day

Two days after last seeing Amelia quite the strangest and most disconcerting thing that Sophie had ever experienced in her twenty six years happened to her at the Sunningdale Retirement Village.

She had arrived as normal in the morning, with a plan to try to catch up with Amelia. Thoughts of the old lady's story filled her every waking thought, and she had even found herself dreaming of travelling through time with Amelia, visiting far off places and borrowing lives. They were fantastical and wonderous trips through history, and she always felt sad when she woke up and they were over. Borrowing the lives of others was her new favourite obsession and her thirst for more of the excitement that Amelia's stories could bring could only be sated by seeing her.

Sophie signed in at reception before going to find David who was in in his office. She popped her head through his door.

'Hi, David,' she said. 'Just to let you know that I'm here for a couple of hours this morning. Anything you wanted me to do today?'

'Ah Sophie I was hoping you would be coming in today. Would you be able to do me a favour, would you be able to go to visit Maureen in flat 12. She's been very under the weather, we're waiting for the community nurses to visit and give her a check over, but I just don't think she should be left alone at the moment. I'd send one of our care staff but I'm down two people already today. It shouldn't be for long, no longer than an hour. It will just give the nurses time to get here and for me to organise some longer term plan for looking after her.'

'Of course, not a problem.' Sophie said. 'I can pop in and chat with her for a while. I was hoping to spend a bit of time with Amelia Hawke today, but I'm sure I can stop in on her later.'

'Thank you so much, here take a pass key it should get you into Maureen's flat, she won't be able to let you in herself, she's so unsteady on her feet at the moment.' He threw a lanyard with a keycard attached to it towards Sophie who snatched it out of the air with a speed and agility that even surprised herself.

Sophie whistled a tune unknown to anyone including herself as she walked down the corridor. It was a habit of hers which she knew annoyed some people, but she just couldn't kick. As she neared Maureen's flat, she suddenly felt a chill, as if the temperature in the building had suddenly dropped ten degrees. This was odd as normally the whole of the Sunningdale retirement village was a collection of overly warm buildings, housing a group of older people who felt the cold and required layers of knitwear on an almost unnatural level. Sophie wondered whether one day when she passed the age of sixty, she would suddenly start to feel as if the whole world was suddenly an Arctic tundra, requiring thermal underwear, thick woollen cardigans, and a constant flow of warm weak tea.

She reached flat 12 and knocked lightly on the door. There was no reply, but she could hear Maureen's television blaring at a deafening level from inside. She waved the keycard over the lock and pushed the door open.

'Maureen! It's Sophie!' she called but there was no response. 'Maureen!' she called again, walking through into the living room, where she found Maureen sat in her tall wing backed chair fast asleep. The noise of the television dominated the room, a wall of noise that made it hard for Sophie to think. She picked up the TV remote and turned the volume down to a level acceptable to anyone under the age of seventy. On the screen a well-worn, middle aged man was wandering around an old property, tapping the walls, and scoffing at the state of an unkempt and unloved garden. 'Look at the state of this place!' he exclaimed. 'Whoever takes on this project will have to shell out some serious cash. I don't think it's worth saving, let it go, I say.'

Sophie tapped Maureen gently on the arm saying her name once more, but the old lady did not stir. Maureen was pale and her sleeping breaths were ragged and crackled. One hour David had said. The community nurse would be here in less than one hour. She wondered what she should do. It was probably best to let Maureen sleep, but it was all a bit weird to be sat in a stranger's home while they slept. Sophie knelt next to the chair and pulled her cardigan a little tighter around her shoulders, she really had expected Maureen's flat to be a lot warmer than it was. She looked around the room, any available surface was filled with hundreds of photo frames and porcelain trinkets, all meticulously placed on lacy linen doyleys.

Suddenly Maureen's breathing sped up a little, becoming shallower and raspier.

'Maureen.' Sophie said placing her hand on the sleeping Maureen's arm. 'Maureen, can you hear me?'

Of course, Maureen did not reply, but Sophie would have sworn she felt another presence in the room. She heard a man's voice, it was faint, but she could definitely hear something. Sophie turned to the television, but the voice had not come from the programme, where the presenter was becoming increasingly aggressive in his deconstruction of the shabby property.

'The brickwork is a mess!' he scoffed. 'I'm sure there's damp in here. I'm not sure I'd be wasting my money on this old pile of rubble. Yes, it was nice once, yes it has a lifetime of memories, but please, those times are gone, time to bring in the bulldozers and consign it to history.' Sophie turned the television off. She could still hear the voice.

'Goodbye, Maureen,' the voice said. A distant echo but the words were as clear to Sophie as if they had been uttered close to her ear. Suddenly a stillness came over the room, whatever had happened, whatever had been going on at that exact moment was gone. Sophie let out a gasping breath, not noticing that Maureen had made her last.

The hairs on the back of Sophie's neck suddenly prickled. A wave of energy flowed across the room, thick and powerful, Sophie could feel it running over her body. She felt dizzy, she felt nauseous, and she raised her hand to her mouth. The room suddenly felt charged, the air overflowing with electricity. Sophie wanted to get up and run, but she couldn't move. It was then that she saw her.

Stood in the room behind the chair where Maureen sat motionless was a tall woman, dressed in white. Not just tall but huge, her head was close to the ceiling. It felt like someone had rubbed Vaseline in Sophie's eyes, as everything in the room was suddenly blurred, nothing could be focused on. Tightness gripped Sophie's throat and she cried out, a sound that made the tall woman quickly turn and look directly at her.

The woman was young, almost ageless, and dressed in a long white gown. She had flowing dark hair, fine features and eyes which shone so brightly Sophie wondered if they were actually eyes at all, they could have been just piercing blue lights, as if the woman was a ball of pure energy which was escaping from her. The dense fog of light in the room was reaching an almost unbearable weight, it pressed hard on Sophies body, constricting, and choking her. She was sure she would pass out at any moment.

'Who are you,' Sophie managed to say, although it took all of the energy she could muster to do so. The woman did not reply but instead leaned down to where Sophie was knelt until their faces were inches apart. The brightness from the woman's eyes now lit up Sophies face, and the woman smiled warmly. In that moment, despite everything, the sickness and the choking, the fear left Sophie in an instant. A calm, contented feeling washed over her like a gentle wave on a tropical beach. Everything was… good. Sophie felt a rush of unrestrained bliss rising up through her body, electrifying her, filling her with peaceful happiness. She had never felt so full of wonder, so full of ecstasy. Sophie felt like screaming with happiness and joy, and she felt tears running down her cheeks, each drop alive with wonder.

And then in an instant, in a blinding flash of light, the woman was gone, and suddenly Sophie was alone again, knelt on the floor next to Maureen who had breathed her last, and who sat peaceful and serene, a smile on her pale still face.

Sophie wept.

# Big Web, Small Machine
## Yetzirah

Zophiel Melaku was exactly the type of being that most normal people would hate to be stuck in a lift with. That is not to say that she was a horrible being, not in the slightest; she was sweet, good natured, helpful to those in need and a fierce friend to have on your side. She was known to be clever and insightful; she could tell a good joke when prompted, and she would never ever tell a terrible truth if it meant hurting someone's feelings. If you were to ask her friends and those that had spent any time with her, they would tell you that she was one of the nicest beings they knew. All in all, she was the kind of being that we could all do with having around, except if you were stuck in a lift with her.

You see, despite all of her most wonderful attributes, she had one terrible flaw in her nature - she hated silence. Now what is wrong with that I hear you say, it is a good thing to enjoy the sounds that the universe has given us, from gentle birdsong, the laughter of children, even the rumble of distant thunder; sound was a blessing, noise was something to be enjoyed. But what about those moments of peace and tranquillity? What of those brief interludes between the hustle and bustle of the day where it is a beautiful thing to sit and enjoy gentle sound of nothing? We all need them sometimes. Well, all of us except Zophiel.

Zophiel despised any moment when there was not sound and as such filled any space between the sounds around her with constant chattering, whistling, singing and where none of these were possible the tapping of her feet or the drumming of her fingers on any potential surface she could find. Those that spent anything but the shortest amount of time in her presence were the unwilling victims of this. Some bore it well, they stayed quiet, inwardly seething but not wanting to hurt her feeling by just telling her to shut up for a minute. Others, like her friend Totfiel, didn't like to stand on ceremony at all and constantly told her to be quiet. It annoyed Totfiel but not enough to keep her from his company, and perhaps secretly inside he did quite enjoy the friction that it was prone to cause between them, he suspected that Zophiel did too, and it was the reason that she was particularly loud and annoying when with him.

She whistled now, as she took the elevator to the bottom floor of the Machanon building where Hariton had told her the Machine containing the concurrence was kept.

'It's a very small unobtrusive room, Zophiel,' he had said. 'Many people just walk past it without the slightest knowledge that kept inside is a machine containing the processor where all life force for Yetzirah flows.'

Zophiel was sure that planting the tracking device that Hariton had given her was going to be easy. She had kept the device, which resembled a small metal flying insect no bigger than button, within her robes when travelling down to Assiyah on her first day back at work after her recouperation time.

The job should have been straight forward and perfect for the task, as it was a single death with no other messengers involved. However, something happened during the visit to Assiyah earlier that day that caused Zophiel to rush to see Hariton as soon as she returned to Yetzirah to tell him what had happened.

As she appeared in the room, she instinctively knew that something was not quite right, and her first thought was that now would not be the time to plant Hariton's tracker in the cloth bag. For a start, and completely unexpected, she found that the deceased Newman was not alone. Knelt by her side, and frozen in time was a young woman holding the hand of the old lady who had passed. The young woman had a kind face Zophiel thought. Something about her eyes which told Zophiel that there was no malice in this person whatsoever. Her hair was long and tightly curled like Zophiel's although it was shorter and a little more unkempt. Zophiel did not often take the time to study the other Newmans whenever she went down to Assiyah to do a job.

There was a feeling in the room unlike Zophiel had ever felt on Assiyah before, it was if the air had been charged with magic, it felt thick and tingly on her skin. It was not an unpleasant feeling by any means.

Zophiel was suddenly aware that she was staring at the kneeling woman, and that she had an important job to do. On the lap of the old lady, who seemed to be in a soft dreamless sleep was a small cloth bag, which Zophiel immediately retrieved.

Pulling the tracker that Hariton had given her from her robes, she dropped it into the cloth bag without taking her eyes from the young woman sat on her knees at the deceased lady's side. As she attached the bag to her belt, she leant down to look into the eyes of the woman. She was sure that she saw them move. Their faces were close now, Zophiel could feel warmth coming from the frozen woman, and for one brief moment thought to reach out and touch the woman's cheek. Touching any Newman other than the one whose life force had been taken was strictly forbidden for messengers. Zophiel did not know quite what would happen if she did do it but knew that now was not the time to be drawing any undue attention to herself from a deputy arch.

She withdrew from the kneeling woman, stood up straight and shot upwards back to Yetzirah before she fell victim to any temptation. As she returned to Yetzirah she knew that by the time she arrived the tracker would have already entered the concurrence and be under the control of Hariton.

'It was weird,' Zophiel said as she sat in Hariton's apartment later that day. 'I felt seen. That never happens. In all the thousands of times that I have gone down to Assiyah and picked up a life force…'

'Empty bag'

'Shut up. In all the times I have been down there to pick up a bag which I still believe holds a life force, I have never had such a feeling of contact with a Newman before. It was as if they saw me and were trying to talk to me.'

'Preposterous,' announced Hariton. 'It could never happen; I should know because I helped designed the whole process of life force collection and put safeguards in place to stop that happening. Just think of what life on Assiyah would be like if every time someone popped their clogs some tall, winged being suddenly shot down from above and tinkered with the body. There'd be uproar, on a daily basis.'

'But she spoke to me, I could hear her voice, although it was only faint, and her eyes moved, I'm sure they did.'

'My dear Zophiel. You've been through an awful lot of trauma recently. It's not every day that someone jumps you in a place where no one is supposed to be moving, stabs you, and leaves you on the ground bleeding to death. It's only natural that your senses were heightened on your first trip back to Assiyah. The Yetziran mind, as evolved and brilliant as it is, is still a deeply flawed bit of kit. It will play tricks on you; it will make you think that irrational things are real. All brains do it, whatever the species. How do you explain the fact that Newmans believe in astrology, or religion, bloody hell some of them even believe that Assiyah is flat, or that national pride, fervent tribalism and flag waving is beneficial to society. The brain by its very nature is a malfunctioning computer that talks bollocks and should generally be ignored. It's supposed to be there to keep the physical body alive and nothing more. All the other random notions it comes up with are blips in the system, short circuits in the wiring, farts of the mind.'

'You're probably right, annoyingly.' Said Zophiel slumping further down into his sofa and wearing, what Hariton called her grumpy child face. 'There was just something about the whole thing, it was almost like a dream.'

'Exactly,' laughed Hariton. 'Dreams – another prime example of flatulence in the brain. Move on, we have bigger problems as a result of your weird experience. I'm not receiving any data from the tracker.

'Well, that's nothing to do with me if you can't build things properly. Do you need me to plant a better one?'

No, the one you planted was fine, I am thinking however that in all the bizarreness that you claim to have experienced when you dropped the tracker into the concurrence, that you forgot to turn on its transmitter.'

'Transmitter, you never told me about that, or about any switches that I needed to press.'

'That's because I did my normal trick and assumed that other people had a least half the intelligence of me, and would have thought to turn the tracker's transmitter on before getting rid of it. It's a common problem I have, it happens to me daily, but it now means that you have given yourself another job. I need you to go to the room where the concurrence is kept.'

'Brilliant,' laughed Zophiel, another spy mission that I can make a mess out of. If it wasn't for her charming nature, Hari I would refuse to be your slave.'

'Yes, yes, now run along, little idiot. Before I find you a worse errand.' Hariton waved her away and resumed studying his tablet, the conversation was over.

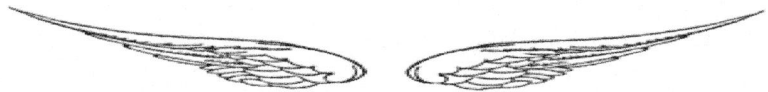

Hariton's instructions had been very clear, get to the room where the concurrence was kept. Find a way in and stand within an arm's reach of the box containing the concurrence, which will be clear to see, and switch on the device he had given her. The transfer of the information the tracker had received would not take long, provided she stayed close to the machine.

'Why can't you go and do it?' Zophiel had asked when she had collected the drone device earlier that morning.

'Because I'm certain I'm being watched.' Hariton said. 'I was only there a couple of days ago, if I return so soon then they will be immediately suspicious and, it wouldn't be long before they discovered that a drone has been released.'

'Can I remind you that I'm probably higher on their radar at the moment, I mean they aren't just following me, they've tried to have me murdered.'

'True, but they'll probably just think that you're being your usual nosey self, snooping around the room where the concurrence is kept, and besides, you're so much better at all this spy stuff than me. I'm just the geek with the gadgets, remember? Once you switch on this device I will have direct control over some elements of the concurrence. It will mean that I can scan a much larger range, cause minor disruptions to flush the rogue life forces out of cover. It will help us catch one in the act and hopefully find out what is going on.'

The door had been as Hariton had said, it was arched and a pale lemon yellow and with a sign on it which had no words but just the symbol of a set of concentric circles with a mass of small arrows pointing towards the centre. Her first thought was to knock, as she was polite, but this was not part of the plan. The room was manned most of the time, and if she knocked now the chances were that she would get no further than the doorway, which was in no way close enough to the concurrence. It would not be locked, and the best method was to just walk in, which she did. She pushed the door open.

'Excuse the interruption, I'm looking for…' The room was empty.

Yetzirans were well known for their minimalist approach, but this room was something quite extreme. It was white walled and bare apart from a shiny white worktop in the middle of the room. Sat in the centre of this worktop was a rectangular black box which would have been small enough for Zophiel to be able to pick up and secrete within her gown. There was only one socket, and one wire attached to the box. It was just sat there. The only signs of life from it were a series of four small lights, only two of which were lit green at the moment. Hariton had told her she would be surprised when she saw it, but the utter shock of seeing something so small, but which contained something so inordinately large almost took Zophiel's breath away. For the briefest moment she forgot the task that she was actually in the room for.

Snapping herself out of her sudden stupor she withdrew the device given to her by Hariton from her pocket and pressed the large blue button on it. Immediately all four lights on the box lit green and began to flash rhythmically. Hariton had warned her that this would happen, and that it meant that Hariton was in the process of receiving information from his tracker inside the concurrence. Once the flashing stopped, she would be able to leave, her task completed. The door behind her suddenly opened and she spun around. An elderly Yetziran had entered and looked utterly dumbfounded to find Zophiel there.

'Who are you!' he demanded. 'You shouldn't be in here.'

Zophiel stepped to the right so that her body was blocking the box from the Yetziran's sight.

'I was looking for Maziel, Maziel Eversby, I was told he would be here on the lower floors, but I can't seem to find him.'

'Well, he's not here is he, any fool can see that,' the old Yetziran blustered. 'You must leave immediately. Who did you say you were looking for?'

'Maziel Eversby, I'm sure you'll know him, tall fella, reddish hair.' She took a quick glance over her shoulder; the lights were still flashing.

'No one of that name works on this floor, and this room is restricted. I will ask you to leave, once more, before I have to call for security. This is not somewhere that you can just be wandering into.'

'Of course, I was just going. Can I just ask though? What is this room? I was told that the bottom floor of Machanon was just for storage.'

'It is for storage and nothing that you should be concerning yourself with. Now I shall be calling security.' He reached for the communicator on the wall and Zophiel took the opportunity to glance over her shoulder once more. The lights had stopped flashing.

'No nee,' said Zophiel. 'I'm going now, but if you do see Maziel. Please do tell him that I was looking for him.' She moved quickly towards the door, gliding past the old Yetziran, and was gone.

# Time catches up

## Finlay, Five years ago

Number 16 Genevieve Gardens, in the small Scottish town of Finlay, was as normal a place as you could imagine an elderly, retired couple to live. It was a quaint dormer bungalow with a well-kept privet hedge on its front border, a short, concreted path lined with Lupins and foxgloves which led to a brightly white painted house, lilac wisteria framing its front door and living room window. There was a small front lawn, fastidiously maintained by the occupants, who could often be seen tirelessly pruning rosebushes, trimming lawn-edges, and joyously pulling weeds free of the earth. The term often used by visitors to describe all of the houses in Genevieve Gardens was 'Chocolate Box' and number 16 was the most perfect example of this.

It was certainly not the kind of place you imagine a meeting of two of the oldest beings in the known universe.

A small terrier, sat forever on guard on the sofa next to the bay window, began to yap furiously as if its life depended on it, as the tall, well-dressed young man lifted the latch on the gate and made his way towards the red painted door. The yapping became an almost feral frenzy when the man had the audacity to press the doorbell making a short ringing sound through the bungalow.

When the owner of the bungalow opened the door to the young man, he recognised him immediately although he had never seen his face before. He paused for a moment looking deeply into the eyes of his visitor. Something which the object of his attention did not shy away from in the least.

'You'd better come in then.' The old man said, turning and walking back down the short hallway and into the living room, where the small terrier, despite not being brave enough to come out and greet the visitor was now in a state of complete apoplexy. Something which only stopped when the young man entered the room and took a seat on the sofa. The dog hid behind the legs of his owner, who in this life went by the name of Alan, and who had taken a seat in a well-worn green leather armchair.

Alan thought of offering the visitor a cup of tea, but he made terrible tea, and he hoped that this visit would not last that long. The last time he had seen the being sat before him had been a hundred lifetimes ago, on a battlefield thousands of miles and thousands of years away. He had watched this powerful being die. The light dimming in his eyes as he was dropped to the floor, his life ended. He knew then that it would not be the last time they met, as they had planned for such an occurrence. Many contingencies had been planned by Helel Bene Elim, his brother and leader.

Finally, the young man spoke.

'Did you think you could avoid me forever, brother? You're not so clever that you are impossible to find, even when you hide yourself in the back end of nowhere. You've certainly been the most difficult to find. Always one step ahead of me. But every few lives you always seem to return here.'

'What can I say, I'm attached to the place. I like it.'

'You are a terrible liar, Armaros. You return here for her.' He gestured to the wedding photograph, sat in pride of place, and surrounded by porcelain trinkets.'

'She is special to me yes, but Finlay is my home.' Alan said, his voice a mixture of tiredness and surrender.

'Shulon is your home!' Helel snapped. 'How quickly you forgot your task, Armaros. How long did it take you to jump ship and continue your love affair with these petty life forms?'

'They are not as petty as you think them to be, Helel. Some would say that spending thousands of years on a contrived revenge plot is pettiness in the extreme.'

Helel took a deep breath, and slowly placed his hands on his lap in a display of control which he was not used to exhibiting. 'Armaros,' he said. 'They killed our children. You were there. You saw them.'

Alan's face wavered a little, a short quiver in the cheeks, his lips moving almost imperceptibly. He knew how close he was to a permanent death. His next words would have to be very carefully executed.

'They did, Helel. I know they did, but look what our children had become. They were monsters, they would have wiped out humanity, they would have destroyed the world.'

'And I would have applauded them for it. I will destroy this stupid vanity experiment in our children's honour. I will take the life of every human on this planet and laugh doing so, I will watch as they're so called gods wither and die without their food.'

'I cannot help you with this, Helel. You are my brother, I love you, but I cannot help you to destroy everything that I have ever loved – everyone that I have ever loved.'

Helel smiled. 'Ah yes, the skinny village whelp, who you manipulated, and moulded. Tell me, in all your hundreds of years together, have you ever even bothered to tell them the truth?'

'She doesn't need to know the truth. If she knew what I was, what I was guilty of in the past then I would lose her forever.'

'And yet here I am about to take you away from her.'

Alan's grip on the arms of the green leather chair tightened. 'I've told you I will not help you. Have you seen our brothers? They will give you the aid you need if you can find them. Go ahead with your plan if you must but I will not be a part of it.'

'You talk like you have a choice in the matter, dear brother. You have only have two choices. Come with me now and you both will live, refuse me and I will kill you both and feed on your souls in the concurrence. No more time skipping, no more borrowing of lives. Your little adventure in love will be over.'

'But she will die when you destroy this world.'

'Of course she will die, she was meant to die hundreds of years ago. Killed by the axe of a Viking invader not four hundred yards from here! These humans are meant to die, they are not immortal like us! They are not gods. This world and the concurrence which it lives within will be turned to dust. It is the only way to end this.'

'We are not Gods either, and there is a flaw to this plan, What if the Yetzirans do not concede? Can I remind you, brother that once this world is destroyed, then we will be as doomed as the rest of the Yetzirans. We will starve and fade away just like them.'

'Good.'

'Excuse me?' Alan looked visibly shocked at this new turn of events.

'I said good. The Yetziran race were meant to die thousands of years ago. I for one welcome the abyss if they will not bow to my demands. If our plan fails, then I am determined to take every living thing with me.'

'But the plan was always different. The plan was just to threaten to destroy the concurrence. To call their bluff. To get them to return our children to us.'

'Plans change.' Helel said smiling.

'Then you are as mad as they said you were all those years ago, and I cannot be any part of it.'

Helel exhaled, his eyes softened. 'But brother I need you by my side.'

'Erm… You threatened to eat my soul not two minutes ago.'

'Bluster, rash words. You know that I am prone to them, allow me some room to flex myself. You are important to me, and I need you with me at the end.'

'A bargain then?'

'A what?'

'A bargain. I come with you now and you let Amelia live. Give her another few years, another few lives. Come now, brother surely a little delay to your plan will not hurt. Let her live and find love and happiness again. Do this for me, and I will follow you to the end knowing that she found peace and love without me.'

Helel closed his eyes for a moment and took a deep breath. What was another few years? He had all the time in the world, and still things left to do before the end. He would let her play the game for a little longer, and then she would die with the rest of their cursed race.

'Very well,' he said. 'Follow me, do the tasks requested of you, the tasks which you should have started two thousand years ago, and I will allow her to live on for however much longer it takes us. Then, if the Yetzirans do not bow down to us, she will die with the rest of us, and we will all know peace. Cross me though, Armaros, and I will force you to watch whilst I will feast on her soul. You have two days left with her. In two days you will die, and I will be waiting for you with the others.'

'They are all still with you?' Alan asked. 'You haven't had to 'eat' any of them?'

'They are all still with me, some took more persuading than others. Samjaza was weak as always and had submitted to his greed, I reminded him of the benefits of not disappointing me. Penemue was lost in his studies and obsession with knowledge. I helped him remember how stupid it would be to not keep his promise.'

'And the twins?'

'Your sisters had become distracted torturing Newmans. They have the right idea in many ways. The vermin were born to be made to suffer, but Azazel and Sariel do tend to lose sight of the bigger picture. All of them will be there though. As will you. You know what will happen if you're not. I am being gracious with you, much more so than I would have been with the others. You have two days left here before you must complete our work. Do not disappoint me.'

'Two days,' said Alan solemnly. 'Thank you, brother.'

Helel got to his feet. 'You know you really have wasted an awful lot of your time on this pitiful race.'

'I did not do it for the human race as a whole, just for her, and you are mistaken, she is not pitiful, and my time was not wasted. I found love, Helel. I found a love that has lasted for hundreds of years, never dimming, only becoming greater. Tell me, does that sound like time wasted to you?'

Helel sniffed and brushed imaginary lint from his tweed jacket. 'You are a fool, Armaros,' he said. 'I shall see you where we planned, and I trust you will have something to report to me by then. If you're not there she dies forever as you watch, and then you'll follow her.' He left without another word.

Alan watched him through the netted curtains, the tall figure striding away from the house and towards the end of the road, and a tear appeared in the corner of his eye. A sudden noise startled him, and he turned to see the love of his many lives.

'Who was that?' Amelia said.

'Just a salesman. He was trying to get us to invest in loft insulation and solar panelling.'

'Oh, I was just coming to see if you wanted some tea. I hope you didn't agree to anything stupid on my behalf.'

'Who me?' Alan laughed. 'When have you known me to do anything daft.'

# Getting Fat on Life

## Yetzirah

It was on the top floor of the hallowed halls of Machanon Building that Falafriel Hemister, Archangel in charge of life force collection sat at his desk, as he did every day staring at the screen in front of him and tutting loudly.

Zophiel entered the office uninvited with a hurried spring in her step. She was the last person he expected to see, as he had heard that there had been an incident of some kind on Assiyah.

'Miss Melaku.' He said with a little surprise. 'I heard you were still on leave from your duties. Should you not be recovering somewhere?'

Zophiel ignored the question and strode right to the edge of his desk.

'Sir,' she exclaimed. 'I've found them!'

'Found them, wonderful. Who are them?'

'The jumpers, sir, the ones I've been tracking, I think I have them, or at least one of them, maybe a couple, but I have them.'

'And what, pray, are jumpers?'

'They are detailed in my report, sir. You'll have read all about them.'

'No, I think I may have missed that report.'

'It's quite extensive, I'm sure you can't have missed it, sir.'

'Oh yes, that report.' Falafriel had a faint memory of receiving a lengthy piece, which he had read the first page of and consigned to the bottom draw in the filing cabinet marked 'Idiot stuff'. It was mad scatter-brained stuff really, detailing how there were unseen forces moving about Assiyah and out of the control of Yetzirah. Zophiel was a good worker in most respects, but she had some very strange ideas that were not worth paying much attention to. Assiyah had been created from scratch by Sustina Homvettiner and her husband Malik, the Newman race had been formed in their laboratory, the very idea that there was anything on or around Assiyah that wasn't fully under the control of the Yetzirans was preposterous. He had asked his assistant to file the report away and hoped never to hear of it again. He should have known it was a foolish hope though seeing that Zophiel was involved.

'Forgive me, Zophiel,' he said. It's been a hectic few months. Remind me again.' He made a mental note to ensure that his assistant, the recently demoted Michael, did not just let Zophiel into his office without a prior appointment that Falafriel could postpone ad hoc. Falafriel was busy enough without having to deal with Zophiel's musings and obsessions.

'You'll remember, sir, Totfiel and I attended Assiyah to pick up some life forces that were not there. You sent Araqiel down to see us about it. He said that he would report it.'

'I do not recall it. You need to be more specific. Of all the messengers working for us, Zophiel, you have created the most multiple reasons for me to take one of the sub arches away from their busy office, and very busy work schedule to go on some wild goose chase. There have been numerous occasions when you have not reported back to Yetzirah within the allotted time frame because things were 'not right'. I assume you recall the time that you did not retrieve the life force you were sent to collect because 'The bag smelled funny', or perhaps you remember when I was called from a very important meeting of the Archangels for an 'emergency' only to find that you had accidently dropped the bag containing the life force and couldn't retrieve it.'

'It was down a well, sir. My wings were too big for me to fit down there.'

'It doesn't matter now; we retrieved it and the 'emergency' passed. What I am trying to say in the most obvious way possible is that there haven't been five years gone by when I haven't sent someone to come running because you have decided that something's a bit iffy, or you've been clumsy in the extreme. Be more specific!'

'It was a village, 7$^{th}$ Century Scotland, there was an old lady and a young boy, no sign of any life force anywhere. Araqiel turned up, scowled at us a little, disappeared off and when he came back, he told us not to worry about it.'

'And yet you decided to concern yourself with it to the point of producing a 500 page report that you expected me to read. Do you realise how busy I am, Zophiel? I oversee the life force transactions of over 150,000 Newmans every day. If one or two go missing, which I doubt even happens, it is not the end of the world.'

'But that is my point, sir. I think that it is the end of the world. You see it happened again in 16th century Bohemia, dead body, empty bag - this time it was a prison guard. Again, Araqiel came down, told me not to worry about it and that was that. But that's twice that it's happened to me, and I know for a fact that it's happened to others too. Always the same thing – the messenger goes down, there's a body with an empty bag, some deputy arch turns up and tells them not to worry as its being dealt with and nothing happens. This is not something that is a rare occurrence. I think that it is happening a lot, and has happened for thousands of years, and I think that it's getting worse.'

'If it happened a lot then I would surely know about it. Do you think I'm so incompetent that I would miss something like this?'

Zophiel paused for a rare moment of silence from her, probably not the best time or place to do this. 'I can prove it, sir.' She said finally.

Falafriel sighed and placed his hands on his forehead as if trying to force the incoming headache away. 'Go on.' He muttered.

'Well, you know that each life force has a signature, a particular and very small fraction of a genome that stays the same once we have collected the life force from Assiyah, taken what we need from it, and reassigned the trimmed down version into freshly born Newmans.'

'Of course it is the basis of life force production. We grow it on Assiyah, we prune it, and we replant the seed. Every Yetziran knows the process. It is what keeps us alive.' Falafriel was seconds away from calling security on the winged annoyance stood on the other side of his desk.

'Yes, sir, but you see I have a friend who is a scientist, he worked with the Homvettiners when they discovered the process and assisted in the design of Assiyah. He was primarily involved in the creation of the concurrence, sir. I'm assuming you are aware of the working of the concurrence?'

'Of course, I've heard of it. I don't know it's full workings but that's because I'm not a scientist.' Falafriel scoffed. 'It's part of the life force processor, it's where they go after they've been removed from Assiyah, it takes them to the core where they are managed, trimmed and redistributed.'

'Exactly! Well, it's in the concurrence that the weirdness happens. You see, there are life forces that have entered the concurrence to be processed but have never come out again. I think we can probably even identify them through their genomes if we wanted to. I think they're up to no good in there.'

'What kind of no good?'

'I think that they're going back to Assiyah, I think that they are inhabiting and borrowing the lives of those that pass on.'

'That's a ridiculous idea, how would they manage that?'

'I have no idea, sir, but it would explain why they've never made the journey for processing and redistribution.'

'And so, what if they are? A handful of rogue life forces aren't going to bring about the end of the world, are they?'

'But they are, don't you see? They are getting fat on life.'

'Pardon?'

'These rogue life forces, they are increasing in size the longer they keep doing what they're doing. They live on Assiyah, their life force grows within them, they die and that is when we would normally take the excess and redistribute them, but they're just diving back down to Assiyah and living again. Each time they do and the longer they live on Assiyah they grow in size and power, eventually they will destroy the concurrence, and all the life force within it will be lost forever. Assiyah will not survive but Yetzirah will lose its primary source of life. We will all die.'

Falafriel drummed his fingers on his desk, and stared blankly ahead, this was not the news he had been expecting this morning.

'You realise how preposterous this all sounds, Zophiel. Why should I believe you?'

'Because when I was attacked on Assiyah and almost died, for a brief moment I entered the concurrence, and saw for myself. I have glimpsed these rogue life forces in action. I have seen our end.'

Falafriel stared a Zophiel for a moment. 'Wait, you were attacked? I was told there had been an incident where you were injured, but I didn't realise you'd been attacked. Were you badly hurt?'

'Erm... I was stabbed in the chest and left for dead.'

'But why did no one tell me this? All I heard was that there was a minor injury and that you were recovering quickly. No one told me you'd been stabbed. This is insane. How could I not know this?' For the first time in the many thousands of years of knowing the Arch, Zophiel could see genuine concern in his face.

'It's fine. It hurt a little but I'm better now. In fact, I'm glad it happened because somehow I got to see the inside of the concurrence. It's what made it all make sense to me.'

If it was any other messenger telling him this Falafriel would have already had them thrown out of his office. Zophiel could be flighty, she could have some strange ideas, she could be a little persistent in her querying the world around her, but she would not knowingly lie. She really believed this, and then there was the attack on her. This had never happened in the history of Assiyah. Violence was not something that the Yetzirans ever had to fear. If Zophiel had been attacked, then there was reason for all Yetzirans to worry.

'Sir?' Zophiel said suddenly shaking him from his stupor. 'Sir, what are we going to do?'

'Do? Do? I... er...' he pulled the keyboard on the desk towards him and typed something. 'You say that you reported this when it happened before?'

'Yes, both times and others have reported missing life forces too, I've listed the ones I know about in my report, if it helps. Surely you should have been told though, when they happened?'

'Yes, surely I should have been.' He looked at his screen, a list of Yetziran employees appeared which he studied briefly. 'I'll tell you what we're going to do, Zophiel. We are, for now, going to keep this between us. Who else knows about it?'

'I've only spoken to Totfiel, my scientist friend Hariton Molechi, and Caphriel Erikson, and even they do not know the full extent of what I have told you. Should I tell them?'

'No, let us keep this between us for now. I have some work of my own to do, so for now leave it with me. You say you've tracked one or two of these rogue life forces?'

'Yes, sir. Hariton designed a tracker drone which we sent into the concurrence to find life forces that were larger than the norm. We think we've found one that entered the concurrence and then returned to Assiyah. We've narrowed down a small area where at least one of them maybe two are at present. Strangely it's the same place where I first encountered the empty bag, so it's a place that obviously holds some meaning for them. If we act quickly enough, we can catch them in the act, and I'm sure that if we find one of them it will lead to others.'

'Leave it with me,' Falafriel repeated. 'Let me read your report and do some investigations of my own.'

'You mean re-read the report surely?'

'That's what I said,' Falafriel snapped, and Zophiel knew that the meeting was over.

She nodded and started to leave his office before turning as she came to the door. 'Sir,' she said. 'Does this mean that you actually believe me?'

'Well, of course I do,' said Falafriel. 'Close the door on your way out.' As the door closed Falafriel pressed a button on his desk which summoned his Michael, who appeared within moments.

'Sir?' the Archangel's assistant said.

'Michael, dig me out a report by Zophiel Melaku. 'And I want a full list of deputy Arches and their current assignments. Be quick.'

'Of course, Mr Hemister,' Michael said. 'Is there a problem?'

'No, probably nothing,' Falafriel lied. 'Just a small issue which I'm sure will be of little importance.'

As Michael left the office, Falafriel slumped down into his chair, wondering if it was time to start thinking about retirement.

# We're Going on a Bear Hunt

## Finlay – Present Day

Sophie had not slept well for the past two nights. She had been caught up in her work at the small jewellers in town, and had not been able to go to visit Amelia, but had rung David when she could, and probably too often for his liking, asking him to keep a close eye on Amelia as she was worried about her wellbeing. When David queried her sudden concern Sophie just said that Amelia had been stewing over the loss of Alan a lot more recently. This of course was true, but she did not let on that there was a risk of Amelia attempting to join Alan in the afterlife. If Sophie knew one thing it was that Amelia would be spurred into action with the sudden intervention of medical staff attempting to talk her out of taking her own life.

The other reason for not sleeping well were her dreams, which had taken a disturbing turn. She had continued to dream about travelling through time with Amelia, but now the dreams were tinged with darkness and dread. They always started well enough, an exciting adventure somewhere in time, but then an element of fear would begin to creep in, a feeling that something was not quite right, which would grow and build to terrifying levels. The dreams always ended in the same way, she would be running with Amelia, Reapers would be chasing them, getting ever closer until finally Sophie would trip and fall. A reaper would be immediately on her, pinning her to the floor and but rather than take her life they would remove their mask revealing a human face underneath. It was not a scary face, if she had seen it in real life, she was sure she would not pay it any attention at all, but something about it made Sophie immediately wracked with an overwhelming terror that made her wake, shaking and drenched in a cold sweat. She would struggle to get back to sleep properly and would often spend the rest of the night sat awake, drinking tea, and cursing herself for being so silly.

Sophie locked up the shop for the evening, before posting the keys through the letterbox of the adjoining door where the owner lived. She would not be back in the shop for three days, and would be able to keep a closer eye on Amelia herself during this time. She thought of calling David again for an update but decided instead to go home via Sunningdale. She approached to small collection of flats where her friend lived and pressed on the door buzzer. It was answered remarkably quickly.

'Hi, Amelia, it's Sophie. Can I come up to see you?'

There was a pause before Amelia answered. 'Well, I was just on my way out actually. What do you want?'

'I just wanted to speak to you. I suppose I could come back tomorrow.'

Another pause. 'No tomorrow won't do. Let me just get my things together, I'm coming down.'

Sophie waited for a couple of minutes until finally, through the frosted glass she saw Amelia approaching. The old lady paused a moment, before opening, Sophie saw that she was wearing an overcoat and carried a small suitcase. Amelia smiled when she saw Sophie.

'Sophie,' she said, 'this is unexpected. Did you leave something here last time?'

'Yes... in a way I did. Is it a bad time?'

Amelia chuckled, 'Well, as you can see, I was just on my way out, I have an important errand to run. You can walk with me if you like.' She walked out of the house, closing the door behind her, and trotted up the path. Sophie followed.

'Where are you going? You're not leaving here yet, are you?'

'Leaving? What do you mean?'

Sophie paused for a moment. 'It's just when we last spoke you were talking of following Alan. I've been very worried about you. I've been calling the office at Sunningdale to check on you.'

Amelia laughed. 'Ah, well that would explain why I've been having so many people come knocking on my door. No, don't worry, I'm not planning to shuffle of this mortal coil just yet. Things to do and all that.'

'Where are we going,' she called. But Amelia did not reply.

By the time they reached the edge of town, the light was starting to fade, and the road narrowed. Sophie was becoming concerned now and pulled her phone out of her pocket, wondering whether she should ring for help. No service. She sped up in order to catch up with the old lady who was moving away from her.

'Your story,' Sophie called. 'The one you've been telling me. It was mesmerising. Have you ever thought of writing it down?'

'No, why would I need to? It's all in my head, who would want to listen?' Amelia moved at quite a pace for her age, and Sophie struggled to keep up with her.

'Well, I thought it was a magical story, it obviously means something to you, I just thought that if it was written, it would feel more solid to you. It would help.'

Amelia halted suddenly. 'Help? What do you mean help?'

'Well... with Alan, you know. It would help you to come to terms with it better. If you didn't want to write it, then I'm sure someone would. A friend of mine from college, he writes stories, I'm sure he would love to help you record it.'

'You still don't believe me, do you?' Amelia reached out a hand and placed it on Sophie's shoulder. 'You want to believe, you really do, but there's something stopping you.'

'I do... I do want to believe but it's all so... so impossible.'

Amelia grinned, 'Come on. You can help me with my errand. It's starting to get dark, I don't want to be out all night, and I've got a big day planned out for me tomorrow.' She trotted off again, and there seemed to Sophie to be a skip in her step. It was impossible, Sophie thought. It was all just in her mind, and here she was, an elderly lady heading off into the night with a suitcase in her hand. Sophie raced to catch up with her.

'This way!' called Amelia, from up ahead. Pushing open a field gate and disappearing off the road and into the darkness.'

'Wait, Amelia. I don't know if this is a good idea.'

'Rubbish,' replied the little old lady, turning on a flashlight in her hand. 'Of course it's a good idea, you'll see, and then you'll believe. It's just up the hill.'

Sophie had no choice but to follow, she could not let Amelia go off like this. She thought of the newspaper headlines 'Woman missing from care home, last seen walking into nearby countryside.'

They traipsed through the fields, Sophie wishing she had worn more sensible footwear, as the mud had begun to cling to the soles of her shoes. The hill was steep, and by the time they reached the top of it she was out of breath, Amelia however seemed just as sprightly as when they had set off.

'Nearly there!' She exclaimed, 'Come on, stop wheezing and keep up. It's just in those trees.'

They approached a small copse and Amelia came to a stop. 'Here we are, let's go and find his spot.' She said pointing her flashlight into the trees.

It did not take long for Amelia to find what she was looking for, a huge tree, the largest in the small woods. She shone her torch at its base. 'There you are.' She said, 'Just as I said, this is where he keeps his valuable possessions. We're going to add a couple of bits.'

Sophie stared at the lighted spot and saw that there was indeed, as Amelia had told them earlier, a sign carved into the bark. Sophie even gave a little snigger when she saw it as it was in the shape of a web. It was still impossible, she thought. Just because someone has cut into the bark of this tree, it didn't mean that Amelia and her dead husband were immortal time travellers.

Amelia had begun to dig in front of the carving with a small trowel that she had pulled out of the pocket of her overcoat. Sophie just stood and watched, not knowing what to do for the best. She checked her phone for a signal and wondered if this was a suitable use of the 'emergency calls only' option. Even when Amelia stopped digging and pulled back a thin stone slab, exposing a hole beneath, Sophie did not fully believe. Coincidence, storytelling and coincidence, that is all it was.

When Amelia pulled a small wooden box out of the hole it suddenly started to feel impossible not to believe. The box was opened and inside, by the light of Amelia's torch, Sophie saw all manner of objects; Jewellery, gold coins, photographs, and small notebooks, for such a small chest it was amazing to see what was held within it. Amelia opened up the small case and pulled out a pouch which she kissed and added to the chest. 'Our wedding rings, and his favourite watch.' She said. 'Now I just need to check on one thing before we go.' She pulled out a piece of parchment, it was old, tattered and looked as if a strong wind would blow it into pieces. There were words written on it, but they were not in anything that Sophie could understand, in fact they were in a different script from anything she had ever seen before.' Amelia looked down the list, reading and mumbling under her breath in a language that Sophie did not understand in the slightest. With a broad grin she folded the parchment up once more and placed it back before closing up the chest and returning it to the hole, which she began to fill once more.

'What was that piece of paper?' Sophie asked.

'A treasure map.' Amelia laughed, adding the last of the dirt to the hole and pressing down on the soil with her hands as she crouched on the ground. 'We're going on a treasure hunt, you and I.'

'But it was just words, wasn't it? Strangely written words, it wasn't a map of anything.'

No, no pictures, just times and places, times and places where the treasure will be.'

'Do you not think it's a bit too late Amelia. It's getting dark, perhaps we could come back tomorrow.'

'Nonsense, we're off to find my treasure!' Amelia exclaimed raising her fist in happiness.

For a brief moment Sophie wondered whether this had all been a terrible mistake and Amelia really was a number of sandwiches short of a picnic.

A sudden noise in the woods startled them both and Amelia jumped to her feet with way more agility than Sophie would have given her credit for. 'I don't think we're alone.' Amelia whispered. 'Come on, time to go.' And she took the now dumbstruck Sophie by the hand and began to lead her out of the trees.

The sound of disturbance in the woods continued and Sophie, despite being now pulled along by the old lady, glanced backwards. She could have sworn that she saw something white moving in the darkness of the trees. It was a bright shape, as if lit from within.

'Faster!' Amelia hissed pulling them onwards. 'Faster, Sophie. We cannot let them see us!'

They stumbled onwards and Amelia tripped dropping her torch which went out immediately. Sophie bent down to pick it up.

'Forget it, there is no time, and we can't take it where we are going. They are coming!' Amelia called, almost joyfully.

Sophie glanced over her shoulder again, and saw them hurtling out of the undergrowth into the clearing beyond the trees. They were tall, white, and carried long staffs.

'Reapers!' called Amelia. 'We must get away from them.'

Suddenly the ground seemed to give way beneath them, and they found themselves falling forwards towards the edge of the hill. Sophie clawed at the grass as she tumbled and stopped herself before grabbing hold of Amelia's arm. They climbed to their feet.

They stood on the edge of Giant's Leap. Finlay lay far below them, the town seemed so small to Sophie now, everything had changed. Sophie suddenly felt dizzy as she looked down to the sharp rocks below and she clasped on to the old woman at her side.

'There's nowhere to go, Amelia. We're stuck!' she cried.

Amelia looked up at her, a mischievous smile on her face. 'Stuck? Stuck? We're anything but, young lady. The world and all time are at your disposal if you want it badly enough.' She pulled Sophie down so that she could whisper in her ear.

'Time to leave. We're going on an adventure together.'

Amelia gave a sharp tug on Sophie's arm, and they fell from the cliff into the web.

# Two Men about Town

## Paris - present day

Attalius de Laustre was having a simply perfect day. He had already visited all 195 countries and had been present for, and ensured the successful demise of, 42,000 people. Things were going along just swimmingly. He was nearly a third of the way through his usual daily quota of deaths and had found time to have slap up breakfast in Caracas, had stood and admired the sun coming up from the Lhotse Wall camp on Everest, and had indulged in a bit of stand up paddleboarding in the Aitutaki lagoon in the South Pacific, as far as jobs went, his relatively new role as the Grim Reaper couldn't have been better.

Now he sat at a table in a roadside café on Boulevard Saint Michel, sipping on someone's expresso and feeling very smug with the absolute wonder of his life. He had taken on the role of the Angel of Death forty years ago, after the last holder of the job had retired, which made him an utter idiot in Attalius' book. Who would actually want to give up this life? Attalius wondered. Who would actually throw away the greatest job on the world? A job where the whole of the Earth was at your disposal, where you could literally, in the blink of an eye, transport yourself anywhere in the globe and take advantage of the fact that the human world around you was seemingly frozen in time.

Attalius had been in the job for forty years, but his time ran a little different to the humans. For him each human day lasted approximately ten years, it gave him time to get around the globe collecting the life souls of the imminently departed, and also gave him the time to enjoy his surroundings, take in the finer things that the world had to offer, all whilst never having to communicate with another living soul. Perfection.

He looked at them now, stood stock still around him, busily hurrying about their day, but to him as unmoving as a photographic snapshot. He enjoyed his coffee and mid-morning pastry, which some poor soul, had ordered shortly before suffering an aneurysm, and marvelled at just how wonderful the world was.

The young woman in mid-death, seemingly frozen in time, had been removed from their chair by Attalius and laid on the pavement at the Grim Reaper's feet. As soon as he had finished his opportunistic coffee break Attalius would put the unfortunate expired back in her chair and remove her life force, in a way which although initially disturbing to Attalius, after forty years he had now managed to stomach a little better. Once the life force had been extricated, he would place it with a small brown cloth bag and leave it next to the now dead woman. There it would be collected by a messenger from on high and taken back to Yetzirah for processing. What exactly happened to it, Attalius was not sure, he didn't really care. Attalius knew the life force collection process well, as he had indeed been one of these messengers for over a thousand years before fate gave him the opportunity for a deserved promotion.

It was as Attalius took a last sip of his coffee that the tall man appeared from around the corner.

'Hello!' he called, and Attalius nearly fell off of his chair in surprise. The humans weren't supposed to be moving. The interloper into Attalius' cosy world was young, bearded and of perhaps North African descent. He wore a perfectly tailored light brown suit, his hair was shoulder length and swept back from his forehead, and he had sharp active eyes which seemed to take in everything around him. He approached the table where Attalius sat, unceremoniously pushing a frozen man out of a chair and taking the seat for himself.

'There you are,' he said, a broad grin spreading across his face. 'You are quite difficult to trace you know, always moving. Always working.'

Attalius put down his cup. 'But of course, it's a busy job I have here, you caught me taking five minutes. Normally it's non-stop, make sure you put that in your report.'

'What report would that be?' The man said, his voice languid and soothing.

'I know all about it, I should do, shouldn't I? I did your job for a very long time. Before they recognised my potential and promoted me. You're a bit early, I've not drained the life out of him yet. Tell me, has the dress code changed? I was always forced to wear a white gown, and where are your wings?'

The man laughed. 'I think you must have me mistaken, I'm not a soul messenger, and my wings went before this world was born. When they return the world will be changed forever.'

Attalius looked bemused. 'So Falafriel hasn't sent you?'

'Who?' The man looked genuinely puzzled.

'Falafriel Hemister, you'd know who I mean if you'd met him. Tall, grey haired, stupidly large golden wings, very officious chap, always bothered about rules and such. He's an Arch you know.'

'An Arch you say? Interesting. No, I don't know who you mean, although I was never really involved in politics as such. I tended to follow my own path, I'm not one for rules myself.' The man touched the coffee pot on the table, checking its heat before pouring himself a small cup.

'Oh, you'll be from another of the departments then. They don't often visit down here.'

'No. I'm not from one of the other departments, I'm what you would call freelance.'

'You are from Yetzirah then. I can tell you have the eyes.'

'In a round-about kind of way, I've not been there for a very long time though. Not since just after this place was built. I've spent most of my life down here, and elsewhere.'

Attalius drew a sharp intake of breath. 'You'll have been here a while then?' As far as conversations went, and this being the first one that Attalius had engaged in for forty years, he actually found himself to be enjoying it.

'You could say that.' The man sat back in his chair, resting his coffee cup on his knee in an assured manner. 'I've been all over the world, and the places beyond. I've never got to meet the Grim Reaper himself though, I came close a few times, but I've never seen you in person.'

'Ah, well you wouldn't have seen me anyway. I'm new to the job, there was another fellow before me, miserable bugger, not very people friendly, he had none of my unique skills. I'm much better at it, I always knew I would be. It's just a matter of fitting the right person to the right job, and I was made for this. He was a bit of a waste of space, good riddance I say.'

The man raised his eyebrows. 'Oh, did the last Grim Reaper actually die?'

Attalius laughed. 'No, not yet. He retired and chose to become one of these idiots. His day will come though, and I'll be there when he does.' Attalius rubbed his hands together in mock glee.

'Really? Why would anyone choose to be mortal? It must be so depressing.'

'Exactly! That's just how I feel,' exclaimed Attalius slapping his hand on the table. 'I used to be one of these things, you know. A very long time ago, I was a Roman Centurion, great times, but I was so glad when I died and moved onto eternal life.'

The man laughed. 'No life is totally eternal. Even us immortals can die, you know?'

'What? I think you'll find you are mistaken there; I cannot die.' Attalius smiled and relaxed back into his seat.

The man's face darkened somewhat. 'Ah, well you see I think it is you that are very much mistaken. You can die, and you will.'

Attalius smiled nervously, the conversation had suddenly altered. 'Oh, so what are you then? I expect you are just some great harbinger of doom, come to warn me of my mortality? You don't scare me though, I don't know who you think you are, but I am Attalius de Laustre, and I am immortal.'

The man stood slowly from the table, towering over the Angel of Death. 'No, I'm afraid you are not immortal, Mr de Laustre. You see my name is Helel Bene Elim, and I am here to kill you.'

When Zophiel arrived at the café on Rue St Michel she wondered why she had been sent alone as there were two bodies lying on the pavement outside Café deux Magots. The first was a woman perhaps in her early thirties although Zophiel had found that age was a very difficult thing to distinguish nowadays, in the age of plastic surgery, endless online make up tutorials and living conditions which had advanced at an alarming rate over the past one hundred years.

For many years Zophiel enjoyed playing the game of guess the age of the deceased as, for the most part, life expectancy for the many was always relatively low, medical interventions barbaric to the point of high danger, and anything resembling a healthy diet was non-existent. Zophiel was pleased that things had advanced so much for the Newman people in that they now often had healthier and longer lives, but there was a part of her that longed for the days of always being within two years of correctly guessing a dead person's age.

Zophiel collected the small brown bag which lay at the feet of the woman and attached it to her belt. From what she could tell the woman had died from some irregularity of the heart (another great game for Zophiel was guess the cause of death) as she was blue in the lips, pale as a linen sheet, and (a most excellent clue here) she was clutching her chest in a very dramatic fashion.

The second apparent victim was a very sharply dressed man in a black suit. He had short blonde hair, scraped back from his face, and seemingly held by some sort of wax, angled cheekbones that Zophiel herself would have quite literally killed for, and a well-toned immaculate complexion evident of a man who took very good care in his skincare and beauty regime. There was however no small cloth bag next to the body. Zophiel had a good scan around to make sure that the situation was as she thought and sat down on the floor next to the well-dressed man and awaited Falafriel who she knew would be attending.

She did not have long to wait, a matter of seconds perhaps before a blinding white light from above shot down sending the whole area outside Le Deux Magots into a scene of quite dazzling brightness. When the light faded it was Falafriel Hemister who stood at the edge of the pavement staring at the two bodies laid outside the cafe. Zophiel knew that he was keeping a closer eye on her now, but this was quite a surprise.

'Oh bugger.' Falafriel said.

'Pardon?' said Zophiel.

'I mean oh dear.' The archangel gathered his thoughts quickly before continuing. 'This is a very interesting scene and not at all good.'

'It must be serious for you to come down yourself. I was expecting you though, I knew you'd be watching me.'

'Miss Melaku, I am quite capable of coming down to check on things whenever I like. I have actually been known to visit Assiyah before, you know. I'm a frequent visitor in fact. I was just here in France not that long ago. I came to collect the life force of Nostradamus; it was one that we wanted kept apart from the rest and to not go back into the system. We'd thought there was something not right with him, making predictions and all that. Some of us thought that perhaps he was a Yetziran that had sneaked off down to Assiyah.'

'Sir, that was five hundred years ago.'

'Exactly. Not that long at all really.' He took a brief moment to look around. Walking over to a passing vehicle which travelled not much slower than normal Paris traffic speed, and as such seemed to not be moving at all. He seemed bemused by the car and gave it a bemused but gentle kick, the same way that a lot of men kicked the tyres of cars to try to look like they knew what they were doing.. 'It's all changed a bit down here, hasn't it? Where are all the horses? I helped design those, you know. Well not specifically horses, I designed unicorns, but they were all left behind in the big flooding reset.'

Zophiel was aware of unicorns, like horses but a bit more pointy, was how she had described them to Totfiel once. They littered Assiyah in picture form, appearing in paintings, posters on children's walls and on the sweatshirts of middle aged people who really should know better. She had never actually seen one in real life however and now she knew why, perhaps they were too busy being dreamy and fantastical to make it on to the Ark on time.

She pointed to the body on the floor. 'Is it another one without life force?' she asked, expecting to be given the normal middle management spiel.

Falafriel took his eyes from the deceased and looked at the messenger as if trying to read her thoughts, before speaking again. 'The body has a life force, it's still in there somewhere, you can be sure.'

'How do you know this?'

'Because this is not a Newman, he is a Yetziran, although not by birth, we adopted him for our sins. This is the being whose job it is to remove life forces. This sad soul laying out on the pavement and looking like he has had a mountain dropped onto his head is who the Newmans refer to as the Grim Reaper.'

'Bloody hell!' exclaimed Zophiel. 'I always thought he'd be bigger. Who did this to him?'

Falafriel knelt down next to the body of Attalius and placed a hand on the side of the Grim Reaper's face. 'I am not sure; we should return him to Yetzirah immediately to find out.' In a display of strength surprising even to Zophiel, Falafriel stood picking up the body of Assiyah's Soul collector one handed, holding him under his arm as if he weighed nothing at all.

'Come, Zophiel let us return to Yetzirah and get to the bottom of this mystery.' He looked skywards and was immediately enveloped in a dazzling light which sucked him into the air at blistering speed. Zophiel, not wanting to miss out on anything, followed immediately.

# Yetzirah

Attalius awoke slowly stretching his arms out wide and yawning loudly. At first he thought of rolling over and continuing his slumber, it had been so comforting to rest, it felt like years since he had had a really good sleep, but then his brain reminded him that he did not sleep, he had not slept for a very long time, he was the Angel of Death, and there is no rest for the Grim Reaper as there is always someone dying somewhere in the world. He sat up with a start and saw Zophiel stood by his bedside. 'Where am I? What's going on?' he exclaimed before seeing Falafriel behind her. 'Oh, it's you.' He said disdainfully.

'Good morning, de Laustre. I trust you've enjoyed your little rest?'

'It was enjoyable, but I didn't need it, you know that I'm not one for slacking on the job, I'm a very important person, you know. Why have you brought me here?'

'I brought you here because you were laid on the floor on the pavement of a Paris café, the life force within you dwindling like dying ember. We returned you to Yetzirah in order to revive you. I am already beginning to regret it.'

'Someone tried to kill me.' Attalius said the memory suddenly appearing on the edge of his mind.

'You don't say.'

'Yes, it's coming back to me now I was sitting at the café enjoying a coffee and someone tried to kill me.'

'Then you are lucky that we found you when you did and brought you back here. Hopefully you will be fully recovered in a few days.'

'But what about my job, If I'm up here who's collecting the life forces down on Assiyah?'

'Don't worry about that, I've set someone else on the job for now, we don't want a reoccurrence of the last time our collector went missing from their duties.'

'Someone else? But it's a very specialised position, I must get back down there as soon as possible.'

'And you will. Don't concern yourself, I want you away from Yetzirah and out of my sight as soon as I can allow it. But for now, I need to know what happened to you down there, who was it that tried to kill you,'

Attalius thought hard, it was all so hazy though one moment he was sat in the mid-afternoon Paris sun enjoying a coffee, and then...

'There was a man, a tall man, he wasn't a Newman though, he was something different. He had powers, I assumed he'd come from up here. He told me he was going to kill me to send a message.'

'A message to who?'

'He said that my death would be a message, a message to God that Assiyah was in its last days, as was Yetzirah's. He said his name was Helel Bene Elim.'

Falafriel's face dropped when he heard the name, 'Oh bugger,' he said for the second time that day. 'It would seem that we are all in a terrible amount of trouble.

# Who Watches the Watchers
## Beriah – Present Day

Falafriel Hemister sat down behind his desk and bade the small group stood in front of him to take seats. They were an odd looking group, not as individuals but, put together as a team that Falafriel hoped would save the future of his race, they were certainly a rum bunch.

Firstly, there was Zophiel, who despite Falafriel knowing that she had a sharp mind and enough go in her to power a football stadium, was currently sat shaking her legs, clicking her fingers, and whistling a tune all to different rhythms. Sat next to her was her friend Totfiel, again someone with a keen mind and who you could definitely rely on in times of trouble, but who at this very moment had his eyes closed and looked for all the world as if he would much rather be back in his apartment and asleep. Next to him was Hariton, probably the smartest Yetziran to ever draw breath, but devoid of any common sense, understanding of social norms, or empathy. Then there was Caphriel, huge of build, probably strong in a fight, but with all the fire, intelligence, and nous of a partially lame bullfrog.

Finally, there was Attalius. Attalius de Laustre who Falafriel had sincerely thought that he had seen the back of when he gave him his dream job of Collector on Assiyah. Falafriel did not believe his luck when Attalius had requested the post as reward for his slim efforts in saving Assiyah forty years earlier. He had long been a thorn in Falafriel's side on Yetzirah in his previous job as a messenger retrieving drained life force bags. That is not to say that he was bad at his job, he was actually very efficient, it was more to do with his smug attitude, and his flawed feeling of superiority over his peers and indeed his superiors, Falafriel being one of the latter. Attalius sat bolt upright in his chair not even attempting to hide the sneer on his face as he looked at his new colleagues.

'Many of you will remember the great reset on Assiyah. The time when Tertira Grammaton herself gave the decree that all but a very few life forces were to be taken from Assiyah.'

'Remember it?' sniffed Hariton. 'It was the worst time of my life. All the work I had done, the creation of the concurrence, the planning of Assiyah's history from beginning to end, all ruined. Just because of some bright spark in senior management decided that Assiyah needed the Watchers to guide it along.'

'Yes, the Watchers.' Falafriel said. 'The greatest mistake we ever made when we created Assiyah. It was a sound plan in theory, have a small group of volunteer Yetzirans enter the concurrence and take relatively normal lives on Assiyah with the Newman people. There they would live secretly alongside the Newmans, they would teach them the skills they would need to push forward society, so that life forces were created at a greater pace, ensuring a stable and secure constant supply of life force from a large population. There were many Watchers on Assiyah, but they were led by six generals. Samjaza, Armaros, Azazel, Sariel, Penemue, and the most powerful of them all Helel Bene Elim. They ruled over the other Watchers on Assiyah, guided and managed them, and were meant to ensure that their influence on Newman culture remained just that, influence and not direct engagement or change.

'The problem with the plan is that it did not consider the intricacies of the Yetziran mindset, namely that, despite millions of years of evolution and development, we are greedy, irrational, self-serving, and on the whole stupid. For the first few hundred years there were no problems. The Watchers wandered Assiyah, ingratiated themselves with the Newmans, quietly taught them new skills and generally pushed along the development of the Newman race. Each of the Watchers had a specific skillset which they passed on, such as weaponry and warfare, language and writing, science and nature – all the things a new race of beings needed to develop and grow.

'As time passed however, and Assiyah developed, the Watchers began to get bored of their seemingly administrative role in the world. Stupidly left to their own devices by the powers that be on Yetzirah, and trusted to make sensible decisions, they fell victim to lapses in judgement, lust for power over the Newmans, and eventually an attempt to change Assiyah into a world which they could control.

'Following a decree from their leader Helel Bene Elim, they made the Newmans aware of their presence among them, and announced themselves as immortal overlords sent to Assiyah to rule over the Newman race. In some cultures, they were seen as gods among us, in others superior alien life forms. You don't have to look very far into ancient writings, carvings on pyramids, or architecture to see their presence in the early civilisations.

'At first the Yetziran administrators including I am ashamed to say myself, paid this no mind. It didn't seem to affect the regular flow of life force, and if anything, it made the whole project a little more interesting. So, what if a few of our agents on Assiyah decided to have a little fun with their role, as long as the world kept developing and the life force kept flowing it did not matter. Everything changed however with the coming of the Nephilim.

The Nephilim were the answer to the question of what would happen when the Watchers lost control of their lust and began to breed and have children with Newmans. Huge abominations, the Nephilim grew to the size of giants. Ugly, cruel, and prone to fits of wild murderous temper, the children of the Watchers soon became a terrible risk to the continued growth and development of the Newman race. At first there were only a few, wild gigantic beasts who ravaged the land slaughtering all Newmans in their wake and invoking fear throughout Assiyah, but the Watchers, rather than being embarrassed and horrified by the destruction that their children wrought across the world, saw the Nephilim as the natural progression of life on Assiyah. The Watchers decided that Newmans were there to be the slaves and concubines of the Watchers, producing Nephilim children who would inherit Assiyah.

'It was at this point that senior management finally woke up to what had been happening. Initially it was cordial, a group of Yetziran emissaries were sent down to Assiyah to negotiate with the Watchers. To tell them that their path would lead to the death of all Newmans and as such could not continue. They were told to destroy the Nephilim and return to Yetzirah for punishment. The Watchers did not take this suggestion well. The Yetziran emissaries were brutally executed and with their wings cut off were sent back up to Yetzirah.

'Nobody wanted a war, least of all Tertira Grammaton our leader, and that was where the idea of the great reset came into effect. Can any of you remember the solution that the Archangel Uriel came up with?'

'Put all the things they wanted to keep on a big wooden boat and drown the rest of them!' exclaimed Caphriel, very pleased with himself.

'Exactly. A messenger was sent to Assiyah who identified a Newman who was given the top secret job of building a big boat. They would then very sneakily get as many living things on the boat as they could before a monsoon of literally biblical proportions hit. The Newman chosen however was an absolute fool and couldn't help but brag about his 'special mission' and how God himself had spoken to him. It wasn't long before Helel and the rest of the Watchers caught wind of the plan.

'On the thirty-ninth day of the rains, the boat was loaded and ready to go when Helel Bene Elim appeared with his generals and an army of other Watchers and Nephilim. Yetziran forces were sent down to Assiyah to protect the boat, and a great battle ensued. Many lives were lost that day, on both sides, and the fighting only ended when Tertira herself appeared.

'The battle was over within moments as most of the Watchers prostrated themselves and begged for forgiveness. Most of the Nephilim were destroyed, although there were some that escaped to high ground to survive the rising waters, however these giants were so spread across the world that they had difficulty finding mates, and their race eventually died out completely.

'Helel and his five Watcher generals were captured and sent straight to Gehinom for eternal confinement. There they would be kept, and the plan was that there would be no risk of them ever being released again. The rest of the Watchers and their terrible children the Nephilim were all left behind when the rains came.

'It would seem however that our friends on Gehinom, either maliciously or through sheer stupidity, decided that these highly dangerous individuals should be sent back to Assiyah to live a Newman life. These are not Newmans though, they are powerful Yetzirans who have clear memories of the time they spent on Assiyah before, the Nephilim that they created, and of the war that ultimately destroyed their bloodline and consigned them to an eternity of solitude and suffering in

Gehinom. They know the workings of the concurrence; they know how it can be abused and have taken advantage of it for their own benefit. I can only assume after the attack on our collector, and the message sent through him, that they desire revenge.

'From the information gathered by Zophiel and Hariton, it would seem that the Watchers upon being released back to Assiyah have been travelling throughout the concurrence, taking over the bodies of those that have just passed into the concurrence, and living borrowed lives. What damage the Watchers have carried out on the world have been small and insignificant so far, but they are smart beings, there will be an endgame to all of this and, through the message sent through our recently attacked collector, their final coup de grace is imminent. We must stop them as soon as possible.'

'Ah,' Said Totfiel. 'A simple case of preventing our inevitable downfall and extinction. Sounds easy, any other simple tasks you wish us to complete today?'

'Contrary to popular belief, and despite your best efforts, Totfiel, sarcasm is not actually the lowest form of wit. Falafriel sighed. 'I think even the Newmans of Assiyah discovered a long time ago that rudeness lacks the cleverness and subtlety of sarcasm, and I'm afraid you have neither the skill nor intelligence to carry out either. May I carry on, or are there any other genius interjections that you wish to make?'

'Forgive me, father for I have sinned.' replied Totfiel with a grin.

'Of course, our task to stop them will not be easy,' Falafriel continued. 'It will be dangerous and there is a very real danger that we may not succeed. However, we must try. I am proposing that a small team of Yetzirans, namely yourselves, enter the concurrence to hunt down, and capture these rogue life forces, returning them here, where they will be able to be dealt with appropriately.'

It was Zophiel's turn to interrupt.

'Sir, can I ask how they've managed to get away with this for so long? Surely someone must have known that they were loose in the concurrence, that they were hopping from life to life, growing more powerful and more dangerous with every new life they took on? I spotted something was up and I'm not even that observant.'

'This is very true, Zophiel.' Falafriel replied. 'Sadly and very worryingly I think that there have been inside elements here within the organisation, Yetziran workers who have been aiding the Watcher's efforts within the concurrence. This is why our operation must stay as secret as possible. We do not know who is listening to us.'

Suddenly the room fell very silent, as if they were all aware that someone could be listening to them at that moment. All but one in the room.

'Excuse me,' said Attalius. 'This idea that we're all going to die and that we have to capture and probably kill these Watcher fellows is all very serious and worrying, but I'm still very concerned about who is doing my job. It's a very special position you know, a very important job that everyone in this room relies upon, you can't just expect any old idiot to do it.'

Falafriel did not respond immediately, but instead gave the biggest idiot in the room a sardonic glance.

'The job is being done, and well by all accounts,' he said. 'But do not concern yourself. Once this special task is over you will be able to return to your job,

'Good.' Said Attalius. 'I refuse to be demoted and replaced by a lesser being. Now, about this task, what is the reward?'

Falafriel placed his hand on his head for a moment and fought hard against breaking the Yetziran law which prevented him from causing bodily harm to others.

'The reward is to not be killed. You were very lucky that Zophiel found you when she did, Attalius. Five more minutes and you would have been an ex-collector. If it's some kind of medal you require for doing this task, I'm sure we'll be able to knock one up.'

'A medal would be nice, maybe some kind of new title to go with it.'

Falafriel moved on, turning to the others, in the vain hope of find some kind of sanity.

'Now I have provided you each with outfits to disguise your identity to the Newmans should you have to enter Assiyah to apprehend a Watcher,' he continued. 'They are a little dramatic, but the aim is to bring fear into the hearts of the Watchers, and as a cover for any Newmans that happen to see you about your work. The Newmans will think that you are alien life forms of some kind, they love that kind of thing, and your actual appearances will become lost among all the other supposed incidents of aliens visiting their planet, and abducting people to probe them in various orifices or whatever.'

Totfiel let out a sudden, loud laugh, followed by a childish snort. A giggle which Hariton and Caphriel quickly joined in with.

'Does this amuse you?'

'Well,' snorted Totfiel. 'First of all, orifice probing, always hilarious, but secondly, they are not wrong. We really are aliens to them.'

'Ooh, I've always wanted to be an alien,' said Hariton.

'Yes, and believe me you certainly are very alien. Besides you don't get to enter the concurrence, I need your supposed skills out here. Now can we move on from the schoolboy humour please? You were supposed to be one of the sensible ones in this outfit, Hariton.'

'I'll try, sir,' said Hariton, barely suppressing a grin. 'It'll be hard though, as problems go, it's a stiff one.'

'Good,' continued Falafriel, ignoring the sniggering in the room. 'You will each be given a staff, simply touching this staff to a Watcher will be enough to immediately incapacitate them and send them to a secure facility here. It is very important that you only use these staffs. Do not attempt to engage with a Watcher by hand, they are incredibly powerful and dangerous individuals. They will show no hesitation in killing you in an instant if threatened.'

'I think you'll find that I am more than a match for any Watcher, Hemister,' said Attalius with a sneer. 'Remember, I'm the one that captured the original so called Grim Reaper when he went AWOL. Do these plebs know that I'm a hero?'

'Oh yes, everyone has heard of your exploits,' replied Falafriel. 'How could they not of heard of the absolute abomination that you made of your simple task to bring the collector in. It was only through luck that the task was completed and the world of Assiyah survived. This is why I'm sending a few of you along, I learned the hard way that sending one lone fool to do a job could have disastrous consequences.'

Attalius raised his hand to speak again but was hushed by Falafriel as an assistant came in carrying a set of uniforms and three staffs.

'I think we're one short,' said Caphriel as he took his staff from the assistant and twirled it in both impressive and annoying way.

'No there are only three of you in this team. I have another task for Miss Melaku,' he smiled at Hariton, who winked back at the Arch Angel.

Zophiel raised her arm to speak 'Erm… excuse me, sir. Can someone explain to me what is going on? Maybe I want a staff and a smart new outfit. I'm not wanting to stamp my feet and be loudly dramatic about all of this, but can you tell me what is going on before I stamp my feet and get loudly dramatic.'

'Patience, Zophiel. I will talk to you once the others have left. I have a special task for you, one that I think you will enjoy a whole lot more.'

'Will I get a uniform and a staff?'

'No'

'Then I might be about to kick off… sir.'

Falafriel laughed and, with a sharp clap, dismissed the others who were excitedly trying on their helmets and waving their staffs around like broadswords.

'Gentlemen!' he called. 'If you would like to head into the next room. Michael will give you your instructions and send you on your way on your first mission. I think it's a medieval start for you lot, just to stir the pot up and get things moving along. I have things to discuss with Miss Melaku. And remember, this operation is meant to be…' But they had already noisily left the room. '… Top Secret.' Falafriel finished to himself. 'Please, take a seat Zophiel, and I will tell you what I want you to do.'

The next ten minutes were probably both the most surprising and shocking moments of her very long life.

# Black Holes and Revelations

## The Concurrence

Despite hearing earlier how Amelia described the concurrence, the initial shock that the being of light that had once been Sophie Pratman felt when entering the giant web for the first time was quite astonishing.

Much later she tried to think of a time in her twenty six years when she had felt similarly surprised, but the only thing that sprang to mind was the very distinct moment in her life when she realised that being an adult wasn't quite as much fun as she'd thought it would be. She could pinpoint the exact moment, she was nineteen, she had dropped out of higher education after falling foul of the University's quite outdated rules on behaviour, alcohol consumption during lectures, and sexual conduct with your professors, and had subsequently discovered that getting a job which actually paid well, and was enjoyable, was an impossible task of almost Herculean proportions. She felt totally lost that day, unable to see where her future lay, and no idea what to do next. Much like she felt now, as a blob of luminescent ether in an endless and oppressive void of blackness.

She had no eyes, but she could see the web around her, she had no ears but could hear the gentle hum which ran along the lines of stars which travelled toward the giant phosphorescent ball of white far in the distance. She had no body as such but could feel the warmth and comfort of the passage to the centre. She began to wonder if Amelia had left her behind and Sophie found herself being drawn into the crowd of souls in the queue and pulled along.

'Did you forget?' came a voice which although sounding nothing like her, Sophie immediately knew to be Amelia's. 'If you follow that lot the adventure is over before it's began. Come over here.'

Sophie's light pulled to a stop and guided itself over to where the voice was coming from. There, away from the travelling stream of lights floated a solitary star, alone in the black void between. She knew that was where she should be heading. She pushed herself against the grain of lights trying to pass her until she reached the edge. Just as Amelia had described to her it was colder on the edge and, as she forced herself onwards, the biting cold began to burn.

'Keep coming, Sophie. You're almost through,' Amelia's light called, and despite the sharp pain which seemed to envelope them, the light that once was Sophie finally broke free of the chain of souls and into a comforting warm blackness beyond. By the time Sophie reached Amelia's light it had already set off again.

'Where are we heading?'

'Onwards, away from these lights and away from Finlay's Hollow, we need somewhere to stop and plan before the next part of our journey.'

They floated through the blackness, occasionally passing bright holes in the web, where balls of light were appearing. As they passed Sophie took the opportunity to glance into them, and immediately remembered why she shouldn't. Each hole contained a scene of death, the passing of someone from a life on earth to the vast concurrence of time that spread about her. Other than the recently deceased Maureen, Sophie had only witnessed one death in her lifetime. She was seven and she had been with her best friend Rachel walking home from school. The friends had been talking about their day and Rachel had victoriously pulled a handful of loose change out of her pocket, declaring that the sweets were on her tonight. Some of the coins had flown into the air and into the road, sending Rachel scuttling off of the pavement and after them. As Rachel bent down to pick them up, she did not see the car approaching from behind. Sophie had though, and screamed. The memory that stuck in Sophie's head the most was her friend's face as it turned to look at her. Sometimes Sophie saw it still, at random times, when she least expected it, like now whilst floating in an endless black void.

How stupid, what a thing to think of at this very moment. The whole of the workings of the universe had been laid bare to her, everything she thought she knew about life and death had been torn to shreds, and here she was thinking about how sixteen years ago she had seen the accidental death of her best friend. Up ahead Amelia's light was nearing a hole on the web, it paused for a moment. 'Nope, not that one.' It said flitting onwards.

'What are we looking for?' Sophie asked.

'Somewhere safe to hide out for a while before we set off to find them.'

'Who?'

'Alan, of course, or whatever he is deciding to call himself when we catch him up.'

'But he said he was bored, that he was heading to the centre, that he was going to give it all up.'

'Poppycock,' laughed Amelia's light. 'He is the most self-centred, greedy, and deceitful being that ever drew breath, and I should know I've met enough in my hundreds of years throughout history. There is absolutely no way he would be able to help himself from looking for his next project. The only thing he was bored of was probably living life as an old man in a quiet Scottish village. No, he's out there somewhere and I intend to find him and give him a piece of my mind.'

'But how will you know where he is?'

'Do you remember the piece of parchment I looked at, in the stash of belongings that he keeps buried just outside Finlay's Hollow? I think it's some kind of map, like a trail. I think that if we follow the trail, we'll catch up with him at some point. I've memorised the symbols on the parchment, but I have no idea what they mean. We need to find somewhere safe, away from the Reapers, recreate his map and work out where to go next.'

'I'm confused though,' said Sophie whose life seemed to be one long journey of confusion recently. 'Even if we know where he is, he could be disguised as anyone, he'll be impossible to spot.'

'To you maybe, at the moment, but I see people a little differently from most. I can see their hidden light. Do you remember, just before I told you my story, I pinched your arm a little and said that I could see the light in you? Well, I really could. It's a very faint glow in almost all people, some shine brighter, like you, as they are travellers like me. Alan has wandered the world and borrowed lives for thousands of years, he is positively beaming with a light, he shines wherever he goes, although only a very few can see it. If we get anywhere near him, I'll know, and that's how we'll catch him.'

Amelia's light had stopped at another hole, Peering down inside. Suddenly a shock wave ran through the web, shaking Sophie's light and causing her to begin to drift away from Amelia.

'What was that?' she called.

'Reapers. They're trying to flush us out. Be very careful, and do not panic. They are probably scanning the web now looking for a sign that they've unnerved us.'

Another wave vibrated through the blackness, stronger this time and Sophie struggled to stop herself from fleeing as far away as possible.

'They are getting closer; I'm going to have to cause a distraction. I need you to do something for me, Sophie. You are going to have to be very brave, but you have to trust me, you will come to no harm, and I will look after you.'

It's a funny thing about human nature, although the trait is also common in many other species. If you are told not to panic, if you are told to be brave, and to trust someone despite what you might be about to experience, more often than not it is the single greatest thing that will actually cause discomfort, fear, and the desire to run screaming from a situation. Think of your last time in the dentist's chair, or that time when you were very young and one of your parent's told you that school would be fun, shortly before abandoning you into the care of a group of sociopathic, and often angry monsters, who were never more than one cup of coffee and a naughty child away from committing murder.

At that moment, after those words of comfort and encouragement from Amelia, there was nothing Sophie wanted to do more than scream at the top of her voice and run away into the depths of the void as fast as her non-existent legs would carry her.

Another vibration, another wave of rising panic within Sophie's soul.

'Follow me, stay slow and calm, and do not lose me,' whispered Amelia, although Sophie was still unsure where the voice was actually coming from. Amelia's light joined the trail of other lights heading towards the centre of the web, and it immediately became almost impossible to focus on which of the lights she was, even though she was slightly larger than the others.

'Sophie, I want you to drop into the next hole when I give the signal, don't worry, the Reapers won't see you do it as they'll be too busy chasing me. I'll find you.'

'What? You're leaving me?' cried Sophie. 'You can't leave me, and how will I know what the signal is?'

Sophie did not have long to wait as suddenly Amelia's light shot away from the rest and off into the void, swiftly followed by three other lights. The hole was close now, and Sophie had never felt so much fear in all of her life. She wished she'd stayed in bed this morning and not been so bloody nosey about the mad old woman in the retirement village.

Before she could talk herself out of it, she dropped into the hole to start her new life, and almost immediately regretted her decision.

# The Damned

## Omo-Kibish, Ethiopia 2045

To an outsider, the dry, barren hills of Omo-Kibish were a strange place for the end of the word to be planned. There were no buildings here, no sign at all of human habitation or history; indeed, there was nothing for miles around this place where six immortal beings now sat around a small fire under a sky lit by a million stars above them.

The six were an odd collection, not the types that you would expect to be seen together and certainly not to be meeting on a hillside in the Ethiopian bush, miles away from any sign of civilisation. There was a blue haired Drag Queen, dressed in a pink velour track suit. Two teenage French boys who looked terribly bored by the whole idea of spending time with their family and were idly flicking stones at each other. A small white bearded man dressed in a thick woollen overcoat who looked like he had lost his fishing boat. A short bespectacled woman who was keeping one eye on her mobile phone as if expecting a call at any moment, and finally a large bald headed man. As wide as he was tall and who looked as though he could crush all of the other assembled Watchers within his great shovel of a hand.

'Well look at this,' Samjaza, the drag queen laughed. 'As family reunions go, we certainly know how to throw a wild party. I reckon next time we should all come as the Village people, I'll be the cowboy, obviously. Unless you'd all prefer the Spice Girls.'

'No that wouldn't work.' Said Armaros, the fisherman, 'There's only five of them, unless the twins both fancied coming as Ginger Spice, that would be quite funny.'

'Scary, said one of the French boys with a grin, 'Scary would be a better... fit.' He flicked another stone at the face of his twin, who responded immediately and caught the stone in mid-air grinning.

'Image isn't everything, said the bespectacled woman, nervously twitching on the cushion that she sat on. 'Have you all not learned anything? It is what's going on in your head that counts not the shell you wear.'

'But what's the point of all your brains, Penemue if you don't look fabulous! I don't even have to try anymore, darling.' The Drag Queen tossed her head back, flicking their blue hair and showing off an array of expensive rings on their fingers. 'Whatever we come as, we need to have a bit more fun, I reckon. After all the boredom of the past couple of thousand years we all need to pep it up a bit.'

'Enough! This is no party, brother,' snapped Helel, 'You have had more than your share of parties over the last two thousand years. It is now time to concentrate on what we actually returned to this flea pit for.'

'Look we're here. We came as you asked, Helel,' said Armaros. 'Mostly because you threatened to kill us and eat us if we didn't, but that's by the by, we're here now. You told us to learn the ways of the concurrence, and to create as much mayhem as possible, we would then bargain with the Yetziran's to give us our children back, and let us have a world of our own. We may be a little late but now we are here. I already know that the plan has changed, but have you bothered to tell any of the others yet?'

'It's a simple plan, it's not changed much, just altered to our advantage,' Helel shrugged, 'We all need to make a concerted effort to travel throughout the concurrence. We want as much mayhem and death as you can possibly create. Plague is the easiest option, but any kind of war, man-made disaster, or genocide will do. But this is where the plan has adjusted, as I was unaware of what happens when you eat pure life force in the concurrence. Once the deed is done you are to enter the web sit back and let all that lovely life force come flooding up to meet you, and you had better be hungry. The more we eat, the stronger we'll get, the stronger we get, the easier our final task will be. Sooner or later the Yetzirans will work out what we're doing and come after us, that's inevitable, and also part of the plan. They already have an inkling, that's what the Reapers are all about. They are onto us and mean to stop us before we get too powerful to handle. For now, we skip through time causing chaos. If you see a Reaper, run.'

'In these heels?' laughed Samjaza. 'But what if we get caught?'

'Part of our plan has always been to bring Newman stooges along with us for the ride. Some of us seem to have taken to this better than others,'

His eyes flicked towards Armaros. 'Some of us have lost ourselves engaging with the Newmans. Make sure you have a stooge with you if you can, and give them up when you have to, or simply use them as a shield while you escape. If the worst happens and you are caught by the Reapers, I have people on the inside and it won't be for long. Now you know the time and the place of our final meeting. Go now, eat life, and get as strong as you can. I will see you there, and we will win the victory and the world that our children deserved.'

'I think that's not all that you told me would happen, Helel. You said that you were willing to destroy Assiyah, the Newmans, The Yetzirans, and even us if you couldn't get what we wanted. You would end everything if we didn't win.'

'Exactly, brother!' exclaimed Helel, noting the look on his siblings faces. 'That is exactly what I want to happen if we cannot win. Do you think that they're just going to send us back to Gehinom again. The risk would be too great for them. No, this is now a suicide mission, it's them or us, and they have to know and believe that too, if we are to have any hope.'

There was silence for a few moments, the only sound on the hilltops were the crackling flames of their campfire. Finally, it was Samjaza that spoke. 'Well, I'm not altogether keen on properly dying, but if you're going to go then why not in a blaze of glory.'

'We are with you,' said one of the twins. 'It's all getting very boring anyway. Time to either start something new or end it for good.'

'Armaros?'

'You are right, of course, brother. We are backed into a corner, there is no way out for us apart from fight or die. As much as I hate to turn my back on the Newmans, I am in this until the end.'

Finally, Helel turned to Penemue. 'And what of you, brother. You have remained very quiet.'

'I think as Armaros has said, we have very little choice in the matter. They are on to us now, and sooner or later they will catch up. I think we all know that it won't end well that way. One small matter - You mentioned you had people on the inside? How can we trust your spies.'

'Ah, now there is a stroke of luck for us. I was approached by a Yetziran group soon after arriving back on Assiyah. They call themselves The Brotherhood of Impending Death, and no, they do not realise how stupid their name sounds. The Brotherhood of Impending Death believe that the Yetziran race should have died a natural death thousands of years ago, before Assiyah was created, and around about the time when Yetziran immortality began to fail. They see the continuation of the Yetziran race as a failure to comply with the laws of the universe, and actually welcome their doom. It's perfect for us, they are Yetzirans that actually want to see the destruction of Assiyah and the slow natural death of their own people. I literally couldn't have wished for a better group of people to meet.'

'Idiots are everywhere.' said Armaros.

'Indeed. Now, none of you have been aware of this, but the reason we have all prospered and been able to survive until now has very much been as a result of this group helping us along, turning a blind eye to our shenanigans, and allowing us to not be noticed for thousands of years.'

'I did wonder how we've got away with it for so long.' Penemue muttered. 'Some of us haven't exactly been subtle.' They cast an accusing eye at the French boys who were grinning broadly.

'Don't blame us for enjoying ourselves.' Azazel laughed, flicking a stone into the fire, and causing sparks to fly up into the evening sky.

'Exactly,' smiled Sariel. 'What is the point of all of this if we can't have some fun doing it.'

'The pair of you could have fun in a morgue, and probably have done on many an occasion,' sniped Penemue, something which brought fresh giggles from the two teenagers. He had never understood his sister's love for cruelty and causing misery, and much preferred to carry out his business, when he had to, in a more indirect and quiet manner.

'Oh shut up,' added Azazel. 'At least we're not dull like you. You're not happy unless you've got your head stuck in a book. Next time we see you like that we may have to slam the book shut on it!'

'Enough!' Helel had heard enough bickering.

Suddenly there was a flash of bright light and all but Helel immediately jumped to their feet fearing a visit from Reapers. As the light faded a tall wiry Yetziran stepped out.

'Do you realise how dangerous it is to summon me down here, Helel?' The Yetziran snapped. 'If it is noticed that I am away from my post I could be sent to Gehinom, or worse.'

'Araqiel.' Helel slowly stood and held an outstretched hand to the new arrival who tentatively grasped it. 'Do not worry yourself, it will all be over soon. I was just telling everyone about our agreement. I trust all is well with you and your colleagues on Yetzirah?'

'Things are progressing as planned, Helel. As I hope they are with you and yours. We will wait and keep watch on you as we have always done. The Brotherhood of Impending Death will act swiftly if you should fail in your endeavours.'

At the mention of the group's name Azazel and Sariel smirked. It was an action mirrored more subtly on the faces of Helel's other siblings, but Helel shot them all a sharp glance of warning and they straightened their faces.

'We will not fail,' said Helel. 'Assiyah will fall and Yetzirah soon after, you and your associates will all have the slow death you all desire, I can promise you that.'

'Good,' affirmed Araqiel. 'It is for the good of the Yetziran people as a whole that this charade ends as quickly as possible. Our people should meet their destiny and move on to the next world.' He scanned the frankly bizarre group of individuals sat around the campfire for a moment and wondered if any of them other than Helel himself really had the guts to go through with their plan. 'I must go, before somebody notices that I'm not in my office.'

'Of course, my friend,' said Helel shaking the Yetziran's hand once more. 'Prepare your people, and wait for my signal.' I will see you in the afterlife.'

There was another blinding flash of light and Araqiel was gone.

'What the bloody hell were you both going on about, all that afterlife and next world talk?' Said Samjaza. 'There's no such thing. Yetzirans discovered that millions of years ago. When you actually die, you die for good, its common knowledge.'

'Of course it's true,' laughed Helel. 'But never underestimate the all reaching nature of gullibility. Araqiel and his fellow idiots are our back up plan, a kill switch we can flick if the Yetzirans defeat us. The fact that they are naive and believe any rubbish they are told makes them willing martyrs. Naivety makes all worlds go around. Come on, Newmans on Assiyah still believe in superstition and astrology, they even believe in true love.'

'I believe in true love,' muttered Armaros. 'I thought you did too. That's what we are doing all of this for isn't it? True love for our lost children? You always said that was what we were doing it for.'

'If you ever believed that this mission was based on love then you are a bigger fool than I took you for, Armaros, and you will die with the rest of them unless you wake up,' snapped Helel. 'It is about power, justice and making things right.'

Armaros knew then that Helel would not be satisfied until everything was turned to ash.

'Anyway, meeting over, time to move on!' announced Helel, pulling out a small black box from his pocket and flicking a red switch, which detonated the explosives buried under the ground where they sat, instantly vaporising them all, and sending them back into the concurrence.

# Sophie Pratman is on Fire
## Woolpit, Suffolk 1594CE

The moment Sophie entered her new body she knew she was an awful lot of trouble, and her first action in her new life was to laugh, loud and long. She was tied to a large wooden pole set high on a pile of logs and brash which were at this very moment ablaze, the flames climbing high, with the supposed aim of killing her.

This was not going fully according to plan for the crowds of onlookers who surrounded the stake in the town centre, and very quickly they had gone from baying mob cheering the death of a witch, to cries of fear and anger as they saw that Sophie seemed unworried by the fire, and in fact was laughing at it.

Fists were waved, pitchforks thrust into the sky and assorted vegetables were hurled at her, as the crowd seemed to be aghast at the fact that, this time around, they had actually caught a real witch who was being protected from being burnt by Lucifer himself.

Sophie could feel the heat of the fire, but it did not burn her, and she was reminded of cold winter nights spent at her grandmother's house when she was a small child and sleeping in a put up bed with a very warm electric blanket under the sheets. It was a comforting warmth and one that she felt the urge to snuggle into. Quite why she was not turning into a barbecued servant of the devil she was not sure but for now, while the flames tickled her arms and chest with their cosy licks, she decided to appreciate the moment while it lasted.

The townspeople added more wood to the fire whenever the flames looked like abating, consuming Sophie with fire and enveloping her in a cosy warmth that she continued to enjoy. She had stopped laughing now, she realised that the more she laughed the angrier the mob would become which meant more wood added to the fire. Amelia had warned her that upon taking control of her new body she would be invulnerable to death for a period (something about the Grim Reaper being a very busy being who would not return to the same body twice within a few hours) but she didn't want to test this theory too far. The binds holding her to the stake had now burnt away, and she thought of just jumping free from the fire and running but knew that she would not get far before she was recaptured, drowned, or crushed by rocks or something, and that really would be testing timescales with the Angel of Death somewhat. Amelia had told her to wait, that she would find her, and so that was what Sophie decided to do, and so, seeing as she was so warm and cosy and a little bit tired from the day's activities, she leant back sunk down into the flames, feigning death and had a little doze.

When she awoke it was late in the evening, the flames had gone, and Sophie was very cold indeed. She found herself sat in a hollow of smouldering charcoal which gave off little or no heat anymore. Much of her clothing had not survived the whole being burnt at the stake experience, and Sophie found that she was more concerned at scorched near nudity than being discovered to be still alive. The crowd had gone, and the town square deserted, most people having been very happy at their day's work and retired home for the evening plotting which unfortunate woman to accuse of witchcraft next. Some had just gone to the tavern across the square to celebrate their great victory over Satan and all of his imps. Sophie could see the lights in the tavern from her perch on the burnt woodpile and could hear the jollity and raucous humour which comes from burning innocent women for doing something evil and radical like curing the sick, reading a book, or owning a particularly suspicious looking cat.

She was beginning to wonder whether she should sneak off and find something to wear, when the door to the tavern opened and a very drunk man fell out into the gutter. Sophie immediately feigned death again as the drunk regained his feet and staggered over to her. A rough throated man, he sang as he wobbled closer.

*'Fair Lady, throw those costly robes aside,*
*No longer may you glory in your pride;*
*Take leave of all your carnal vain delight,*
*I'm come to summon you away this night.'*

The man stopped singing as he reached the pile of smouldering wood. Sophie dared to open her eyes just a touch to see what was happening. The man stared at her, and she felt even more aware of her lack of clothing. As if hearing her thoughts, the man spoke.

'You want to be covering yourself up, missy. The flames are gone now, and you'll be catching your death if you don't get some decent clothes on you.'

Sophie remained silent and supposedly dead. The man let out a little laugh.

'Or perhaps death is what you're wanting. Not happy with this new life then? Want to jump back in the web for another game of roulette?'

Sophie opened her eyes and looked up at the man. If she'd expected to recognise anything of Amelia in the man's face, she was to be bitterly disappointed. He was middle aged, scruffily dressed in a dirty torn shirt, brown worryingly stained breeches, and soft shoes which looked as though they were all but waving a white flag. He wore a wide brimmed pitted hat under which shone lively eyes, full of humour and mischief. A rough beard finished the look and Sophie knew then that the choice of bodies you inhabit really was a game of chance, no one but an utter idiot would have chosen this appearance.

'Amelia?' she said, still not entirely sure that the little old lady from Sunningdale Retirement village was indeed stood in front of her.

'No, my name's Talbot, William Talbot, I know who you are too. You're the talk of the town, Wicked Mary Lyghtfote, apparently you steal babies and eat them, after you've sacrificed them to your lord and master Satan.'

'Really? Oh God, that's terrible.'

'It would be if it were true. From talking to the locals in the tavern there, your worst crime is probably nothing more than being a single woman in a town where most poor girls are married off before they're out of their teens. You're a rebellious one, you, and your card was marked from early on. All it took was a bit of religious fervour, a king that's obsessed with Witches, and these idiots took their chance. Come on, let's get you somewhere indoors and find you some decent clothes.'

'Hang on a minute, how long were you in the tavern?'

'Oh, a couple of hours, enough time to have a few drinks and chat to the locals, it's always good to catch up with old friends before moving on, I find.'

'Old friends? So, you've been here before?'

'No, this is my first visit to Suffolk to be honest. Poor old William Talbot expired from drinking too much and falling into a ditch two winters ago. Terrible shock it was waking up frozen solid and face down in ditch water, still that's time travel, body swapping roulette for you. I've been waiting for you to turn up and here you are, in a blaze of glory, and all that.' He reached out a hand to help wicked Mary Lyghtfote down from her place of death. 'My house is not far from here; we need to get you warmed up before we shuffle off of this particular mortal coil and find some other poor souls to inhabit.'

'You mean we're not staying here?'

'Oh gosh no. It wouldn't do at all. We have Reapers on our tail, it won't be long until they catch up with us again, and besides if any of the locals see you walking about, they'll have another go at sending you back to Lucifer or something like that, and they may be more successful next time. Bloody awful things they do to these poor girls once the mob gets their hands on them - idiots.'

'But how will we leave?'

'Poison, I have it back at mine. It's the best way to do it really, no pain and whoosh off we go to our next life. I'm thinking that we should head further afield than Suffolk next time to try to shake the reapers off our tail, I have a few ideas in mind. Come on, Sooty Mary. Time waits for no being of light in a bag of flesh, and all that.'

# The Mission

## The Concurrence

Attalius De Laustre was having a fantastic few days. For a start he had actually cheated death itself and survived a brush with eternal limbo by using nothing more than his inner strength and physical prowess. Then shortly after coming back from the afterlife, he had been specially requisitioned to take part in a dangerous mission to save not just his people, but probably the entire universe, which could only enhance his already legendary status. Finally, he had been given a snazzy new uniform and a dangerous weapon which he thought made him look even cooler than normal, if that was even possible. Just to have those things happen in a couple of days would have been memorable but then, once he'd put on his new kit and had an impressive twirl of his new staff, he had been led to a top secret room where he had been sent into a giant spider's web larger than a planet.

Before leaving, the Yetziran known as Hariton, who was obviously some kind of nerd, gave them some instructions. As far as Attalius was concerned, the instructions were directed to him more than the other two proles, as Attalius was probably the leader.

'So, this is how we're going to start proceedings.' Hariton said, pointing to a hole in the floor similar to the one that Attalius used to use before he was given the incredibly important job of Grim Reaper. Back then he was just a lowly, but highly skilled and well respected messenger. 'You're all going to jump into this hole as if you were heading to Assiyah, but you're not. You're going somewhere much more exciting. It's called the concurrence and it's the place that all the used life forces travel through on their way to processing.

'What, like a sewage pipe?' said Totfiel holding his nose and smiling at Caphriel.

'No, not like a sewage pipe at all. It's a huge black void that is full of holes of light. It looks very much like a web. When a Newman dies on Assiyah their life force will appear in one of the holes. It will then travel to the centre of the concurrence where it will be processed. When you arrive, you'll be floating in the void, and you'll have a bit of time to orient yourselves once in there. I'm sure you'll soon get the hang of it, but there are few things you'll need to fully understand to avoid total disaster.'

'Sounds ominous.' Said Caphriel.

'Very,' replied Hariton. 'Firstly, you need to understand that the further away from the centre of the web you are the earlier you are in the existence of Assiyah, if you want to see cavemen and the ice age, head right to the outer reaches. Obviously, this means that the closer you are to the centre, the closer you are to the end of the world, the time when Assiyah ends, and the Newman race ceases to exist. So, if its futuristic space age times you want with all the technology, creature comforts and social anxiety, then that is your place. Understand?'

'Of course. Outside old stuff, inside sparkly stuff,' said Attalius, 'I'm not stupid.'

Hariton eyed him for a moment before Caphriel decided to chip in.

'Can I just ask, if this world is all going to end won't we run out of life forces once it's dead?'

'That's a remarkably good question, Caphriel. Time within the concurrence is concurrent, it all runs at the same time, it all happens at once. Once the harvested life force has left the concurrence it is trimmed and sent back in at another point in Assiyah's history. That way the flow of life force is continual and never-ending, even though at some point the space in which it operates ends. Does that make sense?'

'You lost me at concurrent, to be fair,' said Caphriel, 'but it's not important to me anyway, please continue.'

A part of Hariton's soul died at that very moment, it was something that happened whenever he spoke to Caphriel. He counted to ten in his mind before continuing.

'Secondly when you enter the concurrence you will be big balls of light, you will not have a body as such. This is to hide you from Watchers roaming the concurrence and help you creep up on them. You cannot however take on a Watcher in the concurrence, that is highly dangerous, and you will probably be eaten.'

Totfiel suddenly choked on his own breath. 'Excuse me, did you say eaten?'

'Yes, a Watcher in the concurrence is incredibly dangerous and able to consume you in an instant. They have not just been growing through taking over spent lives, they also have the ability to eat other life forces whilst in the concurrence. It is why you do not tackle them there. I will occasionally send ripples through the concurrence, a vibration that should unnerve them enough so that they break cover from hiding amongst all the other life forces. If you see one, and you will know when you see one as they will be a lot larger than any other thing in the concurrence, you should observe where they go. Once they return to Assiyah through one of the holes, follow them and confront them there. On Assiyah they won't be able to eat your eternal soul.' He paused for a moment. 'That I know of.'

The statement was true enough, and they didn't need to know it, but it cheered Hariton somewhat to see the sudden terrified looks on their faces. 'Find them on Assiyah where all you have to do is touch them with the tip of your staff, that will be enough to send them to a holding cell here on Yetzirah. Caphriel, do you get it? No heroics in the concurrence. They will feed on your eternal soul.'

'Got it. Don't get eaten.' Said Caphriel, who had gone back to trying to master staff twirling. Hariton had a very sudden feeling that everything they were doing was doomed to utter failure.

'Once you catch up with a Watcher on Assiyah you will be able to spot them as they will have an effervescent glow about them, invisible to the Newman eye, but clear as day to you or I as they will be full to the brim and overflowing with hundreds of years of life force. They shouldn't be hard to spot. Got it?'

'Yes, yes, yes,' sighed Attalius, who was getting a little tired and eager to get to the mission.

'Finally, and this is vitally important, stay together. Do not split up under any circumstances. You are a team, and you need to act like one.' Hariton paused for a moment as Attalius had put up a hand. 'Attalius, you have a question?'

'Yes, the whole team thing. I'm much more of a lone wolf kind of guy, I don't like to be dragged down. How important is the staying together thing?'

'Vitally. If you are separated from your team, you are vulnerable to attack. You do not want to test the Watchers, they have been gaining power for thousands of years, they will end you in an instant if you are caught on your own.'

'Fine,' hummed Attalius. 'So, if we're a team does that mean that there's a Team Leader. I have a lot of experience in this type of seek and destroy mission.'

'No leaders, just the three of you working together. You have all of Assiyah's history to go at, I'm sure you'll get the hang of it. I'm going to drop you into the concurrence close to an entrance to Assiyah where there has always been a lot of suspicious activity. It's a good place to start. Are you all ready?'

Totfiel nodded and attempted a salute. Caphriel, thinking it was something you had to do, tried to copy him. Attalius shook his head wondering how long until the pair of them would be eaten by a Watcher, and he would be able to get on with this special mission on his own.

Despite Hariton's warnings the shock after jumping into the hole and being transported into the concurrence was one that Attalius, although he would never admit it, would probably never really recover from. One moment he had been looking incredibly smart in his sleek new uniform and wielding a powerful staff, the next he was floating in a void, his uniform and staff had disappeared, and his body had transformed into something that could only be described as a luminous blob. As if the humiliation of this wasn't bad enough, to add to it he was floating in an inky blackness with absolutely no idea what to do next.

Beside him were two other floppy balls of light which he could only assume were Totfiel, and Caphriel. One of them spoke, although Attalius could not tell where their mouths were.

'I thought Hariton told us we'd know where to go.' It was Totfiel. 'Where's this entrance he said we'd be close to?'

'What is that thing over there,' said the other, Caphriel. 'That looks like a hole in the blackness.'

'Where?' Totfiel asked. 'There are hundreds of thousands of holes.'

'Over there, where I'm pointing.'

'You are not pointing; you are a lump of gelatinous light with no arms.' Totfiel groaned.

'But I'm pointing at it, I'm sure I am.'

'Then where are your arms? Where is your pointy finger?'

There was a moment's pause before Caphriel replied. 'Erm... in my head?'

'Brilliant. I am paired with fools,' said Attalius, in his head but he was sure the others heard the sound. He hadn't meant to say it out loud, but it was the first time he had tried to utter anything in the concurrence, and he hadn't quite got the hang of it yet. He hoped that they couldn't hear all his thoughts. 'Perhaps,' he said trying his hardest to intentionally speak aloud, 'Perhaps, as you have no observable arms, you should try to move towards it.'

'Ok, how do I move? Hariton never told us that.'

'I don't know, try flapping with your invisible wings?' Attalius offered. He thought of trying but didn't want to be the first to make an idiot of himself, but then immediately regretted thinking that, in case they had heard it. There was no immediate response, so he guessed he was safe.

'Hang on a minute,' Caphriel said, and made a grunting sound much like someone trying to open a particularly difficult jar of olives. The light that was Caphriel began to move. 'I did it!' he cried starting to slowly float away from them. 'Now I just need to work on direction.'

Totfiel's light made a similar grunting sound, although not as loud or painful, perhaps similar to an old lady getting up from a comfy chair, and started moving also.

The fear in Attalius's mind at that moment was almost deafening. He did not want to be left behind but was also petrified of making an embarrassing noise. He created the thought in his head of moving but did not budge. The other two were floating away now and there was a very real danger of Attalius being left behind. He concentrated with all his might, thinking of the direction he wanted to go, thinking of speeding through the web and catching them up. There was an audible noise, not unlike the squeal made by an angry squirrel, and Attalius realised that it had come from him. He began to move. The other two were ahead of him now, heading for a hole of light and colour ahead of them, a hole through which a lump of light had just come from. He was doing it! He was flying through the air! He had succeeded!

It was then that he realised that he was moving at an increasing speed, accelerating through the web in a way that he did not know how to control. He flew past the other two, and towards the closest hole in the web, managing successfully to not let out a scream as he did so, and deciding to style it out, even if he was about to meet his end.

'I'm going on ahead, making sure it's safe for us,' he called somewhat shakily.

'Go, Attalius!' shouted Totfiel, who could plainly see that Attalius had no idea what he was doing and was probably going to crash somewhere.

Caphriel let out a whoop, hoping that he could be as cool as Attalius one day.

The former Grim Reaper disappeared into the hole and now did let out a small scream, which was heard by the rest of his team. They followed him through the hole.

Hariton had been right, they were indeed in the medieval period and they both landed gently on the wet dirt floor next to Attalius, who was cursing and trying to wipe the mud from his previously shining white uniform.

'I misplaced my landing,' Attalius said. 'It won't happen again.' He realised that the more he wiped himself down the more he was spreading the muck over himself before continuing. 'Do either of you know where we are? Looks like we're on the edge of some kind of peasant village.'

It was the evening, although the village was lit up by a bright moon which reflected off of heavy snow which lay all around. Totfiel studied the buildings and looked upwards, paying particular attention to the night sky. The village was surrounded by tall hills and at the far end of the valley was a large body of water. 'It's weird,' he said. 'I think I've been here before, although not in this time period.' He paused for a moment and fought hard against the temptation to remove his helmet to take a better look. There were no Newmans to be seen and Totfiel suggested that they move into the village to see where they all were, surely the village wasn't deserted.

They passed a few small wooden houses until they saw a large hall ahead of them, it was well lit and with the noises of music and laughter coming from within.

'I reckon that's where we find our Watcher,' said Attalius striding forward staff in hand. 'Fall in behind me!'

The other two glanced at each other for the briefest of seconds. They could not see each other's faces, but both knew that they were thinking the same thing. Nevertheless, they followed him.

As they approached the front of the Hall, one of the doors opened and a portly man came out and began striding down the steps, laughing and whistling as he went. Totfiel could see no Watcher glow about him, this was not their target. Attalius however had other ideas.

'Watcher, I have come for thee!' cried Attalius as he charged the man and attempted to strike him with his staff. The man's response to suddenly being attacked by three seven foot tall, staff wielding beings in white was to immediately scream and faint.

'Well, that was easy,' said Attalius poking him with the end of his staff. Nothing happened.

'Attalius, I don't think that was a Watcher,' said Caphriel looking up to see others coming out of the hall to see what all the commotion was about. Within moments all was chaos, screams and cries rang out through the village. At the top of the stairs a group of Newmans suddenly appeared at the doors armed with swords, one of them shone with a golden light which at first dazzled the visitors.

'There!' cried Totfiel. Charging up the stairs towards him. The man took one look at them and ran back inside. His colleagues, seeing him run followed.

As Attalius, Totfiel, and Caphriel burst into the hall the sight before them was not one they were expecting. They paused for a moment trying to understand what was happening. In the centre of the Hall, surrounded by cowering villagers two tall men, each of them shining gold, one significantly brighter than the other, were locked in a tight embrace. The light from them illuminated the room bathing everyone around them in a warm orange glow. It was then that Totfiel spotted the knives in their hands.

'No!' he screamed running towards them, in a tone which was much more high pitched than he intended.

They each plunged the knives into the nape of the other's neck, and collapsed onto the floor, the light within them immediately extinguished.

The Reapers first mission was a failure and it was Attalius that spoke first.

'Bugger.'

# East India or Bust
## Fort William, Kolkata 1817

It was a day similar to any other in Kolkata, the afternoon air was oppressively thick with heat and moisture, and most sensible people were keeping themselves inside where the environment could be kept significantly cooler and tolerable. Two Scots pretending to be middle aged Englishmen walked the walls and drew incredulous, but well hidden, looks from the men of the East India Company army who had no choice but to stand in the blazing heat.

Colonel Stanley Penwell, and Major-General Sir Henry Worsley, were positively melting in their quite unsuitable uniforms. They also had little choice in being upon the wall of the Fort, searching as they were for a fellow time traveller who always seemed one step ahead of them.

This was the fourth place and time that they had searched for him since Sophie had been burned as a witch in Woolpit, four different lives they had taken on together. She'd been a portrait artist in 14$^{th}$ century Florence, a nurse in a Spanish hospital shortly after the First World War, and a Roman centurion in Mesopotamia. Each life borrowed had only lasted a few months and each time the pattern was the same. Firstly, she would arrive in her new body, and after getting over the initial shock, she would keep her head down and wait for Amelia to find her, which she unnervingly but thankfully always did. Then they would search for Alan, and in each case so far, not catch up with him. The closest they had come was in the Athenian port of Piraeus, when they had actually seen Alan or whatever he was then called, onboard a vessel pulling out of the port. Sophie and Amelia had stood on the dockside, as a pair of, at that time, very angry Roman soldiers watching the bright glow of Alan's light heading off into the horizon. By the time they had acquired places on the next ship to sail he was long gone, and the trail had gone cold.

Sophie had begun to develop the ability to be able to spot the glow of light which she could see on Amelia clearly now and, as her time jumping in and out of the concurrence borrowing lives continued, start to see a glow on whoever's body she was inhabiting at the time. At times she had even seen the glow in others, and Amelia had pointed out that they would be fellow life hoppers such as themselves. Often they would speak to them, trying to find additional clues to Alan's whereabouts, but so far none had been at all helpful, most denying their time travelling ability altogether.

The life force of Sophie Pratman now resided in Henry Worsley and looked positively uncomfortable wearing a woollen uniform in the oppressive heat.

'I must admit,' said Henry pulling at the collar of his jacket. 'I'm struggling with the whole gender thing. I didn't think I would, I thought it wouldn't be too much of a change really. Perhaps I'm just not happy being a man. I don't think it's my greatest ever achievement.'

'Most men think that very same thing at some point in their life, if they're really honest with themselves.' Stanley replied, idly twiddling with his impressive moustaches. 'Most aren't honest though and stumble through life full of bluster and testosterone, ignoring the glaringly obvious warning signs that make them miserable inside. A great many of them are deeply unhappy with their lot, and never admit it. Don't worry yourself too much, Henry, you have a great advantage in that you're able to look at things from a female prospective.

'In time you'll get over it completely, once you realise that it really doesn't matter what you are, male female, queer, pansexual, asexual, agenderous. I've done them all and it doesn't matter one hoot. It's what you do that makes you, not what's hanging between your legs, or what gender you actually feel you are in the deepest recesses of your mind. Do I like being a man? Probably not. Do I feel like I'm more of a woman? No, I don't think so either. Take away this flesh bag that I'm walking around in, and I'm just a ball of light and energy. You're one too, you can see it for yourself now. Does the fact that in one body I can give birth make me a different person, does it bollocks. I've done the whole pregnancy and birth process when I've lived in a body that can do that kind of thing, I've done the whole dad thing when I've lived in that kind of body too. Does that make the birthy one a female and the daddy one a male? No, it's actions that count, it's being a parent that counts, it's loving your children and giving them everything that they want and need.'

'So you've had children?' asked Henry. 'You've never mentioned any of them before. How many children have you had?'

'Just the two.' Stanley said, their voice a little quieter.

'Two? But you've lived for hundreds of years? 'Why only two?'

'It's a hard thing to do to leave your children, Henry,' the older man said. 'It was the closest I ever came to being caught by the Reapers. They came for us once when we lived in France, 18th century it was, around the time of the revolution. Both children were under the age of ten, beautiful, innocent things they were. Alexander and Babette.' Stanley suddenly turned away to look out over the port. 'It's not an easy thing to leave your children for the last time, especially when they are so young and vulnerable.' He said. 'After I left them, I promised myself that I would never put myself or my children through that again. I hope that you'll never have to experience the feeling.'

There was an awkward pause, and it was clear that Stanley did not wish to continue this conversation any longer. Henry tried to change the subject.

'So if we don't find him here where will he go next?' Henry asked.

'Well if he's not here then there's a spot in England during the plague that he has on his list, that should be a delightful trip. After that, I'm not sure. I'm going to have to return to Finlay to have another look at his map. We'll head there for just after we both last left, as there's a risk that we would bump into ourselves, and that's never a good thing.'

'How come, does it cause some kind of temporal rift in the space time continuum that could alter time and make us obsolete, or something?'

Stanley laughed. 'Oh dear, you really shouldn't take too much notice of Back to the Future, dear. No, it's just that you may get to actually see yourself as others see you, which is always disappointing. Mirrors may sometimes be the work of the devil when you're having a bad hair day, but to actually see the state of yourself and the unexpected size of your arse will give you horrible flashbacks forever.'

'I can imagine. Fair point. But what are the rules to this time travel business? Are there actually any really important rules?'

'Not many to be fair,' said Stanley grateful for the chance to move on. 'The main one is that you can never go back. You can never re-inhabit and live a life that you've already borrowed. I'm not sure why. I asked Alan once and he said it was something to do with glitches in the concurrence, causing a ghost in the machine that would make us easier to track and be killed by Reapers. I'm not sure if I believed him. He was often making up bollocks like that.'

'Ok, so I can't ever go back. Not a problem, my first life was a bit chaotic to be honest and I'm not in a rush to return, although I did have the leftovers of a takeaway in the fridge that will be turning pretty gamey by now. Any others?'

'Not really, the other of his so called rules were fairly common sensical – don't travel too near the centre of the web, be careful of inhabiting babies as the parents freak out when you start talking at a few weeks old, and baby food is bloody awful no matter what period of history you visit. Oh, here's an important one: never, and I mean never ever borrow the life of a telesales caller. It's a total waste of time and you'll probably end up topping yourself within a matter of hours, I did. The same goes for anything in banking or politics. Utterly pointless and terrible for your soul and your eternal wellbeing in the long run.'

'What about animals?' Henry asked. 'Can I be a cat? I've always wanted to be a cat.'

'You could be an animal if you so wished, I thought about trying it once but thankfully stopped myself before carrying it out as it is frowned upon by every other traveller. You see after each jump you take something with you, a personality trait, a mannerism, a habit, or way of thinking. You may have noticed that already, but sometimes it comes so naturally that you don't realise it. You have no control over it, you cannot choose the thing you take with you. It may seem like a fantastic idea to be a dog or a cat, but if then in a subsequent life, and in polite company, you suddenly have the strong uncontrollable urge to eat your own vomit, or lick your own bits, it can be a bit of downer. It's also harder to kill yourself if Reapers catch up with you.' Stanley paused for a moment. 'Can you see him? Over your right shoulder four o'clock.'

Henry took a quick but gentle glance behind him, seeing a bright golden glow coming from the corner of the wall some two hundred yards away. 'Yep, who are they?'

'Short woman, bringing drinks to the guards and talking to them. She has her back to us at the moment, we need to move quick before she see us and runs.'

Walking quickly is a funny thing. There is no subtle or graceful way to do it no matter who you are, and the sight of two British Army officers waddling at pace along the walls of Fort William would have raised eyebrows upon anyone lucky enough to see it as they came within arm's reach of the short Indian woman, Stanley could not restrain himself any longer.

'Alan?' He said, calling out to the woman who turned around to look at them.

The woman turned; her face set with shock. 'Really? Do I look like an Alan to you?' she said.

'You know what I bloody mean!' Stanley motioned to the guards to leave the area which they did immediately and without question, whilst wondering what in Heaven's name was going on.

'You really thought that I'd believe you, didn't you?' Stanley continued. 'You really thought that I would think you'd had enough and wanted to shuffle of the mortal coil for good. I could hit you, liar!'

'And I wouldn't blame you if you did. It was a terrible move on my part, but one that I had to take.' The woman took a seat on the edge of the parapet, placing her tray of drinks on the floor at her feet. 'I'd try to explain it all to you, but it's best for your sake if you stayed ignorant to it all.'

At that moment Harold fully expected Stanley to take a full blooded swipe at the Indian woman sat on the edge of the wall, such was the anger in his face.

'What do you mean?' Stanley hissed. Just tell me what is going on! I thought you actually loved me.'

'I do,' said the woman, a pained look across her face. 'And that is why I have to protect you. Please trust me and let me go.' Her voice shook a little, and for a moment Stanley actually thought that he could see a small tear in the eye of the woman. 'Stop chasing me, Amelia... sooner or later you will catch up with one of the others by mistake and they will kill you, for good.'

'Others? Who do you mean? I've met other travellers, we've met other travellers, together. They've never threatened to kill me before.'

'They weren't my brothers and sisters. Trust me, sooner or later you'll run into one of them and it won't end well. Run far away, find a nice quiet life for yourself and your new companion. Live a happy life and forget you ever knew me.' There was a pleading edge to the woman's voice now. Whatever Alan is saying Sophie thought, he really did believe. Either that or he was an even better liar than Amelia gave him credit for.

There was a dull popping sound that they both recognised immediately, followed by a blinding flash of light on the other side of the wall, it was clear to them that they had company. They all turned to see a hole in the air. Three Reapers appeared from the hole and immediately started running towards them.

'I think it may be time to leave.' The woman said. 'I'm sorry Amelia, I truly am but you must forget me. I am a terrible person, and you are better off without me, and besides, I've got places to be and people to inhabit, so…bye.' And with that the woman threw herself backwards off of the edge of the fort where she landed in a crumpled heap in the dry moat which ran around its high walls.

'Don't worry, I have him!' yelled one of the Reapers waving their staff with a flourish and creating a black slice in the air in front of them, before diving headfirst into the void. It was the first time that Stanley had ever heard a Reaper speak, and although it was in a garbled language, the thought that these things might actually talk was shocking in the extreme, she'd always thought of them as silent assassins.

'Attalius, no!' cried one of the remaining Reapers. But it was too late he had gone.

For a brief moment all time seemed to stop, as the two British Officers looked down from the wall at the now dead and empty body far below them, and the two remaining Reapers standing dumfounded looking at the air through which their companion had just leapt and disappeared. It was as if the Reapers had no idea what to do next and it was Stanley and Henry who reacted first.

'Run,' whispered Stanley, and his friend need no further encouragement. They sprinted as fast as their 19th century legs would carry them.

'And where is Attalius now?' asked Falafriel when the two remaining Reapers returned to report in.

'We have no idea,' said Totfiel. 'Probably still chasing the Watcher around the web? Who knows. I'm half hoping that he has been eaten to be honest.'

Falafriel wanted so much to agree with Totfiel. The blessed idea that he was finally free of Attalius would have been a relief. However the slim chance that the pompous idiot was now running wild throughout Assiyah's history causing all kinds of disasters would cause innumerable problems to Falafriel, especially if word of it got back to the other Arches or even worse Tertira Grammaton.

'And you said that there were two others there?'

'Yes, their glow was not as bright as the Watcher's, one of them only had a dim tint.' answered Caphriel.

'But you didn't give chase.'

'Well, we tried,' said Totfiel. It was all a bit strange, what with Attalius being stupid and everything. By the time we made our move for the other two they were running, and had leapt off of the wall too. The life forces were out of their bodies and off into the concurrence before we knew it.'

Falafriel sighed.

'Hariton are you able to trace Attalius?' he said half hoping that the answer would be no.

'Probably,' Hariton replied. 'I am a proper genius remember. I'd leave him in there, but the damage he may be causing is frightening. I'll see what I can do.' He pulled out a tablet and began tapping on the screen.

Falafriel turned to Totfiel and Caphriel who both looked exhausted from their experiences of hopping through time.

'Got him!' Hariton suddenly exclaimed. 'From the looks of things, he's in 8$^{th}$ century BC Abyssinia, the kingdom of D'mt to be precise. From what I can tell he's been bounding his way through the concurrence like it's an underground train network and he has a free travel pass. Either he's still chasing the Watcher we found in Kolkata, or he's utterly lost. Whatever he's up to I think it's fair to say he decided to go off on his own.'

'I want him back here now!' exclaimed Falafriel. 'We cannot have him running riot throughout the concurrence causing untold disasters at every turn. The ripple effects of his careering through Assiyah's history could destroy everything quicker than The Watchers at this rate.'

'I'll drop you back into the concurrence close to his place and time.' Hariton said to Totfiel. 'You should be able to catch up with him pretty quickly. He's not going to be inconspicuous or anything.'

'Get it done.' Falafriel pleaded. 'The whole point of sending you three into the concurrence was to catch Watchers, not to aimlessly chase each other around. We do not have any time to waste.'

Hariton laughed. 'All the time in the world and you still feel like we're running out of it. It is a concurrence remember? Or am I the only person that actually understands all of this?'

'I am aware of the science behind all of this, Hariton.' Falafriel wondered if Attalius really did have the biggest ego in the known universe. 'Yes, it is all happening at once, but that actually means that the end could come at any moment, while we're here celebrating our own intelligence and running around trying to find our own people.'

Hariton paused for a moment before speaking. 'I apologise Falafriel, I am an idiot who bows to your simplicity of thought.'

Falafriel couldn't quite work out if he was being insulted, but was glad when Hariton left with the two Reapers. He was beginning to wonder if sending Zophiel off on her special assignment did nothing but remove the least idiotic member of the team.

# Dancing Will's case of Mistaken Identity

## Houghton, Cambridgeshire 1365

Sophie Pratman was immediately in a state of shock upon taking over her next body. She was laid on a small cot bed in the corner of a dark and musty room, which burnt her nostrils. There was no shock in that, she had taken over the bodies of people who had previously died in bed before, but this time it was just a whole lot more disgusting.

For a start there was the smell, it was rotten like a decaying corpse, or an old person's fridge. She at first wondered if she had entered the body far too late and was at risk of actually being a real live zombie, if a zombie could ever be described as live. It was then she realised that she was not the only cadaver in the room and that there were other cot beds like her own each with a dead person in it. It was as she tried to move that she noticed the huge bursting lumps in her armpits and groin, which were seeping out everywhere and which immediately made her retch. It was then that she realised her cause of death. She moved to sit up in the cot, trying her very best to ignoring all the weeping and disgustingness that her new body was putting her through.

As she stood on thin legs, she could begin to feel strength starting to spread through her limbs. It was a feeling that she had become used to with each new body as her energy and life slowly flowed into what had been a corpse not five minutes ago. The festering lumps healed and shrunk, her fingers, which had been blackened and dead suddenly flowed with new blood and turned a healthier shade, and Sophie never felt more in need of a hot shower in any of her previous lives. As she healed, and the smell of her recent death started to abate, she looked around the room to see that she was in a large wood walled building where the soon to be dead were obviously taken to see out their last few moments in the company of the other soon to be croaked unfortunates.

She could see that she was now a he again, as thin as a 1990s catwalk model, and dressed in ragged clothing which included a shirt and waistcoat made of rough hessian and trousers which stopped just below the knee in tattered frays, again like something off of a 90s catwalk. His feet were bare and black with dirt. He had never felt so peasant.

As he pulled back the wooden door and stepped out, he was dazzled after being in the darkness of the hut. He brought his hand up to his eyes to shield them from the bright sunlight, slowly allowing things to focus once more so that he could see properly. Before his eyes had fully adjusted, he heard a shout from the side of him.

'You get away from me, Will Beckett! You get back in that shed, you're not safe to be out here, and don't you touch a bloody thing or breath on anyone until you get back in there!' a woman screamed.

He turned to see a woman to the side of him. If he thought he looked like a peasant he was beaten all hands down by her, who was as tatty as she was loud. He rubbed his eyes to clear them some more.

'I'm fine,' the surprisingly alive Will Beckett said lifting his shirt. 'Look, I'm better now. Much better. I healed up and I'm all well.' Will did a little dance to show just how alive and better he was but the slowly gathering people from the village were not yet convinced, and continued to keep a safe distance away from the dancing man. He was struck on the head by something thrown by a child at the head of the growing throng.

'Ow!' Will shouted, his first thought was to pick up the object and throw it back at the little oik, but he decided that the rabble were already hostile to him and hurling what he could see was a turnip at a small child would not ingratiate him with his audience.

'I'm fine I promise you all. I got better!' Again, he lifted his shirt to show that he had no more weeping pustules. 'I feel so much better, I've never felt so well in years.' He thought of giving another little dance but inside Sophie was sure that showing off her 21st century dance moves to a rowdy gathering of medieval peasants would probably end up with him being stoned to death, buried alive, or whatever other bizarre and primitive ways of killing people they had locally.

The shrieking woman slowly approached him, her eyes squinting as if to better spot his plagueyness, a grimace across her mouth displaying probably every one of the three teeth in her head.

'How is it you be better, Will Beckett, and don't you be lying to me we haven't been married twelve years for you to be able to be telling me no stories.'

Good god, thought Will, if that was my wife, I'd have been glad to get the plague. I probably rubbed myself in rats and dead people to make sure it took a proper hold and did its worst.

'I don't know, just woke up. I can't explain it.' Will said, thinking that acting as stupid as those around him was probably the best way out of this. His wife got closer.

'Take off that shirt!' she said. 'Let me get a closer look at you.'

He did as he was told, probably something that married Will Beckett had been doing in fear for all his married life. He pulled the hessian shirt over his head and dropped it into the mud beside him, a looked down at his thin body in the sunlight. He was painfully wasted away, being able to see each rib clearly defined, his body was filthy, scuffed with mud, and looking like he had not washed in a very long time. There were however no swellings under his arms or on his neck anymore, and the cleaner parts of his skin looked a good colour, probably a better colour that they had looked before he caught the plague. The benefits of having healthy life force flushing through them, thought Sophie. He wiped at his arms a bit, suddenly very conscious that every eye in the village was on him.

'Well I'll be...' his wife said. 'What have you done, Will?'

'Nothing, I told you, I just woke up. It was like I was sleeping and then suddenly I woke up and I feel fine, I feel great in fact... dear.'

'You've been saved.' The wife said. 'I knew it. I prayed last night when they dumped you in the hut. I prayed that you go to heaven, and Jesus saved you!' She shouted the last sentence and suddenly all was chaos in the village as people sank to their knees in prayer, others raised their hands to the sky crying out the name of their saviour. Another turnip hit Will squarely in the ear, and the child was immediately struck themselves around the back of the head for and cursed for attacking God's favourite, as well as wasting good turnips.

The first few hours of taking over a body were always difficult for Sophie, presenting itself with many problems.

Firstly, there was the issue of names and relationships. Sophie had struggled a few times in her adventures in life hopping when she had got her beloved's name wrong after coming back from the dead, or during the time she spent as a eunuch in the palace of the empress Wu Zetian. She had failed to refer to the queen by her proper title and been immediately dragged from the throne room and executed by drowning. The death of the eunuch had been suitably horrible, Sophie had always had a fear of large bodies of water, she could swim but never felt comfortable in doing so and avoided it wherever possible. It was not the most traumatic part of her experience in $7^{th}$ century China however.

She had taken over the body when it was a young child, the son of a kitchen maid, who should have died of a fever. Sophie had inhabited the body which, of course, had miraculously recovered. The recovery, once complete, was just in time for the unfortunate child to be dragged from its mother and taken to be fully emasculated so that they could serve in the queen's chambers. Sophie had been a man a couple of times and had got used to owning a set of male genitalia. She didn't particularly like it, and ignored it as much as possible, but understood that it was part of the whole being a man thing. However, to be only nine years old and be strapped to a table, before having the whole shebang removed with a hot blade, was possibly the most traumatic thing that had happened to Sophie in any of her lives, and something that would haunt her forever. The deaths, of which she had experienced twelve now, were never nice, often painful and the part of the whole history jumping adventure that she hated the most and was sure she would never get used to.

Secondly there was the immediate problem when arriving in a life, of having to explain away how she, or he had returned from the dead, often after suffering terrible wounds. Having to explain away recovery from the worst plague to ever strike the medieval world, by dancing like a fool was nothing compared to trying to explain to the stunned faces around you how that leg of yours which was severed not a few moments ago is now magically reattached and you are able to not just walk but run on it. There had been two occasions where her attempts at explanation had been roundly dismissed and she had found herself very quickly hurtling back into the concurrence not five minutes after she had just left it.

One of those times was on a battlefield where the bloodshed was still very much raging around her, and the second time when she appeared in the body of a gladiator who had just been skewered through the chest with a spear by an opponent who was obviously much better than her. She knew she had a grace period after just arriving in the body where any further injuries would not kill her, but quickly found that running away from a very irate Gladiator with a spear sticking out of your chest was not time well spent.

Sophie was getting better at navigating those first awkward moments in a new body, in a new person's life, but today, seemingly stuck in a stinking plague village, apparently married to the local harridan, and in desperate need of a long bath, she decided to not hang around too long in the life of poor Will Beckett who should have died from the plague and who probably would again if he hung around in this place for much longer.

There was also the burning issue that she had seen Amelia's golden life force enter near here, and Sophie knew that she would not have got too far away yet. She thought about what Amelia would do and where she would head, and decided that there would be no way that she would hang around in a small village in her hunt for Alan. If he were to be found it would be in the very least within a town if not the nearest city.

Once all the furore over Will Beckett's return to life had died down enough for Sophie to find out where he lived, and more importantly find a pair of shoes worthy of walking the road, Will Beckett strode out in the middle of the clear summer night to find the nearest town, leaving his wife snoring loudly in their lice infested bed. He took the road east and by morning had reached the outskirts of St Ives stopping at dawn by the Great Ouse River to wash off as much of the plague village filth from the body of Will Beckett as would come.

It was market day and already the roads were busy as farmers herded their livestock into fenced pens ready to sell, stalls were being set up ready to sell their wares, and the streets were busying up with townsfolk. Despite there being a deadly plague in the air, it was not stopping ordinary people from getting on with their business, no matter if it was just spreading the plague and killing more people. Sophie thought of the 21$^{st}$

century's attempt at living through a deadly epidemic and wondered if any progress had been made in intelligent thinking over the next 700 years.

Will Beckett had a total of three silver coins in a purse. He did not have the slightest idea of their worth, but found that he was able to use one of the coins to buy a small loaf of bread and a pitcher of milk, enough to fill the stomach of a dead man and keep him going for a bit longer.

As he sat at the side of the road eating, his eyes never stopped scanning the townsfolk, looking for the slightest hint of a golden glow that would show him Amelia. If she didn't turn up today it would be time for Will Beckett's body to do what it was meant to do the day before and for Sophie to return to the concurrence and resume her search.

Sophie and Will spent an enjoyable day observing the town going about its business. People watching had always been a great hobby of Sophie's back in Finlay, it was an enjoyable way to spend a day off, and she had discovered that whatever time in history she visited, observing people from a distance was one of her favourite things.

It was late in the afternoon just as the market was beginning to close for the day that Will Beckett spotted a warm orange glow at the end of the road. At first he thought it was a trick of the light, the sun reflecting somehow and causing the illusion of a glow. His eyes fixed on the glow and saw that it was moving slowly through the bustle of people gathering at a wooden platform. Easing himself to his feet he slowly made his way towards the wooden platform and was immediately disappointed to see that there was going to be a hanging.

Whilst having a greater knowledge of the true nature of death than 99% of the planet, Sophie still hated seeing a person pass on and give up their physical body, especially when it was to be taken in such a fashion. She had seen many deaths by capital punishment throughout her jaunts through time and had seen her fair share of murder committed on the battlefield too. It was something that she really couldn't come to get used to and she wondered about the morals, and personality of anyone that could be comfortable with it.

The poor soul in question was a middle aged man, which by medieval standards was late twenties. He looked suitably fearful of his upcoming lynching, the rope badly knotted and hung around his neck. Not that

Sophie imagined many people would have a smile on their face shortly before being strung up like a pheasant. It would be a strange one indeed that grinned their way through their time on the wrong end of a noose. Sophie was a believer that no one should ever be judged by their face alone, she had worn a few herself. The cruellest and most evil of humans could present with an angelic and kindly face, and Sophie always liked to give anyone the benefit of the doubt. The gentleman stood upon the platform however looked like, what Sophie's grandmother had always referred to as, a wrong'un.

A man in what barely passed as a uniform stood next to him, declaring loudly to the assembled rabble a long list of misdeeds which included thievery, battery, arson, and heresy. Sophie wondered how many of these crimes the man had actually committed, judging by the shocked looked on his face when he heard some of them.

At the front of the crowd the golden glow Amelia was still obvious to see and Will Beckett, who before he died was an avid attendee at any public hanging, edged his way towards the gentle light which no other person other than himself could see. The glow came from a painfully thin young man, with mousy blonde hair, who was watching the man on the platform being told that now was the time to confess his sins so that he may have the slimmest of chances at entering heaven. Will felt the sudden urge to shout out that he shouldn't bother as his best hope was to turn into a glowing ball of light that would enter a giant spiders web and trot off to be eaten, but held his tongue. Instead he sidled up to the side of the young man who still had not noticed the sudden appearance of another glowing being beside them.

'I never thought I'd find you again.' Will said keeping his voice low.

The young man looked at him, a startled look jarring across his face.

'Who are you?' he said in a voice that was probably a higher pitch than he intended.

'Who do you think.' Will said with a wink.

'I have absolutely no idea, and whoever you think you've found it's not me. I mean it's not them.' They paused for a moment and looked Will up and down disdainfully. 'Who do you think you've found?'

'Amelia, Harold, Brid, Galasso? Any of those names ring a bell?'

He paused again, his bright blue eyes a mixture of fear and curiosity. 'No that's not me I'm afraid, and I don't know any of those people. I'm just a simple traveller, no one to be bothered about. Did Helel send you?'

'Helel? Is that someone I should know? It's not someone Amelia mentioned at all. I'm Sophie.' Said Will, a little too loud and receiving a bemused look from a woman in front of him.

On the platform the stool had been kicked away and the wrong'un did a dangly wriggly thing before stopping abruptly. In her mind's eye Sophie could see the light of his life leaving him and heading upward into an invisible hole in the sky.

'There goes another.' Will said, as the assembled crowd immediately started to go their separate ways again.

'You're not just pulling my leg, are you.' Will said, as the young man made to leave as well. She had never done it before, but she wouldn't have put it past Amelia to try a joke like this.

'Definitely not. I'm not the fooling type, you know. What are you? You're not a Watcher?'

'I have no idea what you mean. I am a friend of Amelia, I usually travel with her, but we got split up. I thought you were her.'

'No, I've never been an Amelia, not that I can ever remember anyway. I have been doing this a very long time.'

'What is a Watcher? I've never heard of them before.'

'Watchers are the originals. If your friend Amelia is not a Watcher herself then she will most probably have been taught the ways of the concurrence by one. I really shouldn't be telling you this, but it is of no matter, it'll all be over soon enough.'

'Amelia was taught by someone called Analla, they are most recently known as Alan.'

'Ah, that'll probably be Armaros. Yes, he was always very keen on the Newmans, and I heard he had longstanding companion. I could never be bothered myself. Anyway, happy travels, enjoy them while you can. My work here is done, and I really must be moving on. Good day.' They said, and set off.

'Wait!' Sophie called. 'Alan, or Armaros. Do you know where I can find them?'

The young man turned and smiled. 'Come on now,' he laughed. 'You may not know much but even you must realise that they could be literally anywhere.'

Suddenly he shivered, as if feeling a cold draft, and his eyes widened. 'If I were you,' he said with a grin. 'I'd start running,' and he set off again appearing to walk a little bit faster. Sophie thought of following them, but at that moment a bright light appeared at the end of the road. It was dazzling and Will Beckett had to shield his eyes to stop himself from being blinded. The other townsfolk began to shout and scream and suddenly all was chaos. Sophie didn't quite know what was happening and desperately wanted to stay to watch, but felt the unmistakeable urge to run away as fast as Will Beckett's old legs would carry him. The last thing Sophie saw of the light ahead of her made the final decision to run easy for her.

There, bursting from the light at the end of the road and moving faster than any human could were two Reapers, staffs held aloft, as they ran towards the young man. He turned and tried to get away, but did not have the speed of the huge white winged attackers. The larger of the Reapers thrust his staff at the young man, its blue crystal tip touching his body and causing him to drop to the ground immediately. The body of the young man was dead immediately causing even greater screams for the gathered townsfolk. The Reapers stood over the body for a moment, seeming to not quite know what to do next, before one of them looked up and seemed to spot Sophie, who guessed that Will Beckett's body would be giving off a very noticeable golden glow. The Reaper raised his arm and pointed at her. Will Beckett's gangly body started to run.

It is a strange thing to take over the body of another. Each time you did it you had to adapt your thinking to try to learn its abilities and limitations. The body of Will Beckett, which Sophie had less than 24 hours experience of using, had a number of disadvantages. For one it was relatively old, Sophie couldn't get a definite pinpoint on the age but guessed that he was in his forties, which was nearing ancient for a peasant type in Medieval England. Secondly, he was not just old but seriously malnourished, having lived on a poor diet for all of his as yet unknown years. As such the running style of Will Beckett was similar to that of an oversized toddler wearing clown shoes. And before the Reapers had got within twenty feet of him, he had tripped over his own feet and was sent sprawling into the mud. As Will rolled onto his back he suddenly found that the Reapers were upon him. They both raised their staffs to touch him and send Sophie's life force straight into the eternal void, but they stopped.

Their staffs hovered over him, inches away from touching him.

'Please.' Sophie said. 'I'm not ready yet.' And for a moment she wondered if they would actually not see it through.

Sophie's dreams were dashed however with a loud popping sound and another bright explosion of light behind her. She looked towards the sound, to see a third Reaper leaping through the air, screaming at the top of their voice, and thrusting their staff into the body of Will Beckett and consigning the life force of Sophie Pratman to an eternal death.

# Like a Fish in a Barrel

## Yetzirah

'And that is how you catch a fish in a barrel!' The Reaper shouted, pulling off his helmet and revealing the blonde haired, smug faced Attalius. 'I told you all that the best way to catch these buggers was by surprise in a pincer movement.'

'And I told you that we had to be careful with who we decided to poke with our staffs, Attalius,' said Totfiel removing his helmet. 'We should have left you in D'mt living your best God complex life. Tell me did they really believe that you had come down from heaven to rule over them. People are idiots.'

'They were not idiots, Totfiel, they were my loyal subjects, they worshipped me, as they should. If the pair of you hadn't suddenly shown your faces and kidnapped me, I'd still be there being fantastic.'

'Trust me, you could never be that, and besides THAT is not fish.' Totfiel pointed to the body on the floor.

'Excuse me?' said Sophie, suddenly feeling very angry and picking herself up. 'Firstly, I'm not a fish, and secondly you hardly caught me. If I hadn't tripped over my own stupid feet I'd be a lifetime away by now.'

'Shut up, Fish,' snapped Attalius. 'No one asked you, and anyway a win's a win.' Attalius had long worked hard on projecting the impression of being the most important and impressive person in the room, something which he was demonstrating in full at this very moment.

'I'd say this was a loss,' muttered Caphriel. 'That is very much not a Watcher.'

'Of course it is,' exclaimed Attalius. 'I know a Watcher when I see one. And that definitely is one. Look at them?'

'You've managed to catch completely the wrong fish.' said Totfiel. 'You've managed to grab the one that wasn't a Watcher, or are you too daft to even realise that? We could see it plain as day when she was on the floor, are you so dumb that you couldn't?'

Attalius looked blankly at their catch and shrugged his shoulders. 'I have absolutely no idea what you are talking about.'

'Oi! I am not a bloody fish!' shouted Sophie. It was then that Sophie saw her reflection in the large mirror on the far side of the room. If her body was adorned with gills and fins, she would have been less surprised.

'What in Joseph, Mary, and the scabby donkey is going on!' she barked. 'I knew I wouldn't look like I did in my last life, but this is outrageous. What am I?'

Sophie was almost two feet taller than she had been before she had been grabbed. She had the brightest blue eyes she had ever seen on a person, finely sculpted features, long, lustrously curled black hair which flowed down her back and, quite incredibly, a large pair of golden wings which were as tall as she was.

The other reapers took off their masks. 'You, my dear are Zophiel Melaku, Yetziran messenger, most annoying being in the known universe and my best friend.' He held out a long fingered hand to her smiling. 'I'm Totfiel, but you'll remember that soon.'

'What are you talking about? That's a lie. I have never met you in my life. My name is Sophie Pratman, you're crazy. I remember everything about my life, I remember my parents, I remember my little sister being born, my first day of school, the day my friend Rachel died. All of these things happened. They happened to me. How can you even dare to try to tell me that none of this was true!'

'It was true for you, Zophiel. All of these memories belonged to Sophie. She lived that life before she died, and you took her body. You remember those times because we left those parts of Sophie's life with you. It was important that you were kept in the dark about your previous life. You needed to be anonymous to allow you to contact our target. It was Hariton's idea.'

'Who?'

'Hariton, he's another of your friends, he's incredibly clever, but also very annoying. It's why you both get on so well. Don't worry once we help you remember who you really are then everything will come flying back to you in an instant. Sophie Pratman will be gone forever.'

'But what if I don't want Sophie to be gone. I like being Sophie, I'm happy with who I am. There are few people in this world, or even the entire universe that can say that. Not unless they're a total idiot.'

'I like myself,' chipped in Attalius. 'I think I'm great.'

'And that is totally my point. Look fella, I've only known you for less than five minutes and already I can tell. You're a massive arse.'

'Ooh,' hissed Totfiel. 'Zophiel got feisty.'

'SOPHIE will get violent if she doesn't get some answers pretty soon.'

'Then we had better take you to Falafriel. He'll be able to restore your memory. Things will all seem a little less weird then.'

'I doubt it very much.' muttered Sophie.

'So, I was basically just a glorified tracker, a living breathing drone sent to Earth with just a single purpose.' Despite having her memory returned to her by Falafriel, Zophiel was still in a very feisty mood.

'Well, I suppose so,' said Hariton. 'You served a purpose, you got the job done, you were a bit random at times, but that kind of sums you up really.'

'Yes, you did agree to it when I suggested it to you, Zophiel.' added Falafriel as he disposed of the syringe that he had just used on the angry messenger's arm.

'I seem to remember agreeing to a special assignment, hunting down Watchers, but I didn't think my efforts would entail me losing my memory and taking on a completely different persona.'

'That was Hariton's idea,' Falafriel said, motioning over to her very smug friend who looked even more pleased with himself than normal. 'He knew what you would be like if we just sent you down there in disguise. There is no way that you would have kept what you were doing a secret. We might as well have sent you down to Assiyah with a huge sign with Watcher Hunter on it in big letters. No, it was much better to send you so deep undercover that even you didn't realise it. Did you enjoy being Sophie?'

'I did!' Zophiel exclaimed. 'Sophie was nice, my life on Assiyah was nice. That's what makes it even worse. She's gone forever now.'

'I'm afraid so, dear. She was a real person; we dropped you into her body when she unfortunately died as a child. She was hit by one of those big metal automobile things when she was seven.'

'No, she didn't, I remember that accident it was Rachel that died, she dropped her money and it rolled into the road. She ran after it to get it, and the car hit her as she bent over.'

'The car hit both Rachel and Sophie. Rachel's money fell into the road and you both ran after it. Their deaths were sudden, they wouldn't have known anything about it. We chose Sophie to miraculously survive though.'

'Yes,' said Hariton, 'We dropped your completely blank minded body into hers. To be honest, I think I preferred you when you were a blank.'

Zophiel did not respond with words, as she had picked up some rather satisfying finger gestures during her time on Assiyah. Although he didn't know the true meaning of the gesture, he guessed its intention and smiled sweetly back at her.

'But even if my life on Assiyah started with Sophie, I've lived a few lifetimes since then. I've been down there for years. I can't have been doing that good a job if it's taken me so long.'

'Zophiel, you left here to become Sophie two weeks ago.' Hariton sighed.

'What?' Zophiel suddenly felt a bit ill, like she imagined a newman would after a bad curry.

'You really haven't listened to me when I've explained how Assiyah works have you?' Hariton laughed. 'You left here just over two weeks ago. Yes, you have spent years on Assiyah, you could have been there a thousand, but it still would only have been a couple of weeks to us up here.'

'My brain hurts.'

'That would require you to own one, Zoph. I'm sorry, I often forget that I am always by far the smartest being in the room, if not the world.'

'I would say that there's no need to be rude, but I know you can't help yourself. I would have actually missed you, if you hadn't wiped my memory and forced me into the body of a Newman.'

'You did go willingly remember?'

'I probably wouldn't have if I'd have known it would feel actually longer than a lifetime, or two.'

'You were a very good tracker; you took us straight to a Watcher. We have two now.'

'You mean you already have one?'

Falafriel smiled widely. 'Yes, we got our first one a week ago. Samjaza, the second youngest of the brothers. Yesterday we got a second, Penemue. I'm stunned to be truthful considering the team we sent out to do the job.'

'Have either of them talked? Do you know what they are up to and where the rest are?' Zophiel was suddenly very excited to be back in the game, even though she had never actually left it.

'Samjaza is being surprisingly silent on the matter. I always had him down as the one that would be easiest to crack, but he's holding up at the minute. Not saying a word.' Falafriel sat back in his chair and touched his fingertips together. 'I think that Penemue will be even more difficult. Even knowing that we have them, even knowing that their brother Helel cannot touch them here, they will not give him up. Their fear of him is astonishing. If they would talk and we knew their plan I think we would have them all caught very quickly. It's typical though that due to the nature of their skipping through time and swapping bodies, they never seem to bother to write it down or anything.'

Zophiel laughed, a sudden burst of happiness.

'Are you feeling alright, Zophiel.' Hariton asked. 'Has getting your memory back made you a bit giddy.'

'I am fine,' she said, 'but I'm certainly giddy. If it's a plan you're after I think I know where to find one, but you're going to have to send me back to find it.' Zophiel grinned.

# The Truth be Told

## Finlay

Finlay was the greatest place on earth.

It was the town where Amelia was born over 1300 years ago, when she lived in the Laird's Hall with her mother and sisters under the care of her uncle. It was where she had returned to from Venice nearly 500 years later, and where she first fell in love. It was the place where she marched from with others from the town to join up with the Highlanders in 1746, when they gave George II a bloody nose at Falkirk. It was where she returned after spending two years aboard the Caledonian visiting the Arctic on a whaling voyage in 1826. Finally, it was where in 1970 she had settled into a small and inconspicuous bungalow on the edge of town with her newlywed husband Alan.

That was many years and a few lives ago for Amelia, in fact now the name Amelia Hawke was simply one of many he had used. As he stood by a small copse of trees on the hill overlooking Finlay, Peter Cowie, wondered where in time Sophie had got to. The last time he had seen her was as they fell from the wall of Fort William in Calcutta. When he had entered the concurrence, a strong vibration had sent him spiralling off into the far reaches of the void, and by the time he had managed to return to his start point there was no sign of Sophie's light at all.

He was torn as to his next move. He was undecided as to whether he should abandon Sophie to her fate and continue to chase Alan. In the end he decided that Sophie was strong enough to make it on her own for now, and he would find her later. Alan was the priority.

He knew roughly according to what he remembered of the map where Alan would be heading next and, after a few life hops in 13$^{th}$ century England had failed to find him. It was a grim search, he had never really been one for the bubonic plague and, after a dozen attempts, decided on a return to Finlay for another look at the map. Perhaps he had missed a finer detail.

Peter Cowie, a second year English Literature student at Lancaster, had driven home for the summer break a few days ago, although he had never made it. His car had got within ten miles of Finlay when it had swerved to avoid a sheep in the road and had spun into a tree, hitting it with a force that nearly cut his 1998 Vauxhall Corsa in half. When the emergency services arrived, they were stunned to see a completely unharmed Peter Cowie sat by the wreckage of his car. Quite how he had been thrown from the vehicle and survived a crash that would have instantly killed any other person was a mystery to the throng of Police, Paramedics and Fire Service that attended. The mystery would never be solved for them as they could never be expected to understand, or even believe, how he lived, but the truth was that he hadn't survived. His life force had entered the concurrence, and his body had been borrowed for a short while. His parents were of course overjoyed to see him later that night after he had been fully checked over at the hospital in Glenleven. He felt sad that his stay in this life was to only be a short one and very soon they would lose their son again.

Peter found the tree with the mark carved into its base and began to dig gently. The soil was still loose from the last time she had visited here a few nights ago with Sophie. He did not have to dig long before reaching the wooden casket where their trinkets were kept. For such a relatively small chest, the memories of past lives held within it were immeasurable, small leather bound books containing drawings and scribbled notes, jewellery and coins dating back to ancient times, a pocket watch inscribed with messages of love, a few photographs of happier days, and of course there was the map.

To call it a map would be doing it a disservice as it was just a collection of symbols and letters. There had been more than one map according to Alan, each one a transcription of the last when it had become too worn, tattered, and aged with time. The first was apparently a clay tablet, which was then copied onto papyrus, followed by a parchment, vellum, and eventually paper. Each map was identical to the last and each mapped out a important pathway to follow. Back in his first life Brid had just caught the briefest of glimpses of it, but later Robert had brought Galasso back to the trees where it was buried and took it out to show him properly.

'It is written in Cuneiform,' Robert had said, as he unfolded the parchment out in front of them and pointed out some of the symbols. I had thought once of translating it into a more modern language, but decided it best to leave it. The fewer people that are able to read it the better. This one here shows a time in the concurrence, that one is a place, none of it is specific as there isn't much specificity in the concurrence, you drop back down into the world where you can and find your way.'

'But what is the map for though, why do you need to go to each of these places?' Galasso asked.

'Oh I have little jobs to do, to help things along. Nothing for you to worry about.'

'But who gave you these jobs?'

'I told you hundreds of years ago that you ask too many questions, and you haven't changed at all?' Robert laughed, and that was that. He would answer no more.

Over the years, when they had been in Finlay's Hollow together, they had looked at it, and over the years Peter had started to be able to understand what it said. There were some words and symbols which were unknown, but generally Peter knew that if he saw it, he would know where to head next.

He pulled out the paper and was carefully unfolding it on the ground when one of the most unexpected things in all of Peter's unexpected lives happened.

'Hello, Amelia,' came a voice from behind.

Peter spun around to see Sophie stood, dressed in white, arms spread wide and wearing a warm smile.

'Sophie, my God, you gave me a shock. What are you doing here?'

'I came to find you, we need to have a very brutal, very truthful discussion.' Sophie said taking a step towards the stunned young man on the floor in front of her.

Peter immediately began to fold the paper up and stood. 'Didn't I tell you that you can't go back Sophie? Didn't I tell you that it was dangerous, we'll have Reapers all over us. We don't have much time we need to get this chest buried again and get away before they catch up with us.' Peter frantically began putting everything back into the chest.

At that moment another figure appeared at Sophie's side. He was dressed as Sophie was, but was considerably taller, with wings.

'Bloody hell, an angel!' exclaimed Peter almost falling backwards.

'Don't panic, Amelia, please stay calm. I've come to tell you something very important.'

'What do you mean stay calm? There's a bloody Angel stood next to you. He's dressed like a bloody Reaper without his hat on! It's not something you see every day you know. Does that mean my time is up, or are you delivering a message from God?'

'Not a message from God as such, but perhaps a message from a friend. This is Totfiel he is a friend of mine also. I've come to tell you that I'm like him. How you see me now is not really how I look.'

'So, you've passed over to the other side and now you're an angel, are you?'

'No, I've always been one, well not an angel… oh it's hard to explain. If you just come with me, I can make it all clear to you. It's for your own safety. It's about Alan.'

'Oh, what's he done now?' Peter rolled his eyes. 'Don't tell me, he's broken a commandment or something.'

'Well yes… or maybe no. He hasn't yet, but he's about to get himself into a whole lot of trouble. Now I need you to come with me, and bring the map with you.'

'I don't believe you.'

'What?'

'I don't believe you. How do I know it's really you? You could just be a Reaper in disguise.'

'I'm not a Reaper, I'm your friend. I met you at Sunnydale, you told me your story, we jumped off of that cliff right over there and we entered the concurrence together. It is me, I'm Wicked Mary Lyghtfote, I'm Henry Worsley, I'm asking you to please trust me.'

For a moment Peter didn't move or say a word. He looked Totfiel up and down, the tall Yetziran messenger attempting his nicest smile back. 'Prove it,' he finally said. 'Prove you're an angel like him and I'll come with you.'

Sophie looked up to the sky and held her hands in front of her chest in a praying motion. Suddenly she was blurry, like a bad photo, or how she'd look after about ten cans of lager, and she changed. She grew in height, and a glorious pair of golden wings sprouted from her back. Her brown hair began to curl and grow, turning black and running down from her shoulders until it reached her waist. Her face became more angular, her eyes wider and larger. She was one of the most beautiful things that Peter had ever seen an all of his lives.

'Sophie,' he stuttered.

'Yes, I am Sophie, Zophiel is my true name.' Her voice was the same if a little more ethereal. 'This is how I really look.'

'Impressive.'

'Thank you. Now can we go? Bring the map, and take my hand.'

'One last thing though.' Peter said, pointing to Totfiel. 'Does he not speak?'

'He does,' laughed Zophiel. 'But he never says anything worth listening to.'

Totfiel did speak then, using a word which, although not in any language Peter had ever heard before, was curt, to the point and its sentiment fully understandable.

Peter folded the paper and placed it into the pocket of his jacket before reaching out a hand.

'I always wanted to believe in angels,' he said. 'Alan told me that any talk of angels was poppycock. I never thought that I would ever get to actually meet one, and I certainly never thought that I would ever be friends with one. Tell me what Heaven is like?'

'I wouldn't know,' said Zophiel. 'I've never been there if there is such a place. I come from somewhere called Yetzirah, it's where we're going now. You may think it's quite heavenly really. I prefer it down here though to be honest. Come, we've got places to be.'

Residents of Finlay may have been shocked if any of them had been looking to the north of the town in the direction of the small area of woodland close to Giant's Leap. There was an abrupt bright flash of light, like a sudden and silent explosion, that was over in a second.

# The Git

## Yetzirah

'Please take a seat,' Falafriel said. 'May I call you Peter, or would you prefer Amelia? Our mutual friend Zophiel, or Sophie as you know her has told me all about you. You are a quite remarkable being, let me tell you. It is not every Newman that can take to skipping through the concurrence and living many lives.'

'Oh, there's a few of us. I've met one or two through the years, most of them have been doing it for a lot longer than me according to Alan.'

'Yes. It is Alan who I wish to talk to you about. I gather that Zophiel has told you about the Watchers and the Nephilim.'

'Yes, she's told me a great deal since I arrived here, but she said that the Reapers were sent to catch and stop the Watchers. These Watchers sound like a scary bunch. I can't tell you that I've ever met any though to tell you the truth. I'm sure I'd know if I did.'

'Yes... about Alan.'

'Don't even say it.'

'I'm afraid I have to.'

'You really don't.'

'The person you know as Alan in his last life with you, is in fact one of the Watchers. To us he is known as Armaros, he is the brother of Hele Bene Elim, the leader of the Watchers. I'm afraid to tell you that he, along with their other siblings, have been travelling throughout time causing chaos and feeding on the life forces of others.'

'Oh, for God's sake,' Peter cried. 'For hundreds of years I've been in love with the evil villain's henchman. How depressing. I'll kill him!'

'Quite.' Said Falafriel, 'Although I feel that they may only be acting under his guidance through fear. I was rather hoping that perhaps, if we caught up with him, you could persuade him to help us to stop his brother.'

'Well I could try, but he's a devious bugger himself, you know. In all the time I've known him, after all that we've been through together, he still kept all of this from me. I don't even know where he is though.'

'Yes, this is where your map comes in. Do you mind if I have a brief look at it. Zophiel seems to think that it may have valuable clues as to where to look for him.'

Peter pulled the map from his pocket, unfolded it, and laid it out on Falafriel's desk.

'Ah, Cuneiform!' exclaimed Falafriel. I thought as much. It is very similar to our own Yetziran script, you know. One of the brother's Penemue, who we have locked securely downstairs taught it to the first Newmans.'

'Am I a Newman?'

'Yes you are, a quite extraordinary one by all accounts, dancing your way through the concurrence like you did.'

'I had a good teacher,' muttered Peter, 'who turned out to be a complete git.'

'You see here,' Peter said as they studied the Parchment, 'This is when we last caught up with him, in Calcutta. After that there are only two other destinations before the map ends, London in 1926 where I would have been heading next and finally somewhere called Shulon with no date attached. I've never heard of Shulon, do you know where it is?'

'Yes, Shulon is the place where the first great reset happened. Where, following a battle between the Watchers with their Nephilim children, and the grand Yetziran Army, our leader, the one known to you as God appeared and brought a Great Flood to wipe clean the world. It is where the children of the Watchers were either killed or scattered to the ends of Assiyah, and where the Watcher Generals were taken and incarcerated in Gehinom.'

'We think that's where all of this is heading,' said Zophiel. 'Although we are hoping that Armaros will be willing to help us know for sure, if you can persuade him.'

'And how do you expect me to do that?'

'Go and talk to him. Tell him that you know the truth. If he truly loves you as you say he does, then we have hope.'

'What are you suggesting?'

'I think we should send you back to the night when he left you as Alan.' Zophiel said. 'He left that letter in the casket, so he must visit the trees to place it before he goes. We thought that we could put you back on Assiyah as Amelia.'

'Wait, but I was told that I could never go back. Was that another lie then?'

'Of course you could go back,' Falafriel laughed. 'Why would you not be able to?'

'Alan said it was something to do with glitches in the concurrence and drawing in Reapers.'

'My dear,' Falafriel smiled. 'We are the Reapers. You do not need to fear us anymore. And anyway, you will not be taking her body. We will make the body you wear now look like her. If you do not want to appear as Amelia you can simply go as you are, but we thought that the message would come better from a face he knows.'

'Wait.' Peter interrupted. 'If you say that I can go back as anyone, then I have a better idea.'

## Finlay, Five years ago

Alan Hawke was not in a good mood. He had watched his brother saunter away from the house and back up the street, walking like he didn't have a care in the world. He was behaving like he hadn't just threatened to kill and eat his own brother before destroying everything. He had never felt so helpless in all of the seven hundred and eighty two lives that he had lived.

Amelia had returned to the garden, after flicking on the kettle, leaving Alan to make a pot of tea for them both. The kettle was boiling now, and Alan really should have been getting cups out and preparing the teapot, but there was really not much point anymore.

He knew that this day would come sooner or later, in this life or the next but it had still hit him hard. To leave her would take away everything he lived for and, for a brief moment he thought about ignoring Helel's demands. This would consign both of them to an eternal death though.

He could take that himself but if by leaving there was to be a chance that Amelia could continue to live forever, then it was an easy choice. Perhaps there would be some happy resolution to all of this, and the Yetzirans would give in to Helel's requests. Perhaps they would give the Watchers and their children their own world to live on and be free. Perhaps.

Helel had given him two more days with Amelia, but Alan knew the only reason Helel had done this was to make him suffer more. That night as soon as his wife was asleep, he slipped downstairs and out of the house. The walk through Finlay was not a long one, the town was not that large, and very soon he had passed out of the other side into the fields surrounding it. He lit his way with a torch, but really could have made the journey in the pitch dark without one, he had done it so many times, in so many lives before.

He'd brought a small trowel from his garden shed and, upon reaching the tree began to dig. He thought that this must look very odd, a little old man in the middle of the woods at one o'clock in the morning, digging around at the base of a tree. It did not matter however, as he would not be long dropping the letter into the casket, and besides no one was watching.

'Hello, Analla,' came a familiar voice from behind him and he spun around. His jaw nearly hit the floor. There was a young boy, no older than twelve years old, tall for his age, all pale freckled skin and dark blonde hair. 'Is that letter for me?' said Brid.

'What is going on?' Alan stammered. 'What are you doing here?'

'I'm here to ask you to stop,' the boy said.

'Stop what? I don't know what you mean.' Alan's hand slowly slipped into his jacket pocket, settling on a knife which he carried on him at all times.

'Still talking lies, I see,' sniggered Brid.

'I'm not lying I don't know what's going on. Is this some kind of Reaper trick?'

'It is not, but then maybe there is some trickery involved, Analla. You see it's not just you that can talk in riddles.'

Alan did not speak, the shock on his face was becoming set in stone.

'Perhaps,' the boy said. 'If I click my fingers like this, I can do even more trickery.' He held up his hand and clicked his fingers, causing the look on Alan's face to turn from shock to confusion.

'You see, Jarod, I've learnt a few tricks of my own since you ran away,' said Elswyth, looking down on where he knelt. Her red hair was tied into long plaits, and her stern bossy face frowned at him just as Alan remembered all those lifetimes ago.

Click.

'What's the matter, Robert? Are you seeing ghosts, or are you finally losing your mind?' Galasso looked every bit as tall and handsome as Alan remembered him to be.

'Stop,' Alan muttered.

Click.

'Come now, Francisco.' Atlacoya said, slowly circling the kneeling man. 'Don't tell me that you've forgotten all of the time together. Don't tell me that you would be willing to throw it all away.'

'I said please stop.' He was a little louder now, and he clenched his eyes together.

Click.

'Is it safe to say I have your attention now, Alan?'

He opened his eyes and looked up at Amelia, beautiful and serene, the soul that he had loved for over a thousand years and the woman who he had married and settled down with in Finlay forty years ago.

'This isn't a Reaper trick. This is me, I just thought it important to remind you of all those years we spent together. I didn't even show you George, or Rebecca, Baozhai, or Fatima, or any of the others that you have known me to be.'

'You don't understand, I have to leave.'

'No, you don't understand. I know everything Armaros. I know who you are, all about your brothers and sisters. I know all about the Watchers and the Nephilim, and I am here to tell you that you don't have to do it, you don't have to end everything this way.'

'It's complicated,' Alan muttered, not knowing what else to say.'

'Complicated? Do you know, you were born a gifted child from an immortal race,' Amelia said. 'You have lived hundreds of lifetimes, in the bodies of some of the brightest and greatest people that have ever seen life. You have read thousands of books and seen firsthand the mistakes and brilliance of others, and yet you are probably the most pig ignorant, selfish, stupid being that ever lived on this world or any other!'

Although Alan had only just left Amelia this evening, asleep in her bed unaware of what was happening now, the sight of her brought a tear to his eye.

'But you love me though,' he croaked, his hands resting on the knife at his side but with a tremor.

'Yes, I love you. I have loved you for a thousand years, and if given the chance would probably love you for a thousand more, but that doesn't mean that I don't think you're a total idiot. You're infuriating, you could have done so much more with your time, but no, you chose to meddle, to ruin, to destroy. You are a waste of space, and you deserve to end your days miserable. You're the biggest fool that ever lived! Everything makes sense to me now. Each time you disappeared for years on end, each time you suddenly decided we had to move on to another time, no matter how settled and happy we were. All those times and that bloody map!'

'I didn't follow the plan as fervently as the others,' Alan cried. 'I only did it to keep him off my back. You don't realise how dangerous Helel is. He has threatened to destroy everything. All of this. If he hadn't caught up with me, we could have had years and lives left to us yet.'

'And so you decided to sneak off in the middle of the night and leave me a letter?'

'I had no choice,' he pleaded. 'He said he was going to kill you and then come for me. I couldn't let him do that. And anyway it might not happen, the Yetzirans might give him what he wants, and everything will be fine.'

'I have met the Yetzirans, Alan. They will not give in to terror and threats. Despite what your brother and the rest of your family have been doing, you will not win, and you will be destroyed. You have a chance to stop it though, you have a chance to make things right for everyone.'

'You don't understand. There are other forces at work here, the Yetzirans don't understand what they are up against.'

'Then help us understand,' Amelia growled. 'I can't believe that this is it. That this is how it ends for us. I gave you more years of happiness than anyone else that has ever lived on Earth. We had wonderful lives together.'

'I'm sorry, Amelia. I can't. It's for the best, it really is.' Alan picked up the knife raising it to his chin.

'Wait! Before you go, I want say goodbye to you, Alan.' Amelia knelt down in front of him. Her eyes locked on his. 'After everything we've been through, after the beautiful children we brought into the world, and had to leave behind, after all the good that I thought we'd done in our lives together. I just want to say goodbye before you go, and it ends with you doing your bit to destroy it all in the blink of an eye. What a hero you are.'

'Goodbye, Amelia.' Alan said, 'You are the love of my lives.'

'No, I'm not.' She said.

'Pardon?'

'I'm not the love of your lives.' Amelia smiled. 'I'm a distraction, nothing more.'

'Well, I wouldn't put it that way I…'

But he was gone. The body of Alan Hawke was gone and the golden glow within him had disappeared.

'I always wanted to use one of these.' Zophiel said from behind Alan's body as she twirled her staff. 'Good job, Amelia.'

But Amelia Hawke stayed quiet. Looking at the empty body of the man she loved, and silently weeping.

# Ears in the Walls

## Yetzirah

Falafriel made his way down to the cells where the captured Watchers were being kept. For five days now he had been hopping from one cell to another, interviewing them. Samjaza and Penemue had remained tight lipped and were not giving away any clues as to their brother's final plan. Penemue had been affable enough, chatty, almost friendly to his captors, but would cleverly avoid any talk of how Helel meant to bring about the destruction of Assiyah and Yetzirah, instead nattering on widely about the lives he had inhabited, and the good works he had done spreading knowledge and advancing science and learning on his adopted world.

Samjaza was just as coy in his interactions, but when he spoke about his time on Assiyah, all Falafriel could tell that he did there was live wild lives of excess, which he was very proud of indeed. Any turning of the conversation to Helel or the rest of his siblings would immediately cause him to clam up, with a fearful look in his eye, before asking if he was allowed any visitors and whether anyone other than Falafriel would be allowed to see him.

Each of the Watchers currently in custody had enjoyed their time on Assiyah for different reasons, and Falafriel knew that Armaros, who despite keeping the truth from Amelia for hundreds of years, had a closer affinity to the Newmans, and hoped he would be more willing to assist than his brothers.

The cells were kept in the lower levels of the Machanon Building and had been unused for a great many years as there simply had been no need for them. Most unlawful behaviour had been eradicated from Yetzirah hundreds of thousands of years ago, and those that stepped out of line ever since the creation of Gehinom had simply been sent there to spend their days in the eternal fires of Hell. The Yetzirans were not in the business of forgiveness or rehabilitation of offenders, and once sent to the other place, it was thought to be the last time that that any ne'er-do-wells were ever seen. Which is why it had been such a shock to Falafriel that the Watcher Generals had managed to find their way out of the fires of damnation, and onto Assiyah as time hopping miscreants intent on destroying the Newmans and subsequently Yetzirah through their actions.

He arrived at the door of the cell where Armaros had resided for the past day and waited for the door to be opened. The grey metal door slid to one side, Falafriel stepped in, and was immediately greeted by the captive.

'Ah, Falafriel. I was wondering when an Arch would finally show their face. I trust all is well with you, or are you in a pickle?' Armaros was an impressive sight indeed, returned to his true state. He was very tall, even for a Yetziran, towering over Falafriel. He had finely formed but solid features, blue eyes which glowed with life, and his wings were wide and bronze in colour. Falafriel conceded to himself that he would have been quite in awe and in fear for his safety, if Armaros was not strapped to the far wall and quite unable to move at all.

'Good morning, Armaros,' Falafriel said taking a seat in front of the restrained Watcher. 'I thought it was time perhaps for a little chat.'

'I'd love to, but first, how is Amelia? I trust you are treating her well and she is not confined like me?'

'No, of course not.' Falafriel laughed. 'She is being looked after by her friend Zophiel. They are quite a pair. She is staying in guest quarters and enjoying her time on a new world. We do not need to lock her up, as she is not a danger to us - she is simply a Newman after all.'

Armaros smiled. 'I would suggest that you do not underestimate her, Falafriel. She is no simple Newman. She has seen and experienced things in her long life that would turn your hair even whiter.'

'I don't doubt it, following you around for so long. She is quite fond of you, you know. I would even go so far as to say she loves you. Still. Despite all the lies you told her.'

'I did not lie. I just did not tell her the truth. What would she have thought of me if I had told her who I was, and my real purpose?'

'And what is that, Armaros? What were you actually supposed to be doing?'

'Oh, a bit of tinkering here and there. Isn't that what we were originally put on Assiyah to do?'

'Yes, and you did it well, until you decided that you wanted to rule over the Newmans, and created creatures that set about destroying everything in their path.'

'The Nephilim were just children, angry teenagers at most. They would have settled, and as for the world domination thing, that was more for Helel. He always liked to be in charge. I was glad that you stopped him the first time really, I was just enjoying my life down there, but got roped in because of the whole family thing. When I got the chance to get out of Gehinom and return in Newman form, it really couldn't have been a better outcome for me. I just wanted a quiet life really – one that never ended obviously.'

'And what about your companion?'

Armaros stopped for a moment, his eyes seemed far away, as if they were looking at something very different than a small cell. 'I really did love her... I always have, and I still do, and that is why I had to follow Helel. He would have made her suffer and I could not be responsible for that.'

'But she has suffered, she's suffering now, she thinks you abandoned her.'

'I know, and it is sad, I feel awful for doing this to her but at least she is alive, for now. If Helel doesn't get what he wants, we will all be dead.'

'If you tell me what he plans, I can stop him.'

'I can't tell you, because he has spies, in Yetzirah. Have you ever heard of the wartime phrase on Assiyah 'the walls have ears?' Well, I have it on very good authority that most of the walls on Yetzirah actually are ears, and they're all reporting back to Helel. Once it gets back to him that I have talked he will begin the final battle, and if that fails, he will flick the kill switch and we'll all be gone, some slowly and some in the blink of an eye.'

'You can trust me, Armaros. Tell me his plan, tell me who he has working on Yetzirah, and I can make it all go away. I can ensure that you stay safe.'

'But what about Amelia how can you ensure that she is not hurt in this?'

'I will do my very best, but if you do not help me then we may all be doomed. Let's start with an easy one. Tell me what Helel wants, it might be possible to appease him.'

'If you promise me that you will keep her safe. If you promise that she will not be harmed, then I will tell you. I am overdue dying. I do not care for myself, but Amelia must survive. He must not get to her.'

'I will do everything in my power, Armaros.'

'He wants to change the path of history. He wants things to go back to how they were before we were defeated. He wants the world where the Watchers and their children, the Nephilim can live, untroubled by Yetziran interference. The Newmans would be farmed, their life force pruned and sent to Yetzirah to sustain them, but the world of Assiyah would be controlled by him, and believe me his methods of farming would be... less subtle.'

'That can never happen.' Falafriel exclaimed. 'That's not how it works, surely he must realise that?'

'I'm not sure he does. Helel wishes to rule over a world where the Newmans are subjugated, and their life forces farmed on an industrial level. The way he sees it, he can take control of Assiyah and manage the supply of life force to Yetzirah. If they comply with him, the Yetziran people survive.'

'But even if we agree, what is to stop him changing the deal, once he gets bored?'

'Nothing, and the deal will change trust me. He is quite insane.'

'We are aware of just how unstable he is; he was never really the steadiest of minds. Whatever demands he makes, Armaros, whatever deal he wants to force on us, he will find it hard to come away from it with everything he desires. Why would we agree to anything that harms us?'

Armaros smiled, but it was not in happiness. 'Because the alternative is the complete and utter destruction of Assiyah in an instant, followed by the slow death of a starved Yetziran people.'

'That's quite impossible,' said Falafriel.

'Really? Tell me, Falafriel, have you ever heard of The Brotherhood of Impending Death?'

There are no worse beings in the known universe than a smug Yetziran. They were excruciatingly good at it, which made it all the more worse for anyone unlucky enough to have to witness it. Thankfully for the known universe Araqiel was alone when he wore the widest grin he had ever worn. As it was finally happening, the dream he had cherished for over two hundred thousand years. Everything he had wished for would be in effect within a few short hours.

He hurried along the corridor, trying to look as casual as possible and made it to the elevator just as the doors were starting to close.

'Hold the door!' he called, and was pleased to see the doors begin to open again so that he could enter. His happy mood faded away immediately when he saw who had kept the elevator for him.

'Good afternoon,' he said, his eyes never leaving the floor. 'Are you going to interview the captives again?'

'No,' Falafriel said chuckling a little. 'It is a pointless exercise, none of them are willing to speak to me. I am heading to administration to arrange for them to be returned to Gehinom.'

'Really? Gehinom doesn't have such a great record in being able to keep Watchers locked up. I'm surprised it would even be an option.'

'Their escape from Gehinom was unfortunate and will not be repeated. Our leader Tertira Grammaton has spoken to the management down there personally, and they are aware of the terrible and eternal consequences of not keeping any returned Watchers. It would not end well for Gehinom, it would just end.'

'Good job,' laughed Araqiel, perhaps a little too strongly. It's about time she went back to being a bit Old Testament.'

'Where are you heading?' asked Falafriel.

'I'm off to see Petolatel, who is on duty down on the bottom level. He is overdue an appraisal, so I am going to see him to arrange one. It's been a while since I saw him last, and I had a bit of time on my hands.'

'Ah yes, appraisals. I think you're overdue one with me, Araqiel. We must get our diaries together to sort it. Give Michael a call, will you?'

'Of course,' muttered Araqiel, his eyes returning to examining the floor intently.

There were a few moments of awkward silence, before a resounding ding filled the air, the elevator shuddered to a halt, and the doors began to open.

'This is me,' said Falafriel, as he left. 'I don't see you around much lately, Araqiel. Don't be a stranger, come and see me for a chat when you're free. It's been a while since we had a catch up.'

'Of course,' muttered Araqiel, grateful when the doors closed again, and the elevator began to move.

The remainder of the journey was quick and, as Araqiel stepped out onto the Machanon's gaol level, he was more determined than ever, and the smile had returned to his face.

There was not much to the level, it was just a large room with a central desk. Around the edges of the room were large grey metal doors with no handles or locks to be seen. At the desk sat a stern looking Yetziran, who looked up briefly to see the new visitor.

'Hello, Petolatel, how are you?' Araqiel said, walking around the room and looking at each of the doors. 'How are things? How are the prisoners?'

'Everything is fine.' Petolatel replied. 'The prisoners are secure, and my shift finishes soon. I shall be glad when the cells are empty again, and I can get back to my regular duties.'

'Of course,' said Araqiel from behind him. 'The prayer listening service is always desperately short staffed. I've always been confused at how the Newmans are convinced that speaking to an unseen entity will make their lives better.'

'We do listen to them.' Petolatel replied.

'But you rarely act.'

'True, but if we acted on all the prayers, we heard then Assiyah would be an unconscionable place to live. Everyone would be rich, everyone would be happy, and no one would suffer. Their world would be a very dull place indeed very quickly.'

Unlike the Newmans on Assiyah, Petolatel never suffered. The blow that killed him was quick and relatively pain free.

Amelia was sat in Zophiel's apartment drinking a cup of tea, that Zophiel had managed to make using something she called a replicator. It wasn't the worst cup of tea she had ever tasted in her life, but it was pretty close. She was just going to find a sink so that she could secretly pour it away, when the alert came through on the big screen on the wall. The letters were large and flashing, but she couldn't understand a word of it.

'What does that mean, Sophie?' she called to Zophiel who was in the other room.

'What does what mean?' Zophiel's head was wrapped in towelling as she had just got out of the shower. She saw the screen as she walked through and immediately froze. 'Oh,' she said her hand raising to her mouth.

'What's the matter, is someone dead?' Amelia asked.

'No,' muttered Zophiel. 'Very much the opposite in fact. It's a message from Falafriel. I have to go.' She ran towards the door.

Amelia jumped up. 'Wait for me!'

'You cannot come, Amelia. It's going to be dangerous.'

'Do you think I can't handle a bit of danger, Sophie. Do you think I'm afraid of death. I've died a hundred times or more. I'm coming with you. Where are we going?'

# The Golden God
## Babylon, 1724BCE

Ancient Babylon was a glorious city to live in, if you were one of the lucky ones who were born into wealth, and found that you had all of the benefits of rich living in the greatest city in the world at your disposal.

For Allamu Ea-Nasir, who was possibly the wealthiest merchant in the known civilised world at this moment in time, life couldn't be much better. He had an army of slaves, he had doubled his wealth in the past year, and he lived in a palace in the north of the city which would rival even the king's. As he sat at the end of the great hall in a chair which was whispered in the city to be even more ornate that the great king's throne, Allamu was not however wearing a face of happiness and contentment, in fact he was quite furious.

He idly waved his hand, signalling to the doorman at the far end of the room that the visitors were to be brought in for their audience, although to call them visitors would be doing them a great service.

The great doors opened, and three prisoners were pushed into the room, their hands and feet bound by bronze shackles which limited their movement to nothing more than a pained shuffle. The three bearded men were filthy, and Allamu could smell their stench from the other end of the room as soon as they entered, causing him to signal to one of his attendants to raise a spice bag to the great merchant's nose.

The prisoners had been kept hanging in chains in the underground depths of the palace for months, being given just enough bread and water to keep them alive, their bodies kept on the borderline between life and death.

This was until yesterday when they had been visited by Allamu's seers Beltis and Gula, two old women who had wandered into the city from the desert a year ago and walked straight into the palace where they had been welcomed by Allamu like long lost family. Since that day they had been ever present in the palace, offering advice and guidance, or being found in their private apartments conducting terrible experiments on unfortunate slaves sent to them by their master. They were greatly feared by all in the palace except Allamu, who was the only one that did not mutter prayers under their breath or make the sign of the protective horn under their clothing whenever the sisters passed. When the crones had visited the prisoners yesterday, they had ordered all guards out of the room, which they had done gladly, before slowly cutting the throats of the poor men hung from the walls. Their lives had ended, but only for a short moment.

If any outsiders had witnessed what had happened as they died, they would have cried magic, necromancy, and witchcraft, and would have dropped to their knees and prayed to the gods for mercy. No one but the sisters had been there however when the prisoners returned to life, and the wide gashes on their throats magically healed.

Now, as the hobbled prisoners were brought before their captor, they all in unison fell to their knees.

'Well look at what we have here,' Allamu said joyously. 'The wanderers return! I hear the three of you have been on a little holiday.'

'Brother, free us from these chains,' said one. 'Is this some kind of sick joke? Why have you kept us like this?'

'Because, Samjaza I need to know if you have betrayed me. From what I hear from my sources in Yetzirah, you almost gave yourself up willingly to the Reapers.'

'We never told them anything, brother,' Samjaza wore a nervous smile. 'Well I certainly didn't, I'm not so sure about either of them.' He nodded to the two other prisoners to his left, and was sure that if they hadn't been chained like himself, they would have killed him there and then, such was the look in their eyes.

'Penemue? What about you? I hear that at least when you were caught you were doing what you were supposed to be doing and spreading plague. How am I to know that you haven't given us all up once the Reapers got you? Have you been telling tales to your newfound friends?'

The prisoner in the centre of the three gazed up at his captor. 'I have stayed quiet, Helel, but I know that there is no cast iron way to convince you of that. I did not speak a word to them. Make your own decision. You will anyway.' Penemue lowered his head once more, the situation was out of his control, and he knew that arguing the point with his powerful brother was pointless.

'And what of you, Armaros? I hear that you were betrayed by your Newman mate. My people in Yetzirah say that she tricked you. But has your love of the Newmans caused you to flap your mouth once they had you in a cell?'

'As Penemue said,' the final prisoner muttered. 'You will do what you will do whatever. I did not give us up, I wouldn't, what would be the point? You have made it very clear to us the consequences if we do not carry through with the plan. We are all here with you now. If you say that it is time, then I am with you.'

Allamu nodded sagely, stood from his chair, and walked towards the men, keeping the spice bag close to his nose.

'God's you stink. The girls said you gave off a particular odour, but it's worse than cat's business.'

By the side of his chair the two sisters sniggered a little and held their noses.

'The incompetence of the three of you in being taken so early has forced the issue. I had hoped that you would be stronger now, ready for the final fight. I say we leave here now and meet at Shulon. I am bored with waiting for my revenge, and I now know how I am going to win this.'

'There is an addition to the plan?' Samjaza asked, wondering when his chains would be removed, and he could get a long bath.

'There is indeed, Samjaza, but not one that should bother you, although you have a great part to play in it.'

'Anything,' his brother said. 'You know that I would do anything to help, especially if it means being freed to wash and drink wine.'

'I would expect nothing less from you.' Helel circled the prisoners until returning to his chair, where sat again and leant back. 'Unlike the three of you I have been very busy since we last met, I have positively danced through the ages, causing death and destruction wherever I went and then waiting in the concurrence to greedily feed on the life force as it arrived to meet me. I have become strong, stronger than you would believe.'

Armaros looked up to his brother and then to his side, where his sisters, Azazel and Sariel's constant sniggering rose to almost a fever pitch. They almost danced with excitement, they knew something, and suddenly Armaros for the first time felt stiff with fear.

'You see, life force is a funny thing,' Helel continued. 'I always thought that you could never get enough of it. The more I gobbled up the poor souls in the void, the larger and stronger I became, and I imagined that I could just go on eating it forever until I decided that the time was right for the final battle.

'But in the last life that I took over before this one, as I took over the body, I felt something very different inside, as if the life force within me was bursting to get out, as if whatever body I inhabited was full to the brim and could not contain much more of it.'

The prisoners looked up at their brother as he spoke, something was changing within him. They could see the veins on his arms and in his neck bulging and expanding, but they glowed as if his blood were becoming molten.

'What have you done, Helel?' Penemue asked, his voice shaking. His brother stood and slowly outstretched his arms which were now beginning to emit a golden light. Helel's body seemed to grow in size and great golden wings suddenly appeared from his back. Around the great hall the guards began to shift nervously, and back away towards the doors.

'Don't leave, boys,' their master called, and with a wave of his now glowing hand, the doors slammed shut as his once loyal servants began to run towards them to escape. 'You can't leave the party so soon!' Helel called as he threw his hands forwards, and a great beam of light shot from them, hitting the screaming men as they tried to escape the room. As the light hit them their bodies shrivelled to barren husks and their life forces were sucked back towards the laughing Helel, disappearing inside of him, and making him grow in size. He drank in their life, savouring the moment before looking back at his brothers manacled before him.

'I have ascended, brothers,' he smiled. He was a glowing form now, almost doubled in size, and gave off so much heat and energy that it made his brothers wince to be near him. Behind his chair the sisters Sariel and Azazel were now hysterical with laughter, dancing and screaming, a glow starting within them also. 'I have unlocked a power that I did not think was possible and I now know that I have more then enough strength to finish the plan.' Helel stepped forwards to within a few yards of his brothers.

'We are with you,' cried Samjaza. 'We are with you brother.'

'Of course you are, or should I say you will be,' the glowing figure replied.

'What do you mean?' said Penemue.

'Well it's just that I was thinking,' Helel said. If I can grow my power through taking in the energy of a simple Newman who has lived only one life, what could I gain from eating perhaps... A Watcher.'

'No, brother!' cried Samjaza, but it was to be his last words as Helel reached out and grabbed his brother by the face. His life force was drawn from him, the energy gained from living countless stolen lives throughout time, and even more eaten in the concurrence. The body inhabited by Samjaza dropped in a heap to the floor. He was gone.

Helel screamed as his brother's power ran into him, his body grew once more, and he seemed to be floating off of the ground now.

'Oh, I like it, I like it a lot!' he shouted. 'What a rush! I think I want more!' He looked at Penemue, who simply screamed knowing what was about to happen.

A large golden hand took hold of Penemue's head enclosing it and squeezing. The life force flowed from another brother into the golden being, and Helel grew once more now almost touching the ceiling with his size. Again, Helel screamed as he took in the power of the drained Watcher, it was a terrible, deafening sound that echoed around the great hall, and rang in the ears of Armaros who now knew his fate.

Armaros watched as the body of Penemue slumped to the floor beside him. He knew his time was short and he would soon be joining his brothers who were still shackled to him, another drained husk. This was it. He looked up at the monstrous god that Helel had become and waited for it all to end.

Helel looked down at him.

'I think it's about time, Armaros,' he said.

# The Wrong Box

## Yetzirah

'I fear the final battle is upon us,' Falafriel said solemnly as his team arrived in his office. 'If all goes well it'll be over in a short while...'

'And if not?' Zophiel asked.

'Then today is the day that the fate of our world is decided,' he replied.

'And mine is destroyed, or taken over by psychotic despots and their gigantic evil children,' Amelia added.

'Yes, quite,' said Falafriel. 'Believe it or not we do have an actual plan in place, there are however a couple of things we need to do to make it work.'

'Can I just ask,' Amelia said. 'Who came up with his plan? Because from what I can see you haven't exactly got a great track record so far.'

'The majority of the plan is mine and Hariton's however, there has been some input from Armaros in this.'

Amelia choked a little, 'Are you joking? For a start he's a proven liar, he's related to the people we are trying to stop, in fact he is one of them, and it may or may not have passed you by, but he has actually just escaped from your custody and returned to his evil brother.'

'I am aware of this,' Falafriel said, 'and I should just say that his escape was actually part of the plan.'

Amelia didn't respond but simply threw her hands up in disbelief.

'Let me explain,' Falafriel continued. 'Zophiel, yourself and I will go down to Assiyah. By the time we arrive the battle, that has already happened many thousands of years ago, should already be in full swing. If it were to be left with no interference the result would be as it happened. The Watchers and the Nephilim will be defeated, and Helel and his generals, including Armaros, will be captured and sent to Gehinom. However, this time Helel plans to turn up in another body and use his newfound strength, which he has spent years amassing, to turn the tide and win the battle. Are you following me so far?'

'I think so,' Zophiel said. 'Old Watcher generals will be fighting and losing, but suddenly new improved Watcher generals will turn up to change history.'

'Exactly. We will be there simply to oversee proceedings and step in if needed. If all else fails Tertira Grammaton will also be there as she was present at the original battle.'

'So I'm actually going to meet God?' Amelia was a little shell shocked.

'Yes, if you want to call her that. We see her more as a CEO, overseeing proceedings if you will, although she is a CEO that is Omnipotent, Omnipresent, and has a terrible temper when things don't go her way.'

'I've met her!' piped up Attalius grinning. ''She thanked me personally for saving Assiyah and the Yetziran race the last time I did it.'

There was an audible groan in the room heard by everyone, but Attalius it seemed, whose smile had not wavered. Falafriel decided to not give Attalius the satisfaction of commenting further on what he remembered as being a very awkward meeting between all powerful being and an idiot with an overblown sense of his own importance.

'Now there is another unfortunate element to this,' he continued, 'in that Helel has a number of spies working for him here on Yetzirah. If at any point Helel feels the fight is not going his way, they will act.'

'Act?' asked Totfiel.

''Yes, they will go to the room where the concurrence is kept and destroy it, erasing Assiyah in an instant, killing anyone who happens to be inside it at the time, and consigning Yetzirah to a slow painful death as we lose our immortality and begin to die.'

'And you want us to go down there?' the colour had suddenly drained from Zophiel's face.

'Oh, I am not worried in the slightest.' Falafriel said chirpily. 'The fact that we know their plan, thanks to Armaros, means that we are always one step ahead. We'll be quite safe, and all of this should be over very quickly.'

'Or all of us,' muttered Amelia.

Falafriel ignored Amelia's comment and continued.

'Attalius, Totfiel and Caphriel, I need you to go to Hariton's apartment. He is preparing a device for you which he says is vitally important. Once you have it, head down to the concurrence, complete the task he sets you, and protect it at all costs.'

'I don't understand why I can't come with you and the ladies,' Attalius said. It sounds like you're headed into quite a fight. You know that I'm at my best when I'm in the thick of the action.'

The time for cutting put downs was not now, and Falafriel didn't quite have the heart to tell Attalius that in the thick of the action is the very last place that he should be for everyone's sake. Falafriel also knew that it was such a simple task that any idiot could do, and even Attalius couldn't make a mess of it.

'No,' he said. 'Attalius, I need you to be my main man here. Do your job and you'll be remembered forever as the one that saved the Yetziran race.'

'For a second time,' Attalius added.

'Precisely,' Falafriel said, ignoring the incredulous looks from every other being in the room. 'Now,' he continued, 'if everyone does their bit, we should all be back in this room by teatime.'

'Before we finish, can I just ask a stupid question.' Caphriel had been quiet up until now.

'Go ahead,' said Falafriel. 'There are no stupid questions.'

'You told us that Helel has been travelling throughout Assiyah's history, causing millions of deaths and then consuming the life force of those he has killed.'

'Correct.'

'Well, what if he's got so powerful that we can't beat him.'

Falafriel laughed louder than he had done for a very long time.

'Just how powerful do you think he could have got? It's not as if he will have transformed into some huge, all powerful, evil god or anything. I was wrong. That was a very stupid question, Caphriel.'

Totfiel placed the replacement box on the table next to the concurrence. 'They look exactly the same, he's done a good job of copying it,' he said. 'If you didn't know better, you'd never know that it was just an empty box.'

'Of course he's done a good job. He's obviously some kind of simple minded genius, and he's been helped by the fact that he designed and made the original, oaf.' Attalius remarked, as he grabbed the box from the table and examined it. 'Hariton said that it was simply a case of unplugging the original and plugging in the new one, so let's get this done and get out of here, before Araqiel arrives.'

'Do you ever shut up, Attalius,' Totfiel barked. 'You have done nothing but whine on since we left Hariton's place.

'I speak when I think that there is something sensible to say. It's not my fault that I am often the only sensible person in the room.'

'You're always the biggest idiot in the room.'

'Jealousy is not a nice element of anyone's personality. There are those that can contain it well and not look terrible, and then there's people like you. You seem to forget that Falafriel put me in charge of this operation.'

'Can both of you shut up please?' Caphriel said as he began to unplug the concurrence. 'This is actually a really tricky job that I don't want to get wrong.'

'Which is exactly why a dunderhead like you should be the last one doing it!' snapped Attalius, snatching the concurrence box from the table.

'Be careful with that!' shouted Totfiel, grabbing the box and pulling it from Attalius's grasp. 'There's a whole world and all its history in there, as well as my best friend. If you break it, you'll ruin everything.'

'No, that's the fake one,' said Caphriel. 'This is the real concurrence.' He waved the unplugged box in his hand, which Attalius immediately took from him.

'I shall look after it, I am in charge.'

'You are not. Falafriel only told you that to massage your bloated ego, you fool.' Totfiel made a grab for the other box and Attalius immediately lifted it over his head, out of Totfiel's grasp.

'Give it back!' shouted Caphriel, who was the tallest of the three and attempted to snatch it.

Attalius jumped out of the way and ran around to the other side of the table. 'It's mine. It's mine! I am in charge, and I will look after it!' he shouted. He was dancing from side to side now, as the other two tried to take it from him.

Totfiel launched himself at Attalius, bundling him to the floor, and Caphriel dived onto both of them, until they were simply a wrestling mass of Yetziran idiocy, that only stopped when both boxes went flying across the floor hitting the wall on the other side of the room.

At that moment the door opened and Araqiel and two other Yetzirans walked in. Araqiel saw the two identical boxes on the floor.

'Oh.' Said Attalius.

# Fields of the Nephilim
## Shulon, East of Eden

The rains had started on the 17$^{th}$ day of the 7$^{th}$ month, as Noah had been told they would. He had made all of his preparations and had built the Ark as he had been directed by the holy messenger. It sat now in the base of the valley, dominating all around it. Nothing of its size had ever been constructed in the past and it would be many, many years until anything of its like would be seen in this world again. The animals had come, as he had expected, they had been loaded aboard and now, right on time after thirty-nine days of rain, it would soon be the time for the Great Ark to float.

Noah had sealed the craft and had stood looking out over the valley waiting for the flood to begin. At the far end of the valley, also as expected he saw the first sight of the Nephilim. God had told him that the Watchers and their foul children would come and try to destroy the Ark, that they would try to force God's hand and make the Heavens give in to their demands. This sight of the giant beast men charging towards him would have been terrifying on its own, but they were supported by a host of Watchers, tall, winged demigods capable of terrible destruction and led by their Generals Helel Bene Elim and his five powerful siblings.

Suddenly the plain was filled with a brilliant light which poured from the opposite end of the valley, and God's holy warriors arrived in a flood of their own, swarming forwards and striking the Nephilim front line like a powerful wave, forcing them back and keeping them away from the Ark.

The battle was terrible, with great losses on both sides, Angels killed Nephilim with their swords of flame, and the giant Nephilim replied tearing into the Heavenly Host with brutal force. The Watchers led by their Generals used heavy weapons of wood and stone to decimate the Heavenly line, and still the rains came down.

Noah and his family, who watched from the Ark, were helpless and feared for their lives, such was the brute power of the Watchers and the Nephilim, who edged closer to them forcing the army of God into retreat.

It was as the first Nephilim came within touching distance of the Ark that something magical happened. A light, so bright filled the valley, forcing Noah and his family to cover their eyes. He had been warned that this moment may come at some point. He had been told that when God's light shone, no man should lay their eyes upon the Great Creator, and he should take all of his family below deck and wait for the Ark to float, which he did without question.

As soon as the light hit the Watchers and their Nephilim children, they knew that their battle was over. Many of the Nephilim were frozen in fear, many ran. The Watchers dropped to their knees and begged for their souls, only their Generals stood to face their inevitable fate. A slight but powerful figure walked slowly towards them, through the bodies of the fallen.

God had arrived.

'It is over Helel,' Tertira Grammaton, known to those that lived on this world as God, spoke.

The tall Watcher General shrugged 'Oh well, it was worth a try,' he said, turning to his siblings who had themselves now dropped to their knees. 'Get up you fools,' he growled. 'Face your destiny like the gods you are!'

'It is too late,' Tertira said, with a wave of her arm. 'They are gone now, sent to cells in Gehinom where they will spend eternity regretting their decisions.' Each of the Generals toppled onto the floor, their bodies nothing more than empty husks, their souls sent to Hell. 'Are you ready to join them?' she asked.

'I will take my punishment, but I will return.' Helel rumbled, sticking out his chest, his face defiant to the last.

'Doubtful,' the Almighty said, waving her hand once more. 'Goodbye Helel Bene Elim,' and she watched as the leader of the Watchers fell to the floor, joining his siblings in an eternity of torment.

She was about to leave when she heard a gentle cough behind her, as if someone was trying to get her attention. She spun around to see two Newman men and two Newman women stood. One of the men stepped forwards.

'I think you will find that rumours of my eternal demise were greatly exaggerated,' he said.

'What?' The Almighty said.

Suddenly the man lit up like a golden flame, his body burst open revealing a being of pure light within. It grew in size until it was almost as tall as the Ark itself, and it looked down on Tertira Grammaton and laughed.

'I am Helel Bene Elim, returned from Gehinom, a thousand times more powerful than I was before, and I will have my revenge.'

'Really?' said Tertira, waving her hand once more.

Nothing happened.

'I am not so weak that a puny God such as you can harm me anymore.' Helel laughed.

Behind him the two women began to glow and grow, increasing to the size of Nephilim, wide grinning mouths of flame, and fists made of fire.

Helel enjoyed the sudden look of terror on the Almighty's face. All around the Nephilim and Watchers, who until this time had been knelt in submission, began to stand and cheer.

'And what about your brothers. Where are they?' Tertira said.

'Armaros is here,' Helel said, pointing to the man who had appeared with them. 'Very soon he will have our power. Penemue and Samjaza are dead to this world. They failed me, and they knew the punishment. They are still here, but within me, I can hear their sweet cries in my ears like a distant echo.'

Tertira looked at Armaros stood in front of her. Her first instinct of course was to send him straight to Gehinom, but for some reason she decided not to, there was something about him.

'And now Tertira I will destroy you and eat your soul, making me the most powerful being in the universe.' He pointed both hands at The Almighty and sent a stream of fire towards her.

But it didn't hit her. It was blocked by Armaros, who was now glowing himself, a burning bronze which escaped from within him and covered his body in flames.

Helel stared at Armaros in shock. 'What are you doing?' he cried.

'You are not the only one that was busy in their time on this world.' Armaros said, his body growing in size. 'But I didn't have to consume poor souls to gain power. I did it through living. I didn't waste my time on Assiyah being hateful and petty, I didn't go out of my way to hurt and kill. I lived lives, I loved people, I made a positive difference in the world. Something you will never understand.'

'If you are not with me, you are against me Armaros.' Helel growled. 'Sisters, Kill him!'

Azazel and Sariel threw themselves at their brother, but were stopped in mid-air with one swipe of his arm. They hung there suspended for a moment, the fear and shock in their faces plain for all to see. Armaros flicked his wrist sending them flying backwards into the throng of Nephilim and Watchers, who were suddenly very confused as to what was going on.

'You know you cannot defeat me, brother.' Helel screamed.

'It's not about defeating you,' Armaros said, and he sent a bolt of energy at Helel, which struck the golden giant in the chest staggering him. 'It was never about defeating you.'

He fired another, although it burnt his body to do it and Armaros fell to his knees. The bolt struck Helel again, this time full in the face. The huge Golden God staggered backwards momentarily, before righting himself and advancing on his brother.

Armaros was badly burnt, his skin blackened and smouldering, his breath rasping, as his brother, a giant made of flame and energy towered over him. Helel wrapped a huge hand around his brother and picked him up, raising him close to his face.

'If you were not here to destroy me brother, then why are you here? You're a fool.'

'A fool?' choked Armaros. 'Me? A fool I probably have been but not today.' His breath came in tight groans, his long life was over. With a last effort he spoke. 'Today I'm not a fool, just a distraction.'

No one had noticed the small old Scottish lady making her way through the crowds of Nephilim and Watchers, using a long staff with a glowing blue crystal end as a makeshift walking stick. No one on either side had even batted an eyelid when she made her way behind the flaming giant that was Helel Bene Elim and positioned herself at his left foot, or even wondered why she was wearing welding goggles. In fact, even if anyone present had decided to glance in the direction of the little old lady, they would have thought it was an illusion, a trick of the mind. How could it possibly be real?

As Armaros spoke there was an explosion of red flame, brighter than the sun which made everyone, even Tertira Grammaton momentarily blinded.

Smoke filled the air, and the golden giant was gone.

Tertira waved her way through the smoke to where he once stood and found that there was only man laying his body burnt and his breathing ragged. He laughed as he saw the Almighty approach him.

'You lose,' he croaked. 'You are destined to die, all of us are. This battle down here on Assiyah is purely a distraction. Did you not realise that if I wanted to end it all, and end all of Yetzirah all I had to do was destroy that precious little box that you rely on so much. That tiny thing where all of Assiyah, the concurrence, and the life force that you Yetzirans so desperately rely upon is kept. I have people in Yetzirah controlling the portal, you are stuck on your pitiful world now. Destroy me if you like, it doesn't matter anymore. Very shortly this place will be gone and everyone here with it. Including you, Tertira. This isn't just the day that the world ended, it is also the day that I killed God!'

'I think that you'll find that Araqiel will not be successful today.' Falafriel said, suddenly appearing over Tertira's shoulder. 'You see, when he tries to carry out your orders and destroy the concurrence and everything in it, he will find that he is doing nothing more than destroying an empty box. We switched them.'

'You lie!' cried the man his voice weak and pitiful. 'You lie!'

'That's one of the annoying facts about me, Helel. I never lie. By the time this is over, and I have returned to Yetzirah, Araqiel will be residing in a cell deep within Gehinom as will many of his accomplices. There they will give up the names of every one of the hilariously named Brotherhood of Impending Death. I hear that the demons of Gehinom are very adept at getting information out of lost souls.'

'Lies!' the man whimpered. 'You cannot win. I will return...again.'

'I don't think so, you don't catch me out twice. Goodbye, Hele Bene Elim.' Tertira said, and with a click of her fingers the light that was the Watcher general was extinguished.

Almost as one the Nephilim and Watchers dropped to their knees once more. It was over for them.

Amelia found the horribly burnt body of her once husband Alan in the centre of a giant scorch mark in the dirt. The glowing light within him had gone and all that remained was a man lying very still. At first, she thought him to be dead, but as she turned him over, he let out a crackled breath.

'I knew you wouldn't let me down,' he tried to smile but the pain was too great.

'Of course not,' the old lady laughed. 'I'm the greatest warrior to ever come from Finlay's Hollow.'

'You're nothing more than a weak minded fool with delusions of grandeur, boy,' he whispered.

'I brought you a gift,' Amelia said as she withdrew two short blades from her clothing.

'I love you; you mad old bird.' Armaros croaked.

'And I love you, idiot.' Amelia said. 'Time to leave, we're going on an adventure, although it may only be a short one.' she said, and plunged both blades home.

Zophiel appeared out of the smoke and found the body of her friend laid over the Watcher. They had died in each other's arms, as they had done so many times before. Tears appeared and she wiped them quickly from her eyes. Her friend was gone.

Tertira Grammaton turned to Falafriel beside her. 'At some point I want a full explanation as to what went on here, and why you never thought to tell me about it sooner.'

'Of course,' said Falafriel, his smile doing an absolutely pitiful job at masking his fear.

'And please tell me that the box is safe, Falafriel.'

'Yes, don't worry, your greatness, I have the best people on the job, the very best.' He placed his hands together, as if in prayer. 'However, I do think it would be wise if we were to try to leave this place before we all drown.'

The rain started to get even stronger, and the Ark started shifting on its wooden supports. The flood was coming and the great reset of Assiyah had begun.

Tertira and the other Yetzirans needed no further encouragement and in unison they touched their hands together and looked upwards waiting to be drawn upwards to Yetzirah.

Nothing happened.

## Yetzirah

Hariton did not know what had led him to head down to the concurrence room. Perhaps it was the gormless look on Attalius and his companions, as he had explained the tasks they had to complete. He had never been brave by any stretch of the imagination. It was always everyone else's job to deal with all the action side of things. He had no real wish to get involved in all of that business but here he was.

When he arrived in the room, shortly after Araqiel and his colleagues had entered, all was chaos.

Moments earlier when Araqiel had entered the room, Attalius had immediately leapt to his feet and thrown himself at Araqiel stopping the Deputy Arch from grabbing the boxes. The wrestled to the floor, their feet kicking the boxes which spun across the room.

Araqiel's companions dived towards the boxes, but Totfiel was quicker. He grabbed one of them, but watched helplessly as the other was kicked away from his grasp.

Caphriel had got to his feet just in time to be struck in the side of the face by a fist which knocked him sideways. Luckily for him Caphriel's skull was unnaturally thick, the blow, which would have knocked anyone else unconscious, simply jarred him momentarily, and he charged at the intruders shouting at the top of his voice.

Attalius and Araqiel had each other by the throat, neither submitting and both quite pink in the face.

'Get off me, you bloody fool,' hissed Attalius, and he took one hand off of Araqiel's throat to slap him roughly across the face, an action which Araqiel copied.

'I have one!' shouted Totfiel, waving the box in his hand as he tried to get to his feet. He was struck on his back and was sent sprawling to the floor again letting go of the box which flew across the room, bouncing off of the wall and landing in a dented heap on the floor.

Hariton had seen enough, sooner or later the concurrence, whichever of the two boxes it was now, was going to be destroyed. He pulled the tool out of his pocket and walked to where Attalius and Araqiel were rolling around on the floor pathetically slapping each other's faces. He pressed the tool into the back on Araqiel's neck. The electric shock which ran through the deputy arch's body subdued him immediately, and Araqiel's unconscious body rolled into the floor. His two colleagues quickly followed him.

Attalius jumped to his feet a little quicker than he had planned due to the shock of electricity which had run through Araqiel's body into his own.

The unconscious bodies of Araqiel Mardero and his companions lay at the feet of Attalius, next to a smashed black box.

'We had it covered, Hariton,' he said.

'It looked like it,' Hariton laughed. 'I've never felt so not needed,' he pointed to the smashed box. 'I'm glad that isn't the real one.'

'I really hope you're right,' Totfiel said.

'Of course I'm right,' he replied. 'I'm always right. I have never been wrong.'

'Then it's all over then, one way or another.' Caphriel said holding the other box in his hand. 'We better be careful with this one, or we'll be in real trouble.' He passed it to Hariton, who put it back on the table.

After Araqiel and the other members of The Brotherhood of Impending Doom were taken into custody, they left to return to Falafriel's office, all of them feeling very smug with themselves.

It was in the elevator that Totfiel posed the question.

'Hariton, you did remember to plug it back in again, didn't you?'

Twenty minutes later, after a quick trip back to the concurrence room, they arrived at Falafriel's office.

'Mission complete!' declared Attalius as they burst into the office and came face to face with a very soggy Falafriel, Zophiel, and the Lord God Almighty.

# Epilogue One
## Amilly, Loiret, France 1785

Elise and Emmanuel Chartres had lived for four happy years in their small cottage on the outskirt of Amilly in the northwest of France. They had good relations with their neighbours ever since arriving in the area. Soon after moving into the cottage, they had adopted two children Alexander and Babette, who's own parents had died in a terrible incident six months earlier. They loved the children as if they were their own, and the children were glad to have found a safe and happy home with people that cared for them.

The Chartres were well known for their large garden parties to which everyone in the village was invited, no matter what background they were from.

It was at one of these garden parties, one Sunday afternoon when they were visited by an angel.

Elise had returned to the kitchen to collect another tray of pastries, leaving Emmanuel outside, playing the friendly and gracious host, telling tall tales to an adoring audience of townspeople, whilst their children played with their friends in the sunshine.

The angel was sat at the large wooden table a pastry in her hand, contemplating taking a bite.

'Don't give in to temptation, dear,' Elise said. 'Your unprepared Yetziran stomach will not thank you for it.'

'It looks so good though, you're a wonderful cook,' Zophiel said.

'Nothing to do with me,' Elise laughed. 'I couldn't boil an egg. It's all Emmanuel.'

There was a moment of quiet, which was not uncomfortable in the least. Elise broke the silence.

'I knew you'd catch up with us eventually. Are you here to take us in?'

Zophiel smiled at her friend. 'Not at all. According to everyone on Yetzirah, you're both dead. I won't be telling anyone different.'

'Good,' Elise said arranging the pastries on the tray. 'We are happy here and wish to see the children grow up and be happy. Once they are grown and have families of their own, we will move on. I still have places and times I want to visit. Emmanuel and I have a lot of years to live together yet.'

'I'm glad,' Zophiel was still eyeing the pastry hungrily. 'And I'm a little jealous. Who knows, I may decide to join you again in the future, or perhaps the past.'

'I hope you do, and I look forward to it,' Elise laughed. 'I don't think this world is finished with you yet, Sooty Mary.'

Zophiel laughed, taking a bite of the pastry, and immediately regretting it.

# Epilogue Two

## New York, Present Day

The corner of 86$^{th}$ and Lexington was home to one of the Grim Reaper's favourite coffee shops, somewhere that he always saved himself a bit of time to visit when he was in the area, as he was today.

The job had been a straightforward one, involving an unfortunate young lady and a bus. He extracted the life force from the woman and placed it in the small cloth bag, ready for one of the messengers to come to collect it.

Stepping onto the sidewalk he decided to take a moment out of his day and entered the coffee shop, helping himself to a coffee and taking a seat. It wasn't even midday and he had already collected 70,000 souls. Attalius was bored out of his mind.

Ever since the end of his time as a time travelling Reaper, and his return to the daily grind of life force collection, he had felt very underappreciated in his role. It obviously suited that fool Falafriel to keep him away from the action in this pit of a job. Why hadn't he been allowed to stay on the front line, fighting evil throughout history? They had told him that all of the Watchers had been caught, but he was sure that there were some still out there. Falafriel obviously just wanted all the glory for himself.

As he drank his second cup of coffee, he reached into the pocket of his jacket and pulled out the tip of his Reaper staff, a secretly purloined memento of his time in a much more exciting job.

Why not? Why shouldn't he start up his own private enterprise, hunting down the rogue Watchers that were still hopping through time and causing chaos.

He walked out of the coffee shop and onto a sidewalk frozen in time. The poor woman was still floating in mid-air in front of the bus, and the small brown cloth bag containing her life force was still sat on the ground below her, still uncollected.

'Tardy behaviour,' he said aloud. 'It wouldn't have happened on my watch.'

Holding his broken staff in front of him, he slashed the air causing a black hole to appear on the edge of the road.

It was time to defeat evil once more.

He dived through the hole in the air which closed behind him.

With no one left on Assiyah left to collect the life forces of the dead, the great New York Zombie outbreak began.

# Final Epilogue
## Highlands, Scotland

The giant Finlay McBray sat by the edge of the loch and sang the song that his father had taught him many years before. The song that their ancestors from Shulon had passed down to them; the song to bring a wife. His voice was low in pitch and resonated around the valley, echoing off of the mountains surrounding the place he had made his home.

Each night for ten years he had repeated this same performance. As he sang the sound of his voice hit the surface of the loch, sending ripples across the water. With each line of the song Finlay dreamt of a time when a wife would find him, and save him from his loneliness.

As he finished the final verse he stood, rising himself to his great height, and turning to return to his bed for another night. He took one last look to the hills, seeing the trees at the top of the hills moving in the evening breeze.

Except one tree was moving away from the others. A shadow on the skyline was moving, coming down into the valley and down to the edge of the loch.

When the first men arrived in the valley many years later, they found the remains of Finlay McBray. His loving wife was in his arms, laid in the hollow that he had made in the side of the mountain. Their children had long since moved on to find partners of their own, and whether the descendants of Finlay McBray live on today, we will probably never know.

The village of Finlay's Rest was born, created from everything Finlay and his wife had left. The bones of Finlay and his wife had been used to form the foundations of the great hall where they now sat on a night, and from where the Lairds over the years would rule and govern the people. Their hair had been used to make the thatch that covered the houses and keep the rain out, their hands were the small boats used by the first men to venture out onto the Loch each day to catch fish. Their hearts had been buried deep within the earth under the village of Finlay's Rest, where they remain today.

As everyone knows that within the heart of a giant there is a great and powerful magic, and two hearts that stay together can only ever bring long life, love, and happiness.

Printed in Dunstable, United Kingdom

64807432R00161